Last

BLUE

Christmas

Last BLUE Christmas

ROSE PRENDEVILLE

First published by Eridani Press.

Cover by Crowglass Design

Names: Prendeville, Rose, author.

Title: Last Blue Christmas / Rose Prendeville.

Description: First edition. | Nashville, Tennessee : Eridani Press, 2021.

Identifiers: ISBN 978-1-955643-00-9 (trade paperback) | ISBN 978-1-955643-01-6 (large print) | ISBN 978-1-955643-02-3 (ebook) | ISBN 978-1-955643-03-0 (audiobook)

Subjects: LCSH: Police—Canada—Fiction. | Indigenous men—Identity—Fiction. | Adoptees—Canada—Fiction. | Man-woman relationships—Fiction. | Romance fiction. | Christmas stories. | Ontario, Canada. | BISAC: FICTION / Romance / Holiday | FICTION / Romance / Police & Law Enforcement | FICTION / Romance / Contemporary. | GSAFD: Love stories.

Classification: LCC PS3616.R452 | DDC 813/.6—dc23

LC record available upon request.

For DJ, my north star

Toronto,
4 days 'til Christmas

CHAPTER 1

A run-of-the-mill cotton swab packed inside a plastic tube, nestled within a padded envelope and stamped with prepaid postage—that was all that stood between Max St. James and the answers he'd craved for decades. Or so he thought when he swabbed the inside of his cheek last night, before he read the fine print.

There was no point even mailing it now. A DNA test could only tell him as much as he already knew. He'd have to be patient, to wait and see what the Office of the Registrar General would be able to share about his adoption.

His phone rang, the caller ID lighting up with INSPECTOR ST. JAMES, as though his father's spidey senses were tingling, and Max dropped the envelope into the garbage with his over-ripe bananas. He swiped up his keys, answering, "St. James," so it wouldn't sound like he cared enough to screen his calls.

"Maxxy," his neighbor, Selina, trilled from down the hall the moment he stepped outside, and he waved over his shoulder.

"Max, it's your father." The Inspector's voice came through the phone much less cheerful than his neighbor's.

"You been staying up late watching anime on Netflix again?"

Max asked, locking his apartment and waving again at Selina despite her efforts to flag him down.

"I'm retired. I'll sleep when I'm dead." His voice was dry and raspy, like it was squeezing itself into a thin strand to physically travel through the phone. "Can you come by later? We're doing a food drive for the shelter on Gerard and—"

Max glanced at his watch as he crossed the street, passing a monstrosity of a gingerbread house someone had erected for the holidays, where kids were already lining up to meet Santa, which meant he was running late.

"Yeah, I uh—we're working a big case, but I'll get there when I can."

"Sure, sure." His father's words were the creaky timbers of a dam holding back years of disappointment.

"I'll find the time," Max promised, even though he'd have to twist himself in knots to get it done. There never seemed to be enough time—just like he was going to be late for his shift if he stopped for coffee.

But last night was the weekly Kyle Family Zoom Game Night, which meant Maggie Kyle, his partner, would be tired and grumpy and crawling out of her skin on the stakeout. Only a peppermint latte would perk her up.

He ducked into the shop, weighing whether he could get away with flashing his badge and skipping to the front of the line. Coffee was official police business, right?

"What about Christmas?" his father's voice boomed in his ear. "They don't have you working again this year do they? Because if they're sticking you with the crummy shifts and overlooking you for promotions, I can have a word—"

"No, sir, it's fine."

"I still have some weight I can throw around."

"I'm good. Honestly."

"If you're sure," he said, his tone turning icy. "I mean, I don't know, Max. Maybe it's your shoes."

It was the same argument they'd been having for more than twenty years. Reflexively, Max looked down at his non-regulation Chuck Taylors, black on black, and he smiled because they made him happy. Some people like to wear jewelry, others wouldn't leave home without a ball cap. Max didn't feel like himself unless he was wearing his Chucks and his grandfather's wristwatch. Was that so wrong?

"Next," the barista called, and it took Max a moment to realize she wasn't asking an existential question.

Coffee secured, he slipped into the parade room as Dix was reading through the morning announcements. His friend-turned-supervisor shot him a withering look before turning back to the stack of papers he was shuffling, and Max gave him the courtesy of looking chastened before he scanned the room for Maggie.

She stood off to his left, leaning against the wall. Her head drooped to the side and her eyes were half closed as she listened to Dix drone on about the big King case. Her hair was the perfect amount of messy and her shirt was untucked—a far cry from the buttoned-up rookie Max had met a decade back.

That first day she had marched right up to the group of senior officers and asked for help with her radio because the only thing scary to Maggie Kyle was screwing up. Stunned into silence by her plucky raised chin and defiant hazel eyes, Max had shrugged at her and slipped off to switch the assignments on the job board, ensuring the brash new rookie would ride with him instead of Dix.

They had pretty much been riding together ever since. Except today. Max glanced at the job board. Kyle was partnered with Parker for the stakeout.

Someone had obviously made a mistake.

"With all the extra holiday transit, we can't take any chances," Dix was saying.

"I hate Christmas," Maggie muttered to Castillo on her left.

Max swapped the names back where they belonged and stepped up beside his partner, holding out the peppermint latte responsible for his tardiness. "You love Christmas," he told her.

She gasped and her eyes lit up as she accepted the cup, not looking away from the staff sergeant to turn the full brightness of her smile on Max—and just as well. It would have blinded him like driving west into the sun.

He watched her take a sip, closing her eyes to properly savor it. "I do love Christmas," she murmured.

Yep. Totally worth being late.

"Something to share with the class, Officer Kyle?" Dix asked, not quite his usual jovial self.

Maggie's eyes snapped open. "I love Christmas, sir," she said, lifting her coffee in salute.

Dix laughed and shook his head at her. "You might be the only one. Assignments are on the board. Let's go save Christmas for Kyle."

Maggie smirked into her coffee.

"You're out of uniform, St. James," the staff sergeant added as he walked by.

"Yeah, yeah." Max waved him off, flexing his toes comfortably inside his Chucks.

He should probably check in with his old friend after shift. Dix hadn't asked for the mantle of acting staff sergeant when their old boss had picked up and retired to Belize.

But he had stepped in and stepped up, and it meant changes to most of his years-long friendships.

"Looks like we're riding together," Maggie interrupted his thoughts with a slight smirk. Had she checked the board on her way into the meeting? Did she know he made the scheduling switch?

"Ready to roll?" he asked, before she could comment further.

Maggie nodded. "Just let me..." She gestured toward the women's locker room and guzzled down the rest of her coffee.

MAGGIE LOVED HOW MAX ST. JAMES WAS ALWAYS A LITTLE BIT OUT of uniform. Those shoes were the first thing she'd noticed about him when they met.

He'd been standing across the room with Dix and some others, filling out his uniform in the best possible way, as Frankie had pointed out.

Except for the shoes.

"Do you think he forgot to change them?" she'd whispered.

"Oh probably. You should maybe go tell him," Frankie teased.

Maggie had rolled her eyes so hard it hurt, and then Frankie dared her.

Swept up in the moment—and eager to get a glimpse of the handsome officer's name tag—Maggie had marched right up to the group. But the moment he turned his piercing brown eyes on her, she'd lost all her nerve and asked for help with her radio instead.

Somehow she knew he was a man who didn't forget anything, and the shoes were deliberate. They meant something. A tiny rebellious streak—but rebellion against what?

That day, Officer Max St. James had become a puzzle Maggie couldn't wait to solve.

And she had been trying to figure him out ever since.

Tossing her empty coffee cup in the garbage, Maggie entered a stall. She could've sworn she'd been assigned with Parker today, but to her relief and utter consternation, she was riding with Max.

Max, who was the only person she wanted to ride with any day of the week, even when she was feeling short with him because he lacked her ambition and because he had no right to look so good in uniform and because everything about Christmas present was reminding her of Christmases past. Or at least one particular Christmas.

A sign over the sink advertised a precinct-wide gingerbread competition.

"I can't believe they only gave us three days' notice for this," Frankie said, gazing at the same sign as she washed up at the next sink.

"Yeah, good luck getting participants," Maggie grumped.

She hadn't baked gingerbread since she was twelve years old, standing beside her mom in matching chocolate moose aprons.

"Come on," her best friend begged with dancing eyes. "It'll be fun."

"Will it?"

"First prize will be! A trip for two to Puerto Rico? Bikinis and salsa dancing in February? Tostones?"

"Tony will want to go with you."

"Tony can deal. Come on."

"It'll be a disaster," Maggie moaned, turning away from the poster to straighten her tie and double check her boot laces.

"That's the spirit! We could do a tiny replica of the station! Imagine how impressed St. James will be."

For a half second, Maggie wondered whether he would be impressed, but then she shook her head. Showing off for Max was not her mission, not this Christmas. No matter how many lattes he brought her.

She needed to pour all her energy into the Bobby King case. When they closed it, the brass would be so impressed they'd force both her and Max into a detective's rotation, test or no test, and whether Max was interested in the promotion or not.

"You don't even bake," she told her friend.

Maggie glanced in her locker mirror and sighed. She should've begged off last night's Zoom call sooner, or else given herself time for makeup this morning. St. James certainly wouldn't be impressed with the bags under her eyes.

"I bake."

"You burned your kitchen down and had to move back in with your mom."

"One time. That's why I need you on my team." Frankie took her by the shoulders. "Kyle and Castillo, mixing it up like the old days."

Maggie had the sinking feeling she'd be covered in flour before bedtime. "Do I have to remind you of the epic macaron failure of 2019?" she whined.

"You picked the hardest thing to make," Frankie countered.

"The sourdough fiasco of 2020?"

"Luckily, I know enough to know gingerbread doesn't need yeast."

"You sure about that?" Maggie teased, and her friend blinked, not quite sure. "Come on, the guys will be waiting. Don't want to be a stereotype taking too long in the bathroom."

"Tostones," Frankie whispered gleefully, as she skipped out the door and down the hall to the sally port.

CHAPTER 2

"On the fourth day of Christmas, my true love gave to me... four migraine headaches, three massive ulcers, two aching ear drums, and a hole where my heart ought to be," Maggie sang quietly to herself as though Max wasn't sitting right there. She cracked herself up and switched off the unmarked Suburban's FM radio with a flourish, and Max could swear he caught a whiff of cinnamon.

"Maggie Kyle, your Christmas spirit confounds me," he told his partner. He was pretending to watch a Buick creep down the street a little too slowly so she wouldn't guess how attuned he was to the earnest timbre of her voice or the wry quirk of her lips. She was trying too hard to act casual with him, and he couldn't figure out why.

Maggie forced another laugh. "Christmas spirit," she repeated, skimming the crossword puzzle in her lap before glancing back across the street at the rundown residence of Bobby King. Its peeling paint, once white, was now a weathered gray, and of the four green shutters meant to frame the front windows, two were broken and one was missing altogether.

"What is a six-letter word for 'lack thereof,' Alex?"

"*Jeopardy*'s not a crossword puzzle," she said, making sure he saw her eye roll.

"Dispatch, we need to put out an APB on Officer Kyle's missing Christmas spirit."

"You going to call in that Buick?" she changed the subject.

"I wrote down the plates," he lied, squinting to make them out so he could record the vehicle in his logbook.

Maggie picked up the radio. "51-19?"

"51-19, go ahead," another officer responded from his own unmarked vehicle around the corner.

"10-15 headed your way. Tan Buick, early 2000s model, traveling east. Manitoba plate: Yankee Lima Echo seven seven eight."

"Copy," 51-19 replied.

Maggie replaced the radio and turned her attention back to the crossword. "Frankie wants to enter that gingerbread contest, and her mom's been playing Christmas carols since before Halloween. I'm not sure how much more I can take."

"Got it. No Christmas carols."

Max drummed his fingers on the steering wheel. When exactly had she lost her Christmas spirit? He could picture her as a little girl—in his mind she wore two long braids and was constantly shaking her bangs out of her eyes—staring up at the sky waiting for Santa to ride out of the stars like a meteor with the same patience she now bestowed on their stakeout. "But peppermint lattes are okay?"

She grinned. "I'll allow it."

"So you only hate Christmas a little bit then?"

Maggie snorted.

Time was, Max didn't mind the odd stakeout. It beat writing parking tickets or chasing shoplifters through the snow. Play some tunes, shoot the shit, pee in a bottle if things got urgent.

With the right partner it could seem like a day off. But everything was like eggshells with Maggie lately, and he couldn't figure out when exactly things had changed.

Today he felt a special kind of twitchy, the kind that made you want to peel off your own skin. Max loved the city—sometimes he hated how much he loved it—but sitting still all week, downtown where the Toronto high-rises blocked out the sky, he was starting to feel caged, like the buildings were closing in from every direction.

Maybe he was psyching himself out after the whole ancestry test situation. The dichotomy of an Indigenous urbanite was turning his brain against itself. Maybe he just needed a vacation.

"Do you believe in nature versus nurture?" he asked.

"What, you mean like, mama tried but Bobby King was born rotten and no amount of church or cuddles or bedtime stories could have stopped him growing up to be a cop-killing gun runner?"

"Something like that."

Maggie shrugged at him. "You missed a button." She pointed at his shirt. "Girlfriend didn't catch that?"

She was obsessed with the idea that he and Selina from next door shared more than a wall. It had only happened once—okay a handful of times. But it was five years ago, and there was no way Maggie could have known, except somehow she did. Even back then there'd been something, in his gait as he walked to the patrol car or a half-guilty look in his eyes; she had known, and if he protested now she'd take it as some kind of proof.

Not that it should even matter. They were partners, not lovers, and he'd certainly been her shoulder to cry on when the asshat from college dumped her and split back to Edmonton.

Max should have made a move on Maggie then, but he was still her TO and besides, he'd been a rebound before. He didn't want to be one for Maggie, and she didn't want him anyway. She'd been singularly focused on making detective since her first day at Fifty-One Division. Until, somewhere along the lines, she hadn't.

And she was right about the button. His black undershirt was peeking through. Did he bother to look in the mirror this morning? After a dozen years on the job, he knew what he'd see. Not his father, not even his grandfather—just a sad imitation, like a kid who got the wrong size costume at Halloween.

His phone vibrated, and he tried to be subtle about glancing at the caller ID.

INSPECTOR ST. JAMES.

Speak of the devil—as though thinking of the past had summoned him the same way his pointless spit test had. He silenced his father's call as a beat-up Chevy Malibu flew by, well above the speed limit.

"Not going to answer?" Maggie asked, tracking the car in her side mirror.

"We're on the job." Max shrugged. "Catch the plates?"

"Too fast."

"Wouldn't risk a ticket if they were really up to anything," he said, actually glad they weren't allowed to leave their vehicle for something as mundane as a speeding ticket. In some white shirts' eyes that would make him a terrible cop, but deep down he really didn't care if people bent the rules a little now and then.

Maggie nodded in agreement, willing to go along with the theory they both knew was BS because she was relieved to be on special assignment too. The difference was, she was always meant for more than traffic duty. Every ticket she wrote probably reminded her she wasn't a detective.

She followed the car out of sight, checked her watch, jotted down a note about the nothing happening in front of King's house. She studied everything, but Max studied her. Her chestnut hair was different today, starting out messy instead of twisted into a French braid that would grow loose and disheveled as the shift wore on, making his throat constrict a little tighter each time another curl broke free.

Down boy, he reminded himself. *Partner. Off limits—even if she were interested. Which she's not.*

Her phone began to vibrate then, and she, too, silenced it without answering.

"Your mom again?" he asked.

She didn't respond, which meant yes.

"She giving you a hard time about staying here for the holidays?"

"I'll take 'Does the earth orbit the sun?' for a thousand, Alex."

King's front door opened and Maggie slid down in her seat as a pit bull terrier emerged to sniff the dead grass that managed to poke above the snow and do its business, unaccompanied by whatever human had opened the door.

"Maybe we could just bring him in because of the pit," Maggie said, only half-joking.

"Collins would have our badges if we even whispered about making an arrest before the case was airtight."

"It might give us an excuse for a warrant though." She crossed her arms over her chest, muttering something about tax evasion.

"Weren't you going to invite your folks out here for Christmas?"

"That was last year."

An uncomfortable mixture of lust and shame surged through Max, from the tips of his ears to his belly, at the thought of last Christmas. He tried to remember her parents being in town, but all that came to mind was the department holiday party and sweaty fumbling in a dark interrogation room. And cinnamon. She had smelled like cinnamon then, too.

Suddenly aware of the sun beating through his window, he had the urge to roll it all the way down, protocol be damned, and he shifted in his seat, trying to adjust his pants without being too obvious.

"Did you bring them around?" he asked, trying to hide the little crack in his voice.

"And force them to miss Christmas morning in Vancouver with their grandchildren?" she said with mock horror, sitting up straight again once the dog was back inside. "Maybe next year I'll plan ahead. Send them train tickets so they can't decline."

"So Christmas with Frankie and the Castillo clan this year?"

"That would be like spending Christmas at Disney World."

"Humid and filled with crying children?"

She laughed. "Magical but overwhelming. No, they've been super great about letting me stay there until I find a new place, but I'm not sure I want to crash the family reunion. I'll probably pick up some extra shifts and keep out of everyone's hair."

A year ago, Max would've said, *You should spend Christmas with me.* Now he chickened out, risked annoying her, brought up the test. "Should be pretty quiet around the barn. Give you time to study. I could help if you want."

"Not you, too. You trying to get rid of me?"

"Castillo just wanted me to make sure you haven't forgotten."

"How could I forget? She wrote it in dry erase marker on the bathroom mirror. She circled the date on the calendar in my locker. She even oh-so-subtly left her study guides in the passenger seat of her car."

"Tenacious." Max nodded, admiring Frankie's efforts.

"I thought you were supposed to have my back."

"You know I do, Kyle. Look me in the eye and tell me you don't want to be a detective, you'll never hear another word on it from me."

He was surprised when she did look at him, held his gaze so long he felt like she was peering inside his soul. But she didn't answer, and the truth was, he wasn't sure what he wanted her to say.

If she said she didn't want it, she'd be lying to them both, just like he would be if he said he wanted her to pass the test and move on without him. He did, and he didn't. It was complicated.

The car radio popped with static and then roared to life. "ALL UNITS, ALL UNITS: 10-33. FIFTY-TWO DIVISION REQUESTING BACKUP."

Maggie's eyes broke from his and shifted to the radio.

"10-100 REPORTED AT BAY STREET COACH TERMI-NAL. REPEAT 10-100."

Her eyes widened and she turned back to him for another long moment before they grabbed their seatbelts in perfect unison.

"Dispatch, mark 51-15 responding," Maggie said into the radio.

Max slammed his foot on the brake pedal and started up the engine. He counted to five before he trusted himself to ease down the street at a painfully normal speed instead of peeling off and blowing their cover.

10-100. Bomb threat.

"GO AHEAD AND LIGHT THEM UP, MAGPIE," HER PARTNER SAID, once they were a few blocks from Bobby King's place and the traffic started to pick up.

Maggie retrieved a dash light from the glove box and flipped the switches allowing the sirens to roar to life so Max could untether his own adrenaline. Then she ran through a mental checklist: her gun was loaded, her vest was on.

If she had finally taken—and passed—the detective's exam two years ago, would she be here now? Racing toward the scene of a possible explosion?

Of course she would. 10-33 meant all hands on deck. She would still be careening toward the bus station—just without Max by her side.

"Probably a hoax like the others right?" she said. "What is this, the third one this week?"

"Two for us, three for Fifty-Two Division," he said.

"Good. I mean, not good, but at least a hoax could have us back on King's house by lunchtime."

Max turned onto Bay Street and slowed down to avoid hitting any of the jaywalkers fleeing the station. "They're all real until they're not. You wearing your vest?"

He was incapable of turning it off, the bossy pants training officer shtick.

What annoyed her wasn't that he did it, but that he did it so well. That she liked it. She ought to be pissed off, but knowing Max was at her side, watching to make sure she didn't screw up, gave her the confidence to do the job and usually not screw it up. Somehow that was a turn-on. God, what was wrong with her?

She rolled her eyes letting the misplaced annoyance show. "No, I'm a rookie. Don't yell at me, sir, it's my first day."

He honked and waved at the cab drivers to move out of the way, finally bringing the Suburban to a stop diagonally across the middle of the street to block traffic, then he returned her sass with a shrug. "Old habits," he said.

Not exactly an apology but just like they say, *Don't go to bed angry,* Maggie's personal policy was, *Don't go into a potentially lethal situation pretending to be angry,* so she let it slide.

Mostly.

"You know, St. James, this is probably my hundredth 10-100."

"Okay, we'll throw a party. Later. For now, treat it like it's your first."

"So I should pee my pants and dig my nails into your arm when the balloons pop?"

"Forgot about that," he chuckled. "Maybe treat it like it's your second then," he added and was out of the car before Maggie had even unbuckled. She took a deep breath and followed him toward the entrance.

Dozens of travelers were flooding outside, but there was no visible smoke, no apparent injuries, so at least nothing serious had happened yet. She didn't know whether to feel relieved or disappointed. Maybe a little of both.

"We should corral and interview these witnesses," she said,

because Max was ready to charge right into the terminal. He'd always reminded her a bit of the captain from *Firefly*, Mal Reynolds. He was the shrewdest cop she'd ever met—when he stopped to think things through instead of rushing in like a big damn hero whose ship was going down in flames. She tried to remember which of the two she'd had the hots for first, but it was a decade-old chicken-egg situation, and now was not the time.

"Need to secure the scene."

"Someone's already here." Maggie pointed to a Fifty-Two Division cruiser parked neatly by the curb.

But Max had already jumped into action, directing the frightened and confused tourists, shoppers, and commuters across the street to a crowded parking lot. "That's it, calm and orderly. It's going to be all right," he assured them.

Was whoever called in the threat among those bystanders? Were they waiting, hoping to see the place go up in flames—or simply to sow a little chaos in The 6ix? And if it wasn't a hoax, if the bomb was big enough, would the parking lot really be far enough away? Would the Greyhounds lining Edward Street provide a shield or increase the carnage? Should they perhaps evacuate the entire block as a precaution?

"Come on folks, put a little holiday pep in your step," Maggie urged, attempting to imitate Max's soothing demeanor as she helped to usher the throngs across the street and away from the wailing fire alarm and hypnotic flashing lights inside the building. "I know it's cold, I know you've got places to be, but the sooner you clear out, the sooner we can let you back in."

She tripped over a kid wearing a baggy gray hoodie, longish brown hair, about eleven years old, who stopped to glance back inside.

"You okay?" Max asked them both. When the kid nodded he said, "Go on across the street. You can wait for your parents over there."

The kid nodded again and scrambled across the road.

As the last few travelers hurried out of the station, they were followed by two fresh-faced officers from Fifty-Two Division.

"Which way did he go? The guy with the gun?" the first officer asked.

"Someone has a gun?" Max drew his own weapon, but kept the safety on.

"Black male, approximately eighteen years old, Jays hat," the second officer said, her head swiveling to scan the crowd across the road. "I'm pretty sure it was an assault rifle."

"You're pretty sure?" Max asked. "Or it was?"

"It was an assault rifle. AR-15."

"And you let him walk out of here like it was the eighteenth hole?" Maggie asked.

"We were securing the station," the first officer protested.

"Someone had to wait for ETF," the second added.

"Yeah, the Emergency Task Force definitely wouldn't be able to secure the building without you two," Max replied dryly, turning toward the gathered crowd.

"See him?" Maggie whispered.

When he looked back at her his eyes flicked down at her vest, answering the question he knew not to ask a second time. He tapped his wrist with two fingers—signaling two o'clock—and Maggie followed his gaze to the young black man in the blue baseball cap.

Slowly they approached the crowd from opposite sides, but the suspect wasn't paying any attention at all. He was texting rapidly with one thumb, bobbing his head to a rhythm from his AirPods.

Maggie wiped one sweaty palm on her pants and eased out her weapon. If he really did have an assault rifle, the only reason to hide in this crowd would be to mow down as many bystanders as possible, but it didn't fit the profile. It would be more efficient to station himself at the door, shooting all the fish on their way out of the barrel, not bide his time in a parking lot, texting and awaiting a more opportune moment.

"What's going on?" a businessman in a well-cut gray suit and polka dot bowtie demanded. Based on the Rolex he kept glancing at and his fancy briefcase, she figured he was in tech or finance. He should be at the airport, not waiting for a bus. He must hate flying as much as her mom did.

Maggie pushed past him. With practiced timing, she and Max reached the Jays fan at the exact same moment.

"Freeze," Max said softly, and the kid looked up, genuinely surprised to see them.

He looked from Max to Maggie, from drawn weapon to drawn weapon, and his face fell. "Seriously?" he sighed, raising his phone in the air, thumb frozen mid-text.

"I need you to step to your left, nice and slow," Max said.

The kid looked at Maggie again, his brow knit in disappointment, but he complied. As he did, Maggie got a good look at the tripod slung over his right shoulder, a camera bag hanging off his left, and shame twisted in her gut like a bad burrito.

"St. James," she said, but he saw it too. A tripod, not a rifle.

His jaw tightened, and he studied the ground for a second, loathing himself and the job. Despising the newbies from Fifty-Two. "I'm so sorry," he told the kid, his voice hollow. "Thanks for your cooperation," he added before glowering over his shoulder at the young cops now positioned outside the station entrance.

"Well if it isn't the Dynamic Duo," a voice called, and Maggie turned to see an old buddy from the Academy, Andrew Boyd of Fifty-Two Division, walking over. The greenest-looking rookie she'd ever laid eyes on was trotting along behind, still tucking in his shirttail and adjusting his holster. "Good to see you, Fifty-One," Boyd said, shaking Maggie's hand. "We can take it from here, I guess."

"What kept you?" Max asked.

"We had a thing at the library. Something about Legos." His

sigh was deep and angsty, like someone who hadn't asked to be a training officer. Maggie recognized that sigh.

"It wasn't Lego, though, it was a RoboZ kit. The pieces don't really snap together the same way Lego do," the rookie interjected.

"Try to find out who was in charge inside, would you?" Maggie asked. "I think the employees have mostly congregated in the corner over there."

"On it," Boyd replied.

"And you," Max added, pointing at the rookie. "Make sure nobody leaves."

CHAPTER 3

Max had forgotten how much rookie cops were like baby deer, stumbling around on too long legs, their wide bright eyes soaking everything in for the very first time.

"Um, sir! Officer…?" Boyd's rookie called, jogging after Max and Maggie.

"St. James."

"Right. Officer St. James. It's just… How? Do I keep them from leaving? Any tips?"

Max looked at Maggie and then back at the rookie in disbelief. "You're a cop."

"Yes, I am!" he said proudly. Then, "Oh! Right."

"Hector!" Boyd shouted from across the street, raising his arms, both a question and a surrender to the inevitable.

"Rookies," one of the young officers from Fifty-Two laughed in the doorway. Max had seen them around. They hadn't been cut loose all that long ago themselves.

"You're out of uniform, there, Chief," the other one said to Max, smirking down her nose at his high tops.

Max's jaw tightened and his eyes flicked up to hers, gauging whether the slur was intentional. Then Maggie touched his elbow, grounding him. Later—he would say something later.

Instead he glanced down at his shoes. "Gosh, I guess I am. Congrats on your promotion. I didn't realize Fifty-One had a new staff sergeant. When does the transfer go through?"

She rolled her eyes and opened her mouth to retort, but Maggie jumped in. "Were we ever that young?" she asked, shaking her head at the rookie, who was gesturing animatedly at a witness and looked like he might do a backflip at any moment.

"My mom always said I was born old," Max replied.

"I heard you were born with a badge in your hand and your daddy's nightstick up your—"

Max cut the Fifty-Two off with a glare. God they were a pair: Tweedle Smirk and Tweedle Smart-Ass.

"So who called it in? Dispatch say?" Maggie jumped in with a super smooth change of subject.

She was like that sometimes—an interrupter—always impatient to get to the point or to come to Max's rescue, even when he'd been a little heavy handed with the senior officer routine. She couldn't help it. Loyal to the last.

When he caught her eye, her mouth twitched at the corner in a self-aware half smile, and he nodded his gratitude, which made her roll her eyes and look away, still smiling.

If all it took to finally put things back to normal with her was a couple of jerkoffs and a bomb threat, he was going to need to send a round of thank you cards later.

"Dispatch doesn't know who made the call. We know it wasn't a cell. Probably came from the pay phones by the storage lockers on the west side," Tweedle Smart-Ass said, pointing toward the cordoned off hallway to the right.

"They still have lockers?" Maggie asked. "And pay phones? Did I fall asleep on the stakeout and wake up in the nineties?"

"Whose taxes are going to pay for a retrofit?" Tweedle Smart-Ass murmured.

"Dispatch tell you the exact words?" Max asked. "How long we've got?"

Tweedle Smirk, the one who had it in for his shoes, checked her notes. "Caller said, 'There's a bomb at Bay Street Station. Come quick.'"

"What did they sound like? Male? Female? Old? Young?" Maggie asked the Fifty-Twos. "Canadian? British? Russian?"

Max should've made her stay across the street, safely interviewing witnesses, but it would have pissed her off to be left out of the action.

It wasn't his job to wrap her in bubble wrap. Besides, she was better at this stuff than him—putting all the details together into one big picture, commanding order from chaos. She made him step back and think when his inclination was to rush in. It's why they made such a good team. She was the brains and he was the muscle.

He'd spent the better part of ten years trying to keep her safe.

"Where the hell is ETF?" he demanded, more to himself than to anyone else.

"Keep your panties on," said a voice right behind him, and Max turned to see an officer in full protective gear holding a chocolate lab on a short leash. "Cadbury had to lay an egg," the ETF hotshot added, patting his K9's head. "Area secured?"

Both officers from Fifty-Two Division gave a curt nod.

"Okay then. Hit it," ETF said, bending down to unleash the dog's harness.

Cadbury trotted through the lobby and down a hallway, nose to the ground, sniffing for bombs the way other people's dogs sniff out crumbs and cat poop. It smelled benches and chairs, wall sockets, even a backpack and half a Snickers bar left behind in the evacuation. It passed by everything, trotting toward the pedestrian walkway on the far end, looking like it might head right on out the door and disappear onto the streets of Toronto thinking, *See ya, suckers,* as it marched off into the sunset.

That's what Max would do if he were a dog named Cadbury.

But it stopped right before the exit to check out the pay phones, the floor, and finally the lockers.

The officers followed at a less than safe distance. Max tried to position himself a step ahead of his partner without being obvious enough that she'd notice. For the briefest second, he thought he glimpsed a face looking in through the exit, but it was gone just as quickly, maybe the light playing tricks on his eyes, like his invisible friend Noah who used to haunt him as a child.

Max braced himself, waiting for a whine, followed by an explosion of cinderblock and fur, of fire raining down from the ceiling. He glanced over his shoulder at Maggie, whose face was drawn and pale, but determined.

She didn't give herself enough credit. Sharpest eye he knew and tough as actual nails, she was somehow convinced she wasn't cut out for the next step up, but she never shrank back from the hard stuff, not on the job.

When she caught him looking, he quirked an eyebrow at her in his best Jim-from-*The Office* impression, and she smiled and relaxed.

The dog sniffed at one locker before continuing on a little further. Then it sat down, staring up at one in the top row. No bark, no whine. It sat there, still as a stone and silent as a statue.

ETF held up a hand, as though the other officers needed to be told to freeze, and he chirruped to call his K9 back, but before it reached him, there came an almighty racket. It was like an entire high school drumline was rehearsing a dozen different movements all at once inside a single washroom stall. Smoke billowed out from the locker Cadbury had marked and the sprinklers began to spit water.

"Get down," ETF shouted, another needless order.

Max had already shoved Maggie to the ground where they huddled, breathless, arms covering their heads, waiting for the ceiling to collapse in a pile of flame and ash and shattered ceiling tiles.

He knelt over her, his lips mere millimeters from her face and this, right here, was the problem. This was why he really shouldn't even be her partner anymore. Because it was his job to protect and serve the community, not to protect and serve Maggie Kyle. Because the world could be falling down in flames around them, and all he would be thinking about was how soft her eyelashes would feel brushing against his cheek, and how badly he wanted to kiss the crease between her eyes until it was smooth, and how she smelled like cinnamon and peppermint cream.

But the ceiling didn't fall.

In fact, the cacophony was over in under a minute, and only a sulfurous smoke remained. His eyes met Maggie's once more. Green—they were green today—not a bold, shocking green like last Christmas but muted, mossy, with golden edges like a summer meadow.

"Fireworks?" she whispered, her breath tickling his cheek the way he imagined her eyelashes would, bringing him back to the matter at hand and he shook his head a little to clear it. "Smells like fireworks." She squirmed out from under his protective cover and pushed up on her elbows.

As the sprinklers continued to douse them, Max shrank down inside his jacket. The water heightened everything—cold, sirens, smoke, the goosebumps from such close proximity to his partner. Every unwanted sensation became a thousand times more pronounced when he was wet.

"Ohmygosh what happened?" the rookie yelled, running inside. "Boyd called the fire department. They're on the way."

"Great, just what we need. Hose monkeys traipsing all over our crime scene," Tweedle Smart-Ass grumbled.

"Are you guys okay?" the rookie asked them.

"Where's your partner? What happened to taking statements?" Max demanded.

"I heard the explosion and thought you might need help."

"We do need help. Outside. With the witness statements."

"Everyone either shut up or clear the area," ETF growled, and in the silent seconds that followed Cadbury began to whine.

"Why? Will talking make another bomb go off? Oh my gosh, is it sound activated?" the rookie asked, loudly whispering the last part.

Five heads turned toward him, and if they were all shooting the kid some version of Max's own cold stare it was a wonder the rookie didn't fall down dead right there.

"Hector," Boyd called from outside.

Max turned back to the ETF guy and his K9, who was still whining at the other locker. Had the fireworks been nothing but an appetizer? He'd heard dogs could be trained to detect different strains of the same virus—was this one somehow trained to detect the order of explosions?

ETF's right hand tremored as it reached for the handle of the bottom locker. And who could blame him? He was betting his life —maybe all of their lives—on the cry of a slobbery dog. Admittedly a highly trained slobbery dog, but still.

Max reached out for Maggie to try and shield her once more. He caught hold of her forearm as she reached for his and his stomach did a somersault.

"Are you sure that's a good idea?" asked Tweedle Smirk.

ETF balled his hand into a fist for a moment, then released it and gently opened the door.

Max craned his neck to see what was inside.

"Well?" Maggie asked. "What is it? A dead rabbit or something? Bag full of kibble?"

"Umm..." ETF replied.

Max relaxed his grip on Maggie and pulled away to get a closer look, she and the others right behind him.

ETF stepped out of their way, and there inside the locker, with a tear-stained face and hands clamped over his ears, hunched a shaggy, wide-eyed little boy.

A BOY. A TINY LITTLE BOY SAT SCRUNCHED INSIDE A LOCKER, KNEES to his chin, backpack crammed in beside him.

"See, this right here, this is why they're removing all the lockers from transit stations," Max said, and Maggie felt a hysterical giggle bubbling up inside of her she had to take a deep breath to force away.

She looked at the female officer next to her, but the other woman just smirked. What exactly was the protocol when you found a living, breathing child inside a bus station locker? Maggie knew what the protocol would be if he wasn't staring back at them.

"Can somebody get this damned water turned off?" Max asked, raking a hand through his damp black hair so it stood up all spiky and unprofessional.

Maggie didn't hate the look. Water always turned him into a riled-up alley cat that you kind of wanted to swaddle in your biggest, fluffiest towel and spend a lot of time petting dry. *Stop it.*

"Maybe kill the fire alarm, too, while you're at it?" Max asked nobody in particular. He knelt down in front of the locker. "Hey," he said to the boy who continued to stare at them with wide, frightened eyes. "Think maybe you want to come out now?"

This time, the boy looked away.

"I get it. It's pretty scary out here. Way better than in there though. More elbow room." He flapped his arms to prove it, and Maggie bit her lip to keep from grinning at his antics.

"You don't have kids, do you?" the young male smart aleck from Fifty-Two Division said. Then he turned to Maggie and asked, "Aren't you going to help?"

"I also have no children. Maybe you should help."

"Playtime's over kid. Time to go," he barked.

Max shot the smart aleck an exasperated glare, then turned back to the boy muttering something that sounded a lot like idiot and offering his hand.

What would Maggie have done in his place? Coaxed? Cajoled? Threatened? Begged? Reached in and grabbed the child just to be done with it? She'd have chosen wrong and made the situation ten times worse for sure.

The boy eyed them all a little longer, but allowed Max to help him out onto the floor, where he stood on wobbly legs hugging his backpack tight. Seven, maybe eight years old, with dark brown hair and light brown eyes. He was nearly swallowed by the giant blue U of T hoodie, its moth-eaten hem hanging to his knees, as he blinked up at the water hitting him from the sprinklers.

The others bombarded the boy with questions, but he refused to look at any of them.

Small and cramped, the lockers were stacked one on top of the other in three rows. The little boy had been hiding six to the left and two down from the explosion, sitting inside a metal echo chamber, and though the racket only lasted a minute, it would be a wonder if he could hear anything they were saying to him right now.

"What's your name?"

"Why were you in there?"

"Where are your parents?"

"How long were you in there? How did you even get in there?"

"Did you plant the explosives?"

"Guys," Max hushed them. He pulled up the boy's hood and then took off his own jacket and held it open while the child reluctantly let go of his bag one hand at a time to slip it on.

"You planning to search him first?" ETF Stevens asked, and so Max made a half-hearted attempt at patting the boy down.

Maggie enjoyed seeing this side of her partner. He always took charge, but it hadn't exactly occurred to her or any of the others to offer the boy their jackets. For Max it just came naturally—the big, tough policeman transforming into a gentle giant. Max always dealt with the human side of any problem first. He embodied the *protect and serve* motto—his first instinct was to try to make everything all right, no matter what else was happening.

The other officers' questions burned in Maggie, too, of course. Where did the child come from? How did he get there? Why was he hiding? Was he involved? The sooner those questions were answered, the sooner they could get back to their own precinct, back to their own case, the one that was going to save lives across the city and put Fifty-One Division on the news from Toronto to Vancouver, and force the department to make Maggie and Max detectives together, no matter how next month's test went.

Leaving Max to deal with the little boy, Maggie followed ETF Stevens and the other two officers over to the first locker, which was still smoking.

It was more than a meter off the ground, almost shoulder height, and it was dented all to hell. By the look of the surrounding lockers, some of the damage might have been preexisting, but in a few spots the explosives had blown minuscule holes right through the thin, recycled steel.

"So was it fireworks?" Maggie asked, and Stevens pointed inside, where the remnants of a multi tube cake smoldered.

"But how was it ignited with all of us right here watching?" Maggie asked.

"That's the interesting part," Stevens said, pointing to a partially melted blob of plastic on the upper shelf.

"Are those... Legos?" Maggie asked.

"Lego?" the rookie, Hector, practically squealed, popping up behind Maggie's shoulder. "What!"

He reached up to grab the toy, but Maggie smacked his hand. "Rookie," she said. "Evidence."

"Those aren't even Lego! Oh my god, is that how they detonated it? This has to be one of the sets stolen from the library, right? They said it was a robotics set. It's right here in my notes."

"Where's Boyd?" the female officer from Fifty-Two asked, rolling her eyes and smirking at her partner.

"This is insane! Do we get a commendation for solving the crime the fastest?" he asked.

"Not solved yet, Hector," she said. "Go back to Boyd."

"So I'm confused," Maggie confessed. "How could a bunch of plastic building blocks ignite anything?"

Hector scoffed. "Even Lego have evolved since the nineties."

"Legos aren't just snapping blocks anymore?" the smirky one's partner, the smart aleck, asked.

"Where have you guys been? And the plural is Lego. And those aren't them."

"Is someone else helping your partner with crowd control?" Maggie asked.

"Had to pee. And I wanted a better look at the Locker Boy," he admitted, glancing over to where Max knelt, still trying to get the boy talking.

News traveled fast, apparently. Faster than the request to turn off the sprinklers, anyway.

Max glared at them and then picked the boy up with one arm and carried him over to a bench away from the spray. He was wearing short sleeves today despite the cold, and when he lifted the child his bicep bulged in a way that made the sleeve look way too tight. It made Maggie's throat feel awfully tight, too.

"Parking lot. Now," she rasped at Hector before she let herself get further distracted.

He cocked his head like he was about to argue, but then he thought better of it and headed out of the station with a weird little salute to Max on the way.

"So somebody used this fancy toy to light the fuse on an expensive—"

"Mid-level," ETF Stevens corrected her.

"—firework. Why?"

"That part's your job."

The robot was melted, but there were bits shaped like gears and wires. Somehow the thing must run on a battery or a timer. Maybe it struck a match to light the fuse. It was complicated. A timer would make it even more complicated.

"Could it be triggered over WiFi? The not-Lego?" she asked.

ETF Stevens shrugged and Hector wasn't around to answer.

"You have kids? They have fancy Legos?" Maggie asked the smart aleck from Fifty-Two who had suggested she, as a woman, should deal with the boy.

"Not like those. They're more into video games these days. Watching videos of other kids playing video games."

After a palaver with ETF Stevens, the fire marshal finally got the sprinklers turned off. The boy pushed the damp hood off his head, his hair fluttering when he looked around like he was waiting for something.

"Kids these days," the smart aleck mumbled. "Don't their mothers cut their hair anymore?"

Max motioned Maggie over, and then stood to meet her.

"Hey, Fifty-One? You guys seen my rookie?" Boyd interrupted.

"We sent him back out to you."

"What, you lost him already?" Max teased.

"I mean. Have you tried keeping track of one lately? Like herding kittens."

"Hey, you should call him Jabberwocky," Max said, pointing toward Hector, who was in the corner talking the ear off a clearly disinterested ETF Stevens. "On account of how he jabbers."

"I like it. Come on, Jabberwocky," Boyd called, heading over to wrangle his rookie.

"Jabber—?" Maggie asked.

"*Beware the Jabberwock, my son? The jaws that bite, the claws that catch?* Nothing? Really? Never mind. I know why he looks familiar." Max whispered the last part, nodding at the boy.

"He does?"

"The kid you tripped over when we first got here. Same eyes, same hair, right? Same sort of modern-day Copperfield vibe?"

"He did have the same brand of backpack," Maggie conceded, picturing the first kid's black JanSport, a twin to this boy's red one.

"We need to find that kid."

CHAPTER 4

They put the little boy in the back seat of the Suburban still wearing Max's patrol jacket. No one from Fifty-Two Division tried to stop them, but Maggie crossed her arms over her chest. "You think they were involved?" she asked.

"Not really. Wrong time, wrong place most likely."

"Doubt it. But I'm not sure I care, since this isn't our case. Why aren't you handing him off to Fifty-Two?"

"As the senior officers on scene—"

"Boyd can handle one kid."

"Really? With Tweedle Smirk and Tweedle Smart-Ass and that doe-eyed rookie?"

Max led the way back to the parking lot where Boyd was still attempting to corral the witnesses.

"Tweedle…? You're just going to leave him in the car?"

"I cracked the windows." Max knew what she was doing, trying to get out of taking the case because who wants to blow a case involving kids at Christmas? But honestly, she should be relieved to be off the hook for King. Possibly the biggest case to come their way in years meant a lot of eyes and lots to lose. But she seemed eager to get back to the stakeout. Maybe he didn't know her as well as he thought.

The parking lot across the street was jammed with travelers—men, women, and children anxiously watching Max and Maggie—but none matched the little face that had peered up at him from inside the locker.

Finding the little boy had hit him hard in a way he seldom allowed the job to do. The terror in those eyes, and the hope—dashed when he realized Max wasn't who he expected him to be—they might be permanently seared into his memory.

Even if the kids didn't plant those fireworks, he was hiding in there for a reason, and Max intended to find out why.

"What's up?" Boyd asked.

"Looking for a kid," Maggie told him.

"I thought you had the kid."

"Different kid, bigger," Max explained, holding his hand about chest high. "Looks like my kid. Light jacket, dark backpack, sad eyes. Seen him?"

"Gray hoodie, black backpack," Maggie clarified. "Curly brown hair, maybe four foot eight?"

"You talk to a kid like that, Jabberwocky?" Boyd asked the rookie.

"There's like a hundred kids out here."

"Try again," Max said.

"At least a dozen, all wearing hoodies and carrying backpacks."

"What about the eyes?" Max asked, scanning the crowd once more. He and Maggie had been inside the bus station for a little over an hour, plenty of time for a kid to disappear into the heart of the city if he wanted to. "He wouldn't have gone far. Not with his little brother stuffed inside an old locker."

"Unless he put him there," the rookie muttered the words Max couldn't bring himself to say.

"Nobody leaves." Max pointed at him. "Rookie may be right. If this kid's in the wind, he most likely has a reason to be."

"What are you thinking?" Maggie asked. "Help out with the interviews? Maybe somebody's seen him?"

"We should do a canvas. You go north, I go west."

"St. James—"

"Bring in Tweedle Smart-Ass and his partner to cover—"

"St. James—" she said again.

"I know it's not a perfect plan, but—"

"Look." She caught his wrist again, right below the watch band, causing his breath to catch, too. He wrenched his arm free because now was not the time for cinnamon and foggy thinking.

Maggie nodded toward the far side of the parking lot where a brown, curly head peered out from behind a blue Corolla.

"You go left, I go right?" he suggested.

"Slow and patient," Maggie reminded him.

"You say that like I'm not usually patient."

"Cause you're not," she snickered.

He looked back at her, a little stung because he liked to think of himself as extraordinarily patient. Okay, maybe he was gruff with the rookies on occasion, but being a strong role model was all about tough love.

And wow, when did he start to sound so much like his father? Ugh. Maybe he *should* work on his patience.

"Hey Kyle," he called after her. "Be careful." It was probably just a grade school prank or a science experiment gone terribly wrong, but you never knew. Sometimes kids carried knives these days—or worse.

With a practiced nonchalance, Max worked his way through the crowded lot. He introduced himself, shook hands, passed out business cards, trying to appear busy and engaged, not at all interested in the blue Toyota or the adolescent hiding behind it.

"Are you warm enough, Sister?" he asked a nun in a blue and white habit.

"Me? You aren't even wearing sleeves," she reminded him. "Is your shirt wet?"

"All part of the job." Max smiled, though he was keenly aware of the goosebumps on his arms and how cold the air felt each time it hit his lungs.

The kid was edging around the back of the car. Max was almost close enough to grab him if he really put his legs into it. The kid must have realized the same thing, because he shot out from behind the Toyota like a skink and raced across the lot heading for Bay Street.

"I'll say a prayer for you," the nun said as Max took off after his quarry.

"Thank you, Sister," he yelled back. Then to Maggie he called, "Stay here and keep an eye on the other one."

His Chuck Taylors, already damp from the fire sprinklers, slapped on the snow and squelched in the slush.

An ambulance siren began to wail, echoing off the tall buildings like it was everywhere all at once, but Max guessed it was coming from his left, from the hospital. Sure enough, he emerged from between two parked cars in time to see the kid pivot back onto the sidewalk after nearly stepping in front of the bus. Max grabbed for him, managing to snag only his backpack, which the kid shook off.

"I just want to talk," Max yelled over the wailing siren, but the kid raced down the sidewalk toward Max and Maggie's unmarked Suburban. He sure had a pair. There, right in the middle of Edward Street, he tried to jimmy the handle on a police vehicle.

At least he was trapped by Maggie and Boyd on one side and a line of streaming cars on the other.

"Hey!" Max called.

The kid turned and looked right at him, spoke to his brother through the partially open window, and took off running again. The traffic Max had hoped would slow him down did nothing as the kid scampered across all four lanes of Bay Street Frogger-style. He moved in and out of the flow of cars and trucks almost like he was dancing with them, like they shared a secret rhythm Max had grown up and forgotten how to hear.

It was obvious where the kid was heading, and one thing was sure: if he made it to Eaton Centre, Max would never catch him.

Dodging pedestrians and cyclists before hurdling a small white dog taking its afternoon constitutional, Max reminded himself that the kid might be fast, but his own legs were twice as long and with every stride he was gaining ground. And surely Dundas would slow the delinquent down.

Except it didn't, not any more than Bay Street had. The kid made it across right before the light changed, leaving Max doubled over with his hands on his knees trying to catch his breath before the next round of chicken with the traffic.

"How's it going out there, St. James?" Maggie asked over the radio.

"Kid's slippery," he panted, deciding to head along Dundas instead of crossing it, shadow his subject from this side of the street.

The kid paused outside Canadian Tire. He seemed surprised not to see Max behind him, and his head swiveled from side to side. Max tried to shrink into the shadows of a massive office building, but there was nowhere to hide.

They stared at each other for a minute. He really didn't strike Max as a bad kid, just a desperate one. But desperate people make bad decisions, decisions they might later wish to take back. Maybe the kid was trying to figure out a way to walk all this back —surely he must be running out of steam.

No sooner had he thought it than the kid took off again, and Max lost him in a crowd of holiday shoppers until the kid darted around two men carrying a Christmas tree and ran inside H&M.

Really should have called for backup.

"St. James, what's your 20?" Maggie radioed, like she was reading his mind.

"I'm in, ah, ladies' wear? At H&M," Max said, peering through the racks and down the aisles for the kid.

"Doing a little last-minute shopping, partner? I could use a new sweater."

"Your old sweater's fine," he blurted without thinking. "How soon can you get here?"

"Five minutes."

"Make it four."

Max spun around, scanning the throngs of shoppers. There were too many people, too many floors, too many exits to control this situation, even with Maggie's help. The kid could easily hunker down for days or slip out into the mall, never to be seen again.

Then a disturbance caught his eye. People were murmuring their dismay near the escalators. He knocked over an entire display of nutcrackers when he caught a glimpse of the kid running down the up escalator.

Max raced around to the down side and took the moving steps two at a time.

The kid jumped off the up and was through to the subway before Max could stop him, vaulting over the turnstile and running flat out toward the closing doors of a departing train.

"Hey kid," Max yelled. "What about your brother?"

That made him falter. The kid stopped and glanced back over his shoulder with the most world-weary expression Max had ever seen. Then the train doors closed, and he was gone.

THEY PUT THE LITTLE BOY IN THE SOFT INTERVIEW ROOM, AND Maggie tried to get him talking while Max took a hot shower and changed into dry clothes. But the child wouldn't say a word.

They stared at each other across the table until Maggie realized he was still wearing her partner's jacket, so she went in search of something smaller in the women's locker room.

"Busy day," Frankie said, emerging from a washroom stall, her thick brown hair escaping its bun in wavy tendrils.

"Tell me about it."

"Heard your partner played quite the hero."

Maggie shrugged, trying not to conjure an image of a soaking wet Max and his ridiculous biceps. "You know St. James. Protect and serve."

Frankie snorted, obviously having the same naughty thoughts as Maggie about what her partner was welcome to serve.

"So did you get him anything for Christmas?"

"Who? The kid?"

"St. James. What kid? Who said anything about a kid?"

"Oh." Maggie continued to ransack her own locker. So it was going to be one of those talks. "No. Why would I?"

"Because it's Christmas? And Christmas is a time for friends. And lovers. And friends who want to—"

"Friends who want to stay friends should stop talking now," Maggie said in a sing-song voice, finally turning to face Frankie with her hands in her pockets. "And that's all we are. Friends. And colleagues."

"Yeah of course."

Maggie nodded and turned back around.

"Colleagues who want to bone."

Maggie felt her cheeks catch fire, and she chewed her lip to keep her face impassive. "Frankie—"

"You two are about as platonic as Romeo and Juliet."

"I was no English major, but I'm pretty sure they both die at the end."

"You know what I mean. Canada doesn't need a second Virtue and Moir."

"Virtue and Moir," Maggie chuckled, trying to picture Max on ice skates at all, let alone lifting her in the air in a leotard and tiny skirt, with those taut biceps, spinning her so close they could kiss if they wanted to, while everyone watched, wanting them to.

Stop it.

"Lucky for Canada, I hate to skate." She glanced at the photo of herself and Max taped inside her locker door. They stood shoulder to shoulder in what was meant to be an intimidating pose, except how could it be when she looked so young and Max was wearing those silly running shoes? "Besides, department policy says partners can't date. Not that we want to. He's like an…annoying…"

She couldn't bring herself to say older brother.

"Big brother's hot friend?" Frankie asked.

Maggie groaned. "Can you imagine? Him bossing me around all the time?"

"Mm-hmm."

"When do your folks get in from the Philippines?" Maggie asked, shutting the locker door on romantic notions.

"Castillos started arriving an hour ago. Santoses get in tonight. I swear, if anything goes down with the Bobby King case over the holidays, Ma will kill me. She'll feed you, but she'll kill me. She already thinks I drew a double shift tonight just to avoid airport duty."

"You did."

"Tell her that and no one will ever find your body," Frankie said fiercely.

Maggie laughed and opened the lost and found locker to continue her search. "I was thinking. I don't want to be in the way. I might get a hotel for the holidays."

"Don't be stupid. You're family."

"It's no big deal." Maggie extracted a hideous, frilly green sweater from the jumble of lost clothes.

"Oh, I need that," Frankie said, reaching for it. "Ugly sweater contest."

Maggie passed it over and kept digging.

"Nene," Frankie said, her hand on Maggie's arm. "You're bunking with me, no arguments. It will be fun—like the old days. Go Rams."

Maggie laughed. "Go Rams. You sure?"

"We'll gorge ourselves on adobo and sweet corn and beat all my cousins at Cards Against Humanity. I know it seems like a lot of kids, but I promise the adults will be so rowdy, you won't even notice the kids."

"I don't have a problem with kids."

Her cell phone began to ring as if on cue, and she didn't need to glance at the caller ID to know it was her mother again. She held the screen up for Frankie to see before making a face and silencing the call.

"I have nothing against kids, just against being chastised over the lamentable age of my ovaries and the vacant tenancy of my womb."

"I should probably tell you—"

"I mean a year off sounds fabulous, don't get me wrong," Maggie said, tossing the phone on a bench. "A little boring maybe. What would I even do?"

"Mags—"

"Anyway I do have a career, such as it is. And maybe it's not the one I planned, but it's still a career. Does she really think any of us can walk away for that long and then pick up right back where we left off like nothing ever happened?"

"I'm pregnant."

Maggie froze, her face suddenly burning. It explained the throwing up, at least, and her friend's sudden aversion to the smell of curry. No wonder Maggie wasn't a detective, missing so many signs. "Like... pee on a stick pregnant or pee in a cup pregnant?"

"Both."

"That's so great!" she exclaimed, a little too enthusiastically, pivoting to hug her friend. "Congratulations. I mean it."

"No you don't, but I'll take it. And thank you?"

"It's great, right?"

"Yeah?"

"It's going to be great. What did Tony say?"

"Forget about Tony, I'm going to need a mat leave replacement who can make sure all the testosterone around this place doesn't wreck my filing system."

A tiny thrill ran through Maggie's stomach, followed by sick dread, but she squashed them both down. "Good thing Taylor's on the D's rotation then."

"Have you seen his notes? Anyway, Taylor's not going to stick around. He'll be off to Guns and Gangs as soon as the King case is done. Just think about it, Mags."

"Everyone decent?" Max called from the door, where he leaned gazing out into the hallway.

He'd changed into dry gray Converse and was wearing a long-sleeved uniform shirt, with the cuffs rolled up, exposing his forearms and the mysterious tattoo he usually kept covered with a wide watch band, and my god, what was it about men with their cuffs turned up like that?

"Ready to take another crack at this?" he asked.

Another crack at what now? *STOP IT.*

Maggie took a breath and squeezed her friend's hand before following Max into the hallway. "You know, it's not our case," she said.

Max ignored her, side-stepping into the staff lounge. There were two bananas left on the counter—a perfect yellow one and an extremely ripe one. "Gonna be somebody's case. Why not ours?" he asked, swiping the brown banana before Maggie could, as if it were some kind of contest.

"Because it belongs to Fifty-Two Division? And we're supposed to be sitting on Bobby King. Dix would say we should call Children's Aid and get back to work." She gagged a little, watching him eat the mushy banana which was almost too soft to peel. What kind of sociopath liked brown bananas?

"As soon as the brother hopped a southbound train at Yonge Street, it became our case," Max said between bites. "You want it, don't you?"

He had her there. Maggie liked puzzles, and not the cross-word kind she resorted to during stakeouts. She liked jagged pieces and figuring out how they fit.

"Come on, day's more than half over. What's the harm in investigating a little before we call Children's Aid? There's plenty of eyes on King. Dix won't care."

"Especially if we don't tell him?"

He pointed at her as if to say, Exactly.

It wasn't that Maggie was philosophically opposed to taking a case from another division. It was just—she and Frankie had been besties since college and right on through the Academy. They'd had big plans to disrupt the patriarchy and become the youngest female detectives on the force.

When Frankie succeeded and Maggie stayed behind, everyone expected her friend to bring Maggie up with her—and she was trying, if Maggie would give her half a chance. But each time the detective rotation came up, Maggie didn't even apply, and she half-hated herself for it.

Bobby King felt like her chance to get back on track, a sink or swim moment. Unless they bungled it, and then she'd be pushing paper until retirement.

Maybe Max was right. Maybe the bus station thing was a more enticing puzzle.

She let him lead the way through to the squad room, where Boyd and his rookie had turned up. Someone had strewn the entire contents of both JanSport backpacks across two desks in a haphazard fashion that made Maggie's eye twitch.

"I'm not even going to ask," she said. "You two are going to clean all this up when you're finished?"

"We're off duty." Boyd put up his hands, clearly saying, *Not it*, without saying, *Not it*. "The Jabberwocky found this—I don't know what it is, a Happy Meal toy?—in your boy's locker. Wanted to bring it by."

"That's sweet. And then you were trying to figure out which bag to put it in and their stuff just sort of exploded all over my desk?"

"Yes… ma'am?" Hector stammered.

Ma'am. If that didn't make you feel older than Max's decrepit banana, what would? "Kyle's fine," she said.

"Yes, ma'am."

Max snickered and Maggie glared at him until he flattened his mouth into a straight line and looked sheepishly up at her through long dark lashes that were wasted on a man. Well maybe not wasted. *Stop it!*

"There they are, the flagship of my fleet." Staff Sergeant Dixon emerged from his office and surveyed the mess in his squad room. "MJ? Why'd you steal their case?" he asked, gesturing at Boyd and his rookie.

Dixon and Maggie's partner went way back. Max had explained once that his friend called him MJ because, *There's nothing saintly about you, buddy*. But really, he just thought Dix was lazy.

"Oh, not it," Boyd said, raising his hands in surrender. "I'm not touching this. Your boy wants the case, he can have it. You need my rookie to help? You can have him too."

"Hey!" Hector turned away from the personal effects.

"Call Children's Aid," Dixon said, heading toward the locker rooms. "And change your shoes!"

"Yep," Max agreed, and snatched a granola bar from the rubble.

"Does your rookie know how to check security footage?" Maggie asked Boyd.

The senior officer looked at Hector, who gave a faint head-shake. Boyd sighed dramatically, checking his watch for effect. "All right, I'll stick around, but this is not my case. As far as Fifty-Two Division is concerned, there is no case."

"I owe you one." Maggie grinned at him and he shook his head. There was a time, at the Academy, when she'd harbored a secret crush on her fellow trainee. He was charming and hand-some, with his warm eyes and John Legend smile. Sadly for the fifty-two percent of Toronto's population that was female, Boyd wasn't interested.

"You owe me more than one."

"Two, but that's my final offer," Maggie said, turning back to Max who waved the granola bar. "Hungry?" she asked him.

"Famished. And I bet he is too. For a… gluten-free oatie nut bar. Mmm. Delicious."

"So you're the good cop?" Maggie asked.

"We're all good cops, ma'am," he said, making an after you gesture and then following her into the small informal interview room.

The boy was sitting in a chair with his feet up on the seat, hugging his legs and resting his head on his knees, like a forlorn little Eeyore who'd lost his tail. He sat up when they entered and wiped his nose on his sleeve. Max's jacket sleeve, actually.

"Are you warm enough?" Maggie asked, resisting the urge to take the jacket away and launder it.

Max held up the snack bar. The boy gave him some powerful side-eye, but Max tossed it to him anyway, and he demolished the thing in ten seconds flat.

"So we haven't been able to find your brother," Maggie said. "Any idea where he might have gone?"

No response.

"Maybe home? Or to a friend's house?"

Nothing.

"Are you sure we can't call anyone to come get you?"

Silence.

"I think your brother probably felt pretty bad about leaving you behind when the sirens went off, and now he's afraid you'll be mad at him." Maggie was grasping at straws.

Max leaned against the door, unusually quiet. It irritated her when he took over, but now that he was just letting her do her thing, watching her flail, she found that irritating too.

"Why did he leave you behind?" she pressed.

The boy stared past her, like he was trying to see through the wall.

"Did you do something to upset him?"

Nothing.

There were few things more aggravating to Maggie than being actively ignored. She tried to remember being his age. As the older sibling, anytime she got separated from her younger brother—because he wandered off at the park or was hiding at the grocery store—the guilt she felt over not keeping a close enough eye on him was staggering; but it was nothing compared to how badly she could make Charlie feel about it later. Reverse guilt was a powerful weapon.

She was willing to play the bad cop if it meant an end to this stand-off. Her last shred of confidence was rapidly evaporating as though she'd been handed a grade ten geometry final.

"We don't have time for this, St. James. If he doesn't want to be reunited with his brother, then we better hand him off to Children's Aid. Let them sort it out."

Max raised his eyebrows at her. "Before we even get out the thumb screws?"

Maggie doubled down on her bluff and reached for the door.

"Je vous salue, Marie, pleine de grâce," the boy whispered.

Max's face lit up with delighted amusement, and Maggie glared at him before turning back to the child.

"Was that French?" she asked.

"Le seigneur est avec vous," the boy replied, piercing her with his steady gaze.

"Dixon speaks a little French, right?" Maggie asked.

"Vous êtes bénie entre toutes les femmes?" Max asked the boy, whose eyes widened as he bit his bottom lip.

Maggie was terribly impressed. Since when did Max St. James speak French? "What did he say?" she asked.

Max didn't answer. He stepped forward, leaning with both hands on the table and said, "Es-tu prêt a parler anglais maintenant?"

The boy ignored him, still chewing his lip.

"Look, wise guy," he said, gentle but firm. "We know the bomb threat came from the pay phones across from your locker."

Not strictly true.

"We know your brother was there with you. We know the Legos were yours."

Definitely conjecture.

"The only thing we don't know is why you did it. But you know what? It doesn't even matter. What matters is, if you confess, and you help us find him, you won't get in nearly as much trouble as if you don't."

The boy stared from Max to Maggie—trying to decide which one was more trustworthy.

"No? Tough guy? Cool, cool, cool. Thing is, Officer Kyle here? She needs a win today. There's this other case—I won't bore you with the details. But if you don't cooperate, she's going to insist on a night in lockup."

"Officer St. James, may I see you outside?" Maggie asked.

He opened the door and waved her through to the hallway.

"Yes, Officer Kyle?" he asked, matching her formality despite his teasing tone.

"We can't keep him here overnight. Even if we charge him, he has to be released to Children's Aid or a legal guardian."

"Tactics, woman. He's stonewalling, and I'm tired. Je suis fatigué."

"And since when do you know French?"

"I don't. I know the Hail Mary in French. Which is what he was saying to you because he's stalling. I've seen it a few times from immersion school kids."

"Why?" Maggie asked.

"Because they think they can intimidate anglophones? 'Cause they think it's funny? 'Cause they think you won't know the difference? Take your pick."

"No, I mean, why do you know that prayer in French?"

"Went to Catholic school for a year."

He said it flippantly, with a shrug, and Maggie was baffled. She turned away from him and led the way back to the squad room. How was it possible she'd known him for a decade and there were still parts of his life that were completely foreign to her?

"So what happened? You got kicked out?"

"I didn't like the dress code," he said.

CHAPTER 5

$\mathcal{M}$ax relished the way Maggie stalked around when she was flustered, like a black bear whose fish got away.

"Exactly how much French do you speak?" she demanded.

"Why? Impressed?" He tried not to puff up his chest, but he'd be lying if he said he hadn't been living to impress her every day for the last decade.

"A little."

Noted. "Ah, oui, bon, mademoiselle, mon petit chou. Pample-mousse, jambon, pomme de terre. L'orangeade. Poulet avec fromage."

"Were those all food words?"

"Pretty much. Rookie, get on the horn to the bilingual schools, yeah? See if they're missing any students about yay tall," Max said, measuring out the approximate height of the boy.

"No," Maggie said. "Call Children's Aid and tell them we need a bilingual social worker."

The rookie looked from one to the other and then back to Boyd, who shrugged and grinned, enjoying the show.

"Sure, sure, but do mine first," Max said.

"St. James—"

"I hear you." And he did. Calling Children's Aid was procedurally the correct thing to do, but there was something about this case. He wasn't ready to hand it over yet. "Give me until five o'clock. We don't find him, I'll let you drive for a month."

"You hate driving."

"Fine, then I'll drive. And I'll do all the paperwork."

He knew it wasn't fair to ask her to flout procedure. He also knew she'd do it for him, just this once.

"Fine," she grumbled. "But you're also buying dinner."

"Yes, ma'am."

She raised an eyebrow at him, and he ducked away, chuckling.

"Call the schools, rookie."

"Yes, sir."

"He called me sir," Max said. "I like him."

"Doesn't it make you feel old?" Maggie asked.

It didn't, but he decided to play along. "Well it does now. Thanks for that. Anything on those bus station cameras?" he asked Boyd, who was pretending not to laugh, as he studied the images on his computer screen.

"Not really." Boyd ran the footage backwards so all the players did a weird nightmarish dance. "You can see the Runaway put Locker Boy inside right here." He advanced the tape again slowly.

"Looks like he got in willingly enough," Maggie observed.

"Then big bro runs off stage right. He definitely doesn't stop at the locker with the IED."

"Stage left," Max corrected, and the others all turned to stare at him. "The actor's left. House right."

"Whatever," Boyd said. "He ran toward the Edward Street exit."

"No one else approaches the locker?" Max asked.

"Not until it blows."

"How far back did you go?"

"All the way to the beginning. Tape resets every day at midnight."

"And tapes over the day before," Max finished.

"You got it." Boyd ran a hand over his hair and rubbed his eyes.

"And no one put anything in the locker today?"

"Nope."

"Wait, what was that?" Max asked, as the older boy came back on screen.

"He runs back a few minutes later, but he doesn't appear to stop." Boyd said, sitting up and slowing the footage down once more.

"At the lockers, but what about the phones? The time stamp is right around the time the call came in," Maggie said.

Boyd shrugged.

"Is there a better angle?" She leaned in, itching to take over from Boyd but holding herself in check.

Max smiled. What kind of whirlwind would she be if she just turned herself loose?

"Nope. If he stopped there, we can't prove it."

"We could fingerprint Locker Boy," the rookie suggested, but Maggie shook her head.

"Outside of identical twins, there's not really enough genetic correlation to bother."

An adult-sized person entered the frame, possibly chasing the older kid. "Who's that?" Max and Maggie asked at the same time. They high-fived over their heads without taking their eyes off the screen.

Old habits. Max had a good feeling about this case. They always were at their best working as a team.

"Adorable," Boyd teased, rolling his eyes at them, and Maggie stuck out her tongue.

"So who is it?" Max asked again.

"Haven't ID'd him yet," the rookie said.

"Based on witness testimony, he's most likely an employee," Boyd explained. "A witness said one of the ticket counter guys was chasing a couple of kids shortly before the fire alarm was pulled."

"They say why?" Maggie asked.

"Only that it gave her déjà vu."

"So it's a regular occurrence," Maggie said, more to herself than to anyone else.

"What did the shift lead say?" Max asked the rookie.

"I can't read your writing," the rookie said sheepishly to Boyd.

Maggie peered over his shoulder at the notebook. "It was busy, he didn't see anything, lots of people, blah blah blah. Standard. Useless." She plopped down in an empty desk chair. "Your writing is worse than it was at the Academy."

"It had to get worse to keep you from cheating off me," Boyd teased.

"What about this stuff? Anything incriminating?" Max asked, taking a seat on the corner of the desk where the kids' belongings were still piled up.

"Let's see." The rookie hunted through the mess before holding up a battered children's book about coding. "This could be something."

Max took it and flipped through the pages until a photograph fell out. "Ho!" He held up the picture for everyone to see: two, young dark-haired boys standing on either side of a youngish blond man, maybe Maggie's age. All three stood before a small prop plane, the kind contractors use to fly supplies in and out of remote wilderness areas up north. "A couple years old, at least."

"They're so tiny," Maggie said taking the photo for a closer look, her fingers absently brushing his hand.

He flicked his gaze from Boyd to the rookie, but neither was paying attention. No one had noticed Max's pulse was racing. *Focus, St. James.*

He took a deep breath and flipped through the book again. It was a library book, stamped for Lillian H. Smith Library on College Street. "Hey rookie, which library reported its fancy Legos stolen?"

"First of all, it's Lego not Legos, and secondly, they weren't. Lego." When Max glared at him he added, "Lillian H. Smith Library on College."

"Interesting," Max said, holding up the book.

"You think they stole the not Legos from the library and planted them in the locker?" Maggie asked.

He shrugged. "I wouldn't bet my pension on it. But maybe they know who did."

"Okay, Exhibit B, I guess," the rookie said. "A robotics camp brochure from the same library." He held up a colorful trifold flyer, which Max snatched for himself and then relinquished to Maggie.

"Circumstantial at best," Max mused.

Maggie nodded. "Exhibit C, perhaps? Disposable camera." She tossed the little cardboard box to Max. "For documenting the crime?"

"Bit of a stretch. Couple of Hardy Boys, maybe? Sticking their noses where they don't belong? Get that to the lab, would you?" Max tossed the camera to the rookie.

For Max, the pile of belongings confirmed what he'd already been thinking. Two clean t-shirts a piece and a bottle of cough medicine—these kids had more to worry about than playing backyard detective.

Maggie surveyed the scattered belongings, reserving judgment and weighing each clue. "Bandages. Hand sanitizer. Snacks. A ratty Beanie Baby. A dog-eared copy of *Prince Caspian*. A piece of petrified wood."

"It's a tiger's eye, actually," Max said, cutting himself off to keep from sounding argumentative.

"A flyer for a church choir." She tossed the announcement from Grace Church-on-the-Hill back on the table. "Does it seem like…" Her eyes darted back and forth like a fast-moving type-writer, perturbed by her own thoughts but reluctant to share them.

Max nodded.

"It's everything important." She opened her mouth to say more, and then shook her head. But their eyes met and Max knew what she didn't want to say. Maybe the contents of those backpacks spilled out across her desk was all they had in the world.

He'd asked her to give him until five o'clock to find the brother and he felt the opportunity squeezing shut like a car window being rolled up on his fingers.

Maggie was right, they couldn't legally hold the boy much longer. They'd be forced to call Children's Aid, and then it wouldn't matter who did what or why. Nothing would matter because Max believed with every ounce of his intuition that Children's Aid would send the younger boy off to a home some-where, and the older one might never be found, splitting the brothers up forever.

And if there was one thing Max always tried to do, it was trust his gut.

From their ratty clothes to their unkempt hair, it was obvious these kids were on their own. Sure, they should send the photo around to French schools, that was just solid policing, but they hadn't attended school recently, he would bet his pension on that. These kids didn't have warm beds and gentle words waiting for them at home each night.

He rifled absently through the sad pile of supplies and trin-kets, finally picking up a dark blue choir ribbon and rubbing the medallion between his thumb and finger. All they had to go on was the library book.

"You guys get the CCTV footage from the subway yet?" he asked, standing up and stretching.

"It's processing now," Boyd said.

"Where are we going?" Maggie asked.

"Library," he said, waving the coding book. "Best place to find answers, right?"

"What about the little francophone?" she asked.

"Hey, rookie. Get the kid a pop or something. If he speaks English, call me."

"Yes, sir," the rookie said with a little salute, accepting the toonie Max held out for him.

"St. James is fine."

"Yes, sir. When should we call Children's Aid?"

"Later," Max said over his shoulder as he snatched up the car keys and headed toward the sally port leaving Maggie to trail along behind.

"Hey," she protested.

"Just give me until five o'clock."

THE DISCOVERY DISTRICT BRANCH OF THE TORONTO PUBLIC Library was an imposing post-modern structure situated at the corner of College and Huron. Each time Maggie saw the majestic griffin and lion statues guarding its brick arched entrance, she promised herself to visit more often, to join a book club or spend her next day off immersed in the third-floor sci-fi collection. Somehow, though, she never quite managed to make the time.

The first thing she noticed upon entering the grand, circular lobby was a massive Christmas tree. The next thing she noticed was the lone, frazzled librarian, who bustled back and forth like a biblio-bumble bee, serving the long, snaking line of visitors waiting to check out their holiday haul.

"We may have come at a bad time," Max whispered, checking his wrist out of habit, though he hadn't put his watch back on after showering. Maggie's footsteps echoed through the grand room as they joined the back of the line.

"This is, what, one—two klicks—from the coach terminal?" Maggie leaned in close to whisper and caught a whiff of his sweet earthy scent, aftershave, mint gum, and something else that was pure Max.

He leaned in too and breathed, "Give or take."

Maggie swallowed. She had some ideas about both giving and taking which had nothing to do with this case. *Stop it!* "Twice as far as the City Hall branch," she murmured, trying to get her head back in the game.

"So?"

"So why this one? There must be a reason."

"Like fancy robot Legos?"

"Not-Legos. Get it right."

"Look around, Kyle. Why would anyone go anywhere else?"

Max took in the marble atrium as though seeing an old friend for the first time in years, a small smile tugging at the side of his mouth, and Maggie had to agree. It was maybe the most magnificent library in Toronto.

"I remember when this place opened. I used to love riding my bike here and getting lost for hours."

"What, sneaking the *Sports Illustrated* swimsuit edition?" Maggie teased.

"Sure, but with Farley Mowat tucked inside so I wouldn't lose my street cred." He stepped up to the counter where it was finally their turn.

"Sorry about the wait," the librarian said, glancing from Max to Maggie and back again. "If you're here about the RoboZ, you'll want the children's department."

She nodded in some vague direction and motioned for the next person in line to approach the desk. A young girl stepped up, glancing nervously at the two officers.

"That's not actually why we're here," Maggie said, scooting over so the librarian could still serve the little girl.

"We were hoping you might give us some information about

the person who borrowed this," Max explained, showing her the coding book.

"I'm sorry," the librarian stammered. "That would be a massive violation of our privacy policy."

"Please? A child is in danger," Maggie said. It wasn't exactly stretching the truth. He was out there, somewhere, cold and alone. "We really need to find him."

"I wish I could help," she said, and Maggie mostly believed her. "What kind of danger?" she added, glancing uncomfortably at the long restless line behind them.

"Brenda," Max said, leaning on the desk to read her name tag and smiling sweetly at her, showing off one dimple. A one-dimpled smile wasn't genuine. When he dialed up the charm to try and get his way, he couldn't seem to force the right cheek to pop. "Is it okay if I call you Brenda?"

She nodded, her own cheeks beginning to flush. "Is it okay if I call you Officer Tight-Pants?" she asked with a slightly shocked but somewhat proud look on her face.

Maggie's eyes widened, her smile frozen in place. Max grinned, a hint of the other dimple trying to break free, and Maggie had the sudden urge to start cracking jokes just to prove she could control his dimples better than he or anyone else could.

"Is there somewhere we can speak privately?" Max asked the librarian.

Brenda glanced at the long line again and then offered a noncommittal *what-the-hell* shrug before waving them around the desk and into a workroom. Following along behind like a rusty caboose, Maggie noticed that somehow the navy cargo pants, the perpetually ill-fitting bane of every female officer, did rather flatter Max's backside. They showed off just the right amount of curve. *Stop it.*

"Thank you so much for your help, Brenda. The thing is, this kid? We found his little brother crammed inside a bus station locker."

The librarian blanched, and Maggie stepped heavily on Max's foot in warning. He knew better than to divulge details of an active case.

"He's alive," he said quickly. "But traumatized, as you can imagine. We're trying to locate his family. Do you think you can help us?"

"Our policy is pretty clear," Brenda said with less conviction than before.

"We won't tell if you don't." Max grinned suggestively.

The flirting really didn't bother Maggie. It didn't. In fact, it probably should have. Not for herself of course, but for all of womankind, because Max St. James thought he could get whatever he wanted with a few friendly words and those dimples. But if the other women didn't take offense then why should she? They always flirted right back—except when they didn't, and then Maggie took a perverse pleasure in his rejection. But not because the flirting bothered her.

"Maybe I could pull up the account. Maybe I could give them a call and tell them to contact you?" Brenda suggested.

"That would be incredible. Thank you." Max handed her the book.

"Oh." She frowned and pointed to a Friends of the Library stamp on the interior cover. "This one isn't in circulation anymore. It was sold in one of our book sales."

"I'm guessing you don't have a record of that?" Maggie asked.

"No, I'm sorry. Anyone could have bought it. But are these the kids?" She pointed to the photo Max had left tucked inside.

"Do you recognize them?" he asked.

"Yeah, I mean I think so. It's kind of an old picture, but I'm sure they're in here all the time."

"With their parents?" Maggie asked.

Brenda shrugged. "Maybe? You should probably ask the children's librarian." She pointed out some bookshelves off the atrium.

"Do you know their names?" Max asked.

"Sorry. I really wish I did. Regina might."

"Thank you so much, Brenda," Max said, handing her his card. "If you think of anything else, please don't hesitate to call."

"I won't hesitate," the librarian said, looking at the cluttered workspace and then tucking his card safely into her bra.

Maggie had no doubt Brenda would be thinking of something else real soon.

THE CHILDREN'S DEPARTMENT WAS WARM AND INVITING, IF A BIT quieter than the late afternoon assault on the circulation desk. A handful of kids browsed the shelves with their parents while the wiry, gray-haired librarian cleaned up the remnants of an arts and crafts explosion.

"Officers," she said brightly. "How can I help? Are you here about our robot?"

"Indirectly," Maggie said. "We hoped you might know these two boys?"

Max handed over the photograph and Regina's face lit up instantly. "Yes, I know these two! Harry? And… Oscar? No, that can't be right. Oh, it's on the tip of my tongue—"

"Have you seen either of them this afternoon?" Maggie asked, trying not to let her impatience show.

"I see them most every day." She frowned. "But not this afternoon, no."

Max pointed to a corner hidden from view by bookshelves and made a circle with his finger to let Maggie know he was going to walk around, scoping out the hidden nooks.

"Are you sure?" Maggie pressed the librarian. "Maybe the older one came in by himself today?"

"Oh, he's never by himself," Regina said, smiling and handing the picture back. "Those two are always together."

"What about him?" Maggie asked, pointing out the man in the photo.

"I don't recognize him. But then, I don't pay much attention to the parents."

"Thanks." Maggie slipped the picture back inside the coding book. "Every day, huh? What do they do here?"

"Oh a little of this, a little of that. They read, do homework. Sometimes they play on the computers or participate in crafternoon. They joined the robotics camp a few months back. Or was it the Minecraft camp?" she asked herself, pausing to stare into the depths of her memory with one hand full of pipe cleaners and the other, popsicle sticks. "I don't suppose it matters. We had a few last-minute cancellations and it seemed a shame to let the kits go to waste."

"Kits?" Maggie asked, nodding at Max to rejoin her. He did, shaking his head once to say he hadn't spotted the brother. "Kits like the one that's missing?"

"Yes. Maybe not the exact same, we have a few. But similar."

"Do the campers keep them?" Max asked.

"Goodness no. Do you know how much those cost? We got ours through a special grant. We reuse them for other camps and lend them out to scout troops and primary schools."

Regina put the craft supplies in a bin on her desk and then led them to a filing cabinet which she unlocked and opened. It contained at least a dozen zip-top bags full of pieces.

"A grade four teacher checked them out last week. That's why they weren't locked up. I was still making sure all those tiny pieces got back into the right bags."

"You can build any kind of robot with these?" Max asked, picking up a bag full of colorful blocks and gears.

"If you can dream it, you can do it, as they say."

"Can you also program it to do anything you want?" Maggie asked. "Could it strike a match and light a fuse?"

The librarian frowned. "The programming would need to be

very precise, but maybe if you glued a match or two in each little hand… it could strike them against each other?" She imitated the motion as she envisioned it. "Why do you ask?"

"Curiosity," Maggie said with a smile. "Other than the stolen set, were any pieces missing?"

"Yes, actually, a wheel and a few gears. They must have been misplaced in the stolen bag. I really hope you find it. I'd hate to have to reduce our camp size, but the board won't approve replacements any time soon."

"What about security cameras?" Maggie spotted one aimed at the librarian's desk.

"I told the officers this morning. You'll have to make a formal request to the board. It would be a major violation of our privacy policy to share footage," Regina said, closing and locking the cabinet once more.

"Even when a crime's been committed?" Max asked.

"I'm afraid it's the policy."

"What's the point of having the cameras then?" Maggie asked.

The librarian pointed to a sign that read SMILE, YOU'RE ON CAMERA. "It's a powerful deterrent," she said reverently.

"Until it's not," Max said. "Tell the board we don't have a prayer of recovering your missing kit without the footage."

Maggie resisted the impulse to add, *At least not in more than one melted piece.*

CHAPTER 6

$\mathcal{A}$fter another quick walk-around to confirm the brother wasn't hiding elsewhere in the library, Max and Maggie headed back outside, no closer to finding him than they had been an hour ago.

They stood on the library steps for a moment, looking out at the long shadows cast across the sidewalk. It would be dark soon and cold.

"Three kilometers between here and the church," Max said. "Long walk for two little kids."

"Maybe they take the bus. Kids ride free."

"Why though? Harry? And Oscar...? That can't be right," he said, imitating the librarian.

"It's a shame. Even librarians don't remember names anymore," Maggie said, shaking her head.

"People don't listen when other people talk," Max replied, heading to the patrol car.

"People don't, huh? What's Boyd's rookie's name?"

"Hector."

"Touché," she conceded.

"Ma'am," he said with a nod and a grin.

She shook her head, trying to hide the smile she didn't want him to see. "We'd better get back to the barn. At least it wasn't a complete loss. We have means and opportunity."

"Come on. You really think they stole that set from the library?"

"You honestly don't?" Maggie asked, her voice high with surprise although he didn't see why. She was fixated on circumstantial evidence and conjecture.

"I know you hate coincidences, but I'm having trouble putting together a motive."

She leaned against the hood of the patrol car with her ankles crossed, waiting for him to continue.

"What would possess two generally well liked and well behaved children, according to Regina the librarian, to steal from a place that's been good to them? And then turn around and use those stolen goods to destroy public property? To what end?"

"Piss poor judgment? Mad at their parents? They thought it would be funny? They wanted attention? They have nothing and robots are cool? Why does anyone do anything?"

Max shoved his fists deep in his pockets and rolled his neck. The windchill was beginning to bite through his uniform shirt. And the kid was out there with nothing but a hoodie. They needed to find him, not argue about theories.

"You really don't think they had anything to do with it?" Maggie asked.

Max shook his head.

"I never pegged you to prefer coincidence over an outcome you don't like."

Now she was twisting his words. What happened to innocent until proven guilty? But he couldn't say that or it would hurt her feelings and her confidence and turn into a whole thing. "Friendly wager?" he asked, working the dimples instead. "Chaos theory versus synchronicity?"

"You already owe me a month's worth of paperwork and dinner. What else is there?"

"Loser's prize from the White Elephant."

"Deal," Maggie agreed, surprising the heck out of him. "Pick something good."

"I always pick yours," he said holding her gaze, and he didn't know why he was confessing to it. Now wasn't the time or the place, not that there would ever be a right time and place to end a ten year partnership by confessing to *feelings*.

"What?" she laughed. "The White Elephant Exchange is anonymous."

"I can tell which one's yours." *Shut up, Max.* "You wrap like you're getting graded on it, and you've used the same roll of paper for at least six years. Santa Claus in space."

She opened her mouth like she had some pithy retort, but then closed it and turned away, moving toward the passenger-side door. "I'll have to buy something good then."

"Like it's not already bought and wrapped in the back of your locker?" he teased.

"Maybe it is, maybe it isn't," she snapped, yanking open her car door. "What's really going on?"

He shrugged and tossed her the keys even though he had promised to drive for the foreseeable future. "We caught a case. We've got to see it through."

Maggie wasn't buying it though. "I get it," she told him, crossing to the driver's side. "But it was criminal mischief at worst. Don't you want to get back to the King case like everyone else?"

"King'll get booked with or without us. Those kids... they're on the precipice." Max's voice broke, and he looked out the window because he didn't want to see if she was looking at him.

She adjusted her mirrors and merged into traffic before finally answering. "I understand your concerns about the system. I do."

She really didn't though. It wasn't her fault, but she didn't understand at all.

"I mean, it's not perfect, but we have to give the system a chance to work."

"And when it fails? What then?"

"I guess then we figure out how to help."

But in Max's opinion, by then it would be too late.

YOU COULD CUT THE AWKWARD WITH A KNIFE AS MAGGIE DROVE back to the station. Max often asked her to drive, but this time he had practically thrown the keys at her. Was he mad at her because they'd have to call Children's Aid, like somehow it was her fault they hadn't found the kid before his self-imposed deadline? Or because she tried to deflect his—his what? What even was that about her gift-wrapping?

Since when did he pay such close attention?

She jumped when his phone vibrated. "St. James," he answered.

A female began speaking immediately. His new librarian friend, perhaps? Maggie slowed the car, waiting for the signal to turn back to the library.

"Yes, good point, Selina, if I had checked caller ID, I would have known it was you… On the bright side, I probably wouldn't have answered, so—"

Selina? Maggie mouthed questioningly at him, but he waved her off. She was pretending anyway. She knew *Selina* was the neighbor he insisted he wasn't dating.

"No, I haven't looked into it yet, I—" he began, but she kept cutting him off. Apparently *Selina* was feeling chatty. "Because it's been a very busy day… No, not writing speeding tickets," he said, pinching the bridge of his nose. "No—Selina, I've got nothing for you on the gingerbread house. Because I—kind of on a deadline here. Can we talk about this later?" He took the phone from his ear, but she kept talking. "Gingerbread. Got it. Gotta go," he said, stabbing at the touch screen to end the call.

"So, gingerbread?" Maggie asked. "She helping you enter the contest?"

"What contest?" he asked, distracted. "No, she's on about this—it's nothing."

"Didn't sound like nothing," Maggie said, making a left turn onto Front Street.

"I guarantee—ninety-five percent, it's nothing."

"And the other five percent?"

"Still probably nothing."

"*Selina* clearly thinks it's something," Maggie said, pulling into the parking lot behind the station. She hated herself for being incapable of saying the poor woman's name without infusing it full of meaning and venom.

"It's like a playhouse for kids to go inside and tell Santa what they want for Christmas. It's nothing. Last year she was convinced carolers were casing her place to rob it. The year before that, thieving Santas were following her around the city pretending to raise money for charity. I assure you, this gingerbread thing is nothing."

"Didn't the Santa larceny ring turn out to be real?"

"Whose side are you on?"

"Yours," she said. "Always yours." She bit her lip, hoping it didn't sound weird, but it was important for him to know. It shouldn't even need to be said, except maybe it did.

"Good. Let's get this over with."

The moment they entered the squad room, Hector waved them over. "I was starting to think you'd never come back. I found something!" he called.

"You did?" Boyd asked, looking over in surprise.

Why were they even still here, helping on a case their division didn't want? Maggie glanced at her phone, but there were no missed calls or texts.

"Rookie doesn't have a phone?" Max asked Boyd.

"May have dropped it in the toilet," Boyd said, while Hector turned three shades of red.

"No," Maggie groaned.

"I'm not saying he did. But maybe he did."

"So what is it?" Maggie asked Hector.

He looked up at her with big puppy dog eyes, brimming with excitement. She imagined him wagging an invisible tail—swish, swish, swish—as he twirled side to side in his computer chair. "You're not going to like it," he said.

"Well then lay it on us." Max pulled up a chair beside Hector and straddled it the wrong way around, like the rebel he thought he was, and Maggie had never realized she might have a thing for rebels, with or without a cause. Or at least for improper seating.

"Promise you won't get mad?"

"Why would we get mad?" Maggie asked.

"Just don't shoot the messenger, you know?"

"Hector!" Boyd snapped. "What did I tell you about ripping off bandages?"

"The kid's gone," he blurted out.

"Gone?" Max jumped up to check the soft interview room.

"Not Locker Boy. The Runaway."

"He was already gone," Maggie said as Boyd rolled his chair over to hear more. "We've been looking for him all afternoon."

"Look." Hector pulled up some footage on his computer. "This is the west side of the bus station." The grainy, jerky image showed a small figure in a hooded sweatshirt approach a semi truck and speak to the driver before racing around to the other side and presumably climbing in.

"How long have you been sitting on this?" Max asked. He kept his voice calm, but his clenched jaw gave away his mounting temper, at least to Maggie.

"Like maybe an hour, hour and a half."

"What's the time stamp on the video though?" Maggie asked.

"Two thirty."

"Two and a half hours," Max said, his voice shaking a little. "He climbed in a truck more than two and a half hours ago. He could be halfway to Ottawa by now. He could be halfway to anywhere."

"Take a breath," Maggie said. "It's a lead." But she could already see in his eyes that Max wasn't going to pass this lead to the proper authorities.

"You have a phone," Boyd chastised Hector, picking up the receiver of the desk phone and shaking it at him before slamming it back in the cradle. "You have a training officer with a working cell that sends text messages, and by the way you can text over email, and you thought this was information that could wait?"

"I'm sorry," the rookie said.

"You don't sit on things for the glory here, all right? We're all one team. It's the case that matters."

"Yes, sir," Hector said, and Maggie thought his puppy dog eyes might burst into tears at any moment.

"Any idea where the truck's heading?" she asked.

"No, how would I…?"

"Did you notify OPP? Put out an APB? Issue an Amber Alert?" Boyd demanded in full TO mode, being hard on Hector to drive the point home—probably being hard on him because he was angry at himself for not paying the rookie more attention.

"He wasn't in imminent danger—"

"Are you sure? Do you know what the truck was carrying? Where it's going? Whether the driver's a pedophile?"

"You think he's a pedophile?"

"He could be anybody, that's the point," Max said. "Drug dealer, human trafficker. Slow it down?" He pointed to the video as the truck began to pull away from the loading dock. "Can you read the logo?"

The rookie froze the footage and tried to zoom in, which only made it more blurry.

"Does it say Kindersley?" Max asked.

"Maybe?"

"Rookie you have exactly ten minutes to figure out where that truck is heading," Max said, tapping the controls to zoom the picture out and back it up until the kid was in the frame again.

"On it," Hector said, sliding over to another computer and tapping away at the keyboard.

"It's five fifteen, St. James," Maggie reminded him.

Max took a picture of the CCTV footage with his phone and another of the photo they'd found inside the coding book. "No more French," he said.

The boy met them at the door as soon as they entered the room.

"Can I go yet?" he asked in perfect English.

"You ready to talk yet?" Maggie asked, guiding him back to the table where she took a seat.

The boy hovered near his chair, chewing his lip and thinking it over. "Ver says to let him do the talking," he finally said.

"Ver? Your brother?" Maggie asked. "What's that short for? Vernon? Everett? Avery? Denver?"

"If he were going to take off somewhere, where would he go?" Max tried.

The boy shook his head. "He wouldn't go anywhere without me."

Max leaned on the table like a TV character about to flip the whole thing over. He held out his phone for the boy to see the grainy picture of his brother speaking to a truck driver. The little guy looked at the picture and squinched up his face.

"That's not him," he said.

"Sure looks like him," Max replied.

"Ver wouldn't leave, not without me. He especially wouldn't get in a truck with a stranger, not even for a second!"

"Camera says different," Max told him.

His voice was so gentle that it almost broke Maggie. He didn't even know these kids but he was trying so hard to make everything okay.

"So in a crazy, upside down world where he did leave, where would he go?"

"He takes care of me," the boy whimpered.

"He put you in a locker," Maggie reminded him, trying to be as gentle as Max.

"Just for a minute. Just to hide."

"Hide from who?" she asked. "Why did you need to hide?"

He frowned again, realizing he'd said too much, and looked away.

"Come on, kiddo," Maggie said. "A witness told us the ticket counter guy was chasing a couple of kids. You wouldn't know anything about that, would you?"

"What I don't get," Max chimed in, setting his phone down and taking a seat next to Maggie, eye level with the boy, "is why he'd be chasing you, if you didn't put those fireworks in the locker."

"He said we were loitering. He always says that. But we weren't though. We never are."

"What were you doing then?" Maggie asked.

"Waiting."

"That's what loitering means," Max said.

"No it doesn't. Ver says it means hanging around for no good reason. But waiting is a reason."

Maggie tilted her head at Max. Kiddo had him there. "So, what, you were waiting for a bus?" she asked.

He looked down at the table and plopped heavily into his chair. "Sort of."

"Sort of?"

He heaved a deep sigh. "We were waiting for our mama. We wait for her every day."

"You were expecting your mom on the bus?" Max asked.

"No. Not expecting. Waiting just in case," he said.

A couple of years before Maggie was born, one of her mother's greatest anxieties was set in stone and left to ripen. It had started with a little girl, abducted and likely killed, while Maggie's mom was completing her nursing program in Edmonton. The urge to solve such an awful old case so her mom could finally exhale was probably the root of Maggie's desire to be a cold case detective.

The news broadcast of the girl's distraught parents pleading for the return of their child left an indelible mark on Charlotte Davies-not-yet-Kyle and informed her anxious approach to childdrearing for years to come.

Like the time she took Maggie and Charlie to Bower Place Mall in Red Deer, where everyone pretty much knew everyone. Maggie was about six, so Charlie would have only been four. He claimed not to even remember Charlotte sending them into the candy store with pocket money to spend, but they had felt like millionaires deliberating on the best kinds of chocolate and taffy and jaw breakers. Until they emerged from the shop to find her gone.

At first Maggie and her brother had sat down to wait, assuming their mom had popped into another store. They watched all the people go by and ate candy until their stomachs hurt. But after a couple of hours, they grew frantic and Charlie began to cry.

Maggie had known they couldn't sit outside the shop forever, but she was paralyzed with indecision. What if they left just as their mother came back for them? How would they ever find each other then?

Finally she had decided to go find help, so she left four-year-old Charlie outside the candy store in case their mother returned while she was gone. After wiping her runny nose on her sleeve, she had approached a kind-looking young saleswoman and told her she was lost. When asked her mother's name, though, Maggie worried she would be angry about being paged, so instead, she asked them to call her father.

An hour later, with the whole family reunited, Maggie learned the awful ordeal had been a test—one that she had failed spectacularly. She'd forgotten everything her mom had tried to teach her: don't hesitate, don't split up, don't talk to anyone but law enforcement. Twenty-seven years later, the mistake still haunted her. Ironically, it might also be the reason she never took the D's exam.

Was this little boy the victim of a similar test gone horribly wrong?

"How long have you been waiting?" Maggie asked him.

"A long time. Ver says it's better if we don't try to keep track, but I've had two birthdays," he said, and Maggie's heart collapsed, folding in on itself like a supernova.

CHAPTER 7

As soon as they got a name out of the boy, Max threw open the door and strode through the squad room to the staff sergeant's office.

"Name's Henri," he called to Boyd and the forlorn rookie, who slammed down the phone like it had bitten him.

"Sudbury!" the rookie yelled. "Truck's going to Sudbury."

"Did you tell them to hold it there?" Max asked. When he was met with a frozen, blank stare he motioned for the rookie to try again.

He didn't wait for a response before barging into Dix's office.

"Thought I told you to change those shoes," Dix said without looking up.

"You gotta give us the case," Max told him, sitting down and pulling his chair up close to the desk.

"What case? You have a case." Dix closed a file folder and dropped it on the pile growing from the floor beside his desk. "Bobby King. Illegal weapons trade. Ring a bell?"

"The bus station."

"Not only is that not a case, it's not my case to give. No one got hurt, no property of any value was damaged. It's not even our division. I don't have enough detectives to make that a case. You've turned the kid over to Children's Aid, right?"

"Kyle and I have it covered. Who needs detectives?"

"That reminds me," Dix said, getting up to rifle through his filing cabinet. "I'm looking for volunteers to train next year's rookie class. I'd like to put your name forward. You did a good job with our girl there. We could use another dozen like her."

Max made a noncommittal grunt. This was not the conversation he wanted to have, and he was burning daylight. Figuratively. The sun was already beginning to set.

"Fine. Whatever. But a new rookie might take your mind off the old one."

Max didn't react but maybe his friend had a point.

Dix turned back to face him. "You know, MJ, you step in a puddle in those shoes, you're going to have wet feet. Cold, slippery-soled, smelly wet feet."

"Probably."

"Wet feet will give you pneumonia," Dix said.

"I think trench foot is more likely."

"I won't come visit you in the hospital. Leah won't make you soup—"

"The case, Dix," Max interrupted.

"I told you—"

"Fine, I'll train your new rookie." It was the one thing he could offer—the one thing he didn't want to give up—that might change his friend's mind. Dix seemed to think with Max out of the way, Maggie would take the D's exam. Max wasn't so sure, but if they solved this case, maybe she'd get the adrenaline rush she needed to actually go through with it.

"Great!" Dix said. "You want to investigate pranks instead of being part of breaking the Bobby King case, go for it. But wherever it leads, you don't leave the city, understood?"

How did he know? Did he hear the rookie shouting Sudbury? Anyway, he had to say that, he was the boss.

Max nodded and turned to leave.

"Want to go out later?" Dix asked, frowning at all the paperwork on his desk.

"Tonight?" Max cleared his throat, thinking fast.

"Yeah. Drinks? Darts?"

Max cleared his throat again. "Rain check?" he asked. "I, uh, think you were right—about the shoes—or maybe I'm out of shape." He coughed. "I was going to drop by a clinic and call it an early one."

"Oh," Dix regarded him, probably debating whether to call his bluff on the obvious lie. "Sure, yeah, feel better. By the way, what are you getting Kyle for Christmas?"

"What—I—what?" Max froze.

"I need ideas. For Leah."

"Why are you asking me?" Max rubbed the back of his neck. He really didn't have time to play marriage counselor.

"Who else am I going to ask?"

There was no bite in his tone, but it made Max feel shitty. Dix had been buddies with most of his officers for years, but only Max really ignored the new chain of command.

"Leah… I don't know, brother. A gift card to the place with all the boxes? You know, for organizing stuff?"

Dix gave him a long blank stare. "Useless, MJ. We were talking about my wife, not your work-wife."

"Funny," Max said. "You're funny. I dunno man, what's the one thing she's always asking you for?"

Dix stared at him again, but then the clouds cleared, and he said, "You mean I should get myself one of those flying phone booth thingies?"

"Uh…"

"Bigger on the inside? I was watching *Dr. Who* with the girls, and Emmy said I needed one so I could find more hours in a day."

"Date night kit," Max said. "I meant a date night kit."

"TARDIS. I think that's what it's called."

"You know *Dr. Who* isn't real, right?"

"Not with that attitude. What's a date night kit?"

"It's a—you know, a date night kit. Whosits brought one to the White Elephant last year. You get some microwave popcorn, her favorite candy, a bottle of wine, maybe a new fuzzy blanket. And a gift certificate to a movie rental place."

"Places still rent movies?"

"Good point. Netflix."

Dix nodded, thinking it over. "It's not the worst idea," he said. "Thanks, buddy."

"Yeah, well, if I save your marriage, you can buy me lunch."

Max should probably feel bad for ditching his friend to disobey the direct order he'd just been given, but he didn't feel anything except the urgent drive to go after this kid. It wasn't even up for consideration, it was the only right thing to do, whether anyone else realized it or not.

He slipped out to the squad room as the rookie was getting off the phone again.

"They said they'd try," he reported in a small, disappointed voice. "To hold the truck."

"Good."

The young cop nodded and turned back to his computer. God he really was young, wasn't he?

"Hey," Max said. When the rookie looked back at him he added, "You did good."

The young cop smiled a sort of sad half smile and then turned back around again.

"Do me a favor?" Max asked, and Hector nodded eagerly. "Take a few friends to this address after work." He jotted it down on the rookie's notepad. "Ask for the Inspector, and help him out with whatever he needs?"

"Yes, sir."

That was his father taken care of at least. "I'll owe you one."

Maggie emerged from the interview room as Max was

selecting a set of keys. He chose the oldest undercover on the lot, a 2000 Chevy Impala with so many kilometers on it that according to Maggie, it could have driven to the moon. It smelled like old fried fish and damp socks, and the A/C was busted, but the heat still worked the last time he'd checked. No one would miss it.

"They figure out where he's headed?" Maggie asked.

"Sudbury."

"He'll practically be there by now. You're really going after him?"

"Someone has to. Dix gave us the case."

"Why not someone on the Sudbury force?"

"They've got a lot of ground to cover up there. What's one more stray from the city?"

Without another word, Maggie turned and went back inside the interview room.

So that was it. Max had finally trampled the eggshells he'd been dancing around all day, and he wished more than ever that he could read her mind. Was she pissed at him for leaving? He'd thought she understood.

Pulled in both directions at once, like he'd swallowed two repellent magnets, Max knew he should go after her. But it was only his feelings at risk, and Maggie would still be here tomorrow. The kid needed him now.

"Hold down the fort," he told Boyd and the rookie.

"This isn't our fort," Boyd reminded him.

Max waved over his shoulder and headed out the sally port.

"St. James," Maggie called after him.

He turned to see her crossing the parking lot with his patrol jacket and the tightness in his throat eased.

"I tried to clean all the snot off the sleeve with a wet wipe," she explained. "I'll find something else for the little guy."

"Thanks, Magpie," he said, hit by a rush of warmth which had nothing to do with putting on the jacket. They were standing close—too close.

The fruity scent of her shampoo washed over him, lapping at the edges of his memory until things were apt to spin, and Maggie leaned up and kissed his cheek, whispering, "Good luck," but then she stayed there, in his space, her lips inches from his. Again.

She's your partner, Max reminded himself, sirens going off somewhere in the distance.

He pushed his forehead to hers and Maggie opened her mouth, welcoming him. The sirens grew louder. This wasn't what she wanted, this was an emotional reaction to a gut wrenching, adrenaline-fueled day. Max exhaled heavily and stepped back, out of her space, leaned against the Impala.

"Disregard?" he asked.

He couldn't let himself be tomorrow's regret.

She blinked up at him, but nodded. "Disregard."

"Four hours each way. Should be back in time for a nap before shift. Can you put off Children's Aid until then?"

She tilted her head and took a breath, never one for breaking rules, not because she liked rules, but because she didn't want to flunk out for breaking them. "Children's Aid won't necessarily split them up, you know. It's not like... their goal."

"Maybe."

"What if the brother doesn't want to be found?"

"Kyle," he sighed. "Running away decreases the likelihood a kid will graduate high school by ten percent, did you know that? Twenty-two percent of runaways abuse prescription drugs. Twenty-eight percent engage in survival sex, and that's within the first forty-eight hours. Thirty-two percent attempt suicide. I don't really care if he wants to be found."

Max was pacing back and forth in front of the old car. It surely made him look unstable, too emotionally involved, so he forced himself to stop and cross his arms instead.

"He left Henri trapped, believing it was actually a real fire. Could be he's just some terrible kid who never deserves to see his little brother again, but maybe it was the worst, dumbest mistake he's ever made, and it might ruin both their lives."

She looked at him then, working him out like he was a puzzle, studied him and saw him in a way that made it hard to breathe, so he turned away and pretended to inspect the tires.

"Is this about you? Do you have a brother somewhere?"

"I don't know. That's sort of the point."

"Couldn't you ask your dad?" She said it cautiously because she knew he never would.

"It's not about me, okay, it isn't personal."

"Kind of seems like it might be though."

"I gotta go. Like you said, he'll practically be there by now. I can't expect the driver to hold the kid hostage forever."

Maggie hesitated like she wanted to say more. She always looked like she wanted to say more, but she pressed her lips together, frowning at him again, her eyebrows all knit up in a little furrow. But her eyes held—not sadness or pity, exactly. More like deep sorrow.

"Be careful," she said. "If you need to lock him in the back and take a nap, do it. You're no good to me dead."

HE DROVE AWAY LEAVING MAGGIE STANDING THERE WISHING HE'D at least asked her to go too. But the only thing he wanted from her was the one thing she couldn't give. She wasn't willing to risk disciplinary action because he had an unhealthy suspicion of social services. She wasn't mad at him exactly, he was obviously working through some things, but what the hell kind of request was that?

She wasn't even going to try to unpack what had almost happened back there. It was a moment of weakness brought on by a few minutes of mortal peril, worn-off cologne, and peppermint latte. A kiss on the cheek was no big deal, but then once she'd done it, she hadn't wanted to stop.

And she knew better. She'd been down that road before and found nothing but awkwardness and bruised emotions.

Back inside, she stared at the vending machine in the staff lounge, trying to evaluate its contents for nutrition in a way she never had before. Was there anything close to a suitable dinner for a child? Doritos and a Dr. Pepper would do it for her. Had done, more than once.

"Kyle?" Sergeant Dixon asked, poking his head into the lounge. "St. James around?"

"He had to take off," she said.

"Ah. What about you, pal, want to grab a bite? Maybe some beers and pool before you go home?"

"Yes, definitely. I want to do that. But I can't tonight. I'm sorry, I… have a date."

"A date? Oh. Wow. Well, you look fantastic. The lucky guy better hope he deserves you."

Maggie tried not to blush. For a half second she wished there really was a lucky guy. Get a few things out of her system, if nothing else. Like brown eyes, spiky hair, and a wrist tattoo.

"Rain check?"

"Sure, sure. You two get the kid squared away with Children's Aid?"

"Mmmm," Maggie muttered and turned back to the vending machine. "You know what I can't figure out?" she asked, to change the subject.

"Lay it on me, Ace."

"Gluten. Who the heck even knows what it actually is—I mean, really?"

"Gluten? Uh—the stuff they make from horse hooves, right? It's in jello."

"That's gelatin."

"Isn't that what you said?"

"Gluten."

"Oh yeah. I hear it now. Not a clue." He patted the doorframe. "All right, I'm going to head out. Rain check," he added, pointing at her.

"Rain check," she agreed.

He started to leave, but then turned back. "Hey, uh, when you called Children's Aid, was it Leah you spoke to?"

"Leah?" Maggie repeated. Dixon's wife, Leah! How had she forgotten the woman was a social worker for Children's Aid? How had Max not immediately called in every favor under the sun? "No, Sarge. We didn't talk to Leah."

He nodded distractedly and then turned and left.

"You want something to eat?" Maggie asked Henri. "All we've got here is chips and pop."

"Pop will rot your teeth," he told her.

"Good thing yours are all baby ones then. They're going to fall out anyway." She held out her own navy jacket for him. "Come on, let's take a drive."

"They're not all baby ones!" He bared his teeth at her so she could see the too big grownup teeth in the front of his mouth. Made him look a little like a chipmunk. "Did you know, if we take the number one train to St. Clair West, we would get to Grace Church in forty minutes? Thirty if we run."

He was so sure—so certain his big brother would be waiting for him that Maggie almost believed it too. Maybe he would open up when he saw he was wrong, or maybe he wasn't wrong, maybe Max was off chasing his own tail. Either way, Henri was never going to let it go, so what was the harm in taking him?

His face lit up when he saw they were borrowing a patrol car, and he begged her to use the lights and sirens all the way to Lonsdale Avenue.

The church looked tight as a fortress, but Henri jumped out of the car undaunted and ran up the steps to the big double doors.

"Ver!" he yelled, cupping his hands to the glass and peering into the darkness. "Ver!"

He tried tugging at the heavy door handles and hammering the glass with his fists so hard Maggie was afraid he might actually break it.

"Ver, it's me! I'm sorry I'm late, open up!"

"You're going to wake the dead," Maggie shushed him.

He looked back at her, horrified, and whispered, "But they're ashes."

She blinked and said, "Just quiet down, okay? He's not here."

"Yes he is," he said, pounding the doors a little more softly, and then trying to fit his fingers into the crack to pry them apart. "He just can't hear me. Maybe he's in the washroom." He smacked the glass with his open palm. "There's another door over here," he said, racing back down the stairs and over to the childcare wing, where he started the whole routine over again.

Maggie put her hand on his little shoulder, like a bony robin's wing even through her patrol jacket. He twitched like he was going to shrug her off but changed his mind. His head hung so low his chin almost touched his chest, and his breaths were coming in shallow gasps. In retrospect, bringing him was an awful idea, maybe the worst. She had wanted to prove she was right, but that meant proving he, a desperate child, was wrong. In the process she stole the one thing he had—hope.

Was she actually a terrible person? If nothing else this was evidence she'd be a spectacular failure as a mother. She should've called Leah.

"Where is he?" Henri whispered.

And Maggie's heart broke for the second time in a day.

"Officer St. James will find him," she said. "You know what? It's really cold. I think I need some cocoa to warm me up. What about you?"

"Can I have it with soy milk?" he asked, allowing her to take his hand and lead him back to the car, but he didn't say a word all the way to the coffee shop.

"I have to use the washroom," he told her when they walked inside.

"Hang on, you need a code from the receipt," Maggie said, stepping up to place their order.

"I can get one out of the garbage."

"No, hang on—"

"Finally. Can you do something about him?" the barista whispered, leaning across the counter. "He's really bringing down the mood." She gestured toward the window, outside of which a homeless man in his late sixties sat on a bench carefully counting his nickels and dimes.

Maggie looked back at the barista. Was she joking?

No, of course not, people don't joke with cops. She glanced around at the other clientele, most of them sporting AirPods or otherwise entranced by their smartphones, as oblivious to the desperate man outside as they were to the tiresome "I Ain't Gettin' Nothin' for Christmas" screeching from the cafe speakers.

Why didn't she change clothes at the station like everyone else? Once the uniform was on, people stopped seeing her. All they saw was the uniform. If she were a detective, she wouldn't have this problem. She could fly under the radar, camouflaged in plain clothes.

"We called you guys like an hour ago," the barista said.

"Did he come on the property? Threaten anyone?" Maggie asked.

"No, but look at him. Would you want to come in here and buy a coffee?"

"Not anymore," Maggie agreed. "But I'll take a large decaf, tomato soup, turkey club, and a soy hot chocolate."

"Oh," the barista said. "And him?"

"I'll speak to him."

The girl gushed in appreciation, and Maggie collected her order, leaving the smallest tip her conscience would allow.

"Okay, here's the deal," she told Henri as she punched the code from her receipt into the lock on the washroom door. "I'll be waiting outside by that bench. Come right out when you're done, got it? Make me chase you, this goes straight in the garbage," she added, holding up his cocoa.

He nodded and went into the washroom, and Maggie exited through the side door to join the homeless man on his bench.

He immediately pocketed his change and said, "I was just waiting for the bus."

That was the other thing about the uniform. Instant fear, suspicion, dread. Somehow it drew a certain type of woman to Max like he was freaking Batman, but everyone else wanted Maggie to go away. "I know," was all she said.

He reminded her of her great-grandpa, but he wouldn't look her in the eyes or accept the offered coffee and bag of warm food, afraid it was some kind of trick, so she set everything on the bench between them.

"They asked me to make you move along. You don't have to. In fact, if it were me, I'd probably stay until they close and then come back tomorrow and serve them right. But if you can wait for your bus at a different stop for a few days, it might save you some hassle."

He looked at her then, and the likeness to Grandpa Bob was even stronger—a wizened gentleness in his dark, tired eyes, eyes that had seen things. Probably Vietnam if she had to guess.

"I think I must have missed my bus anyway," he said. "Maybe I'll go enjoy my dinner in the park. Merry Christmas, Officer Kyle," he added, squinting at her name tag in the light of the streetlamp and then smiling warmly at her.

And the pieces of Maggie's broken heart somehow felt a little bit lighter.

Henri joined her as the man was walking away.

"You know Old Bill?" he asked her.

"We were just making friends," she said, handing him his cocoa. The fact that this little boy knew the old man's name told her enough. If she didn't want him to end up like Old Bill, it was time to be the cop everyone who saw her uniform expected her to be, to follow the rules and do what she should have done hours ago. It was time to call Children's Aid. Max would forgive her.

Wouldn't he?

CHAPTER 8

The city melted behind Max, leaving him somehow lighter, and that made him, not sad exactly, but surprised. Wherever he came from, his memories were formed inside the greater metropolitan area, the provincial capital, Queen City, a stone's throw from the CN Tower. He'd never really known anything else, and yet it was a relief to escape, but, like the relief you feel after a high fever breaks, exhaustion soon set in, and he was yawning before he even reached the outskirts of Barrie.

He ought to be home in bed, making up for last night's tossing and turning, not chasing someone else's kid halfway to Hudson Bay. But even at home, would he really sleep, or would it be a replay of last night, staring at the little DNA test that had finally arrived in the mail, mind churning with guilt? If his mother were still alive, would she see it as a betrayal of the love she'd poured into him? Or would she have understood Max needed to know where he came from—which band's blood pumped through his veins?

It was a moot point anyway, according to the instructions. His only chance for answers lay buried in paperwork and bureaucratic red tape.

Yawning again, he cracked the windows, hoping the brisk air would wake him up, and it worked a little. But the wind rushing through the trees and into his car played tricks on his hearing, bringing with it a whisper. *"Little bear,"* it called, his nickname as a child.

"Little bear," the wind sang, and he tried to drown it out with music, talk radio, anything. Try as he might though, the old tuner could only pick up static this far out in the boonies. Max fumbled with the controls, scanning from station to station, until he accidentally turned on the CD player, which fired up with a vaguely familiar tune that resonated deep in his belly.

The turnoff for Parry Sound should be just over halfway, but the clock on the dash already said 9:24. Wondering if it had ever been turned back after Daylight Savings, Max checked the time on his cell phone, and noticed he had a missed call from Maggie.

Heart racing, he played the message.

"St. James, it's me. Listen, don't be mad, but I called Leah Dixon."

He cursed silently. He really thought when she didn't say no, that she would wait for him. It was a mistake—assuming consent. He knew better, and her call was her way of reminding him.

"She had me sign a couple of forms, and now I'm Henri's emergency foster parent. Everything's on the up-and-up, so you're welcome."

There it was. Marvelous, magnificent Maggie found the answer and saved the day. Why the hell hadn't he thought to call Leah? He introduced her and Dix when he was still a rookie, for goodness sake.

"Thing is, you know, my place got sold and Frankie's entire family is here, so we're headed to yours. Least you can do, right?"

She laughed a little, a nervous laugh, meant to hide annoyance. And she was right, of course, it was the very least he could do. He'd have to make it up to her tomorrow. Sushi? Dim Sum? Tiramisu? A massage that might lead to—*Down boy.*

"I'll put him in your room, and I'll take the spare. See you soon."

Good. Perfect. Wait—shit. Not the spare room. Max had kept it shut so long, sometimes he almost forgot he had a spare room, except it was there, like a specter, every time he passed down his own hallway.

And no one, not Maggie or anyone else, should go near it. Not yet. One look and she'd convince Dix to suspend him pending a psych eval.

He swerved a little in his lane, looking for the call-back button. "Come on, pick up," he begged, but it rang unanswered and went to voicemail.

"Kyle. Spare room's off limits. It's… infested… with spiders."

She hated spiders. He'd once seen her beat a garden spider with a boot for ten minutes straight to ensure it was good and dead. She still swore its little spider ghost haunted her desk.

"Real bad, worst I've seen. Put the kid on the couch and you take my bed, or—or put him in my room, whatever," he stammered because he'd basically told her to get in his bed, which was exactly where he wanted her and exactly the last place she needed to be. "Keep the door to the spare room shut. I've got them pretty well trapped in there. Don't want them getting out—"

The voicemail beeped to warn him he was cut off.

"Call me back, I guess," he finished to himself. What a disaster.

There are support groups for hoarders, she would tell him, but that wasn't what this was. It was complicated.

He drummed nervously on the steering wheel, hoping and waiting for her to call, but not at all sure what he would say.

Her ingenuity was impressive. It was why she'd be a good detective—she saw a problem from every angle, big picture and all the smaller ones too. Of course she'd found the perfect compromise, when his judgement had been too clouded—a way to give him what he wanted without breaking the rules. Maybe he should listen to her more, maybe let her make all of his important life decisions from now on.

Except for the ones she would make if she opened the spare room door.

When the phone finally began to vibrate again, he didn't even stop to look at caller ID.

"Kyle, promise me you won't go in the spare room, it's full of spiders," he said. "Poisonous ones, I'm pretty sure. I need to call my landlord again, he's—"

"Um, sir? It's me, it's Hector… the rookie? From Fifty-Two?"

Embarrassment flooded through Max. "Right. Yeah. Did you get the food drive thing squared away?"

"You bet, sir. Boyd and I took care of it."

"Thanks, Rookie. Like I said, I owe you one. I'm sorry if my old man was… a lot."

"No, he was great. He had a ton of career advice," the rookie chuckled.

"Sounds about right."

Hector yawned loudly into the phone.

"What the hell time is it, kid? Are you back at the station?"

"Sorry to bother you, sir, but I wanted to catch you before you got off the Seventeen."

"I'd say you've got about ten minutes then," Max said, dreading whatever news the rookie might have.

"The thing is, sir—the truck didn't wait."

"It didn't wait at the med supply warehouse? Or it didn't wait in Sudbury?"

"I'm really sorry, Officer St. James."

Max sighed. Perfect. Tonight just got more and more… interesting was how his grandfather would have put it. The chase continues? How interesting. "Where am I headed now? North Bay?" he asked.

"Timmins."

"Interesting."

"Sir?"

"Nothing."

"He's going to wait this time. He got a late start and he had to drop off his load before midnight or he'd be fined, but he can't pick up his next haul until four so he has to wait, their dispatch promised. I mean, she promised last time, too, but she only promised to try, and I didn't really trust her. That's why I called back to check. And so I told her this time she better do more than try or I would personally arrest her for impeding an investigation and endangering a child."

Max laughed out loud. "Careful, rookie. Threats can get you into trouble."

"Yes, sir."

"So she promised?" Max asked, calculating that he would be there by one in the morning, and if rush hour cooperated, still make it back in time for his shift. Just.

"Yes, sir. And then she cried."

MAGGIE USED A KEY HIDDEN IN MAX'S LOCKER TO LET HERSELF into his apartment, where she was met with the overwhelming scent of him, his soap and his aftershave and his favorite curry takeout. She tossed the key on the kitchen counter, and threw Henri's empty cocoa cup in the garbage next to a pair of bananas so brown they must be practically liquid inside. It made her gag, but it was good to know even Max had a line.

"Come on, let's figure out the sleeping arrangements," she said, as she pressed play on the first of two messages.

She had visited a few times before and more or less knew her way around. They wandered through the tidy living room and down the hall where Max's bedroom door stood open on the left, revealing a bed with a brown plaid duvet, made up with military precision. Across the hall was the bathroom, cleaner than her own would have been after so many hours of overtime.

The next door was closed, Maggie opened it as Max's voice boomed from her phone warning her not to go in because of a spider infestation.

Spiders, huh? Is that what we're calling it?

The room was piled floor to ceiling with junk. Boxes of junk, bags of junk, piles of junk stacked atop mountains of junk. Okay maybe *junk* wasn't a fair assessment, but with so much stuff crammed into one small space, who could tell? Old dresses and high heel shoes, newspapers and magazine clippings, a first generation Fitbit, an iPod, dishes and teacups and all manner of knick-knacks were strewn across every surface.

For a moment she froze, panicked that she had somehow broken and entered the wrong apartment. But she had used his key and recognized his essence, this was all his. Still, she felt like an intruder discovering a dirty little secret. Had it been left behind by a previous tenant?

"He needs to clean his room," Henri observed.

"No worries," Maggie said brightly, pulling the door closed again. "I sleep better on the couch anyway. You can put your bag in there if you want," she added, pointing back across the hall to Max's bedroom.

She played the second message while Henri stood in the doorway apparently thinking it over.

"Sorry again about the spiders," his voicemail voice said. **"The truck didn't wait in Sudbury, so I'm on my way to Timmins. I'll call you in a few hours."**

Poor Max. His voice was strained with exhaustion and driving in the dark always made his eyes hurt. She should've insisted on going with him—that's what partners were supposed to do. But then she would've insisted on getting a room once it got late, and that couldn't have led to anything good for either of their careers, and anyway, he hadn't wanted her. He wanted her to take the boy.

"You must be tired," Maggie told Henri. "How about a shower before bed?"

"I'm clean enough," he responded on autopilot, and then frowned. "I can't sleep here."

"I know it's not what you're used to—"

"I'm not going to sleep here. I sleep in the loft with my brother and my brown blanket."

"It's just for one night. Max has plenty of blankets, and look how cozy his bed is," Maggie said. "It's brown."

"No, it's not cozy. My loft and my brown blanket are cozy. I have to go find Ver, he misses me."

"He's not there. He's gone, Henri, remember?"

"He's not gone, he's hiding. Because you chased him away like you chased away Old Bill. You guys chase everyone away."

"I think you'll feel better after a shower," Maggie bit out, opening a closet in search of towels.

"No, I won't feel better, and I won't go to sleep either," he yelled, stomping his foot. "You're not my mama, you can't make me. I have to go back to the Church-on-the-Hill!"

That escalated quickly.

Was it too late for Maggie to call Leah and get her to take Henri to someone who would know what to do with him? Max leaving had been a bad idea. Maggie seeking custody had been a slightly worse idea. Taking him to the church, buying him cocoa —every decision made today had been one awful notion heaped atop another. Now Henri was hopped up on sugar after what must have been a traumatizing day—intellectually Maggie knew all that. But she didn't have a clue how to fix it.

"Shower," she said, fighting to keep her voice calm and controlled and holding out a clean towel. If Max were there, he'd know what to do. He'd know exactly how to calm the boy and make everything better.

To her relief, her tone must have been scary enough because Henri looked a little surprised before snatching the towel, stepping into the bathroom, and slamming the door so hard it rattled a frame on the wall—a sketch of the city skyline Max had bought from a street vendor in exchange for witness testimony last year.

The running water couldn't quite drown out Henri's sniffles.

Maggie turned down the covers on Max's bed, then hunted through his drawers to find a large t-shirt for the boy to sleep in. Then she made up the couch for herself with a spare blanket and pillow.

By the time she finished, Henri was showered and dressed in Max's clean Maple Leafs shirt, which fell below his knees. He stood in the hallway, his head hanging low and his eyes, which refused to look at her, rimmed red.

"Sorry for being a jerk," he whispered.

Maggie pulled him in for a hug, and the little boy melted into her side, burying his face to hide another onslaught of sniffles.

"Want to watch a movie or something?" she asked, stroking his long, damp hair.

He shrugged.

"I think *The Grinch* is on."

"I remember that movie," he said, looking thoughtful and far away. "He's green and has a nice dog?"

Just how long had these boys been on their own?

"When I was your age, and my brother and I would bicker, instead of saying, 'Santa Claus will put coal in your stocking,' like a normal parent, my mom would always say the Grinch would kidnap us and take us home with him."

"But he turns out to be nice."

"Yeah, it didn't make a lot of sense to us either," Maggie said, sitting down and turning on the TV.

"What was she like? Your mama?" Henri asked, and his use of

past tense wasn't lost on Maggie as he snuggled up next to her on the couch.

"She's great. I mean, she's scared of everything, a total worrywart, but absolutely the person you want in your corner in a crisis. I guess worrying over nothing prepared her for the real thing somehow."

"Ver's like that."

"Yeah?" she asked, tilting her head to look down at him.

"He worries about everything: that we'll be hungry or cold or sick. But whenever something really bad happens, he knows exactly what to do."

"Like what kinds of bad things?"

He shrugged, but Maggie was starting to learn if she waited long enough he would answer the question eventually.

"Like one time, when I was seven and Ver was ten, the ice cream man said he had potbelly pigs in his truck."

"Pigs? Not ice cream?" Maggie asked, a shiver of recognition running down her spine.

"That's what Ver asked. The man said he used to have both, but the pigs ate all the ice cream. I wanted to see them so bad. I wanted to tickle their little pot bellies. But Ver said no."

"How come?"

"He told the man we had to go home for dinner, but we'd come see them the next day."

"But he didn't let you?" Maggie asked, the shiver turning to a gnawing nausea working its way up her throat.

"No. Ver wrote down everything about the truck and its license plate and stuff. Where it was going to be and what time. He put it on an index card from the library, and left it on the windshield of a police car."

"That was really smart. What did the truck look like?"

"Light blue with puffy white and pink clouds instead of ice cream."

Maggie almost stopped breathing. "That was our police car," she said. "My partner's and mine."

"Oh." He slid down in his seat, rigid. "Are we in trouble?"

"No. Your brother's kind of a hero."

He relaxed again. "That sounds like him."

Maggie had a million questions, but she didn't want to ask the wrong one and make him clam up again. Where did they come from? Why were they on their own? Had anything truly awful happened to them on the streets?

Finally she settled on the rather tame, "How long has Ver taken care of you?"

But this time there was no shrug in reply. Henri had fallen asleep.

She probably could have carried him to Max's room without waking him up. She probably should have, but he looked so comfortable where he was and if she was being honest, the idea of climbing into her partner's bed herself was an exceptionally appealing one, even without him there.

It still smelled like him, but different from the rest of the house, stronger: less curry, more musk. Maggie felt a bit scandalous curling up under his covers wearing only her tank top and underwear, enveloped in his scent. His detour to Timmons meant no chance of him coming home to find her there, and she drifted off to sleep imagining a scenario in which he did.

Buzz buzz buzz. Buzz buzz buzz.

Drowsy and disoriented, Maggie groped for her cell phone. It was almost two in the morning.

"St. James, hey," she answered.

"Did I wake you? I'm sorry, of course I did."

"No, it's fine," she said, rubbing her eyes and trying to make her voice sound less hoarse. "What's your 20? On your way back?"

"Not exactly."

Maggie pushed herself up on one elbow to better clear the cobwebs from her head. "The driver didn't wait for you in Timmins, either?"

"Oh, he waited. Nice guy, actually. Bought me waffles. Real nice guy. So nice he put the kid on a bus back in Sudbury. To Thunder Bay."

"No."

"Afraid so."

"How far is that?" she asked, trying not to let the disappointment creep into her voice.

"I won't make it back in time for shift. You mad?" he asked, his voice strained with exhaustion. Maggie wasn't sure how he was still seeing straight enough to drive.

"Me? No. I'm not mad. You should probably get some sleep first."

"Can't. Gotta make up for lost time. If the little bastard gets off his bus and I'm not there... I don't know. How's our francophone?"

"No more French at least, but he misses his brother. I'm not very good at this."

Max made a harrumph of disagreement, the one that always sounded like if she were anyone else dissing his partner, he'd fight her. It always made her feel like a hummingbird was zipping a path between her stomach and her throat.

"I haven't given much thought to the case," she lied.

"Liar."

True. She hadn't made any progress, but her mind hadn't stopped turning the thing over, examining it for clues, even as she snuggled into his pillow imagining one or two things she'd like to do there. *Stop it.*

"Okay, you're right. I have been thinking about it. I've been thinking I should hand it over to someone who might have a prayer of solving it."

He tsked. "Kyle, believe me when I tell you, you're the only one who can solve it."

"Why?" She hated how small her voice sounded, how badly she needed him to answer, even though she could guess what he would say.

"Because you won't give up on a puzzle. And everyone else already has."

"But what if…"

"Yeah," he agreed. "What if."

"Yeah?"

"What if I don't find this kid? What then? If he's not on missing persons already, who's going to add him?"

Maggie sat up, like she could make him listen better that way. "St. James, whatever happens, what you're doing counts for something."

"I need to make this right."

"You always do."

"I try."

"You do."

"Okay, Yoda."

Satisfied, she laid back down. If she were a good friend or a better cop she might try to convince him to give up the chase, to let someone else handle it. Then he could come home and handle her… *Stop it.*

Case. He could handle her case.

The truth was, she wanted him to choose to come home on his own, to choose her—well, she did, and she didn't. When did everything get so complicated?

Oh right. About the time Henri told her about the potbelly pigs.

"Do you remember the Klondike Killer?" she asked softly.

"Pedo with the ice cream truck, kidnapped, what, a dozen kids, about a year and a half back?"

"Remember how we caught him?"

"Anonymous tip, wasn't it? Good Samaritan saved a lot of kids' lives that day."

"Keep that in mind when you finally catch up to that Good Samaritan in Thunder Bay."

Max was silent for a moment, processing what Maggie had said, and what she didn't say. "You're kidding."

"Henri described the guy, the truck, the contents of the note. He knew it was written on an index card, remember? Because I had forgotten. He even knew about the potbelly pigs."

"Well."

"Yeah."

Lying there in the dark, talking on the phone, it was easy to pretend he was there too, lying beside her. Just a chat before bed. She kicked off the covers, suddenly over-warm.

"Look, I don't know how the fireworks got into the locker. I still think the kids are connected, but no one really seems to care. No one's looking to press charges."

Max sighed. "You want me to turn around and come back?"

It was the olive branch she'd been waiting for. "It was never really about the fireworks for you, was it?"

"No. You want me to turn around and come back?"

"I don't see how you can," Maggie said. "Not without that kid."

"Copy that."

He was silent for a minute, and Maggie almost dozed off again.

"Magpie?" His voice cracked, like it was tight and full, like how a cork might sound right before it pops out of a bottle of champagne.

"Yeah Max?"

He was quiet for another beat and then, "Nothing."

"Disregard?" she asked, disappointed.

"Disregard."

Western Ontario,
3 days 'til Christmas

Somewhere between Ameson and Longlac, the five cups of coffee began to wear off. When he left Timmins, Max filled every cupholder in the front seat, plus one in his hand, but he should have bought more at the last truck stop. Now his yawns were so cavernous he imagined his jaw dislocating itself like a snake's. And he desperately needed to pee.

"So she's finally in your bed and you're not even there," a familiar young voice said, and Max turned to see Noah, eternally teenaged, sitting in his passenger seat. "Is that what they call ironic?"

Max closed his eyes and opened them again, but Noah was still there. Maybe Maggie was right, he should have stopped to rest before he started hallucinating.

"Unfair, brother, but I guess life's unfair. What?" Noah asked.

"It's been awhile," Max said to his hallucination, because it was nice to have someone to talk to even if they weren't really there. Is this what they call a slippery slope?

"I guess," Noah said, but then, he never did seem to have a sense of time, even when Max was a boy. Noah was just always there, popping up when Max needed him, like no time had passed at all. "Can't have been very long," Noah said. "Looks like you're still a cop."

"What else would I be?"

"Touché. Those St. Jameses have blue blood in their veins, am I right?" Noah said, looking out the window instead of at Max.

"Everyone has blue blood in their veins."

"You know what I mean. Except it's not your blood."

Max turned up the volume on the CD player in response. The album must have started over eight or nine times by now. He'd lost count after heading west on the Trans-Canada Highway.

It must have been Maggie's CD, left behind years ago in the rundown Impala after they'd gone undercover at some country-western bar where she tried to make him line dance.

He should've danced with her. If the opportunity ever presented itself again, he wouldn't hesitate.

"What is this, anyway?" Noah asked.

"His name's Jason Isbell," Max quoted Maggie. "And anyone who doesn't love him, doesn't have a soul."

"So are you?" Noah asked.

"What? In possession of a soul?"

Noah nodded at the stereo. "Living the life you chose for yourself?"

"I chose it," Max said. "Nobody made me." Sure, it had seemed like an easy solution to a problem—maybe the noble solution or maybe a cowardly one. Maybe both at once, but it was still his decision.

The social worker at his grade eleven career fair had spoken to him like an adult with valuable opinions—even after he was rude about her own career choice.

"Why would I want to be a social worker? Why would anyone like me?" he had demanded, daring her to ask about his First Nations heritage, ignoring the shame of not knowing his own truth. He hadn't cared if it was cruel or if he was reducing her life's work to a single entry in a book where he learned the

Sixties Scoop was still being practiced well into the eighties, a book that only his grandfather was brave enough to let him see.

But she didn't ask, and she didn't get angry.

The woman seemed to give his question careful consideration, taking him more seriously than any other adult ever had, apart from his grandfather.

"To help," she'd said, and that was what did it.

"Social work?" his father had scoffed when Max came home from school, so excited to finally have a direction. "If you're set on public service you should focus on something with advancement potential."

"If it's what he wants," his mother said, trying to head off an argument.

"I'm not going to let him waste his potential after we saved him—"

"Saved me?" young Max asked skeptically.

"I didn't mean saved. I didn't mean it that way…" His father had backed down, but he *had* meant it. He was a precise, inflexible man. He didn't say things he didn't mean. That was the day Max realized his life was not his own. There were expectations. Strings attached.

"Social work is perfectly respectable," his mom had argued.

"He could be a surgeon or a judge, if he would knuckle down and apply himself," his father replied. "With a little ambition he could be the police commissioner, I have the right ties."

The Inspector ranted on with a litany of other less ignoble professions, ones that would ensure promotions and stable income, but Max didn't hear most of it. He was too busy tearing himself apart and trying to put the pieces back together in a new image—an image he'd rarely allowed himself to conjure, an image he'd always dismissed—of a boy, unwanted and unloved, who'd needed saving.

His father never said another word about it—not even when Max double majored in English and social work in college.

But Max saw it etched across his old man's face the day he signed up for the Academy—as though Max had finally chosen him, and at the end of the day, wasn't that exactly what he'd done?

Jason Isbell, you magnificent sorcerer. How did you write a song about me?

"You chose… poorly," Noah said, impersonating the knight from Indiana Jones.

"Maybe I always do." After all, he disobeyed a direct order not to circumnavigate the province. And if by some miracle he managed to find the kid in Thunder Bay, so far outside his own jurisdiction, forcing this *Ver* into his car would basically be kidnapping.

"Nah," Noah said, studying Max in his stoic way. "Not always, brother."

Max looked back at the teen, trying to detect any trace of translucency, until the Impala drifted onto the shoulder and hit the rumble strip.

"Watch the road."

Noah had been visiting for as long as Max could remember. When he was little, Max believed he was an invisible brother or friend, as real as anyone, except only Max could see him. But in his teens, he realized Noah didn't age, didn't change his clothes, didn't change at all. He couldn't be a real, living, breathing person, invisibility aside. And Max decided his friend might be a ghost.

Now he wondered if the boy was a symptom of psychosis, some manifestation of the version of himself he wished to be.

After all, they wore the same shoes.

He'd never told anyone about his ghost, never revealed that part of himself, not even to Maggie, and now he supposed it was for the best. Believing in ghosts—plus his spare bedroom—maybe she'd be right to think he wasn't fit for duty. Still, a tiny part of him felt sad she didn't know.

WHEN SHE AWOKE, NESTLED UNDER MAX'S DOWN COMFORTER AND surrounded by his scent, a tingling below her stomach as dreams of soft murmurs and caresses faded into daylight, it took Maggie several seconds to remember where she was. The TV was on in the living room, high-pitched cartoon voices and zany sound effects intruding on her own intrusive lie-in.

She dressed quickly, opting to put her dirty uniform back on rather than her partner's cozy-looking sweats, because people might not notice the uniform, but they would definitely notice the sweats. And aside from the part where it would be breaking every rule, who wants to deal with the gossip that you're banging your partner without the perk of actually doing it?

Stop it.

After battling her tangled hair into something resembling a bun, she felt ready to face the day—and the child in the living room.

"Good morning," she very nearly chirped.

"Is Ver coming home today?" Henri asked, not turning away from the flickering images on the screen.

"That's the plan."

If her math was right, Max should arrive in Thunder Bay in a couple of hours, and if luck was with him, turn right back around with the brother in hand. They'd be in Toronto tonight. Maggie just needed to figure out what to do with Henri for the next ten hours or so, while she attempted to solve the bus station case sans star witness.

"What do you like for breakfast?" she asked, surveying Max's austere fridge and pantry. There were a few eggs, but she hated eggs, and his bagels were cinnamon raisin. Did anyone actually like raisins? Maybe only the sociopaths who enjoyed brown bananas.

"I ate an Oatie Nut Bar."

Maggie added water to the coffee pot and some kind of aromatic blend with chicory. Then she popped a bagel in the toaster. She could always pick out the raisins.

"Sleep okay?" she called to Henri.

When he didn't answer, she stepped back into the living room. After so long without TV, the child was even mesmerized by the commercials. Max had been right, the Klondike Killer had been brought to justice eighteen months ago—but how long were they on their own before that? Henri had said two birthdays.

"Hey," she said and this time he turned to face her. "Can you turn it off and come in here a minute?"

He looked like he might argue, but to her relief he found the remote and complied.

"Did you remember anything last night? About the coach terminal?"

"Like what?" he asked, dropping into a kitchen chair and studying the choir medal around his neck.

"Anything really. Anyone you saw or heard who might have wanted to cause trouble?"

He traced the ridges of the medallion with his finger. "Is Ver dead?" he asked quietly.

"No," she gasped. "Of course not."

"You don't have to pretend. I can take it," he said, his soft words like tiny punches to her gut.

"He took a bus west."

"Is that a eu—eupher-cism?"

Maggie suppressed a chuckle. She'd have to remember to tell Max about that one. "No. He got on a bus in Sudbury. Where'd you learn a big word like euphemism?"

"Ver taught me."

"What else did he teach you?"

"Don't talk to strangers. Look both ways before you cross. Lots of things in French. Celiac means no gluten. Gluten is the glue in wheat but not rice or oats or corn."

Maggie thought she saw his lip quiver before he decided to stop talking.

There was a rhythmic tap on the front door, and then it swung open. Maggie reached for her sidearm, but she'd left it in her locker at the station. Instinctively, she stepped in front of Henri before a woman's head peeked in, followed by her whole body, all five feet and maybe ninety-five pounds of her (on a high-sodium day).

"So what did you—oh!" the stranger exclaimed, tucking a runaway strand of shiny black hair behind her perfect, tiny ear and stepping back as if to double check the apartment number. "I was expecting Max."

"Who's Max?" Henri asked.

"Officer St. James," Maggie reminded him. Then to the woman she added, "He's not here."

They awkwardly sized each other up while Maggie's coffee beeped its readiness.

The woman was gorgeous—probably about Max's age, svelte and feisty all at the same time, with dancing eyes so dark they were practically black, and a warm smile. Wearing gray leggings and an oversized sweater she exuded girl-next-door charm, looking effortlessly chill instead of sloppy,

Maggie hated her.

"You must be Selina. Can I offer you some coffee?" Maggie asked, though she hadn't really made enough to share, and if she was being honest, she'd like to pour the whole pot over Selina's perfect head.

"Love some, thanks. And you must be the infamous partner, Kyle?" she asked, raising her eyebrows with meaning. It wasn't jealousy, exactly. Maggie couldn't decide what it was. What would Selina have to be jealous about, when Max could see her like this, in a feminine sweater that clung to all the right curves and leggings that revealed them, as opposed to the boxy uniform streaked with dirt and sweat he was accustomed to seeing Maggie wear every day?

"The one and only," Maggie said.

"That's Ivan," Henri piped up. *"The One and Only Ivan."*

"And who's the choirboy?" Selina asked.

"Not me," Henri said.

"No? Isn't that your choir ribbon?" she asked, reaching for the medallion around his neck.

"No," he exclaimed, swerving away from her. "It's Ver's and you can't touch it, only I can."

"Yes, sir," Selina said, withdrawing her hand.

Maggie searched Max's cupboards for coffee mugs, but she kept finding everything else instead. "Over the stove," Selina said, and it bothered Maggie more than it should have for this *neighbor* to know her way around, but of course she did.

"I bet your medal came from St. Thomas's, didn't it? I had one exactly like it," Selina told Henri.

"No. Holy Rosary," he said, like it was the most obvious thing in the world. Then he realized what he'd said, glanced at Maggie and clammed up.

She poured the coffee and handed Selina a cup, which the shorter woman accepted with a wink. That, too, galled her. She didn't need help with her case from a buxom, legging-clad civilian.

"So what did you guys find out about the gingerbread house?" Selina asked.

"There's a gingerbread house?" Henri exclaimed.

"There is, and you stay far away from it. Something fishy going on over there." She turned back to Maggie. "Tell me he mentioned it?"

"He mentioned it, but we were a little distracted yesterday."

"That man is eternally distracted. But you'll make sure he gets to it? Today?" she asked.

Maggie looked from Selina to Henri. "I can't promise

anything," she said. "But it would be a lot easier to investigate if I had a babysitter for a few hours."

Selina grinned.

"I'm not a baby. I don't need a sitter," Henri protested.

"Not a baby. Not a choirboy. Do you at least like to sing?" Selina asked him.

"Yes!"

"Perfect. I need singers. What do you say, Ivan, want to hang out?"

"I'm not Ivan, I'm Henri. Ivan's a gorilla."

Selina handed Maggie back her empty coffee cup, raising her eyebrows in confusion.

"I have no idea," Maggie said.

"It's fine. I direct a children's choir. I'm fairly accustomed to having no idea."

The poor woman, even her willingness to help out rubbed Maggie the wrong way. What kind of life did she lead where she could so easily agree to babysit a kid she'd just met at six thirty in the morning? Who had that kind of flexibility? By the look of her, she was probably into yoga, probably super flexible in other ways a man like Max would appreciate. *Stop it.*

Maybe that's what drew him to her. Free spirit was the completely opposite term anyone would ever ascribe to Maggie, but this woman was friends with musicians and leatherworkers and henna artists and probably some muscle-clad brute who forged chainmail for the Renaissance Faire. Hadn't it been one of her friends who made Max the leather cuff which now served double duty holding his grandfather's watch and hiding his tattoo?

"Does he need breakfast?" Selina asked.

"He ate," Henri said, and Selina grinned. She liked him. And damn if it didn't make Maggie not hate her—a little.

"And he's gluten-free," Maggie said.

"Perfect. I'm keto."

Of course you are. "That must be hard, working at the Ren Faire," Maggie said, hearing the snark in her own voice. Since when did she look down on people associated with the Ren Faire? As jobs went, it would be freaking cool, and anyway, she knew Selina was a cellist with the symphony which would have impressed her, if it was anyone else.

Selina cocked her head in puzzlement. "My friends who work the Ren Faire usually bring their own food. Hard to make a profit if you spend it all on fried cod and Scotch eggs, more's the pity."

"That is a pity," Maggie said, trying to leash her insecurities. She had no right, no claim to Max that justified being rude. "I really appreciate this."

"You scratch my back, I'll scratch yours," Selina said with a friendly shrug.

Is that what you do for my partner? Scratch his back? Stop it.

"Right. You be good, okay? No running off, and I'll see if I can get you fingerprinted later. Deal?"

"And then Ver comes home?" Henri asked.

"And then Ver comes home."

THE PARADE ROOM WAS STILL HALF EMPTY WHEN MAGGIE SLID into a seat next to Frankie for morning roll call.

"So you stayed over at Max's last night? Finally?" Frankie asked, raising her eyebrows suggestively, though she didn't look up from her chamomile tea.

"Calm down. He wasn't even there."

Frankie nodded. "Yep. That's on brand. And I owe my mom twenty bucks."

"You bet on me with your mom?"

"I did. Way to let me down. So where was he?"

"Out. How'd it go with Tony? Is he excited? What did he say?" Maggie asked, hoping to deflect any further questions about Max's whereabouts or her own feelings about his whereabouts.

"He said, 'You've had this stomach bug for a while, Franks. You sure it's not your appendix?'"

Maggie side-eyed her friend. "You haven't told him?"

"I can't believe he hasn't figured it out."

"Are you going to tell him?"

"Yeah, I'll tell him. We just, we haven't been dating very long, you know?"

"You love him, right?"

"Of course. He's great. And he won't care that the condom broke, and we'll get married even though it's only been six months, and I'll finally move out of my mom's house. We'll get a place of our own, maybe even a white picket fence. It's going to be great. A little ahead of schedule, but, you know, great."

"It sounds great," Maggie agreed.

"Right?" This time Frankie didn't sound like she was trying so hard to convince herself.

Dixon stormed in, his uniform and hair almost as rumpled as something out of *The Walking Dead*, and took his place at the podium without preamble. "So. Little bit of excitement yesterday. How are we feeling?"

"Sick of the bullshit," Taylor said.

"It's your lucky day then, Taylor, because Officers Kyle and St. James will be taking the lead on the coach terminal case, which means any more bomb threats should go their way, too. Unless it's real. Then ETF will take over."

"As they do," Maggie said.

Her comment drew the staff sergeant's attention. "Kyle, where's your partner?" he asked.

"He… had an emergency," Maggie said.

At the same time the desk sergeant said, "The flu."

"I see." Dixon looked from one to the other, not believing either of them.

"He went to the emergency room, because his fever was so high, and it turns out it's the flu." Maggie hated lying, even to cover for Max, and she could feel herself getting sweaty as Frankie's gaze bored into her.

"Okay. Enjoy the case your partner begged me for."

"Since it's technically Fifty-Two's jurisdiction, can I at least steal their rookie for the day? Corbin Hector?"

"He has a TO in his own division. They're looking into some Lego thing," Dixon said.

"Lego thing *is* the coach terminal thing," Maggie said. "Boyd won't mind."

Dixon sighed. "Fine, whatever, I'll put in a call."

"Thank you, sir."

"Yep. Then unless Officer Kyle would like to make any further scheduling changes?" He didn't sound angry, but his tone was a little less teasing than usual.

"No, I'm good."

"Outstanding. Assignments are on the board. Stay alert, stay safe, and let's catch some bad guys. Dismissed."

HECTOR ARRIVED FIFTEEN MINUTES LATER, LOOKING JUST AS TIRED and rumpled as the staff sergeant.

"What's with you?" Maggie asked.

He yawned. "Late night. Can I drive?"

"Not a chance. Besides, we're staying home today. I need you to make a formal request to the library board for their security footage and get me a list of Holy Rosary churches. Then you can start going through the forensics and finding me suspects to interview," she said, leading the way to the staff lounge. This kid was going to need massive amounts of caffeine.

"Did he seem… overly eager to be rid of me?" Hector asked, trailing along and looking around at everything like it was different and new.

"Who, your sergeant?"

"Nah, my TO. Boyd?"

"Oh, I don't know." Maggie glanced in the fruit bowl. Once again there were only two bananas left, a nice normal one and an over-ripe one, and Max wasn't there to snatch up the over-ripe one.

"You've known him a long time, right?" Hector asked.

"St. James?"

"Boyd," the rookie said, swiping the nice banana for himself.

Maggie couldn't leave the brown one there all alone. It was like leaving an empty roll of toilet paper or returning Doritos to the pantry with one chip left in the bag. "Yeah, I guess," she said, grimacing as she picked up the soft fruit. "We came up through the Academy together and he started here at Fifty-One Division before he transferred."

"Was he always so serious?"

Maggie half-choked on her banana, only partly because of its horrible mushy texture. "Boyd? I'd say more intense than serious. But we all were. We were super driven back then."

"Back then?"

She'd said too much. She didn't want to have this conversation, not with the rookie—not really with anyone. But he was watching her with big, hungry, exhausted eyes.

Maggie choked down another bite of the banana and then threw the rest in the garbage, but Hector was still watching her, waiting for an answer.

"You know, we were fresh out of the Academy, the world at our feet. I don't know what your staff sergeant did when you joined, but every year ours used to make the new rooks stand up and say why we were there. So our first day, Castillo gets up and says, 'I'm going to become the youngest female officer in this division to make detective.'"

"Did she?"

"Sure did." Maggie stared into her coffee, trying to remember what it felt like to be new and fresh and hopeful. "And then I stand up and say, 'I'm also going to be the youngest female officer in this division to make detective, but I'm three months younger than her, so I'll let her go first.'"

"Kyle bringing the swagger!"

"Fake it 'til you make it, right? So then Boyd stands up and says, 'I'll do everything they do, except backwards and in high heels.'"

"No he didn't!"

"He totally did. It was amazing. Please tell me you get that reference, you're not that much younger than me."

"I'm exponentially younger than you," Hector said, flicking his banana peel in the garbage. "And I'm pretty sure most people your age wouldn't get that reference. Lucky for you, my mom's a big Ginger Rogers fan."

"Lucky me. Look, Hector, I didn't want this case, but sometimes that's the job. I did, however, ask for you. I think you're sharp and driven. Just do me a favor and don't screw it up."

"Yes, ma'am."

"And also, don't call me ma'am."

CHAPTER 10

Thunder Bay. Max hadn't been there since Dix's stag weekend over a decade back, one eternal week after his mother's diagnosis. He had skied and rock climbed and parasailed as though his life depended on it, and eventually a stillness had settled his restless soul. On the plane out there, he was certain his life was over, but nestled in their mountainside chalet watching the sunrise, he felt like it began anew.

Something about the scenery—the freedom and ruggedness and unforgiving resplendence of nature filled him up and made him whole. It convinced him his mother would be all right, beat the cancer, live to meet her grandchildren someday.

Now, as he approached the outskirts of the Lakehead, Max felt the opposite of whole. His throat constricted like a bad allergic reaction and his left leg bounced with nervous energy.

"Can you even get there in time?" Noah asked, looking out the window at the Nipigon River.

"It's going to be close." Max let his foot weigh a little more heavily on the gas pedal. According to the rookie, the Greyhound from Sudbury was due to arrive at ten o'clock on the dot.

"You shouldn't have stopped for waffles."

"I'll make it," Max said.

To pass the long hours of the night, he had tried to make a contingency plan. The best he came up with was to get help from the local law enforcement, which wasn't ideal since he wasn't supposed to be west of Etobicoke. Luckily rush hour, if the city had one, was long over and Max parked in the bus station lot with a few minutes to spare.

The brown brick building housed a small lobby, a shipping office, an ATM, and little else. There was space for a cafe, but it looked as though it hadn't been open in years. Fortunately, there was lukewarm coffee in a thermos at the ticket counter.

There were no windows looking out on the bus parking lot, so Max waited outside, leaning against the chilly wall, trying to melt into the shadows where he might not spook the kid.

Out of habit, he checked his watch, forgetting he'd left it behind in his locker hoping both his grandfather's old band and the wide leather cuff that now encased it would dry out after being soaked by the fire sprinklers. Instead, when he pulled up his sleeve to check the time, his eyes fell on the stylized moose inside his wrist, and he yanked the sleeve back down.

Max was deeply ashamed whenever he saw his tattoo. Even in the shower, he had mastered the art of looking away. He had no memory of where he'd gone or what he'd requested—only of waking up with a throbbing pain on the inside of his wrist, of peeling back the gauze to find red angry skin outlined with an image that would be deeply personal to someone, but couldn't be personal to him. Had he asked specifically for the moose? Pointed to the Indigenous art from a menu on the wall? Said he didn't care, just to ink him?

He should have had it removed immediately upon sobering up instead of leaving it there the last five years as a reminder.

"Wicked ink, Copper. What does it mean?" Selina's friend had asked when he acquiesced to join them for hair of the dog.

"It means I shouldn't drink Everclear," he told them. And what else could it mean, tribal art to a man who knew no tribe?

He checked the time on his cell instead and found a text from his father.

Let's talk about Christmas when you can.

Five years since the tattoo felt like an eternity. Five years since his mother passed felt like yesterday.

He and his old man had half-heartedly attempted Thanksgiving the first year, but it was painfully empty. The food had no flavor, the conversation no substance. They sat in a colorless void which his father had attempted to spruce up with some of her old decorations, but she was their lifeblood, and without her there was no them.

Max called Maggie.

"You get him?" she asked without preamble.

God it felt good to hear her voice. "Not yet. Bus should be here any minute."

"How're you holding up?" she asked, and for some reason, not the least of which was probably sleep deprivation, he wanted to curl up and lay his head in her lap and listen to the soothing sound of her voice talking about anything at all.

"I'll be fine. What about you? Survive the night?"

"No spider bites or anything," she teased.

Had she gone in the spare room? Seen the truth behind his lie?

"We even met the famous *Selina*."

Something about the way she said it made Max's stomach twist and his mouth go dry. He didn't feel warm and fuzzy about the two of them becoming confidantes, although from Maggie's tone, he might not need to worry.

"Yeah, she has a tendency to drop in," he half-apologized.

"I noticed. She's gorgeous."

"She's a good friend. Is she still on about the gingerbread thing?"

"Oh yes, not letting that one go. She does seem really nice. She agreed to watch Henri so I could investigate. First, of course, I need to deal with this case you requested."

Max could picture her pursed lips and eyebrows raised in annoyance to match her voice.

Please don't be mad. "I thought I'd be back by now when I requested it."

"Merry Christmas to me, I guess."

That reminded him. "Listen, about Christmas. I know I invited you to Dix's, but I think I have a change of plans."

"Are you… staying in Thunder Bay?"

It was a throw away question, she didn't really think he was. Would she be disappointed if he did though?

"St. James?"

"No, of course not."

"Is this about the exam?" Her voice took on a steel edge. "Because I swear, if—"

"I think my dad wants to get together. So…" A pang of guilt pricked at the corners of his conscience.

"Oh."

The bus rounded the corner, and Max told her, "Gotta go," and dropped the phone into his pocket, relieved to swallow the knot in his throat and focus on the job.

Still, anxiety mounted in his chest, his heart beating faster, his stomach clenching as he waited for the passengers to disembark. Was it nerves over facing down a ballsy pre-teen, or the holidays weighing him down?

Probably he should have stretched, in case the kid made another run for it, especially after so many hours behind the wheel. But all he wanted was a salty cheeseburger and fries, a hot shower, and a long nap.

One by one the weary travelers descended, waiting for their luggage to emerge from the outside bin.

An adolescent kid got off alone, and in his exhaustion, Max

started to move toward him before it registered that he was blond and being hugged by his equally blond mother.

After about ten minutes they stopped coming and the luggage had all been dispersed. Had Max zoned out and missed the kid altogether? Or had the kid fallen asleep and not realized he'd arrived? Maybe he saw Max through the window, recognized him, and was still hiding on the vehicle?

Max followed the driver toward the lobby, keeping one eye on the bus door. "Excuse me," he called.

"Been driving all night. I'm on break," the driver said. "New guy will reload in fifteen."

"I feel you man, I've been driving all night, too, except I don't get a break," Max replied, flashing his badge quickly so the driver wouldn't register that technically Max was out of his jurisdiction.

He made no response, but he at least paused to listen.

"There was a kid on your bus," Max said. "About this tall? Shaggy brown hair. This kid," he added, remembering the picture on his phone and showing it to the driver.

"Oh yeah," the driver said. "The one they radioed about?"

"Exactly. I didn't see him get off yet."

"You wouldn'ta."

"How's that?"

"He got off—oh… Nipigon, maybe?"

"Nipigon? That's, what, thirty—forty minutes back?"

"Nah. It's at least an hour, hour and a half, I'd say."

"You didn't stop him?"

"What am I supposed to do? Leave my bus and go chase him down? You're the cop, not me."

Max counted to three.

"Did you see where he went? Into town?"

The driver shrugged. "Maybe down to the lagoon? I dunno."

Max nodded. He'd been utterly defeated by a kid. "Do me a favor," he said. "Next time—at least call it in."

He turned to leave and the driver yelled after him, "What'd he do, anyway?"

"What do you care?" Max called over his shoulder. "I'm the cop, not you."

❄

MAGGIE STUDIED THE PHOTO OF HENRI AND HIS BROTHER. THE entire plane wasn't in the picture, but you could almost make out the serial number across the wing if you squinted with one eye.

"Do you think this is an eight or a B?" she asked Hector, but he waved her away and pointed to the phone against his ear.

"I understand your policy. What I don't understand is why you bothered to call the police at all if you're not going to cooperate with our—" Hector cut himself off and hung his head before nodding at the person on the other end of the call as though they could actually see him. "Yes, ma'am. I'm sure the people of Toronto appreciate your discretion."

He smacked the phone down on its receiver and laid his head on his arms, making a throaty, grumpy moan.

"Library still won't play ball?" Maggie asked.

"What was that sitcom with the evil librarians?"

"Um…"

"I think maybe they were right." He clicked his computer mouse a few times, and the printer fired up.

"Yes, how dare they stand up for civil liberty," Maggie teased. "I'm going to see what the shift lead remembers. You finish cross-referencing the fingerprints on the pay phone with the ones on the locker. What are you printing?"

Hector rolled his desk chair over to the printer and pulled off a thick stack of papers, but they still kept coming. "You wanted a list of Holy Rosary churches."

"Not for the entire world."

"This is just Ontario and Quebec! Can I help with the interview?"

"No."

"Please?"

"You look pretty busy."

"Come on, ma'am."

"Definitely not."

Maggie hadn't interviewed a witness by herself in a long… ever? Even if she went in alone, Max would be on the other side of the glass—watching, evaluating, ready to jump in if she needed him. The opportunity before her was simultaneously liberating and completely inhibiting. What if she took the wrong tack? Made the wrong move? Said the wrong words?

Boyd's report suggested the witness seemed shy and reserved. Her plan was to play it cool, make him comfortable, gain his trust.

"Vincent Reyes," she bellowed louder than anyone would mean to, throwing open the door harder than should have been possible, bursting into the interview room like a badly aimed bowling ball barreling straight into the gutter.

"I'm Officer Kyle," she said, taking a breath and a beat, visualizing the version of herself that she wanted to be, like Max had taught her. "Thank you for coming in today, Mr. Reyes." She offered her hand to shake, and he sat up straight, shifting his weight around in the chair before hesitantly extending his own hand in return. It was cold and clammy.

Vincent was tall but scrawny, probably six foot three, one hundred and forty-five pounds.

And he was young. Boyd had put him between twenty and twenty-two, but Maggie would be surprised if he was over nineteen.

"Sure, I mean I guess. I told the cops everything yesterday, so I don't know how else I can help." He shifted around in his seat some more, and wiped his sweaty palms on his khakis.

To be fair, though, the chairs were really hard, with a straight back that probably hit him right between his bony shoulder blades, and the heat was turned up way too high for such a stuffy little room.

"Would you like a drink?" she offered. "Water? Pop? Coffee?"

He shook his head, but the offer seemed to relax him. "Nah. I mean, I won't be here long right? They're expecting me back at work."

She smiled at him. "We'll have you out of here in a jiffy. My notes say you were shift supervisor yesterday? That's very impressive, someone your age."

"Not supervisor. Lead," he corrected her. "And not just yesterday. Every day. Since August."

"Lead, got it. Still impressive though. I mean, you were in charge, right?"

Vincent shrugged, but it puffed him up a little. "I guess. Not that you'd notice."

"Do your employees not listen to you?"

"Coworkers," he said. Then he shrugged again. "They're okay."

"Were any of them acting strangely?"

"Stranger than normal, you mean? Why? Did somebody say something?"

"Not so far. Do you think I should question them again?"

"No. They're not very attentive to detail," he said, picking at a spot on the table where an old piece of Scotch tape had been left behind.

"What kinds of things do they miss?"

He looked up from the tape, as though seeing the long checklist of infractions he'd been tracking for months, waiting for someone to ask. "Making sure voucher dates haven't expired. Asking juveniles for ID when they try to buy a ticket on their own. Or cigarettes."

"Not exactly sticklers for the rules."

"You could say that."

"Why don't you take me through your day yesterday?" Maggie asked, leaning back in her chair.

"What, from the beginning? Got to work, made a double-double, took a leak—that kind of thing?" he asked, leaning back himself, matching her posture.

"Please."

"Okay, I mopped down the bathroom floors because it was obvious the night crew hadn't done it. Really more of a spit polish because I was running late, but people don't usually complain as long as their shoes don't stick."

"Why were you late?"

"Traffic."

Maggie wrote that down, and he noticed, craning his neck to try and see what she'd written.

"I mean, I wasn't that late. I clocked in on time."

She smiled. "What time was that?"

"Seven on the dot, like most days. I work first shift."

"And you drive to work?"

"Usually I take a streetcar."

"But not yesterday?"

"It was late, so I walked."

"The streetcar was late? Which one was it?"

"Does it matter?"

She smiled again. "Just trying to get a picture of your morning."

"The five oh five."

"Does it frequently run late?"

"It's a streetcar," he said with a shrug.

"So you walked to work and mopped the floor. Then what?"

"A little of this, a little of that. My job is mainly being there when people demand to see the manager. They don't get a manager, they get me. Until they demand to see my manager.

Then I give them a number to call." He took an official business card out of his wallet and tossed it on the table.

"How often would you say people ask for a manager?" Maggie asked, studying the card.

"Once or twice a shift usually."

"Did anyone demand to see a manager yesterday?"

"Yeah. Two different wrecks on the four hundred had the schedule all out of whack. And one guy was pissy because he bought a ticket for today but wanted to use it yesterday."

"Did you let him?"

"Couldn't. Bus was full. But I got him on one leaving in the afternoon and then he calmed down."

"Anyone ever yell at you? Or threaten you?"

"People mostly just want to be heard."

"Yeah, I guess they do. Was it busier than usual?"

"Busier than usual for Christmastime, you mean?"

Maggie shrugged.

"I guess. Busy enough they needed my help with ticket sales all morning."

"All morning?"

"Except when I had to go chase off a couple of little terrors."

"Terriers?" Maggie asked, deliberately mishearing him.

"Kids."

"Minors?"

"Yeah."

"Unaccompanied?"

"Always. Every damn day like clockwork. In before six, and sometimes they're gone, time I get there, but I see them on the security cameras, you know? Sometimes I come in early to try and catch them."

"Your dedication is admirable," Maggie said, channeling Max's sarcasm, and it made her want to wink at him behind the glass. "What do they do every day?"

"Run up and down the stairs, play on the escalators, eyeball the candy at the newsstand."

"Do they steal the candy?"

"I mean, I haven't caught them yet, but I know they do. Come on, they're kids."

"What do they look like?"

"Stupid little kids? I dunno. Hoodies."

Maggie held up her picture of the boys.

"That's them. Little fart eaters."

"Kids are the worst, aren't they?" she laughed, channeling Max again and trying to think of a way to play both good cop and bad cop herself.

We're all good cops, Max would say. But it wasn't always true.

"You said it. I was too busy to chase them off at first, but give them an inch—you know? Pretty soon they were screwing around with the lockers—opening doors, slamming doors, trying to bust into the locked ones, tripping old ladies with big rolling bags."

"Hoodlums."

"Exactly. I keep telling my manager we need more security cameras around those lockers and to fix them up, you know? Half the locks don't work. Mostly tourists use them, and I mean, who would want to? But especially with those two playing around. He says they're fine and we haven't had any real problems or complaints, so." He shrugged.

"Until now."

Vincent nodded. "So I had to run them off. Part of the job, you know? But they split up. I didn't know where the little one went, but I kept after the older one."

"Did you catch him?"

"Nah, he was too fast. They're good at finding places to hide, and two buses had finally pulled in so there were people everywhere. I lost track of him in the crowd. Then I heard someone yelling 'bomb,' so I pulled the fire alarm and tried to get everybody out."

"Quick thinking. Did you see who yelled it?"

"Not really. It sounded like an older woman, and for a second I wondered if she saw, like, a smart phone for the first time or something. But I decided it wasn't worth the risk."

"Were you the one who called 911?"

"Gross, and touch a pay phone? Do you know how many people use those? More than you'd think, I bet."

Maggie cocked her head. "How did you know the call came in from a pay phone?"

"You guys—what do you call it? Dusted it for prints? I had to clean all that shit off—sorry. Anyway, if it hadn't come in from a pay phone, you wouldn't need to ask who called, right?" He held up his cell phone.

"Good point. So you never use a pay phone? What if you're out and your cell dies?"

Vincent took a small tube from his pocket. It looked a bit like a heavy duty *Star Wars* PEZ dispenser.

"Is that Yoda?"

"Never leave home without him. A spare battery, he is. Lasts forever, my cell does."

"Nice. But what if you can't get a signal?"

"I guess I'd use a signal boosting app, but if you need one in Toronto you're on the wrong network."

"There's an app for that?" Maggie asked.

"There's an app for everything."

"From the ticket counter you could see those two kids messing around by the lockers?"

"I could see enough."

"Did you see who put the IED in the locker?"

"No, but I mean, isn't it pretty obvious?"

"Is it?"

Vincent leaned forward and whispered conspiratorially.

"Look, I don't want to tell you how to do your job or nothing, but it doesn't take a genius to figure out those kids are trouble."

"What about the guy who bought the wrong ticket? Did he hang around?"

"I didn't see. They get a free pass because they're kids?"

"Just being thorough," Maggie said. "Did you ever see them with Legos? Or fireworks?"

"What kid doesn't like fireworks?"

"Do you like fireworks?"

"Sure. Don't you?"

"Less than I did last week. See any other kids? Maybe older kids or anyone who might pick a fight with these two?"

"No, ma'am."

"How long have these boys been coming in?"

"At least as long as I've been there. Sometimes I think they actually live there. Like the creepy twins from *The Shining.*"

"How long is that?"

"I don't know. Seven hundred pages?"

Maggie rolled her eyes at the two-way mirror before remembering she was on her own. "No, how long have you worked there?" she tried again.

"Oh, about a year. Started a little bit after I turned eighteen."

"Pay good money?"

"Pays the bills," he said, fiddling with the Yoda battery.

"Sometimes I think about it, you know? Maybe it would be nice to leave all this and be a security guard for public transit."

"I probably don't have as many bills as you. Kids, mortgage, shopping."

"Alas, no kids, no mortgage. Very little time for shopping. What about you?"

"No. I live with my brother. Sometimes I shop online."

"Sweet."

"I mean, I pay my own way. I just don't have a lot of expenses."

"I get it. So for a year now they've been coming in? Every

morning? Not Monday, Wednesday, Friday, or alternating Thursdays, but Sunday through Saturday before seven, they come, loiter, and then they leave?"

"Yeah, once I come in they pretty much scram."

"Any school uniforms or logos on their clothes?"

"Maybe?"

"Why do you think they visit your bus station every day, Mr. Reyes?"

"To make my life miserable?" he said with a mirthless laugh.

"Ever tried to contact a social worker? Maybe invite Children's Aid for an early morning visit?"

He shrugged. "Look, that's not my place, you know?"

"Not your circus, not your monkeys, eh?"

"You got it."

"Anything else you might have seen or heard yesterday that you want to tell me about?"

"Not really."

"Well if you remember anything, please give me a call." She handed him her card and stood up. "Oh, one last thing," she said. "What buses come in around the start of first shift every day?"

"You serious?"

"Just the out of town ones that were late yesterday."

"Let's see." He tapped his phone.

"You have an app for that, too?"

He ignored her and kept tapping. "You've got Ottawa and eastern origins coming in at six. Sudbury and points north coming in at six. London at six fifteen. And North Bay coming in at seven ten."

"That's a lot of buses," Maggie said.

"That's Toronto."

"Mr. Reyes, it's been a pleasure." Maggie shook his hand again. This time it was dry.

CHAPTER 11

The whole endeavor was turning out to be an epic Failure with a capital F. The kind of Failure that rang in Max's ears with a voice much like his father's.

"Do you want to be a Failure?" he had asked when Max brought home an F in history.

"History's boring. I got B's in everything else," Max replied.

The truth was, Max enjoyed history. But that semester the units focused on First Nations history as it related to white settlement across Canada. The white perspective of the textbook was meant to be politically correct, but every page portrayed the Europeans as brave explorers, white saviors opening up the wilderness to civilization.

Every time Max tried to ask questions about what really happened, the teacher shut him down. As the lessons wore on he could feel the eyes of his classmates drilling into him, watching, waiting for a reaction, comparing him to the figures they were reading about and expecting him to pick a fight.

Eventually he had quit showing up to class.

Failure. The word still rang in his ears twenty years later, even though this time he was trying to show up and do the right thing.

The bus stop on the way into Nipigon was little more than a truck pull-off in between a diner and a Tim Hortons. Max asked at both, but nobody remembered the boy in the gray hoodie with melancholy eyes. The kid might be three hours in any direction, but where was there to go? Winnipeg was still eight and a half hours west by car, Sault Ste Marie was six hours back to the east, and the US border at Grand Portage, only two. He could have hitched a ride somewhere, but even on foot he'd have had time to disappear into the woods or town.

Max was grasping at straws, but he cruised along Fifth Street toward the waterfront, passing first one tiny church and then another. If the boys were raised here, they must have made the trek into Thunder Bay for choir practice, but somehow it didn't feel right.

The marina was deserted, which suited Max fine. He shoved his hands in his pockets and braced himself against the wind, staring out across the lake which reflected a dreary gray sky. He could head back out of town, pay a visit to the provincial police. But what would they do besides put out an APB?

His phone vibrated from a text, and it could only be Maggie. He was going to have to tell her the awful truth, that any reservations she'd had about his fool's errand were well-founded. He'd be coming home empty handed.

He almost didn't answer when it rang a minute later, but he needed to hear her voice, even if it turned out to be laced with disappointment. "St. James," he said, pretty sure his defeated tone would give everything away all at once.

"I can't solve this thing without you, are you on your way back yet?"

Max sighed.

"What is it?"

"Kid got off the bus."

"Yeah… Is he okay?"

"He got off the bus in Nipigon."

"I don't know where that is."

"Well, it's not Thunder Bay, which is where I was. I've lost him. Maybe for good this time."

Max turned into the unrelenting wind and tried to keep his eyes open as it whipped across his face.

"Just… take a step back."

He literally stepped back, sagging heavily onto the hood of his Impala.

"He must be going somewhere that means something to him, right? Your gal pal *Selina*," there it was again, that tone, "tricked Henri into telling her the choir ribbon came from a Holy Rosary. There's not one in Thunder Bay, but for what it's worth, there's one right across the border."

"Minnesota?"

"Yep, Grand Portage. Thought you should know."

"Damn. Do you think they're American? Could the French thing be a coincidence?"

"I mean there's a Holy Rosary in Toronto, too, so who the hell knows. I put Hector on it."

"You're partnering with the rookie from Fifty-Two?"

She was silent for a moment. "Who else do I have?"

Max should've asked her to come with him. They could have split up on foot and canvassed the town rather than following the case from opposite directions. He'd wanted her to come, and she probably would have if he'd asked her to, but it was one thing to risk his career and quite another to risk hers. At least if she'd been with him, though, he could scrutinize her face to under-stand what she was feeling.

"Are you mad that I'm in Thunder Bay? You told me to come."

"I'm not mad," she snapped, and Max didn't believe her. "So now what?"

"I don't know yet." He slid back into the smelly old car.

"Okay. Keep me posted, I guess."

"Kyle?" His voice came out all wrong. Like he was pleading, and maybe he was.

"Yeah?"

He should have said he was sorry. Sorry for taking off on this wild goose chase, sorry for getting her reassigned to a case she didn't want. Sorry for asking her to duck Children's Aid. Sorry for being wrong when she was right. Sorry he would never admit to being sorry. Was he sorry for reassigning her as his partner ten years back instead of handing in his badge? Sorry-not sorry. But also, sorry.

When he didn't say any of those things she said, "Disregard?"

But Max didn't want to disregard. He very much wanted to regard.

"St. James?"

"Go easy on the rookie," he said. "He pulled an all-nighter for me."

"We all did. Drive safe."

Max tossed his phone in the passenger seat and smacked the steering wheel. Maybe asking for the case had been a step too far, but was the last straw not being there to help?

"You abandoned her with a case she told you she didn't want that she doesn't know how to solve," Noah said, looking out the window at the lake. "Thinking maybe you pulled her off the case of the century because you figured she couldn't hack it without you there holding her hand."

"I didn't abandon her," Max said, turning up the volume on the stereo. "If nothing else, the kid's a witness. And I've never been allowed to hold her hand."

"Aren't you also trying to prove something?"

"Like what?"

"You're tracking him, right? Trying to, anyway."

Flames shot through Max's cheeks and down his neck. He knew his people were just people—not mythical, not magical. If a First Nations person possessed superior tracking skills it was because he or she had been trained—by a generations-old body of knowledge and wisdom, but trained nonetheless. If they were attuned to the natural world, to the shifting winds and tides, it was because they lived in nature, not as city boys brought up on Dr. Pepper and *Degrassi*.

Still, a part of him needed to find all those things within himself. He longed for a connection, for a way to prove his father had not erased his heritage through his upbringing, but where would he even start?

"What does it mean," he asked the ghost boy, "to be… not white, not Indigenous, just… adrift?"

"To be you? I don't know, brother," Noah said. "How would I?"

"What if I can't find him? What if I'm not good enough, what do I do then?"

"Then you do you. You find him your way."

Max nodded. He'd come this far—too far to give up. What had Maggie said? The choir ribbon was from a church called Holy Rosary? He tapped it into his GPS. The nearest one was in Minnesota, like she said, but if the kid was headed there, then this was the end of the road for Max. He didn't have his passport, and he was too old to consider sneaking across. God help them all if the kid was attempting to brave the boundary waters. They might find him in the spring.

Excluding all the churches in the States, the next closest one was some place way up north called Pickle Lake, followed closely by Winnipeg, and the rest were all back east.

"What are you thinking?" Noah asked.

"I think we better get lunch. And coffee."

I'm not mad, Maggie told herself again. What was there to be mad about? Sure, she'd almost kissed Max and then he took off never to be seen again. He was probably interviewing to join the Mounties. And honestly, that was fine, because the thought of Max on a horse made her burst out laughing. At least now he'd be on his way home to help her finish this case. They'd be back on Bobby King by Christmas. Nothing to be mad about.

Her feelings thus sorted and packed away, she reread the text her mother had sent after another unanswered call while Maggie was interviewing Reyes.

Since you're not coming for Christmas we should schedule a Skype. You don't want your niece and nephew to forget what you look like—haha. They're almost as over scheduled as you are. Try to take some time off before the job kills you.

It was a masterful takedown of both Maggie and her sister-in-law at the same time, shrouded in a thin veil of concern.

"St. James on his way back?" Hector asked without looking up from his computer when Maggie sank down into the chair next to him.

"I don't know," she said, not ready to go into detail. But I'm not mad, she didn't add. "Did you hear back on the warrant?"

"Judge says if the library doesn't care who robbed them, neither should we."

"Damn. What about forensics?"

Hector passed her a file. "Dozens of the prints off the phone are in the system. I think prisons must actually bus their cons there."

"And?" Maggie prompted. Hector liked a good narrative as much as a resolution.

"And you should start with Michigan Mickey," he said, tapping away on his keyboard.

"The arsonist?"

"Prints are a perfect match, and he was released on parole two days ago."

"Okay. But he sets fires, right? IEDs have never been part of his MO."

Hector shrugged. "Maybe he learned some new skills on the inside."

Maggie nodded. It didn't give him much time to steal the not-Lego set, but it was as good a place to start as any.

"He'll be here after lunch. Can I watch?"

"We'll see."

"Also a Selina called? Said she would drop off Henri on her way to the symphony. Asked how you were coming with the gingerbread house?"

"What did you tell her?" Maggie asked, doodling a gingerbread house on her notepad.

"I said you were in an interview, and she seemed happy."

"Good work. You keep that lady occupied and we're going to get along fine."

"What's the gingerbread house?"

"Nothing."

"Didn't sound like nothing," Hector said, echoing Maggie's response to Max the day before.

"How are you coming with those French schools?"

He sighed and pulled up an email on his screen, inviting her to read it. "Last night I sent the boys' picture to basically every school in Ontario with a French program. Then I thought why stop there, and I sent it to primary schools in Quebec."

Maggie raised an eyebrow. "Busy night," she said.

Hector shrugged. "This lady's a music teacher from École de Château d'Eau in Québec City. She recognized the older kid as a grade one student she taught about five years back. Oliver Thibault. Pretty good singer for a six-year-old, as she remembered it."

Maggie did the math. The kid would be around eleven, which matched up with what Henri had said about the Klondike Killer case.

"Sounds promising. So why'd he head west?"

"Whole family packed up and moved out to the middle of

nowhere. The father was some kind of bush pilot or something, and the mother didn't speak a word of English."

"The middle of nowhere. Fantastic." Maggie stood up again because she needed to pace in order to think properly.

"I know. But she remembered the mom saying something strange. She kept saying, 'La fin de la route.' The teacher was never sure why."

"La fin de la route?"

"The end of the road."

Suddenly, Maggie felt sick. "Do you think he killed her?"

Hector looked up, horrified. "I mean, no, that's not where my head went."

"Really? The end of the road?"

He shook his head. Apparently she was a creepy weirdo.

SELINA DROPPED HENRI OFF AT THE FRONT DESK AND WAS GONE before Maggie got there. She must have been in quite the hurry to not even wait for an update on her gingerbread house.

Henri was bright-eyed and exhilarated from his morning. As they walked to the Celiac-friendly pizzeria Maggie had found, he couldn't stop talking about *Selina*.

"She's amazing. Did you know she plays the cello and the violin and the piano?"

"So?" Maggie said. "I play… charades. And… chess. What kind of pizza do you like?"

Even wearing the baggy hoodie, he looked as though he hadn't eaten more than granola bars and applesauce for a very long time, but he shrugged. "She even directs a choir just for boys!"

"Do you like Hawaiian? People think I'm weird because I like Hawaiian."

"I got to go to choir practice and sing all the carols! Even 'Merry Little Christmas!' What's your favorite Christmas carol?"

"Sounds like a good day," Maggie said, giving up on the pizza conversation.

"When Ver gets back, can he meet Selina too?"

Maggie was saved having to answer by a friendly hostess quickly seating them and taking drink orders.

"Henri," Maggie began after they placed their order, "would Oliver ever do anything against the rules?"

The boy looked up at her with trepidation in his eyes.

"That's Ver's full name right? Oliver?"

"No way, he would never," he said, but his face crumpled up halfway through and he looked intently at the Parmesan cheese shaker.

"You sure?"

"He wouldn't hurt anybody," he almost whispered.

"Did he put the fireworks in the locker?"

Henri looked her in the eye and shook his head fiercely. "He wouldn't have done that and then put me in there too," he said, like it was the most obvious thing in the world.

"Good point," Maggie conceded. "Did you see who did?"

He looked away and shook his head again.

"You didn't see or hear anything at all? Not while you were waiting in the lobby, or while Vincent was chasing you, or while you were inside the locker?"

Henri thought for a long moment. "Shoes," he finally said.

Well… it was something.

"What kind of shoes?" she asked.

He shrugged. "Like the other officer's."

"St. James? You mean running shoes? With stars on the side?"

He nodded twice.

"He's not supposed to wear those on duty," she whispered conspiratorially earning a small smile with the faintest hint of a dimple on the right side. It reminded her of Max. "So they were Converse shoes. High tops?"

He nodded again. "Except not black."

"White? Red?" Maggie asked.

"The rubber part was black. With a red stripe. And red laces and stitches. But the sides were… like checkers, but not square."

"Can you show me?" Maggie asked, fishing out her notepad and pen.

Henri took them and slowly, carefully drew a pattern across the paper. He frowned and stuck his tongue out in concentration, and for some reason that reminded her of Max too, the way his brow would furrow when he was figuring something out.

"Like this," Henri said, passing the notepad back, covered in a familiar pattern.

"So you saw houndstooth running shoes with red accents."

He nodded again. "And…" He bit his lip.

"And?"

"The middle part."

"The tongue? It was red too?"

"No. It had bloody soccer ball skulls."

"Bloody soccer ball skulls?" Maggie repeated, trying not to laugh.

"Yep."

"Okay then. Show me what those looked like, too?"

So he took the paper back and drew what was unmistakably a bloody soccer ball skull.

When their food arrived a few minutes later, like the Grinch's heart, Henri's eyes grew three sizes and after triple checking with the server that the pie was, in fact, free of gluten, he dug in with gusto. Maggie texted the description of the shoes to Hector, and then Googled—THE END OF THE ROAD—but the results mostly referenced the Boyz II Men song.

She pulled up a map of Thunder Bay. All roads led there, from the north, the south, east and west. But the end of the road? The end is wherever you decide you want to go, right?

If you were to drive west out of town on Highway Seventeen, you'd eventually get to Winnipeg. She zoomed in and saw a northern road off Seventeen, Ontario-599. It looked like it ended at the town of Silver Dollar, but when Maggie zoomed in, it kept going north for hours. Pizza forgotten, Maggie traced the route as it wove around lake after lake, like it was never going to end.

She followed it as it curved east and then west and then east again, but always north, past Riach Lake and Hughes Lake and Osnaburgh Lake, Doghole Lake and Pickle Lake and Tarp Lake, on and on until the road actually crossed right through a lake and she realized at some point it had stopped being called Ontario-599 and must have turned into a winter road—the ones only ice road truckers would use year round.

She traced her way back to the last highway designation and zoomed in on Pickle Lake.

It had an airport.

So she Googled that, too—PICKLE LAKE ONTARIO—and the results confirmed everything: ONTARIO'S LAST FRONTIER. THE NORTHERNMOST POINT WITH YEAR-ROUND ACCESS. THE END OF THE ROAD.

She looked up to find Henri watching her. "Whatcha doing?" he asked.

"Trying to figure out where Oliver might have gone."

Henri set down his pizza. "Sudbury, you said."

"He kept going. All the way to Thunder Bay. Do you know where Thunder Bay is?"

Henri nodded, but his eyes were wide with surprise and fear.

"Do you know why he would go there?"

He looked down but didn't answer.

"Could he be going to Pickle Lake?"

The little boy's frown deepened, but he held back any tears and simply lifted his bony shoulders.

"Henri," Maggie said as gently as she knew how. "Is Pickle Lake home?"

"Not anymore," he whispered.

Maggie didn't know quite how to respond so she said, "I grew up in Alberta. I used to think about running away to the city sometimes too."

"We didn't run away."

"You didn't?"

"No. We were sent."

A chill ran all over her body. They were sent. By themselves. To Toronto. And every day they went back to the bus station to wait for their mother, who never came. For over a year.

Oliver wasn't running away. He was going home to find his mother.

CHAPTER 12

Max drove slowly, along the shores of the lagoon. The odds of spotting the kid were slim, but he couldn't bring himself to scarf down a Tim Hortons sandwich and turn east in defeat. Not yet.

When he stopped too long at a three-way intersection, the Jeep behind him honked and then went around him in the on-coming lane, but as Max watched it go he noticed a creaky old cabin called The Musty Moose Diner. The name alone held vastly more appeal than any dime-a-dozen chain, so when Noah nodded his approval, Max pulled into the parking lot.

"Morning," an older man wearing a fleece zip-up greeted him from a stool in front of the counter. He folded his copy of the Red Rock Gazette and added, "You have the look of a man on a mission."

"Just lunch," Max said, glancing around at the otherwise empty diner. It was covered wall to wall in photographs and hockey memorabilia.

"Come to the right place then. Sit anywhere you like. Did you have anything particular in mind?"

"Cheeseburger? No onions."

"Onions are the best part, bud. You got a hot date tonight or something?"

A picture of Maggie in his bed flashed into Max's mind, and he forced himself to laugh before shaking his head.

"Bacon?" the proprietor asked, sliding off his stool.

"Always."

"Fries? Or a side of pie?"

"What kind of pie?" Max asked.

"What kind you want?"

"Apple?" he said because it seemed like a good idea to have some fruit in his diet.

"Aw, shucks. We've only got sugar pie."

"Sugar it is," Max said, his mouth watering as he tried not to think about the post sugar crash he would face in an hour. And hey, sugar grows from the ground, so it's basically a vegetable, right?

"Coming right up. Have a seat, friend. If you need anything, yell for Jerry. That's me."

Max waved at him, and Jerry disappeared into the back, presumably to cook Max's lunch himself.

He wandered the perimeter of the dining room, taking a closer look at the pictures—mostly local sports teams and school mascots, but some of the neighboring landmarks, both natural and man-made.

"Check this out," Noah said, peering intently at more pictures on the wall.

Max crossed the dining room in a few strides to join him before the display. "The wall of wings?"

"Buffalo wings," Jerry called, popping his head out of the kitchen. "Gotta eat two hundred to get your picture up there."

"Two hundred? Wow." Max gazed at the pictures of triumphant diners, all wearing matching glazed looks of over-fullness.

"Interested? Change your order?"

"No thanks," Max laughed. If Maggie were with him they might stand a fighting chance. Yet another reason he should've invited her along.

Mostly the pictures were of men. Men in their forties and fifties going through midlife crises. High school and college-aged boys with too much to prove. But there was also the odd Girl Guide company, too, sporting sauce-covered faces and striking Rosie the Riveter poses, and the occasional hockey team made an appearance.

Max almost moved on, almost turned back to the newspaper clippings he'd been examining before, but the peewee hockey jerseys reminded him of Noah, and even though the jerseys didn't match, Max studied the picture as though he would find his old friend there, a face in the crowd, unchanged through time. He wondered if Noah could be looking for himself, too. But these kids were too young, the photos too recent, whether Noah was a ghost or an imaginary figment or an ageless, invisible human boy.

One face did jump out at him though. Like some kind of haunted Where's Waldo he spotted his quarry enshrined in polaroid right in front of his own nose. He turned to look at Noah, who raised his eyebrows before turning back to the picture.

"Recognize someone?" Jerry set down the savory burger and pie on a nearby table.

"I don't know. I'm pretty tired, maybe starting to see things, but—could be the same kid, right?" he asked, holding up his cell phone alongside the polaroid and zooming in on the kid's face.

"They do say everyone has a twin," Jerry said.

"This team—they're local?"

"Well now, let me see." Jerry took a pair of reading glasses from his jacket pocket and peered closely at the picture. "No, Nipigon are the Elks. They're up here somewhere, oh where did they go…" He began to search the wall collage until Max directed his attention back to the photo he'd found.

"This team are the…?"

"The Lakers," he said. "Yes, sir. Fine group of boys. Very well mannered, and their coach left quite a tip, too, if I recall."

"How long ago was that?" Max asked, marveling at the older man's memory.

"Oh… three years maybe? Passing through on their way back from a tournament."

The door jingled and Jerry moved away to greet his new customers with a warm hug.

The Lakers.

Max's phone began to vibrate, but he didn't want to answer, not yet. He was on the verge of something, he could feel it in the back of his mind, like a gnat buzzing around his ear.

If he drove north there were a million lakes, sure, but… a tingle of a realization danced just on the cusp of out of reach. His phone stopped ringing and then immediately started again, and he sighed. The caller ID showed his favorite picture of Maggie's infamous side-eye, pretending to be annoyed at having her picture taken.

"Magpie—" he answered.

"St. James, his name is Oliver Thibault, and I know where he's going."

"Pickle Lake," Max said as it came to him, finally surfacing from his earlier search for Holy Rosary churches.

She was silent for a moment before saying, "Exactly," in a tone filled with surprise and tinged with disappointment. "You know it?"

"Not really."

"You basically drive north until you run out of road."

"Say, Jerry," Max called. "I'm going to need a box to-go."

"Anything to drink?"

"Coffee. Every drop you have." Pickle Lake was marginally closer than Winnipeg, but it was still another eight hours by car.

STANDING ON THE DARK SIDE OF THE TWO-WAY MIRROR, MAGGIE watched Michigan Mickey chew his thumbnail. Max always said she was the better detective, and she'd be lying if she said she didn't sometimes believe him. She was cautious and analytical, where he followed the whim of intuition. But hadn't he deduced Oliver's destination all on his own, without even Henri's vague help or the cryptic words of their mother?

Still, she'd gotten there too, using the tools at her disposal, and that was something. Maybe if she managed to solve the whole case without Max she would reconsider taking the D's exam.

It would be so much easier if he wanted to take it too, if they could leave the patrol ranks together as partners, Dix's Dynamic Duo, Max and Maggie, the Flagship of the Fleet. But he wasn't interested at all. Beat cop for life, like his grandfather.

Except Maggie didn't believe he wanted to stay put anymore than he wanted a promotion, and if he was going to work a job he didn't want, why not take the more interesting, higher paying one? Maybe he could surprise himself and learn to like it. She sighed.

It was Hector who had put the suspect in Interview Room Two. Maggie had specifically told him to use Room One. She liked Room One, but of course the rookie had chosen Two.

It wasn't his fault. He didn't know.

Maggie hadn't realized herself how standing in the stuffy, dark observation room would transport her back to last year—the department holiday party—her back, cold against the two-way mirror, and her front, warm against Max, as she pretended to be more drunk than she was. And Max—well, she wasn't sure. She'd spent the past year choosing to believe he was drunk too.

He wore a charcoal turtleneck sweater, which was out of character but looked amazing on him. It was soft against her bare shoulders and the delicate skin of her midriff. She almost stopped breathing when his hand slipped under her sweater and teased along the edge of her bra's underwire.

When their lips finally met after so many years of lusting and longing and off-limits collegiality, Maggie wanted to etch every detail indelibly into her senses: the taste of peppermint gum, the scent of something earthy which she now recognized as red clover goat milk soap. Afterward she had tried so hard not to remember that she'd almost begun to forget. But the interview room brought it all roaring back.

The way his heart sped up when he slipped his hand around her waist, and the way his breath caught when she reached over to lock the door, wondering in her giddy stupor why the observation room had a lock to begin with. He kissed below her left ear and the spot where her jaw met her neck. Had anyone ever gotten a bruise from their pulse racing too hard?

She had panicked for half a second when he pushed her sweater up—what if they were on the wrong side of the glass, what if another amorous couple in the dark could see them? But then he kissed her forehead where her brows knit together, and took her lips hungrily, and they were on the right side of everything and uninterrupted as time stood still.

Over the years, Maggie had allowed herself to imagine such a moment. She'd seen it play out in a dozen different ways, and yet somehow the reality did not let her down. Until it did.

Without warning, he had stopped—pulled back—muttered, "I'm sorry," or something equally devastating that Maggie could only just hear through her burning ears. He had pulled back, even as she leaned into him, keenly aware that his sudden reluctance wasn't due to an inability to rise to the occasion. "Disregard?" he had begged.

Maggie had cried herself to sleep that night watching *Bridget Jones* and piecing her armor back together, vowing it would never be pierced again.

Neither of them ever mentioned it.

From their first shift back after the holidays, they both pretended it didn't happen. Or, perhaps more accurately, they both pretended not to remember it had happened. Maybe she was wrong, maybe he really was so drunk he'd blacked out and forgotten.

"How's it going? You good?" Dixon asked, barging into the room and looking curiously from Maggie to Michigan Mickey on the other side of the glass.

Her skin, which moments before tingled at the memory of last year's touch, immediately flushed and she was glad of the semi-darkness. "Yep. Everything's great," she said, forcing a smile.

"Let's try that again with conviction," he replied.

"Just thinking through my approach on this one."

"Where's your rookie? Need me to step in as bad cop?" he asked, a little too eagerly, and not for the first time, Maggie wanted to ask if he missed it, if he had really ever wanted to be in command.

"No, thanks," she said, forcing a chuckle. "I'm good."

"I know you're good—you're the best."

It was nice to hear, from Dix the friend as much as from Dix the boss, but nice words wouldn't help her pass the test or survive the preliminary rotation. It wouldn't even help her solve this case no one seemed to care about.

"You look a little peaky though. You're not coming down with MJ's flu, are you?"

"I'm fine," she said, stepping around him into the hallway. "How's the Bobby King case going?"

Dixon's eyes narrowed and his head cocked to the side. "Second thoughts?" he asked.

"Of course not." She tossed him a tight smile and entered the interrogation room.

"Michigan Mickey." Maggie slapped his file down on the table and shot a confident look at the mirror, where she figured the sergeant was still watching, offering her a goofy thumbs up.

"Detective," Mickey said, scooting closer to the table and tapping it with his hands. "Nice day, ain't it? You ready for Christmas?"

She let the title slide—let him think she was a detective, maybe it would make him more cooperative. "You don't seem too worried about why we brought you in."

"'Cause I know I ain't did nothing," he said.

"Toronto Coach Terminal."

"Never heard of it."

"Funny."

"All right, so maybe I heard of it. But I ain't been anywhere near there. Not for years."

"Your parole officer and your fingerprints on the pay phone say different."

"Oh, you said the coach terminal. Over on Bay? I thought you meant Union Station."

"So you remember being there?"

"It was months ago," he said, fidgeting with his right eyebrow.

"Months, eh?"

"Weeks ago," he tried again.

"You were still in prison weeks ago."

He raised his hands in surrender. "Been having trouble keeping track of time since I got out. Anyway, I only went in for a second to call my mama."

"She verify that?"

"You betcha."

"And after you called her, did you maybe call in a bomb threat?"

"What? No." Damn if he didn't look her dead in the eyes, blindsided by the question.

"It's no secret you like setting fires, Mickey. Watching them burn. Frankly, my staff sergeant wants me to book you right now."

His face grew pale and drawn, and his eyes darted from her to the mirror. "You said bomb threat, though, right? Was it fire or a bomb?"

"Bomb's just another way to start a fire."

"Come on, lady, I don't mess around with that shit."

"Everyone knows a pyro loves fireworks."

"Everybody loves fireworks!"

"You ever start a fire with one?"

"Come on. Fireworks are just potassium nitrate and sulfur. I like to think my fires were—past tense, Detective—more sophisticated than that."

"Sophisticated?" Maggie asked, choking back a laugh.

"Yeah. You know." He waved his hand to illustrate his point. "Elegant."

"Could you make fireworks if you wanted to? Anyone ask you to do that for them?" Maggie asked, sitting down across from him and sliding over a picture of the cake remnants inside the locker.

Mickey whistled. "That would be a strict violation of my parole. And those don't look homemade."

"Where would someone get a cake this time of year? Could it be left over from Canada Day? Do they expire?"

"Not if you store 'em proper. But they were for sale last month for, you know, Diwali or whatever."

Diwali. Of course. There was a huge celebration out at the Hindu temple in Etobicoke, complete with fireworks. The public could have bought them anywhere in the few days leading up to the holiday and sat on them until yesterday.

"If you'd seen anyone leaving fireworks inside one of the lockers while you were on the phone with your mama, would that have caught your attention?"

"Might have piqued my interest, if I'd seen it."

"What about kids? Two boys? Did you notice any kids horsing around near the lockers?"

"Lady, after four years on the inside, I wasn't exactly noticing no kids, you know what I mean?" he said, winking. From some, the expression would have been decidedly creepy, but from Mickey it felt almost ludicrous enough to make her laugh.

"I think I know what you mean." Maggie stood up and leaned against the door with her arms crossed over her chest. "Do you celebrate Diwali, Mickey?"

"I celebrate life!" he said, throwing his arms up and leaning back in his chair.

"I bet you do. I bet your mama was happy to get you back in time for the holidays."

"She baked me a big cake. Red velvet."

"She buy you any fireworks to help celebrate?"

Now Michigan Mickey glared at her. "She won't even keep so much as no matches in her home, Detective," he said, slapping the table.

"Doesn't she trust you?"

"Would you?"

"Got an alibi? Yesterday around ten in the morning?"

"You're barking up the wrong tree, Detective. And the fact you think I look good for this, it hurts my feelings. Frankly, I'm insulted."

"Yeah?"

"Yeah! No pyro's going to try to burn down a building with a fireworks cake."

"Why's that?"

"Because it's gonna do exactly what it did. A whole lotta bang and bluster, and not so much—you know—burn."

"Poetic. So no alibi, then?" Maggie asked, leaning forward on the table, invading his space a bit.

Mickey sighed. "Ten o'clock? I weren't nowheres near the bus station yesterday at ten o'clock."

"Got any witnesses? Besides your mama?"

"About a dozen. I might have been in a fight. At Tim Hortons in Regent Park."

CHAPTER 13

Driving west on the Trans-Canada Highway in the daytime was not altogether different from driving it at night. There were a few more trucks on the road, and Max felt slightly less anxious about watching for moose and deer. Mostly, it was a dull, straight drive, the snow recently cleared, and enough evergreens to make it kind of beautiful if he stopped to notice.

When his phone rang somewhere outside of Ignace, Max was surprised he still had cell service. "St. James," he answered.

"It's me," Maggie said, her voice warm if tired, and that may have been the moment Max began to notice the pretty scenery.

"How's it going?" he asked.

"How's it going yourself?"

"Just... thinking someone ought to send Musk and Bezos letters telling each the other is about to go public with a tele-porter," he said.

"So they can race each other to invent one? I like the way you think, partner. By the way, *Selina* says Dix dropped by your place with pho."

"Am I humped?" he asked, imitating the show she made him watch with her, the space western.

"No," Maggie laughed. "She covered for you. But I think we might actually have to check out her gingerbread house as a thank you."

Max groaned. "How's the case?"

"Ugh. Dead end. Everyone's got an alibi, even Michigan Mickey."

"You'll get there," Max said, slowing the car as a deer wandered a little too near the road for comfort. "What do we do when we get stuck?"

"I go big picture, you go details," she answered.

"No, that's how we get stuck. How do we get unstuck?" he asked, and he realized he wasn't only talking about the case. They'd been stuck in a pattern of advance and retreat since long before last Christmas. But the kiss, that one perfect heart-breaking kiss, had frozen them in space and time, doomed to repeat old patterns.

Maybe the only way out was to tell her how he felt—let the chips fall, as it were. But she was so… skeptical of everything. Would she believe he didn't have ulterior motives like pushing her into the detective rotation?

"St. James?"

"Sorry."

"I said, when you're stuck you usually go for a jog and I organize my cupboards."

"Keep your body moving so your brain remembers how," he agreed. "I'd love to let Noah drive and get out and jog alongside for a while."

"Noah?"

Shit. He'd said it out loud.

"Nothing. Inside joke," Max said, making a righthand turn onto Highway 599, the road north to Pickle Lake. "Disregard?"

"St. James, you're okay, right?" she asked.

But before he could answer his phone beeped to indicate a dropped call.

He rolled his head back and forth a few times. This kid, this Oliver, was turning out to be a huge pain in the neck—literally. A dull ache spread from shoulder to shoulder and there were hours of driving yet to go, at least five of them by Max's estimation.

He probably should have called the Pickle Lake force, put it off on the lone provincial sergeant, and what? Maybe one constable? Let them try to wrangle the kid and bring him back to the city.

But the truth was, he was enjoying the open road, pretending to be some sort of survivalist in a ridiculous way. He wasn't even tired of the Isbell CD yet. It suited the trip and his mood. Because this mission he was on, this crusade—it reminded him of something his mom would do.

She always did have a soft spot for hard luck cases. Why else would they have adopted him in the first place? His father may have agreed to it, some kind of appeasement for being unable to produce an heir, or out of some sense of misplaced pride, like he was doing the world a huge favor. But whatever his father's motivation, Mary St. James wanted Max and loved him fiercely. It was as good as her blood in his veins.

Never knowing a stranger, always willing to push up her sleeves and help—if it wasn't a stray kitten his mom was fostering, it was a homeless person she invited in for a hot meal or an elderly widower she played checkers with on Tuesdays. Max always strove to be more like her, because he feared he was too much his father's son. The same temper roiled beneath Max's surface, yearning to smash plates, the same strict adherence to a personal code that demanded more from others than they might be capable of giving.

Had he inherited this one thing from her—this desperate need to make everything all right for everyone? His helpfulness used to at least restrict itself to the people he loved.

So why was he chasing some stranger's kid to the Kenora District?

Because his father would have said, "Follow procedure." But his mother would have brought Oliver home and fed him. She'd have been proud of him, maybe.

He could only remember his father being proud of him once as a child.

The St. Jameses had rented a cottage on the shores of Parry Sound for Thanksgiving weekend, his parents and grandpa and his father's sister's family. All day the adults sat around a bonfire chatting while six-year-old Max ran wild with his cousins. Being so far from the city seemed to relax Detective St. James in a way that Max had never seen. He taught his son how to fish and throw a baseball, and when his little cousin, Aly, tumbled right off the end of the pier and Max dove into the frigid water to bring her out dazed but unharmed, his father didn't scold him for not calling the adults or for disobeying the stay out of the water rule.

With genuine pride and shining eyes, he praised Max's quick reflexes and confident swimming and registered him for the swim team as soon as they returned to Toronto.

This mission to save Oliver Thibault felt like the first right thing he'd done since then, but would his father be proud of him now?

"You should probably sleep," Noah said. "How are you not delirious by now?"

Max laughed. "I'm talking to you, aren't I? I don't have time to sleep."

"I'll sleep when I'm dead," Noah growled. "Isn't that what your old man used to say?"

"Until I tried to turn it back on him when it was past my bedtime."

Noah laughed at the memory.

"Can I ask you a question?"

"You can ask a second one if you like," Noah said, grinning so a dimple appeared in his left cheek, still the same old smart-ass.

"Is your name really Noah?"

The ghost boy shrugged. "It's what you've always called me. What else is a name?"

"Where'd you come from?"

"Where does anyone?"

"Do you think I'm too much like him?" Max blurted out. After all, if Noah was a manifestation of his own subconscious, he'd like to know what he really thought of himself deep down.

"The Inspector?" Noah cocked his head, studying Max.

"How much of who you are comes from your blood? Rather than the people who raised you? Do you think a family you never even knew—people you don't remember at all—could still be a part of the person you grow up to be?"

"Brother, I thought you were listening to these songs. If you loved them—ever—they're a part of you."

As the CD spun to the next track, Max stared at Noah, scouring his face for a resemblance to his own, for any kind of answer.

"You need to watch the road," Noah said when Max hit the shoulder spraying gravel and snow up behind him.

So Max faced forward and focused on the kilometers stretching away before him, singing along with the music that had become his anthem as the sun dipped lower in the sky.

MAGGIE SIGHED. HER PARTNER HAD BEEN UP FOR MORE HOURS than she wanted to count. He'd be driving in the dark again soon. She should've gone with him, should've insisted. At least she'd have been more useful than she was here.

Two more potential suspects popped in the forensics workup, and she interviewed them both, but motives were thin.

"Look, I know you wish he were here instead of me," Hector said, bouncing his pen on the notepad. "And I get it. St. James is badass."

Maggie reached out to still his pen. "Hector, you're doing great."

"Really?"

"This is the unglamorous side of police work," she said. "You try, and you get it wrong, and then you try again." That was rich, coming from her.

"Good, because St. James may be charming as hell, but he might not have been able to flirt his way to this little chestnut," Hector said, sliding a piece of paper down the desk to her, his anxiety combusting into fresh excitement.

"Rookie, you worked the dimples?" Maggie teased, picking up the paper.

"I mean, it was over the phone," Hector said. "But David at Converse customer support has a soft spot for cops."

"Ew, David," Maggie teased again. "Badge buck, eh?"

Hector shrugged, trying not to look too pleased with himself.

She glanced down at the paper. It was an address in Regent Park. It was Bobby King's address, the house she and Max had been watching on the undercover op. "What is this? Which case are you working?"

"I know, right?!"

"Explain it to me?"

"Your boy's description was a perfect match. Only one unique pair of bloody soccer ball skulls combined with the red piping and houndstooth was ever made. And it was delivered to the home of Bobby King."

"Bobby King?"

"Bobby King," he repeated, beaming.

"*Bobby King?*" Maggie said again, the gears in her mind spinning, trying to catch up.

"Is there an echo in here?" Hector asked giddily. "Bobby effing King!"

"Bobby King bought the shoes our witness places inside the bus station—next to the lockers—at the time of the attack?" Maggie said in disbelief.

"Bobby effing King!"

"But how did he get past us? We were sitting on his house."

Maggie replayed the scene in her mind. She and Max relieved the night shift who drove off ten minutes later. No one in or out except the pit bull.

"Uh, he's a criminal mastermind. So now what?"

"Now we convince Guns and Gangs that we need to raid his house."

Maggie rushed to Staff Sergeant Dixon's office with Hector practically tripping on her heels, and she burst inside, forgetting to even knock.

Her boss set down his sandwich and swallowed slowly. "Officer?" he said to her. "Other division's Officer?" he said to Hector.

"We need to raid Bobby King's house. Sir," Maggie said.

"I thought you were working the bus station thing," Dixon asked, searching his cluttered desk for a napkin.

"He did it, Sarge. We don't know how, but we know he did it," Hector said.

Maggie waved for the rookie to calm down. "We have witness testimony which might place King at the scene just prior to the event."

"What witness?" Dixon asked.

"Henri Thibault," Maggie said. It felt a little strange referring to the boy by his full name after so long.

"The Locker Boy? I thought you handed him over to Children's Aid yesterday?"

"Sort of," Maggie said. "They handed him right back to me, as an emergency guardian."

Dixon found his napkin and took his time wiping his hands. "Why?"

"Because he's a witness." *Leah didn't tell you?* she wanted to ask.

"And you don't think you've tainted your witness by fostering him?"

"No, of course, I would never—"

"In the eyes of the court? Or any defense attorney worth his salt?"

Maggie swallowed. "If we find enough evidence inside, we won't need the witness."

Dixon gave her a look over the top of his reading glasses. "Guns and Gangs aren't going to like it," he said.

"Guns and Gangs are going to hate it, but it's a solid lead. And, bonus, maybe it gives us the break we need in the big case."

Dixon considered her for a long moment, deciding whether to take a chance on her and a rookie from outside his division.

"Yeah, okay. I'll see what I can do. But if the judge wants details on the witness..."

"Thanks, boss," Maggie said, heading back to the squad room before he could change his mind.

"Now what?" Hector asked.

"Now we wait."

The time wouldn't be wasted, though. Maggie sent Hector home to get some rest and then assembled a selection of mugshots, including Bobby King's, to put in front of Henri.

The boy had spent the afternoon in the soft interview room, listening to Christmas carols on Maggie's phone and coloring in a Looney Tunes book Frankie had scrounged up. But he didn't have the calm demeanor such a placid few hours should have evoked.

"When's Ver coming back?" he demanded the moment she entered the room.

"Soon."

"You said that before."

"It's still true."

"Soon came and went," he said, and Maggie almost burst out laughing.

"He had a good head start and went really far away. But I have a fun activity to pass the time." She placed three mugshots in front of Henri. Two were known associates of Bobby King. "Look really closely. Do you recognize any of these men?"

Henri pushed himself up on the table, swinging his legs back and forth, but he looked at the pictures and shook his head. "Go fish."

Unfazed, Maggie laid out three more, including another King associate, recently imprisoned.

Henri gave her an annoyed look before glancing at the photos and shaking his head again.

She laid out another set, this time including King himself, and immediately he shook his head. "Are you sure? You hardly looked at them."

"I don't want to play this game anymore," he said, lowering himself back to the floor.

"Please, Henri? It's important."

"I don't want to," he said, and he poked at her phone, trying to pause the music, but when it wouldn't stop he swept the whole thing clattering onto the linoleum.

Maggie took a breath and retrieved her phone, stopping the music. "Not a fan of 'The First Noel'?"

Henri slumped into a chair, crossed his arms on the table and buried his face. "It's Ver's favorite," came his muffled reply.

Maggie remembered how lonely she had felt at the age of eight when her parents went away for a two week vacation, leaving her and Charlie with their grandmother. Grandma had planned all kinds of interesting activities, but her house smelled different and her food was a little strange, and it left Maggie anxious and restless.

She wanted to cuddle Henri on her lap and make everything

okay, but she didn't want to cross any boundaries uninvited. Instead, she sat down close beside him, stroking his back and hair. "St. James will find him," she said.

"But why did he leave?" When Maggie didn't answer, he peeked his face out of his arms to look at her.

"I don't know," she said. "But I bet he had a good reason." Henri didn't respond, so she held up her phone. "Why don't we play your favorite Christmas carol?"

"I don't really feel very merry."

"Welcome to adulthood," she sniffed.

"Why, what's your favorite one?" he asked, sitting up and looking at the mugshots again. He stared for a long time at Bobby King, touching the edges of the picture absently before looking back at Maggie for an answer.

"O Tannenbaum," she said.

His brow knit in confusion.

"You know 'O Christmas Tree'?"

"I think so."

"It's Tannenbaum in German. My great-grandpa learned it in the War."

"He learned a Christmas carol in the War?"

"He did. One night the Germans laid down their guns, and the French and English and Canadians laid down theirs too, and for one night, there was peace. When the German soldiers started singing, he said it was the most beautiful sound he'd ever heard in the world."

"Thought I heard your voice," Frankie said, poking her head into the room. "I was about to head to your place—I mean, St. James's place. You staying much longer?"

"Just waiting on a warrant and looking at mug shots."

"No, I'm not," Henri said, pushing the photographs away and stomping off to throw himself onto the couch.

Maggie offered her friend Henri's abandoned chair.

Frankie noticed King's mugshot and raised a questioning

eyebrow.

"Long story," Maggie said.

"I brought a few things." Frankie placed two grocery bags full of clothes on the empty half of the table. "My sister-in-law sent them over. They haven't fit Devon for ages."

"You're an angel," Maggie said, pulling a blue flannel shirt out of the bag and holding it up. "Look what she brought you, Henri!"

He didn't look.

"So how's St. James?" Frankie asked, sitting down and opening a ginger ale.

"Still in northwest Ontario."

"Northwest?"

Maggie nodded. "How's..." she gestured at Frankie, "everything? Shouldn't you be home with your family?"

Frankie took a long slow sip of pop. "I'm avoiding my family. Thank you for asking."

"I thought you were avoiding Tony."

"Now he's avoiding me. Keep up, Nene."

Frankie wouldn't meet her eye, so Maggie busied herself examining and refolding all the clothes her friend had brought. "What happened?" she asked.

"Ma let slip to the aunties. Then my niece let slip in front of Tony."

"And you hadn't told him yet."

Frankie took another drink and closed her eyes. "I was waiting for the right time. That wasn't it."

"He'll come around."

"Or he won't." She shrugged. "I just needed a few days to process it before I had to start helping him process it, you know?"

"Makes sense to me."

"Nene." Frankie reached out, stilling Maggie's arm. "You didn't fight Dix taking you off the King case—that wasn't because I brought up the D's exam, was it?"

"No," Maggie said, glancing at Henri to make sure he wasn't

listening. He was playing with her phone, which he must have swiped off the table. "This was all St. James."

Frankie looked surprised and let her hand drop. "How do you feel about that?"

"Haven't decided. He thinks I'm pissed at him."

"Aren't you? I would be."

"Not pissed exactly. Maybe… sort of… vexed."

Frankie burst out laughing, drawing a curious look from Henri.

"What?" Maggie whispered.

Frankie turned her chair to face away from Henri and picked up one of the sweaters Maggie hadn't refolded yet. "Who says that? Who says vex and isn't keenly aware it rhymes with *sex*?" she asked, whispering the last part.

"Not this again."

"Tell me you don't want to."

Frankie was never going to let it go, because she was sweet and supportive and, annoyingly, could read Maggie like a book. A year ago Maggie might've tried to deny it, but maybe it was time to admit everything out loud. Even the embarrassing and painful parts.

"*He* doesn't want to."

"Since when?" Frankie laughed.

"Last Christmas," Maggie said sharply, putting an end to the laughter.

"What? What happened?"

"Nothing. That's the point. We almost hooked up. Almost, and then he shut me down. *Disregard*," she added in a deep, dopey voice meant to imitate her partner. "Like one word can erase everything."

"How have you kept this secret from me?" Frankie smacked her with the sweater she'd been folding. "Did you ask what his problem was?"

"Of course not. I pretended I was too drunk to remember.

And I spent a year convincing myself he was too drunk to perform."

"When's the last time you saw him drink anything more than tonic or Coke on the rocks?"

"Not helping!" But Maggie knew she was right. Just like she didn't remember him tasting or smelling of alcohol, Maggie knew. Max was subtle when the officers socialized, collecting rounds for everyone and requesting his virgin soda in an old-fashioned glass, or volunteering to be the designated driver, but she hadn't seen him actually drink in years.

And besides, pressed up against him in Interview Two, it was plenty obvious performance would not be an issue. "Honestly, that makes it a thousand times worse." Maggie buried her face in her arms like Henri had done.

"Talk to him," Frankie said. "You guys are meant to be. If you don't end up together, what hope do any of the rest of us have?"

"Talk to him, says the woman whose—"

Frankie leaned her head on Maggie's shoulder. "Okay so I need to take my own advice."

"Ya think?"

"But Nene, I've seen the way he looks at you."

Maggie's throat tightened. "And?"

Frankie raised her eyebrows, but Maggie needed her to spell it out. "He doesn't look at me the same way."

"We're partners."

Laughing, Frankie shook her head. "He partnered with Dixon before you. Pretty sure he doesn't look at the boss that way. And Taylor definitely doesn't look at me that way."

Maggie tried to picture Max, staring at her with his intense, dark eyes. The left side of his mouth quirked up in an expression that said she was strong and capable and irritating and maybe a little bit brilliant sometimes.

"You know I'm right," Frankie said. "Don't give up on him yet."

Western Ontario,
2 days 'til Christmas

CHAPTER 14

It took Max a minute to remember where he was when he woke with a start on a lumpy bed in Pickle Lake Lodge. The sky was turning that eerie blue of pre-dawn and his undershirt was soaked with sweat. Panting to catch his breath, he struggled to recall the details of his dream. He'd been running toward smoking wreckage, but he kept tripping over his shoelaces and stumbling into fallen-down trees.

A glance at his phone told him it was past seven. He'd slept eleven hours, when he only meant to take a quick nap, to rest his eyes until they would stay open without crossing.

"We don't rent rooms by the hour," the proprietor had told him when he stopped at the inn on the outskirts of town the evening before.

"Not even for a weary policeman who has driven all the way from Toronto without stopping?" he asked.

"Why would you do something so foolish?" She wrapped her heavy woolen sweater more tightly around herself, not bothering to free the long dark hair trapped inside.

"My old man used to say 'sleep when you're dead.'"

"Then he was a fool too. How did he think you wound up dead in the first place, eh?"

"Can you make an exception this once? For a good cause?" Despite his exhaustion, Max had tried to amp up the charm, working both dimples, but the innkeeper remained unmoved.

"Rate's the same either way, so you might as well stay all night," she huffed. "It's minus eighteen out there and more snow on the way."

"Super."

"Not safe for a city boy like you to be wandering around."

Max laughed. "City boy," he repeated, and then sighed. "That's me."

The woman had studied him then, scrutinized him with narrowed eyes that made the wrinkles around her cheeks and forehead more pronounced.

Max blinked a few times, trying to hold her gaze, and realized she was First Nations.

"Status card?" she had prompted, when he handed over his Visa. "For the tax?"

"I…" he shook his head and shrugged as his cheeks flamed. "I was scooped." If he'd had an official document he wouldn't have tried the DNA test.

"Ah," she said, more gentle than she'd been before. "You look Cree."

"Dunno," he admitted, and it must have been exhaustion making his eyes prick hot. He picked up his room key, an actual key on a carven antler keychain, and tapped it absently on the counter, longing to say more, to ask all the questions, but especially why she had guessed Cree. Longing to talk with her, to learn from her, longing—hell, just longing.

She reached out to cover his hand with hers, stilling his tapping, and the gesture felt so motherly.

"Don't tap the moose antler. It's very old. Get some sleep. Whatever you're looking for, it can wait until morning, eh?"

"I'm not sure it can," Max had said, showing her the photograph on his phone.

Her eyes flicked up to Max's face and back down at the picture. "You're looking for a bush pilot in this weather?"

"The older boy," he said, shaking his head and zooming the picture. "Oliver Thibault."

"Whole family's gone," she said, frowning. "Such a tragedy."

"What happened?"

"You don't know?"

Max shook his head. The innkeeper looked like she might not tell him, like if he didn't already know then he didn't deserve to, outsider that he was. But then she turned her back on him to fix a cup of tea, and she started to talk.

"Marc Thibault," she said, pronouncing the name T'bow, instead of TEE-bow, as Max had, "lived to take risks. Always flew like he had something to prove. But that's why they called him."

"They?"

She turned back placing the mug of tea before him. "Eco tourist at a cottage on one of the lakes had a heart attack. Medics needed to fly in, but a storm was rolling through. Marc's plane was struck by lightning, hours from anywhere. Terrible thing."

Her story took the wind out of Max, leaving him trapped under the weight of his exhaustion. But the hot tea was a little comfort. "And his wife?" he asked.

"Genavié? Her mind started to go, after that. Maybe before. She died a year later, wandering around in the snow. Neighbors thought she was looking for those boys. They hadn't been seen for months by then. We all assumed the worst."

"They're alive," Max had told her. "I've met them."

She nodded sadly and seemed to exhale a long-held breath.

· · ·

HE HAD MEANT TO CALL MAGGIE—DESPERATELY WANTED TO HEAR her voice, to share what he learned, to talk it through. But he'd fallen asleep with his shoes still on, and now here he was, waking up on a strange bed, having slept but not rested, hours behind the kid, Oliver, who must have returned home to an empty house and no sign of the mother he hoped to find.

All because Max had set his alarm for nine in the morning instead of nine at night.

After splashing icy water on his face instead of the hot shower he longed to stand beneath for the rest of eternity, Max ran wet fingers through his hair. He looked more like a madman than a respectable officer of the law, and for some reason it made him chuckle. Except if he saw someone who looked like him trying to lure an unwilling child into his car, he'd pull his weapon.

The mere thought of driving made his back ache, but Max eased into the sedan and cruised slowly down Koval Street to the other side of town.

There was more activity than he would have expected given the weather, but maybe people up here didn't notice cold or snow. A young couple walked three large dogs while an older man pulled a small, sweater-clad chihuahua behind him in a sleigh. When he stopped to check the addresses, a pack of rosy-faced kids darted across the street with toboggans flapping behind them. Had they been friends of Oliver and Henri, once upon a time? It could be helpful to ask them, but Max's presence had not gone unnoticed. Each person glanced at him as he passed, turning curious, concerned stares his way. They were not accustomed to strangers invading out of season, especially not strangers driving unmarked police cars.

When he reached the Thibault house, a green townhouse on the wooded Crescent Road, it looked cold and lifeless compared to the other attached houses. Those were decked out for the holidays with wreaths and lights and all manner of snow-covered lawn ornaments including an inflatable Santa using an outhouse.

In contrast, the Thibault home looked like uninviting pickle loaf wedged between two delightfully toasted slices of bread.

Max tried the front door, but of course it was locked, and there was no spare key hidden under the weathered welcome mat.

Probably, he should have knocked on a neighboring door, explained his mission, asked for help or a spare key. Instead he walked around to the back of the unit to pick the lock—hoping the neighbors wouldn't look out and see him breaking in or demand to know his business from the business end of a hunting rifle.

But the back door wasn't locked and he quickly slipped inside.

It was deathly quiet except for the tick tick tick of the kitchen wall clock. Max flipped the light switch, but no lights came on. The power must be off to the unit. The only other sound besides the clock was the squelching of his Chucks on the linoleum.

In fact the only sign that anyone had been inside the musty house recently was a trail of snow-melt puddles across the kitchen to where the linoleum ended at a carpeted hallway.

Slowly he cleared the house, room by room, and what he found was a life interrupted. The living room walls were still covered with framed photographs of the boys smiling joyfully at kindergarten graduations, of Oliver in choir robes and hockey gear, of Henri toothless and holding up a freshly caught trout. More family photos rested atop the mantle next to an urn. A perfect dust-free circle seemed to indicate the vessel had recently been picked up and moved. A basket beside the sofa held a half-knitted blanket and yarn, as though set aside mere minutes ago, but another fine layer of dust told a different story there too.

In the first bedroom, Max found the closet door ajar and filled with mostly women's clothing.

In the second he found two neatly made twin beds. One had clearly been lain on, though it wasn't warm to the touch. The kids' closet held lots of toys: Lego sets and board games, hockey sticks and so many plastic guns. Hanging on the inside of the door was a gray cub scout shirt with achievement badges sewn all down the right sleeve.

Max had always wanted to be a scout, but his father insisted on team sports and swimming and Junior Model UN.

Absentmindedly Max ran his thumb over the badges trying to guess what skill each one might represent: the one with a maple leaf he knew to be citizenship, the one with a tree—environmental. Photography, home-ec, astronomy, athletics, water conservation; there was one with a microscope and another with gears, there was one for computer technology and another for robotics.

The STEM ones made his stomach twist. Might a Lego-loving cub scout learn enough earning those merit badges to build a rudimentary explosive and plant it in a bus station locker?

He didn't want to believe Oliver had anything to do with the locker IED, but whether the kid did it or not, Max needed to find him. He'd clearly spent the night here, and now he was gone, but where?

Prowling around the house unleashed a palpable déjà vu that pressed into Max's chest until he couldn't breathe. He was no longer inside Genavié Thibault's life interrupted. He was back inside his mother's sitting room, a week after she'd gone into the hospital never to return.

He was surrounded by all of the things his father wanted to be rid of, and he wasn't ready to let any of it go. To let her go.

As his own memories engulfed him, Max was undone by the thought of a boy coming home to find his mother's unfinished tea and toast, her book set down so the pages splayed out, destroying the spine instead of finding a proper bookmark.

Despair haunted every corner of this house, and Max was drowning in it.

His phone rang. "St. James," he answered on autopilot, his voice as skritchy as a needle on a record.

"St. James, I am freaking out. We found a connection between the bomb and Bobby King, and I got Dixon to authorize a raid, and this could be it, you know, the big one, but what if I'm wrong, what if—"

Her voice, frantic with need, brought Max back to himself a bit.

"First, take a breath and stop pacing."

The line went quiet. "I wasn't pacing," she mumbled.

He ignored the obvious lie, because he didn't have time to soothe her with argumentative banter.

"Kyle, you can do this. I believe in you. Dix believes in you. Some judge somewhere who approved the warrant believes in you. That rookie sure as hell believes in you."

"What if I screw it up? Ruin both our careers? Mine and Hector's, I mean?"

Max focused on an old stain in the carpet. This he could do. He could talk Maggie off a ledge in his sleep.

"You're not gonna screw it up, you know why?"

"Because you're on your way back, and you'll be here by ten for the raid?"

"Sorry," Max said, feeling like he was letting her down in the worst possible way. "I left my Tardis in my other pants."

She didn't respond for a long moment, as though she really had thought he could control space and time. But finally she said, "Because it's either this or the opera and I'm a terrible singer?"

"No, because it's either this or astronomy and you couldn't spot a meteor in Toronto with a telescope."

Maggie laughed, her anxiety abating for the time being. "Are you okay? Your voice sounds funny."

Somehow that one question broke him, and when he took a breath it was a jagged shudder.

"St. James, what's wrong?"

He couldn't find the words.

"Max?"

"Yeah. I'm fine."

"Are you really?"

"No." He sat down heavily on the bed, facing out the window. "I'm in their house."

Staring outside, Max could imagine the boys playing in the shared backyard—packing snowballs to throw at unsuspecting neighbor kids, kicking a ball around, launching those homemade rockets with their engines so similar to fireworks. He could see them running around with sparklers on Canada Day and dressed as superhero zombies for Halloween.

Oliver and Henri probably rambled through the woods for hours, likely knew them as well as anybody. The kid could be anywhere out there—and *out there* seemed to go on forever. For all Max knew, he might have gathered up some camping gear and disappeared into the wilderness like D.B. Cooper.

"You found him?" Maggie asked.

"No. I mean, he was here, but he's not now. Kyle, I don't think I can fix this."

"St. James, I say this with all the love in my heart—" his chest flared "—because I know it goes against everything in yours, but maybe you don't have to fix it. Maybe just being there's enough."

Max wished desperately that she was here with him and that he could also be there with her for the big takedown. "Thank you," he rasped.

"For what?"

"For not saying I can't save everyone."

"Wouldn't dream of it," she said, and he could hear the smirk on her lips. "Mainly because you'd take it as a dare."

Max laughed and realized he felt better. How was she magic like that? Even with the distance and everything else between them, she could always make him feel better. Even when she made his head spin and his stomach flutter, she grounded him, too.

He should probably tell her so, before he chickened out again.

"Magpie," he whispered, but then stopped himself, searching for the right words.

"I'm here," she said softly, waiting.

Outside a massive, shaggy brown moose with only one antler ambled into the yard. It was mesmerizing. At a certain angle, it made him think of a triceratops. It moved much more quickly than he would have imagined, and with a stateliness and grace usually reserved for horses in a military display.

Then it stopped and looked right at Max. Watching him through the window. Waiting for him.

"Max?"

He traced the outline on his wrist, the symbol he'd hidden for so long that almost no one knew it was there.

Outside the moose was still staring at him, like its black, watery eyes could see into his past and his future. Like it wanted to tell him something. Like it needed him to follow.

"Disregard?" she asked, giving him an out, only this time he didn't want to take it. But he had no choice.

"No, but I—Kyle, I'm sorry. I gotta go."

In a sort of trance, Max returned to the back door and when the moose saw him, it slowly began to walk away into the woods.

Feeling vaguely terrified but unable to stop himself, as though the moose had hypnotized him, he followed it—right through the middle of the woods, through the snow that rose above his ankles until his Converse were sodden and his toes numb. If only he'd worn regulation boots.

He could abandon the moose—return to the house to see if by some miracle there was a pair of Marc Thibault's old work boots in a closet, but the moment felt almost holy, and Max didn't dare break the spell by turning around. If he did, the creature might revert to its feral tendencies and maul him—or worse, wander off without him, never to be seen again.

They walked silently, only the sounds of shoes and hooves crunching through the top crusty layer of snow, and the moose periodically chuffing until suddenly it came to a stop and Max realized he could hear rushing water.

The moose looked back at him, and, though he knew better, Max reached out, wanting to pet it—to feel its warm fur or rub its velvety nose. But it turned away from him again and walked off to the left, revealing a shivering Oliver clinging to a log in the middle of a swift river.

Five minutes after Maggie's call with Max, Detective Collins from Guns and Gangs stormed into the squad room.

"Your guys were supposed to be watching King, that's all. What's with the warrant?" he demanded of Dixon.

"He's wanted in connection with the bus station bombing," Maggie explained.

"The crude little IED? Wasn't it a kid's toy?"

"It was made out of Lego and fireworks, yes," Maggie said, puffing out her chest to feel less small.

"Not Lego," Hector whispered, but she waved him off.

"Did you know about this?" Collins demanded of Frankie.

"No, sir," Frankie said, refusing to look at Maggie.

"Eight months we've been working this guy—the ring leader of the biggest gun smuggling ring in Ontario. Flooding the streets—our streets—with handguns and assault rifles." He got close to Maggie's face, sneering his disdain. "Ammo that could pierce your vest like a mosquito taking a drink."

"We know, sir," Maggie said, looking from Frankie to Taylor for support, but still they both refused to even glance her way.

"And you want to go after him for some middle school prank?" Collins practically yelled in Maggie's face. She closed her eyes against his flying spittle, but she refused to back up or back down.

"Ever heard of Al Capone? We bust him for this, and we can make the rest stick."

"That's the thing, kiddo, there is no we. You're not coming."

"It was Kyle's tip." Dixon stepped forward to make Collins back up. It was a gallant move, the right move for a leader, but it galled Maggie. She didn't need saving.

"She's not coming."

"Technically, it's her warrant. Looping you in was a courtesy, but you wouldn't have this opportunity if it weren't for her."

"Oh is that what this is? An opportunity?"

"She's going, Detective," Dixon said, pulling rank. And Maggie tried to be grateful, even if she didn't love being forced on the guy.

Collins glared at Dix before turning on Maggie, snarling, "Suit up and stay out of my way."

"I'll change into my SWAT gear," Frankie said, exchanging a glance with Taylor. Maggie was surprised those two were acting put out, like she had stolen their case instead of maybe busting it wide open for them. Did they harbor the same secret fears as her own? Doubt she could close the case without Max there to hold her hand?

Not that he ever actually held my hand.

"Nuh uh," Dixon said, stopping Frankie on her way to the locker room. "Kyle and the rookie can go, Taylor can join if he wants, but you're staying here."

"Excuse me?" Frankie demanded, turning an accusing glare on Maggie.

Maggie shook her head, just as surprised as Frankie was. Her friend couldn't think she'd spilled her secret to the boss, Maggie would never.

"Too risky. Put away your daggers, Castillo, she didn't tell me anything. I have two daughters, I figured it out all on my own."

"Sir, respectfully, it's not your decision," Frankie said.

"No, see, that's the fun part of being staff sergeant. I always get the last word, which makes every decision my decision."

"I'm so sorry," Maggie whispered, and she really was. Frankie's fears about being sidelined by motherhood were already coming true, and selfishly, Maggie wanted her friend with her. If she couldn't have Max for backup, she would have felt much more confident with Frankie along for the ride.

"Whatever. Just don't blow my case," Frankie said, shaking her off and storming away.

JOINING A SWAT TEAM WAS BOTH TERRIFYING AND EXCITING. WAY more exciting than sitting in a Suburban all day watching the dead leaves dance around in the wake of passing cars. Though opportunities were scant, suiting up felt like donning layers of armor, preparing for battle. The preparation steadied Maggie's nerves and masked her insecurities—it reminded her that she may not have taken the D's exam, but she had trained for this and she really was the goddamned police.

Detective Collins sent Maggie and Hector around the back of the house. "Radios on two," he reminded them, though they'd switched to the protected channel before even leaving the station.

Maggie's breaths came quick and shallow as they ran, low to the ground, through the snowy back garden.

Hector tripped over a garden gnome causing a minor ruckus, and they squeezed themselves tight against the walls, sucking in their stomachs, trying not to breathe. She glared at him, and he mouthed, Sorry.

He was pale and breathing so fast Maggie feared he might faint on her.

"Breathe like a musician," she whispered the words Max once told her. "Breathe in four-four time."

She watched as Hector counted his breaths: in-two-three-four, out-two-three-four, in-two-three-four, out-two-three-four, slow and steady until he felt in control. Had *Selina* taught Max that trick?

"On me," Collins said softly through the radio, and Maggie took her own deep breath. Now was not the time to get wound up about her absent partner's neighbor. "Go. Go. Go," Collins ordered.

She nodded at Hector to ask if he was good, and when he nodded back, Maggie kicked in the back door, to find a thug she recognized from yesterday's mugshot game eating cereal at the kitchen table, the pit bull napping beside him. "Police, don't move!" she yelled, but he was already frozen with the spoon halfway to his mouth.

The pit bull jumped to its feet instantly, and Maggie took a dog biscuit from her cargo pocket and tossed it to him.

The thug's other hand was hidden under the table, probably scratching his balls by the look of him, but she wasn't taking any chances.

"Both hands where I can see them. Nice and slow," she said.

The guy looked from Maggie to his spoonful of Cinnamon Toast Crunch.

"Hands on the table now," Maggie said, so the guy ate his spoonful of cereal and then put the spoon down. Slowly he brought his other hand out from under the table. In his hand he held a small pistol.

The dog took a step closer to Maggie, sniffing. She tossed it another biscuit, while Hector trained his own weapon on the thug's head, allowing Maggie to step up and snatch the gun.

"Who else is home?" she asked.

The guy shrugged.

"Let's see your feet," she said, handing Hector the gun.

"I ain't had a pedicure lately, sweetheart," he said.

"Yeah, well, I ain't interested in your toes," Maggie replied, jerking his chair away from the table, causing him to drop the cell phone hidden in his lap.

The dog sat at attention, daring them to come near its thug again. Maggie stared right back, tossing it a third treat and then snatching up the phone and passing it to Hector, too.

"Anything interesting?" she asked, glancing down at the guy's fuzzy purple slippers before re-establishing eye contact with the dog.

"He sent someone a warning," the rookie said.

"Kitchen's clear. One suspect in custody," Maggie told her radio. "Who'd you text?" she asked.

"My mother."

"Your mom's initials are BK?" Hector asked.

"She works at Burger King," the guy replied with another shrug.

"Be aware, suspect has warned King," Maggie told her radio. "Repeat, Bobby King knows we're here."

"First floor clear," Taylor reported.

"Heading to basement," Collins replied.

"Hector, will you do the honors?" Maggie asked.

"You bet!" Hector took out his cuffs and stepped toward the thug, but paused when the dog growled at him.

Maggie tossed it another treat as Taylor entered the kitchen.

"Can you deal with him?" Maggie asked, scooping most of the dog biscuits out of her pocket and handing them over before heading for the staircase on the other side of the room.

Taylor nodded, and Hector practically ran to join Maggie.

"I'll go first. Follow me backwards, gun out," she told him. "Please do not shoot me in the back."

Every creak, every groan of the staircase sounded a thousand times louder than Maggie knew it to be, but still, there was no way any occupant didn't hear them coming.

"Basement clear," Collins radioed, and Maggie turned the

volume down low. Only the second floor was left. If Bobby King was on the premises, she would find him.

She stepped onto the landing and whispered, "Last step," to Hector, who tripped anyway.

Together they cleared the first room. It was simply decorated with a bed and dresser, every inch of which was covered in gadgetry. A laptop, a tablet, an external storage drive, and thumb drives scattered across the surface like spilled jelly beans. It would take weeks for forensics to catalog everything. There was also a stack of DVDs, mostly superhero flicks. What there wasn't, was any sign of custom-made shoes—or guns.

The small washroom, too, was clear. It had a sliding glass panel instead of a shower curtain, grubby and soap-scummed but nothing to hide behind.

A scuffling in the final bedroom was too large to be an errant squirrel. Maggie put her finger to her lips and pointed for Hector to take up a position behind the door, covering her.

Ever so silently she crossed the remainder of the hallway. But when she reached the threshold, close enough to see the butt cleavage of whomever was bent over a duffel bag between the bed and the closet, a loose floorboard betrayed her.

"Police! Freeze!" she yelled, before the man inside could react. "Hands in the air."

Obviously experienced with cops, he put his hands on the back of his head without being told to.

Maggie circled around to face him. He'd been stuffing large amounts of cash into his bag—hundreds of thousands, by the look of it—moving the bills from shoeboxes into the duffel. Nike, Puma, Roots—but no Converse.

"Bobby King," she said. "Looks like you're going somewhere."

"Making a deposit. No law against that."

"What, you don't keep it in your mattress?"

"Mattresses are for kooks. I just don't trust banks. This is my savings account right here, nice and liquid."

"How'd you make so much money, Mr. King?" she asked, knowing she didn't have cause even as she cuffed him.

"I'm an astute businessman. Thrifty."

All Maggie could think was that she was making the bust of her career, without her partner by her side. It wasn't right, and it wouldn't stick, and maybe Max's absence was the reason why. If they didn't find the goods he'd be out before lunchtime, and she'd be sunk.

"Cool, cool, cool," Maggie said. "I'm going to have to search your closets. Where do you keep your shoeboxes that aren't full of cash?"

$\mathcal{M}$ax took in the scene before him. A log spanned the width of the river. Oliver must have tried to walk out on it and slipped in. He was holding on, but bobbing under the water periodically and coughing when he popped back out. Trapped in a dam of brush and reeds just out of reach floated an urn matching the one on the Thibault mantle.

"Sorry," the kid kept saying. "Sorry."

"Oliver Thibault," Max yelled, getting his attention, but when the boy looked his way, Max didn't quite know what else to say. "How's it going?" he asked.

"Pretty great," Oliver yelled back, and Max delighted in the sarcasm at such a moment. But then Oliver said, teeth chattering, "Gonna let go."

"No. You keep holding on, tight as you can. I'll come to you."

"Can't."

Oh no. No telling how long the kid had been in there.

"Yes you can," he yelled to Oliver. "I'm coming." Max stripped off his warm jacket quick as he could—no point getting everything soaked.

"No," the kid said, and Max realized he was giving up. He could hear it in the solemn tone of that one simple word.

"What about Henri?" Max yelled. "I promised him I'd find you and bring you back. I don't like breaking promises."

He scanned the riverbank, looking for a large stick to keep him upright and searching for the best point of entry.

"He okay?" Oliver asked.

"He's fine."

"Doesn't need me."

"Are you kidding?" Max asked, settling on a branch from a nearby tree and heading downstream in case the kid did let go. "You're the center of his whole world."

Oliver didn't respond. Max saw his head dip under again, and he plunged into the water.

Jesus it was freezing—the kind of cold that felt hot. He slipped on some rocks and almost went completely under, but he recovered his balance with the muscle memory of a former skater. "Oliver?" he called. "Henri would be lost without you. You're all he's got."

"Couldn't take care of him," the small voice said, breaking a little.

"You took care of him real well," Max said, picking his way gingerly against the current. The water rose above his waist, his manhood shrinking up inside himself. "I wish I had a brother like you when I was a kid."

Oliver didn't reply.

Max panted, the water rushing past him so shockingly frigid that it literally whisked his breath away and he might never catch it again.

"Hang on a little longer, okay, kid? I'm almost there."

About another meter would do it, but then Max slipped, turning his ankle when the riverbed dropped deeper than he expected, and with a splash he went all the way under, dropping his stick, knocking the side of his head on a rock. He washed downstream quite a ways, sprawling like an upside-down turtle trying to regain its legs.

"What happened?" Oliver called, trying to look over his shoulder at Max.

"Everything's fine," Max said, but if he didn't get them both out soon then everything would not be fine, not at all. "Oliver, listen to me. I need you to let go and let the current bring you to me."

"Can't," the kid said.

So there was some fight left in him after all. Good. "It's too deep, kid. I can't get to you. But I will catch you, I swear to God. You have to trust me and let go."

"No. I can't," Oliver repeated.

"You have to. It'll be okay, I promise."

"Already tried."

No, no, no. "You pinned?"

"Can't move my arms. Think they're frozen? Will they cut them off?" he asked, the pitch of his voice escalating with each question.

"You need to calm down," Max said. "I'm coming."

"Said you couldn't."

"I will." Max heaved a deep breath and pushed off from the nearest rock, propelling himself against the current, swimming hard—harder than hard.

His lungs felt like bursting and his arms were heavier than leaden oars. Max had never cared much for swimming. Benched from the swim team because it seemed like such a pointless sport, his dad had pulled him out and put him in hockey, where at least there was an outlet for his anger.

But like that long ago holiday with his American cousins, this time there was a point, a very real one, and Max dug deep, thinking first of every time he'd been made to feel like some great disappointment, and then thinking of every time Maggie looked at him like he wasn't. He should have told her. If he survived this, he would tell her the truth—she gave his life meaning and he loved her more than any man had a right to love, more than the sun loved the earth and more than the tides loved the moon.

And when he thought he couldn't take one more stroke, he imagined never seeing her again, and he pressed on even harder and suddenly he was clinging to the same log as Oliver.

"Hey," Max gasped.

Oliver just looked at him, shivering, his teeth knocking each other like rolling dice.

Max gasped for air, but each breath was a dagger of ice straight into his lungs. Each breath left him needing more. Like Maggie.

"Now what?" Oliver gasped.

Up close the kid was so pale he was almost blue.

"Really can't move at all?" Max asked.

"No."

Summoning all the strength he had left, he kept one arm over the log and clumsily unbuttoned his shirt with frozen fingers. Then he pulled the soaked shirt off, switching arms to keep hold of the log. He looped the sleeves around Oliver.

"Don't freak out," he said, before backing up to the kid so he could tie the arms around his front. He had to fumble with frozen fingers to make a simple knot.

Then he twisted himself at an awkward angle and grabbed the one wrist he could reach. Oliver groaned in pain.

"Sorry. Hang on."

With a grip on the kid's wrist and their torsos essentially tethered together, Max moved down the log inch by inch, pulling them both across the thick, icy current by his free arm, until finally they reached the shore. He dragged Oliver out of the water and onto the snowy bank and then rolled on his back panting and coughing. He looked up into the nose of his one-antlered moose, which snorted hot, steamy breath on his cheek before turning and walking away.

THE GUNS AND GANGS UNIT TORE BOBBY KING'S HOUSE APART. There weren't any custom Converse shoes—no Converse of any kind, for that matter. No hidden stash of guns, either.

"Your careers are over," Collins snarled when they arrived back at the station. "Both of you," he added, sweeping Hector out of his way.

Maggie watched him storm out of the squad room, and then her gaze fell on Frankie who observed the whole exchange with disappointed detachment before turning her back and following Collins down the hall.

"I'm sorry," Hector whispered.

Maggie shook her head. "It was a solid lead," she said. "And the raid wasn't your call, it was mine."

The rookie smiled weakly at her and headed for the locker room, and Maggie completely deflated.

The whole failed op was one more sign that she didn't know what she was doing and had no business playing detective. Even Max, who winged it so often he could have been a pilot, had warned her not to make a move too early.

Dixon opened his office door. "Kyle," he called, standing aside to allow her in.

She didn't want a debrief with the boss, she wanted to go hide in a toilet stall and cry. But she forced one foot in front of the other until she found herself standing before him.

"Sir?" she asked.

"Stop it." He leaned back against his desk, arms folded over his chest.

"Stop what?"

"This. Self-pity, self-doubt, self-flagellation bullshit. Whatever it is you're telling yourself right now—stop it. You made a call based on the evidence before you. It was sound. It was also wrong. Move on."

Maggie swallowed her inclination to argue with him.

"Come on. We're going to lunch," he said.

"I'm not really hungry."

"I don't really care," Dixon replied, grabbing his jacket off the back of his chair and holding the door open for her.

Maggie followed him to the patrol car for a painfully awkward ride. She couldn't bring herself to speak, so he filled the silence with dad joke after dad joke.

"Goodbye, foggy weather," he said, looking out at the sun peeking through some clouds. "You won't be mist." Maggie glanced at him and he added, "Come on, that's some of my best work!"

She cracked a smile, and he grinned back.

"You were pretty good back there with the rookie. If you're really not going to take the D's exam, maybe you should think about being a TO."

"I dunno," Maggie said. If she wasn't going to partner with Max, what was even the point?

Dixon parked in a fire lane at the Eaton Centre, and Maggie looked around, confused.

"Sarge? You brought me to the mall for lunch?"

"I couldn't decide if you needed a burger, a crêpe, or Thai."

"You didn't ask."

"It's Christmas. It's festive. You love Christmas, remember?" he said, gesturing broadly at the trees and decorations and throngs of shoppers.

Did he know about Max and the interview room? No, Dix looked earnestly eager to make Maggie feel better. It was sweet.

"All right. But I wish there were tacos." When his face turned crestfallen she quickly added, "Kidding. Crêpes. Always. A savory one and a sweet one."

"Perfect," he said, opening the door. "And after we eat, I was hoping you could help me with my Christmas shopping."

Maggie was taken aback. "Like… your PA?"

"What's a PA? That's a... an intercom, right?"

"A secretary, Sarge," Maggie said, taking her place in line at Suzette's Crêpes.

"What? No!" Dixon exclaimed, genuinely affronted by the misunderstanding. "As a... friend," he said with a shrug. "I don't know what to buy. You're second guessing your day, I'm second guessing my... list. Match made in heaven."

"Oh." Since his promotion they'd done this awkward dance trying to negotiate the whole friendship-supervisor-employee thing. "Then sure, but it's been a long time since I was a preteen girl. I don't even know what to buy my own niece anymore." It was sweet that he was stressing over Christmas presents instead of leaving it entirely up to his wife. Or maybe it was simply an excuse to reach out.

"Not for the girls. For Leah. She..." He looked away, focusing on the large, garish tree. "She kicked me out."

"What?" Maggie asked a little too loudly, reaching for his elbow.

"It's not a big deal. Only, you know, completely life-changing, right? Who needs to manufacture a midlife crisis? I'm just not sure what I'm supposed to do. I mean, maybe it's actually a good thing? More time to focus on me, focus on getting the promotion for real—permanently. Maybe even start dating again, 'cause that's not terrifying—"

"Dix—"

"I just—do I get her a gift, do I not get her a gift? Do I give her something impersonal like a blender?"

"Don't get her a blender. What happened?" Maggie asked as gently as she could. Normally she wouldn't pry, but it seemed like he needed to talk about it.

"It's hard. Being married to a cop for thirteen years, you know?"

"I know, but—"

"It's hard. It takes a special kind of person. Not that you're looking for advice, but when you find your person—the one who understands the job, the demands—don't ever let them go, all right, Kyle?"

"Sure."

"Do you copy?" He looked into her eyes more directly than he ever had before.

"When I find him, I won't," Maggie lied. Dixon looked like he wanted to say more, so she turned away to place her order.

"Maybe I should give her jewelry?" he went on, while they waited for their crêpes. "Something understated but really classy."

"Like an apology? For being so busy?" Maggie asked. "I tend to think apologies and proposals should be separate from Christmas presents. They should be their own thing. But I'm not even sure you should apologize, I mean, you're doing good work. She knows what the job is—"

"I flirted," he blurted out and his whole face crumpled. "She caught me flirting at a neighborhood thing. I didn't mean to, I… There's a gray line between friendly banter and flirtation, and I sidled right up to it and sort of moseyed along beside it for a while, and then I just stepped right over that line."

"Maybe you were feeling like she didn't have time for you either. Two kids, plus the weight of every motherless child in the city? It's a lot."

"It's not an excuse though, is it?"

Maggie was relieved to turn away from him and collect her tray, to turn her back and search out an empty table. The truth was, she felt a little disappointed. There was never a time in the past decade when she would have questioned his devotion to his wife. He cherished his family. Always put them first, from what she could tell.

When he joined her at the table he was searching her eyes for forgiveness, and she realized it wasn't hers to bestow. Dix was as human as the rest of them.

"How do you want your story to end? Do you want it to end? To date?"

"I don't know. That stupid flirtation was the happiest I'd felt in a long time. But it was just… new. And different. And a little bit more dangerous than sitting behind a desk."

Maggie reached out and squeezed his arm.

"She doesn't want me to get the promotion," he said. "Acting Staff Sergeant's bad enough."

"Do you want it?"

"How else am I going to put two kids through college? On a lieutenant's salary? Ha!"

Somehow scholarships and work-study programs seemed like a conversation for another day. "There are ways that don't have to mean the end of your marriage."

"Pretty sure robbing a bank would still mean the end of my marriage."

They ate in silence for a minute, listening to the tinny Christmas carols under the din of shoppers and diners and squalling children.

"So a gift," Maggie finally said. "My mom has this charm bracelet."

"Thanks, Kyle, but she's not a twelve-year-old girl."

"No, it's classy, like you said. Real gold. And every year my dad would get her a new charm. A diamond for my birthstone, a sapphire for my brother's. Peridot for grandma, opal for their anniversary. Each one was a reminder of the past they shared and a promise for the future."

"That's really beautiful."

"Maybe start with the girls' birthstones. To remind you both."

"Thank you. You're a gem yourself, Maggie Kyle."

"Aw shucks, boss."

"What do you think?" he asked, tossing down his fork onto the empty plate. "Should I grab some more pho on my way out?

Drop by to see St. James? He could probably use another hot meal."

"I don't know. Did you get your flu shot this year?" Maggie asked, because Dix was even more afraid of needles than he was of the flu.

He shuddered, right on cue. "Picked a hell of a time for it, but I guess it's going around."

"Guess so," Maggie said.

"Blue Flu, we used to call it."

She froze. The Blue Flu was when police effectively went on strike, all calling in sick the same day. So either Dixon was making an eerily apt joke, or he was suspicious. And why wouldn't he be? He'd known Max longer than anyone.

"Anyway, maybe he's doing you a favor, getting sick right now."

"How do you figure?" Maggie asked, eating but not tasting the chocolate and strawberry crêpe that had been so delicious a few minutes earlier.

"Giving you the chance to spread your wings a little. Work a case without him."

"'Cause that's going so great."

"Okay. Giving you a chance to screw up then. Learn from it. Make it right. Be the TO instead of the rookie."

Max wasn't exactly one for grand plans, but at least that would mean he didn't prefer his own solitude over her company.

"Don't get me wrong," Dixon said. "You two are my dream team, flagship of my fleet. But, I don't know. Sometimes the band has to make a solo album. You hear me?"

"I hear you," she said, but she didn't want to be a solo artist, to spend the rest of her life thinking, *Man, remember how good it used to be?*

"But are you hearing me?" he asked again.

"You said yourself we make a great team."

"So did Simon and Garfunkel. But imagine the world without *Graceland*."

Maggie tried to think of a cutting retort, but there wasn't one.

"There's a detective's exam in three weeks," he said. "If I could write you up for not taking it, I would."

"I haven't studied."

"Good. Then maybe you won't psych yourself out this time."

MAGGIE HAD PLANNED TO TAKE THE D'S EXAM AT LEAST THREE OR four times over the years—enough times that she'd lost track of her excuses. Except for the last one. It was late and they'd come off a particularly tense shift. The department shrink would say calling it tense was sublimating or something. During takedown, the perp managed to knock Maggie to the ground and get his hands around her throat, choking her until Max knocked him out with the butt of his gun.

It rattled her. More than rattled her. But when Max asked her to go for a drink after, she turned him down. She couldn't stand the way he was looking at her, all big piercing eyes and furrowed brow, like she was a fragile baby bird, in need of protection. She told him all she wanted was to get home—to take a bubble bath and drink Sauvignon Blanc in her PJs, and then prepare for the exam the next day.

But she was still on edge, even after the hot bath. Every sound, every silence made her imagination more wildly dramatic.

And then the sounds started coming from inside the walls like some kind of tell-tale heart, clawing and scratching and gnawing its way through the drywall. It was too much. She thought maybe she was having a breakdown. So at one thirty in the morning she had called Max, and he was there by one forty-five.

She wasn't imagining it, though, he heard the sounds too. In fact, he had arrived moments before a massive black squirrel pushed its head through the wall causing Maggie to scream.

But Max was apparently a squirrel whisperer. Without considering rabies or god-knows-what-else, he corralled the rodent in her bathroom, coaxed it into a towel, and carried it outside to safety in the most impressive catch and release Maggie had ever witnessed. It would have made the Crocodile Hunter proud.

He stayed with her for hours, teasing her back into good spirits. And it occurred to her, somewhere in between rounds of Slapjack and peanut butter chocolate chip cookies, that while they might remain friends if she became a detective, they would no longer be partners. And maybe next time he wouldn't be so quick to come when she called.

She never showed up for the exam.

Maybe it was an excuse, an easy way to ignore her test anxiety —convincing herself that she didn't want to be a detective as much as she wanted to keep her partner. But being an excuse didn't make it any less true.

CHAPTER 16

Slogging back to the Thibault house carrying the sodden eleven-year-old while his own wet clothes grew heavy with ice took much longer than following the moose to the river had. Each step was a marathon, and Max had to force his limbs to take orders from his brain.

Oliver didn't say a word. Adolescent boys are sensitive creatures, and Max was sure being carried hurt the kid's dignity, but he closed his eyes and silently endured it.

"Don't fall asleep on me, okay?" Max said, worried the kid might be suffering from hypothermia.

One eye fluttered open to glare at him.

"When's the last time you ate?"

"Last night. Old graham crackers. Juice box. From my hockey bag."

"After a feast like that, I guess you probably don't want any lunch? Burger and fries? Chicken wings? My treat."

"Spaghetti and meatballs?" the kid asked.

"I'll see what I can do."

When they got back to the house, Max set the kid on a

kitchen chair and walked down the hall searching the closets for towels.

"Her ashes," Oliver said. "I forgot her. I have to go back."

"What?"

"I didn't scatter them yet."

Max returned to the kitchen with an armload of towels and blankets.

"I dropped them," Oliver said quietly, like the shamed whisper of a confessional.

"It's okay." Max wrapped one towel around the kid's shoulders and another around his legs. "The current will take care of it."

"I have to go back."

Max draped a blanket around him, on top of the towels. "We need to get you warm," he said, vigorously rubbing Oliver's feet with a third towel.

"I can't leave her there." Oliver yanked his foot away.

Max's instinct was to yell, *Wasn't that the whole point?* But the kid was so sad and angry, unable to hold is eye. "Look," he said. "It isn't her inside that canister. It's just dust. She's already gone."

It was what he had repeated over and over to himself as he'd lifted his own mother's casket onto his shoulder, and again as she was lowered into the ground. She's not inside. It isn't her. It's only dust.

"It's all that's left."

"No. What's left is here," he said, tapping the kid's chest.

Oliver looked like he could cry, but he didn't—instead he laid his head on the table, shivering inside his towels and blanket.

It shouldn't have been so easy. He suspected it wouldn't have been, if the kid weren't half frozen, but there wasn't any fight left in him. So Max returned to the boys' room and hunted through the closet until he found a warm-looking pair of sweats.

"You should change," he said, holding out the dry clothes. "You'll feel better."

"Those were Henri's. When he was six."

"Then go pick something else," Max told him. Again to his surprise, the kid complied, heading down the hall to his room on wobbly legs.

Max followed, stopping in the main bedroom to search the closet and all the drawers for something, anything, he could change into. The only piece of clothing that looked remotely like it might fit was a pair of old sweatpants which hugged him too tightly across the crotch and stopped halfway up his calves. But they were dry, and for the moment that was enough.

"Those are ladies' pants," Oliver said from the doorway.

The kid was now dressed in a pair of jeans two inches too short but loose at the waist. He wore a sweater that bagged around the torso of his lanky frame despite the sleeves stopping before they reached his wrists. He looked down at a Université Laval hoodie for a moment before holding it out to Max. "This was my dad's," he said.

"You sure?" Max asked, touched by the offering.

Oliver nodded. "You're that cop from Toronto."

"Yes."

"Why'd you chase me?"

"Why'd you run?" Max asked, pulling the hoodie over his t-shirt.

The kid stepped into the closet, closing his eyes as though absorbing his mother's presence—or maybe only her scent. Max knew a little something about that.

"How did you know to find me here?"

"I'm a really good cop."

"You going to arrest me?"

"Is there a reason I should?"

Oliver seemed to think it over, then shook his head. "So what happens now?" he asked, leaning back against the doorframe.

"Do you want to take anything? We should hit the road soon. You want to spend Christmas with Henri, don't you?"

The kid nodded almost imperceptibly and returned to his old bedroom where he stood in the middle, between the two twin beds, looking small and lost. He glanced at the closet full of toys, at the cub scout shirt full of patches. Then he turned to the far bed, the one which had not been slept on, and he looked under the pillow. There was a small, plush panda with fur that had been well loved to a dull, grayish hue. He picked it up tenderly and sat down on the bed.

"Is Henri really okay?"

"He's fine. We haven't even glutened him yet."

"Good, because that's no joke."

Oliver handed Max the panda and returned to his mother's room. He scanned her dresser and the happy faces looking back at him from dusty frames. Then he opened a drawer and took a deep breath, inhaling the essence of her that seeped out. He opened a second drawer and removed a jewelry box, running his fingers tenderly over the necklaces and earrings inside. From the same drawer, Oliver removed a lipstick. He opened it and stared at the color, then placed it to his lips, almost like a kiss. Then he selected one of the necklaces from the box and put it around his own neck.

Feeling helpless, Max wanted to reach out to him, to offer him a hand or ask if he was okay. But the boy looked around the room once more in surprise. "No suitcase," he said.

"We can cram as much as will fit in the car," Max told him.

Oliver shook his head. "What would we do with it all?"

While Max was trying to think of the right words, the kid went on. "She was supposed to come with us. To the city. But she forgot her suitcase in the car, she said. She went back to get it and missed the bus. It's stupid but, I sort of thought it would be here, packed and ready for her to come find us."

"Maybe she—"

"I don't think she even packed a suitcase," Oliver said, and Max ached a thousand lonely nights of his childhood for the kid.

"I don't think she ever meant to come. Mrs. Tevis, our neighbor, left me this note." He frowned at the soaking wet piece of stationary.

Max took it, but the pages were stuck together. "What did it say?"

"There was a tumor. In her head. She wouldn't tell where we were except to say we were safe. But she didn't know that."

"I'm sure she hoped you were."

"It's not the same thing though, is it? What happens now?" he asked, repeating his earlier question, but Max still didn't have an answer.

"Do you have any other family here? Or in Quebec? Grandparents? Godparents? Anyone I could call for you?"

"No." Oliver shook his head. "There's no one but me and Henri."

The kid looked exhausted and resigned standing there in the middle of his dead parents' bedroom with sagging shoulders and a drooping head. If he'd had the yoke of adulthood on his shoulders before, he was being crushed by it now. Max was reminded of the river, of his fear that the kid was giving up, and a chill coursed through him that had nothing to do with his wet hair or icy plunge. He remembered what it was like to be a kid, feeling lost, without any hope at all.

"That stuff back there," Max began cautiously, waiting for Oliver to turn and face him but the kid didn't move. "About letting go?" Still no reaction, but Max pressed on. It was too important to wait. "It was because your arms were weak from holding on so long, right?"

The kid didn't answer, but his breathing changed; he was listening.

"Oliver?" he said in his gentlest tone.

"Of course," came a husky reply. "What'd you think?"

Max sat down on the edge of the bed so he'd be at eye level

with Oliver's reflection in the mirror. "Listen to me, okay? No matter what happens—no matter what—if you ever feel that tired again, just… tell someone, okay? It doesn't have to be me. It's okay if it is, but it doesn't have to be. Maybe a friend or a teacher, your brother when he's a little bit older. But… tell someone and let them hold on for you for a while, okay?"

"Okay," Oliver whispered, but he still wouldn't meet Max's gaze.

"Promise? Oliver?"

"Fine, I promise, weirdo. Can we get going already?"

WHEN MAGGIE RETURNED FROM LUNCH SHE FOUND HER SUITCASE in the locker room, and Frankie washing up after another round of morning sickness.

"You kicking me out?"

"Relax," Frankie said, but her tone didn't hold its usual warmth. "I brought your stuff in before the op."

"Oh." Maggie opened the case to see what her friend had packed. It was mostly socks and underthings, along with her favorite hoodie and the sweater from last year's Christmas party.

"It occurred to me that you hadn't had access to clean underwear for a few days. Much as I delight in the idea of you wearing your partner's, I thought you might prefer your own."

So it was a peace offering, even if Frankie had brought the bag in before there was a need for peace.

"I'm really sorry about the case," Maggie said.

"The funny thing is, it was the most St. James-like thing you've ever done, and he's not even here." Frankie stood with her hands on her hips.

"I—"

"You trusted your gut, which I would never tell a cop not to do." Frankie seemed to become aware of her stance and put her hands in her pockets instead.

Then why does it feel like everyone wishes I hadn't?

"Don't become him, Mags, just because he's not here. There's a reason he doesn't want to be a detective. He always shoots from the hip, but that's not you."

"We followed the evidence—"

"Well the evidence wasn't there. So I guess you didn't follow it far enough."

And then Frankie—Maggie's best friend in the world after Max—walked out of the locker room, leaving her alone.

She stood there, the morning's scene replaying on a loop in her mind until a knock at the door made her jump, and she turned to see Hector in the doorway with his hand over his eyes.

"Officer Kyle?" he called. "Ma'am?"

"You can open your eyes, I'm decent." It made Maggie smile to remember when Max used to do the same thing, back when she was a rookie herself.

"What do we do now?"

"Let's take a drive," she said.

"Where to?"

"Coach terminal."

"Why?"

"Because when you're stuck, you go back to the beginning." Because when she was stuck, she looked at the big picture, and Max looked at the people involved.

So that's what they would do.

THE STATION WAS BUSY, PACKED SHOULDER TO SHOULDER WITH holiday travelers jostling Maggie and Hector, annoyed to find them stagnating in the middle of the stream.

"Who stood to gain by putting an IED in a locker the week before Christmas?" Maggie asked.

"Scrooge McDuck?" Hector said. "Old Mr. Potter?"

"Seriously. What was accomplished?"

"A couple of hours of chaos? Some people had to take a later bus."

"Exactly. Which means either our bomb maker should look for another line of work, or it was never meant to hurt anyone," Maggie said.

"Some buses had to be rerouted to other stations. Maybe a passenger on one of those was the real target?"

"Maybe. But I haven't picked up any chatter about a related assault, have you?"

"No, but I mean, it was firecrackers. I'm not sure even an eight-year-old would really expect it to blow up the building."

"I agree. Which means the intent was to create a stir."

"The Joker then?" Hector said.

"Bomb threats all over the city, but only one had fireworks. And nothing since. Why?"

Hector shook his head.

"Why would Bobby King want to cause a stir?"

He shrugged. "Because he hates Christmas?"

"Maybe he had a delivery coming in by bus."

"Not that I want to agree with that dick-hole Collins, but what if he was right? What if the kid made everything up and got lucky?" Hector asked.

"You believe in coincidence?"

"I mean… I think I believe it's a coincidence before I believe anyone could see much detail from inside one of those lockers. There aren't even slits in them, just a tiny crack at the bottom of the door."

Maggie hated to admit the rookie was right. It was a stretch to imagine Henri saw much of anything through the gap where the old door was slightly bent from being closed on too-large luggage, let alone the level of detail he'd described. If only they could know for sure. She looked from the locker to Hector, who stood about five foot one on his tip toes.

"What?" the rookie asked. "I don't like that look, what's that look?"

"Let's test it."

"How? Put the kid back inside the locker? That kind of seems like child abuse."

"Not Henri," she said, and then he caught on.

"No."

"Come on. You'll almost fit."

"Rude."

"Please?"

"No way. When does St. James get back?"

"Do it for science?"

"Is that an order?"

"Do you want it to be?"

"I hate you," he said with an exaggerated sigh, but Hector opened the nearest locker and poked his head in.

"Not that one," Maggie said, and she pointed to the one they'd found Henri inside. Hector glared at her in protest. "Try?" she begged.

"You owe me. You'll never be able to repay me, not even if you win the lottery, that's how much you owe me," he said before squeezing himself inside.

Maggie reached for the door.

"Wait, it's claustrophobic in here. Not all the way," he said, but she pushed it closed anyway, or else the angle wouldn't be right.

"What can you see?" she asked.

"My life flashing before my eyes. I've now realized the moment of my downfall was getting assigned to this case."

"Seriously, Hector, what can you see?"

"Nothing, Kyle. I can't see a damn thing. And I'm getting nauseous."

"Can you see my socks?" she asked, lifting her pants legs

to reveal West Highland Terriers wearing red and green scarves. She'd found them in the back of Max's drawer and put them on in an effort to locate her missing Christmas spirit.

"Come closer," he said, so she came up right next to the locker. "Too close. It's really hot in here. I can't breathe."

Maggie stepped back and a few paces to the right, toward the fireworks locker. It still smelled of burnt sulfur. "How about now?" she asked.

"Still nauseous," he said.

"But what can you see?"

"Nothing but floor. How did Henri stay in here so long? Can I come out now?"

"Maybe try shifting around so your head is closer to the gap?" she said.

No answer.

"Hector?"

A scuffling followed as shoes banged the back of the locker and elbows rattled the walls.

When the string of curses ended, Maggie positioned herself right in front of the locker once more, practically leaning against it. "What about now?"

"Only shadows. I'm legit going to puke."

Disappointed, she opened the locker, and Hector fell out, panting for breath.

"How did you get into the Academy?" Maggie asked. "You barely lasted two minutes."

"I think you're going to have to face the fact—your boy played you," he said, holding his head down between his knees.

But Maggie wasn't ready to believe it. "Not being the truth, doesn't mean it was entirely a lie."

"Isn't that the exact definition of a lie?"

"Why would he lie? What did he stand to gain?"

"Why does anyone lie?" Hector asked, pushing himself up off

the ground. "Were you being relentless? Did the answer make you relent?"

The way he said it, Maggie couldn't help but laugh. "Yeah, I guess it did."

"But you still believe him."

"If he made the whole thing up, I'm taking him to play the horses at Woodbine."

CHAPTER 17

*A*bout an hour outside of Pickle Lake, Max stopped to fill up with gas. The station doubled as a grocery store, selling no hot foods but plenty of snacks and semi-fresh baked goods. Max stocked up on trail mix, beef jerky, and bottles of water, but the kid still insisted on spaghetti, happy to settle for cold Spaghettios and a box of Ritz crackers.

"I'm not sure you're supposed to eat those cold," Max said, but Oliver glowered at him and picked up a second can.

They got chocolate chip cookies, too, because what was a gourmet Italian meal straight from the can without a poor man's cannoli?

Back in the car, Max turned the ignition key, but nothing happened. He tried again and got a sad little whir before he stopped, so as not to flood the engine. On the third try, the Impala finally choked to life.

"Come on, old girl. Just a few more klicks," Max said, patting the steering wheel. When he checked his rearview mirror, there was Noah sprawled out in the back seat with an amused expression on his face.

"Looks like you're okay at this after all," the ghost said.

Max glanced at Oliver, half afraid the kid would hear his invisible friend, but he was completely absorbed by the Spaghettios, which made Noah laugh harder.

The drive back down south somehow felt even longer, despite having a living, breathing companion in his passenger seat. Max tried to make small talk, but got little more than grunts and side-long glances. Noah was a better conversationalist.

Maggie called a couple of times, but he didn't think he could talk to her again without blurting out his feelings, and he didn't want to do that from halfway across the province. He needed to see her face, interpret her reaction. So each time, he silenced the call, feeling a little bit more awful.

"Been gone a long time, huh?" he asked Oliver, trying to take his mind off Maggie's latest attempt. "Does it look any different?"

The kid made a non-committal sound and kept staring out his window.

"Must have been hard—not only looking after Henri, but with his food allergies and everything? Couldn't have been easy."

The kid shrugged.

"Tough guy, huh?" Max said, more to himself than to Oliver, but it earned him a sad little snort. "What?"

"That's the last thing my dad ever said to me. 'Boy, you better toughen up, or when I get back, I'll have to toughen you up,'" Oliver said, using a deep, macho voice.

Max glanced at the kid. "What the hell was that supposed to mean?"

"I don't know. Hit me, I guess," he said into his empty can of Spaghettios.

"Did he? Ever?" Max asked, the words catching in his throat.

Oliver shrugged. "I know you don't believe me, Officer, but I'm not a bad kid."

"I believe you." Even if Oliver had set the IED, maybe there was a reason that justified it in his pre-teen brain.

"I didn't leave him, okay? I thought that Vincent guy pulled the alarm to trick us into coming out. He was always on our case. When I realized it was real, I tried to get back in but you guys wouldn't let me. I went around to the side door, but it was locked or jammed or something. And then there was an explosion and—I thought he was dead." Oliver set the can in an empty cup holder and put his hands inside the belly of his sweater.

"That must have been pretty scary."

"But then you arrested him."

"I didn't arrest him."

"Looked like it. I figured I could turn myself in for whatever you thought he did, but then he'd go to foster care and I'd go to juvie. Or I could leave him with you for a few days where he'd be safe, and maybe I could find my mom and—" his voice broke, "—and she'd know what to do."

"I'm sorry," Max said.

"If he's not in jail, is he in some kind of orphanage now?"

"No, my partner's been looking after him while I looked for you."

"Why would they do that?"

"Because she knew it mattered to me."

"Why? You don't even know us." He almost sounded angry.

In some ways I think you are me, Max didn't say. "It was really dangerous, hitchhiking across the country," he said instead.

"I know."

"You should have come to us. Trusted us to try and find your mom." Like he himself would have trusted a cop—even his own father? Like he trusted the system to work in their favor now? Max knew the kid didn't need a lecture, didn't need a reminder of his disappointing failure, so he changed the subject. "If I don't have some music I'm going to fall asleep. You care?"

The kid shook his head, so Max turned the Isbell album back on and tried not to sing along.

It was strange sharing the music with Oliver. The entire record felt so personal, like it was written about Max St. James—

the baby, the boy, the man—his life, his loneliness, his pain, and no one else's. Even though it was only music to the kid, Max felt exposed and vulnerable.

After a while, though, he started to sing under his breath. It really was the only way to stay awake.

Suddenly Oliver reached out and punched the button to switch from CD to radio, abruptly replacing the music with the loud roar of white noise.

"Okay," Max said. "Static is good too."

"I know what you're trying to do," Oliver told him.

"Keep myself from driving us into a snowbank?"

"You're trying to torture me into confessing, right? But I didn't do it. Whatever happened at that bus station—a pipe bomb or whatever it was—I didn't do it."

"I just really like this CD," Max said.

"Did you join the police so you could harass kids all day or something?"

"No, I joined because it was the family business. Look, maybe it makes me a bad cop to admit this, but I don't really care if you did it or not. I mean, I guess if you did, I'd want to know why."

His honesty seemed to make the kid uncomfortable, and Oliver started spinning the tuner trying to pick up a signal, but they were too far from everything.

"I'm sorry my singing feels like torture," Max said.

"You're different from other adults," Oliver told him, sizing him up.

"Yeah well. You're pretty different from most of the kids I've met."

"And your singing sounds like a lynx and a bear fighting," Oliver said with no trace of mirth, but from the corner of his eye, Max thought he caught the tiniest smile.

"Hey, I used to be a chorister, you know. Try switching it over to AM, maybe find a station playing Christmas tunes," he suggested. "Or we could sing them. What's your favorite carol?"

"I don't sing anymore," Oliver said, and then after a few minutes of roaring silence, "Why, what's yours?" he asked, grudgingly.

"Mine? 'What Child Is This?'"

"Most people just say 'Jingle Bells,'" Oliver said, but he seemed intrigued by the answer.

"My mom used to sing it to me. Her name was Mary, and she would rub my back while she sang, and I used to think she was actually singing about me. Except for the Jesus part, which I conveniently ignored."

He was babbling. If he wasn't careful, he'd give Oliver insight into both his mommy issues and his daddy issues. He waited for a smart-ass comment, but instead the kid reached out and turned the CD player back on.

As the music filled the car and Max sang quietly to himself, he suddenly remembered where the CD had actually come from. It hadn't belonged to Maggie at all.

"There they are," Dix had said. "My stars, my aces, the flagship of my fleet. A little mood music to get you ready for the op." He handed them the CD before they got in the Impala to go undercover as a hot and heavy couple. Max had at least remembered the country-western bar correctly.

It had been Dix all along, trying to—what? Set them up? Force them to acknowledge the elephant in the room?

A little on the nose, there, weren't you buddy? And yet, it hadn't mattered. Max had never allowed himself to say the words he needed to because then what? They wouldn't be able to ride together, and what other partner could keep her as safe as he would? And what if she didn't feel the same? There was a time when he thought that would be the worst possible torment, but maybe he'd been wrong.

When it got to the humming part of the refrain, another voice joined his, and he looked over at the kid, who was deliberately looking away from him, out the window, humming along.

"'The First Noel,'" Oliver said when the song ended. "That's my favorite one."

MAGGIE LEFT WORK EARLY, PICKING UP A GLUTEN-FREE PIZZA IN AN effort to bribe Henri into looking at mugshots again. They bundled up in all the warm clothes they could find and built a snowman in the apartment courtyard, and then warmed up with big mugs of homemade cocoa. The moment she pulled out the mugshots, though, Henri got up from the table and asked, "Can I go visit Selina?"

"You spent all morning with her," Maggie said, trying not to feel jealous. What was it about *Selina* that held the entire male population in thrall?

"So?"

"Maybe tomorrow."

"I thought Ver was coming back tomorrow."

"He is."

Max had left a voicemail while she was at the coach terminal with Hector. It was short and sweet: **"Got him. See you tomorrow."**

She wanted to speak with him desperately, to find out how it all went. Hearing him on her voicemail was like a teaser, and she needed more, needed his easy laugh and smug sarcasm. But he didn't answer when she tried to call back, and she hadn't heard from him since.

To feel close to him, Maggie put on a hoodie she found in his closet. Maybe she could absorb some of his deductive skills by osmosis. Max and Oliver wouldn't reach Toronto before noon, but it still wouldn't be enough time for her to solve the case.

"Maggie?" Henri asked, his face close to hers, snapping her back to the present. "For real, tomorrow? Or soon?"

"For real, tomorrow," she said.

Henri grinned a timid smile. "Can I talk to Ver on your phone?"

"I don't think they have service right now, buddy."

"They didn't pay the bill?"

"No, they're out of range. Tell you what, why don't you draw them each a welcome back Christmas card? You brought the crayons and sketchpad home with you, right?"

He nodded and went to get his art supplies. Maybe whatever he drew could be a segue to talk about the bloody soccer ball skulls that weren't.

A knock at the door brought the child racing back into the kitchen, probably assuming *Selina* had dropped by.

Maggie plastered a friendly smile on her face and opened the door.

It was Frankie. Disappointed, Henri slumped off to the living room.

They stared awkwardly at each other for a moment before Maggie stood back to allow her friend inside.

"I'm sorry," Frankie said. "I got it in my head that the King case might be my last chance to prove myself before I get thrown behind a desk forever, and I took it out on you."

Maggie enveloped her friend in a tight hug. "Prove yourself? You were the youngest woman to make detective in division history," Maggie murmured.

Frankie pulled her face away from Maggie's chest. "And I've spent every day since trying to prove I deserved it."

"Do you want a—" Maggie wished she could offer a glass of wine—"ginger ale or something?"

Frankie nodded, so Maggie set about fixing the drink. She finally knew her way around Max's kitchen pretty well. "How are things with Tony?" she asked.

"Radio silence. I figure it will go one of three ways."

"Yeah?" Maggie handed over the pop, which Frankie accepted but didn't drink.

"He could leave. I could raise the kid alone."

"Not completely alone," Maggie said, squeezing Frankie's arm.

Frankie nodded. "Or, he might stay. But he won't want me to keep being a cop. So we'll compromise, and I'll take a desk job. We'll get a house in the 'burbs, and he'll get a real job to compensate for my salary change."

"Sounds… domestic."

"Yeah," Frankie replied, but her voice was morose. Neither of them had joined the force to sit behind a desk.

"So what's behind door number three?" Maggie asked.

"He takes paternity leave, and I'm back on the force in a week."

"Come on." Maggie led her friend to the living room, and then stepped into the hall to gather extra blankets from the closet.

"Are we building a fort?"

"The Ursid meteor shower has been going all week, and I haven't had a chance to watch. Maybe you'll get lucky, get to make a wish."

"When have you ever seen a shooting star in Toronto?" Frankie asked.

Maggie handed her a blanket. "Never. But I haven't stopped looking."

"Can I come?" Henri piped up.

"Grab a blanket," Maggie told him, opening the door to Max's balcony.

"How are things going here?" Frankie asked in a low tone before Henri joined them.

"I'm sure it's connected to King somehow, but I don't think I can solve it without St. James. He's always sort of been my north star," she added, gesturing up at Ursa Minor, the little bear constellation. "Sorry if that makes you want to barf. I know it's corny."

Frankie sat down in one of the deck chairs and laughed. "Everything makes me want to barf right now. But I meant…"

"What?" Maggie asked, taking the other chair, delighted when Henri climbed onto her lap. He'd found *Angry Birds* on her phone and from the look of it, would beat all the levels she'd never gotten around to playing, but she didn't really mind.

"With—" Frankie nodded at the little boy. "But while we're on the subject, why can't you just admit you've been in love with Max St. James since the first day you met him?" Her voice was more tender than teasing.

"What? No, I haven't. Have I? I don't—I don't think that's true…" Maggie glanced nervously at Henri, but he was absorbed by his game and didn't seem to be listening. "Max was scary."

"Scary? St. James is about as scary as a hot teddy bear."

"He wasn't your training officer. Back then, he was scary. Like, super intense and serious. And really strict. He had so many rules."

"St. James? Who's never worn regulation boots in the entire ten years we've known him?"

"He held my future in his hands, Frankie. I had to impress him all the time or he could tell the staff sergeant to cut me loose." After about a day, she'd known he would never do it, but he could have.

"Yeah, that's why you wanted to impress him," Frankie said, hiding her grin behind her ginger ale and pretending to look for shooting stars. "Nothing to do with his cute butt or smoldering eyes. Or those dimples."

Stop it. "I had a boyfriend, remember?"

"That guy—what was his name? Derrick?"

"Darren."

"He was an ass."

"He was jealous of St. James."

"Of course he was. Because even he could see you were into him."

"He was jealous of anyone with a—" Maggie was going to say dick, but she remembered there was a child on her lap and cut herself off. "He hated us spending all day together, hated how St. James was tough on me instead of treating me like a pretty princess and carrying me around keeping me safe."

"I guess that's sweet?" Frankie said, but she sounded like she wanted to vomit again.

"It used to piss me off so much. It wasn't because he cared about me, it was because he didn't believe in me. Not like St. James did."

"St. James, who you aren't in love with? Just to be clear."

Right. Definitely. Hundred percent. Infatuated maybe. Captivated? But not in love.

"I mean. I guess he did sort of spoil me for other men." *Stop it!*

"Uh huh."

"Okay, now that I'm saying it out loud, I can see how you might make that leap."

Frankie snorted her ginger ale and started to cough. "You can, huh? You can see how everyone might make such a 'leap,'" she used air quotes, "but not how it is one hundred percent facts?"

Heat flooded Maggie's face, but it felt somehow disloyal to Max to keep denying it.

"What are you so afraid of?"

"Screwing everything up, don't you know that by now?"

"I'm afraid of ghosts," Henri piped up, not taking his eyes off the green pigs he was blasting with brightly colored birds.

"That's just good self-preservation," Frankie told him. "God, how many opportunities have we let go by because we were scared?" she asked, standing up to lean on the patio railing and gaze out across the city.

It was beautiful at night. What the light pollution stole from the cosmos, it made up for in the twinkling buildings and signs, allowing the world to sparkle like a Christmas tree.

"Missed opportunities? Thousands, probably," Maggie agreed.

"I wasn't going to go quite that high."

"Did you know I wanted to be an astronaut? That was my first dream."

"Hah! Nerd," Frankie laughed, turning back around. When she saw Maggie's face she said, "Wait, you're not joking?"

"I was going to solve the mysteries of the universe like a damn space detective."

"Why didn't you?"

Maggie lifted her eyebrows in response. "Because math is hard. And test anxiety is real. And maybe some mysteries are better left unsolved."

"Oh." Frankie sighed and raked a hand through her hair. "I gotta call Tony."

Maggie nodded and slid a sleepy Henri onto the chair so she could stand to hug her friend.

"You may be a hot mess and an awful test-taker, but you're also the most tenacious person I know. Don't forget that part, Nene," Frankie whispered. "And don't give up on all your dreams because you're afraid you'll wreck them."

"What other reason is there?" Maggie asked.

Frankie shrugged. "None that's good enough. I don't want you to give up on them at all."

Maggie kissed her friend's cheek and squeezed her hand.

"Call me later if you need to bounce around ideas about your case," Frankie added. "Or anything else."

"You too," Maggie said.

But what she wanted right then, before she talked herself out of it or lost her nerve, was to tell Max how she felt. No matter what happened next, at least it would be out in the open.

CHAPTER 18

There was nowhere to stop for dinner until Max and Oliver reached Thunder Bay, and they were both ravenous. He let the kid choose, and the kid chose poutine, which was the correct and only answer. Soon they found themselves in a trendy restaurant surrounded by hipsters and families sporting their Christmas sweater finery.

After giving their drink orders, Max wanted to change out of the too-short sweatpants and back into his mostly dry uniform.

"Don't you need to pee or something?" he asked Oliver, half afraid the kid might bolt if he left him on his own.

"No."

"At least come wash your hands then."

Oliver frowned at him. "I'm not going to the washroom with you," he said, a little too loudly, so Max banked on him being too hungry to take off before his meal came.

He changed quickly, and hurried back to the table to find Oliver exactly how he left him, chin resting wistfully on his fist and staring into space.

"Your phone buzzed," he said.

It was a video from Maggie, so Max connected to the restaurant WiFi and let it download. When he saw it was a video of Henri, he propped the screen up where Oliver could see it too. They were building a snowman in the courtyard behind his apartment complex.

The little boy was dwarfed inside Maggie's coat. When she entered the frame wearing Max's leather jacket and Maple Leafs toque, his heart sped up into double-time.

"You have to pack it really tight and sort of melt it with your hands a little so it sticks together," Henri instructed her as they worked.

"Like this?" Maggie asked.

"Yeah that's really good."

Oliver smiled watching it, but there was sadness behind the smile.

Then Henri peeked mischievously around the snowman when Maggie went to retrieve her phone from wherever it was propped, and pelted her with a snowball.

Oliver held his breath, waiting to see her reaction, while Henri threw a second one.

"Oof," she grunted. "Come here you rascal!"

Then the camera shook as she chased after him while he laughed maniacally.

"I'm going to get you," Maggie called, and the phone fell in the snow, catching Maggie in closeup as she hastily formed her own snowball, winked at the camera, and then took off after Henri again, tossing it at him, as he pretended to fall tragically to the ground, and they both collapsed laughing.

It was everything Max had ever wanted.

"Looks... pretty cold," he said, clearing his throat. "At least we've got poutine."

Oliver laughed, a small snort of a laugh, but it was something.

"Man you really missed out earlier. A guy in the washroom had candy cane colored dreads."

Oliver shrugged.

"Guess you've seen your fair share of interesting people hanging around the coach terminal. Was there ever anyone who seemed a bit… off?"

"Sure. Usually two kinds. People who I guess are mentally ill. They mostly shuffle around and talk to themselves. But you have to keep an eye on them because they swear a lot and sometimes they'll grab you thinking you're someone else. And then there's the guys who watch Henri a little too close, and you have to walk in circles for hours before heading back to the—the place you stay."

"Grace Church?"

He shrugged again, and Max couldn't decide whether he was embarrassed or simply cautious. It killed him that this kid had to be so aware, to think strategically all the time. He definitely didn't sound eleven. He was the very definition of an old soul, a forty-year-old trapped in a kid's body. Henri was lucky to have him.

"Anyone else? Anyone messing around with the lockers? Inspecting them a little too thoroughly?"

"People always do. Wouldn't you?"

"But you didn't see anyone place anything inside one?"

"I didn't see a man twirling his handlebar mustache and holding an armful of dynamite, if that's what you mean."

Max tried not to laugh. He knew the sarcasm should've annoyed him as the actual adult and police officer at the table, but it made him like the kid more. "What about the phones? Did you—"

"Are you just not able to turn it off? It was a normal day like any other day. Until it wasn't."

"Ready to order?" the waitress asked tentatively.

Max smiled up at her, relieved by the interruption. He chose pulled pork, and Oliver picked the classic, and the waitress left them again to stare at each other in silence.

"So what do you want to be when you grow up?" he tried.

"Seriously dude?" Oliver shook his head in disgust. "How come every adult seems to think kids spend all our time thinking about our future careers instead of pizza or wrestling or dogs or something?"

Absolute honesty had worked on the kid before, and Max didn't have the energy for anything else, so he said, "I guess… because so much of our time is spent on our careers, and we miss being young and filled with endless possibility. And kids make us a little uncomfortable, so we don't really know what else to say to you. You didn't want to talk about the bus station—this is the best I've got."

Oliver blinked at him and picked up his straw wrapper, bending it in half and folding it into an accordion. "It's a dumb question. I want to *be* grown up. I want to be old enough to get a real job and sign a lease. To earn plenty of money for food and cough syrup, and not be too hot or too cold. I want to grow up so I can take care of Henri better. How I do it, what kind of job, doesn't matter. Who cares?"

Max picked up his own straw to fiddle with, still wrapped out of respect for Maggie, who despised them. *What about the turtles?* she would always say, pushing her own straw back toward the server.

"So what did you want to be before you grew up?"

Oliver looked him in the eye then, like Max's simple acknowledgment that his childhood had been ripped away from him was all the validation he'd been looking for in the world.

He shrugged, his go-to response. "A conductor, I guess."

"Trains or music?" Max put the straw down before the wrapper ripped off and made it unusable by someone else.

"Music. I wanted to play every instrument and not have to choose one or two. A conductor would have to know all the parts and how to arrange them all together. Maybe even compose."

Such a detailed vision from a boy who claimed he didn't care. Max couldn't help grinning.

"What?"

"Hold on to that dream."

Oliver shook his head. "It's artsy-fartsy."

"Artsy—it's great!"

"What's even the point? It's a stupid waste of time."

"Just… Hang on to it, even if it's a tiny sliver of a corner of a dream tucked away in your pocket. Don't let it go."

"Why? Didn't you always want to be a cop?"

Max laughed. "I never—" he began, but stopped himself, realizing how sad the admission was, despite being true. "I never wanted to be a cop."

"What did you want to be then?"

"Mr. Rogers."

"Who was that? Your teacher?"

"What? No, Mr.—won't you be my neighbor? Look for the helpers? Nothing?" Max asked, crestfallen. God, how could the kid be so young and so old at the same time? "Thanks for making me feel like a rusty old man."

"Feel?"

"All right, wise guy, be nice or I'll eat your poutine." Max leaned back so the waitress could place his steaming pile of french fries on the table in front of him.

"You said before that you became a cop because of your dad?"

"And my grandad."

"What was he like? Your dad?"

Max shook his head. "Ordinary."

"What's that mean?"

"It means eat your food."

But Oliver kept staring at him, trying to force the conversation Max didn't want to have. Kind of reminded him of Maggie. Who he should call. Or at least text.

"He was strict, I guess," he finally said with a sigh.

"Like clean your room and make your bed?"

"Kind of. He has a… code… a set of rules he lives by, and he expects everyone else to do the same. If you don't, he acts disappointed even if he's not, so you can't help but do better next time."

"My dad should've followed the rules more."

"Yeah?"

Oliver set down his fork. "The air traffic controller told him not to go up."

"Maybe he felt like he had a good enough reason to go."

"Yeah. I guess we weren't a good enough reason to stay. I begged him not to go, but he said he had to. So I hid in the closet and wouldn't come out to say bye. I yelled at him through the door that I hoped he would crash, and then he did."

"You didn't make it happen, kid."

"Maybe I did. I put it out there. A wish or prayer or…"

"I saw all your scout badges. You know science doesn't work that way. If it did, I'm not sure my old man would still be kicking."

"The guy he was trying to save died, too," Oliver whispered.

"You must have been practically the same age Henri is now," Max said, changing the subject. "How did you know what to do to survive?"

"I didn't. I just… had to figure it out. I had to take care of him."

"Did you ever try to go home before now?"

The kid leaned back in the booth. He sighed, and in the depths of his sigh, Max heard the heartache of a thousand losses and a grief so deep no child should know, and all he wanted in the world was to find a way to make it better.

"Go home to what?" His lip trembled. "She sent us away and never came to find us. We'd either be going home to someone who didn't want us or going home to nothing at all. Plus, like you said, it was stupid dangerous. I wasn't going to let Henri do that. It was better to let him hope. Like Santa Claus. Waiting for her to come made him happy."

"Your dad would be really proud of you for taking such good care of him."

"You think? He never said."

"Sometimes people don't. For what it's worth," Max said, reaching across the table to pat Oliver's hand and deciding at the last minute to tug his sleeve instead, "I'm really proud of you."

Oliver didn't meet his eyes, but his mouth turned up in a kind of half smile, and Max withdrew his hand.

"Kind of wish I'd never gone back though. Yesterday I was a lot of things—a street kid, I guess, a brother, a son. Now I'm an orphan."

"Just a word. Only has meaning if you let it." Max tried to keep eating, but the food clogged in his throat like so much dust.

"I've read Lemony Snicket. I know how people feel about orphans."

"I don't know what a Lemonade Snippet is. But, kid, everyone becomes an orphan if they live long enough."

"No one wants them around though."

"Someone wanted me," Max said through the potato lump that seemed to be expanding in his throat.

"You?" Oliver asked, finally looking up.

Max nodded.

"Were you a full-grown kid?"

"Maybe half grown."

"You were a baby."

Max tilted his head in concession. "Toddler."

"That's not the same at all."

"No, I guess it's not."

"Is Mary your real mom or your adopted one?"

"She was the only one I ever knew."

"Was? Sorry."

"Thanks," Max said, poking at his dinner. He really needed to eat, but his appetite was gone.

"What was she like?"

"She was the kind of person who always had your back," he said, realizing he could easily be describing Maggie too. "But boy did she have a temper." He grinned at the memory. "As long as you tried your best, she would be right down in the trenches digging alongside you. But if she didn't think you were giving it your all—and she was shrewd. She knew. Then the fire of the furies would come down on you. And God help your soul then," he added with a laugh.

"Mine had a temper too… She only ever spoke French, and our dad spoke English. And when she got mad, I mean really mad, she would let loose with a string of French cuss words. We knew they were cuss words because she wouldn't explain what they meant, and we would laugh so hard, which made her even angrier."

Watching Oliver reminisce, the knot in Max's throat began to loosen and he could swallow again. It was the first genuine smile he'd seen from the kid. Maybe things would be okay.

"Man. I know so many French swears, but I have no idea what they mean," Oliver said, shaking his head. "I was going to Google them at the library, but I was afraid they'd throw us out."

Max laughed out loud, and they both managed to dig back into their dinners, fortifying themselves for the long drive ahead.

Maggie's mind was even more cluttered after Frankie's visit than it was before. Logic was beginning to elude her. She kept turning and turning the pieces of the case, but like a Rubik's cube, the whole picture refused to come together. Except once upon a time, she could solve a Rubik's cube blindfolded.

And then there was Max St. James.

Was it illogical to keep him at arm's length? Or the ultimate act of self-preservation? The evidence suggested they were great as friends, but anything more could ruin everything. Last

Christmas proved that. So why did it feel like ignoring her feelings might end up risking even more?

Max had a habit of turning Maggie inside out and upside down until she was as jumbled as his spare room, crammed full of cobwebs and old junk. Maybe that was the problem. Maybe messy rooms were contagious.

When she had her own place, Maggie would clean top to bottom, all hours of the night, to find perspective and order her thoughts. But she wasn't at home, and the spare room wasn't hers to organize.

She peeked inside it again. How he could stand it—orderly Max St. James who liked everything just so? Maybe it was a case of out-of-sight, out-of-mind, but Maggie was one hundred percent certain if she had such a chaotic room at home, it would haunt her night and day.

Maybe organizing it would be the best Christmas gift she could possibly give him. Maybe such an intimate act would help erase some of the awkwardness hovering over them like a storm cloud since last year.

Or make it worse. Fifty-fifty really.

Ignoring the little voice in her head screaming not to, Maggie grabbed a roll of garbage bags from the kitchen and pushed her way into the room.

"Where to start?" she asked the room, but the room offered no reply.

Go to bed, the little voice begged her, as though she'd ever be able to sleep.

Instead she started with the books. Paperbacks, mostly. Mysteries and romance, and the ones falling somewhere in between, their spines worn and cracked. She bagged them by genre, taping post-it note labels to each bag, and with the books out of the way there was a clear path into the room.

She found the photo albums next, erasing any doubt the clutter belonged to her partner: pictures of him as a tiny toddler, a little boy, a sulky teen. Photos of him with his parents, his friends, his hockey team, his grandpa. There was one of him in uniform from his Academy graduation, and god he looked young, more little boy than tough policeman, but still a hint of the handsome man he would become. He stood alongside a white shirt officer that Maggie recognized as his father. They stared past the camera, stiff, each uncomfortable in his own skin, and Maggie marveled at the resemblance. Even though they shared no blood, their mouths flattened into the same thin line as they raised their chins with cookie cutter posture.

Tucked in the back of the album was a program from Mary St. James's funeral. Maggie remembered it clearly—how stoic Max had stood, a little apart from his father, leaving enough space between them for his mother. She'd been their bridge to each other, Maggie suspected, maybe the only connection between the two at all.

Maggie had watched him so closely from her distant seat in the church, waiting for tears, for him to break down so she'd have an excuse to go to him. But the tears didn't come and she stayed back.

And suddenly Maggie understood—everything in the room— all of it belonged to his mother. Instead of going through it at the time, Max had schlepped it all to his apartment and enshrined it in the spare room like a little mausoleum, where he wouldn't have to see it and also would also not have to let it go.

Stop now, the voice in her head cried. *Put it all back and pretend you never opened this door.*

But no. She had always felt like she'd been unable to adequately support him at the time. Now was her chance. She'd have to be beyond careful not to throw out anything important— to label everything so he could find it later—to give him the final word on what stayed and what could go.

Maggie put the photo album down and moved on to the clothes, tossing out the undergarments, bagging up the dresses, sweaters, and slacks for charity, but saving out the Maple Leafs apron just in case.

Tiptoeing to the kitchen so as not to wake Henri, she dug a few flattened boxes out of Max's recycling and taped them back together. Using the tea towels to wrap china and cut glass vases, she packed it all away—except one pretty vase, which she filled with the sea glass she had found in a zip-top bag. It was starting to look like a room again.

In stacks and towers and tumble-down heaps she found so many magazines. Things most people would have thrown away, Max had been unable to part with. There were glossy gossip rags and periodicals about knitting, crochet, quilting, embroidery: a treasure trove of patterns and techniques for the modern handicrafter. She bagged them and marked them like everything else. Maybe a library or a collector would want those.

She saved out her favorite of the handmade quilts to put on the bed, and when she came across his mother's wedding and engagement bands, she placed them inside a small jade box on the nightstand.

It didn't have to be like this. If Max would've let her in back when his mother died, she could have helped him then. She'd wanted to be there for him, but he'd shut her out. And, as she cleaned, she realized she'd felt hurt, and she had held on to that hurt for five years. Maybe it was why she always let him see her at her worst—in the hopes he would reciprocate the vulnerability. How foolish she was.

Underneath a layer of postcards scattered across the dresser, Maggie found newspaper clippings—a few about the younger St. James, and a few more about his father, but the rest were about his grandpa, who had been something of a hero in his day. Alongside those she found a blue and yellow ribbon from which hung a large cross, the police Order of Merit, and another with a silver medallion, the Exemplary Service Medal. Next to them lay the badge once belonging to Officer Evan St. James. Then she remembered the empty scrapbook and shadowbox she'd found wedged under the bed. Mary must have been planning a display to honor the patriarch, but she never got the chance to assemble it.

Maggie would have to finish it for her.

IT WAS WELL PAST MIDNIGHT WHEN SHE FINALLY GOT EVERYTHING put away—all except a photograph she must have dropped when she gathered the newspaper clippings.

She picked up the picture and slumped exhaustedly on the edge of the bed to look at it: two Indigenous boys—one was very young, little more than a baby, but already with a dimpled smile. It was strange how much a grown man could resemble himself as a baby. Little Max sat on the lap of the older boy, probably fifteen or sixteen years old. His dark, shaggy hair hung in his eyes and he grinned a cheeky grin she'd seen on her partner's face more than once. Baby Max looked up at the boy—his brother? Or maybe a cousin? Max's face was pure adoration, and the older boy gazed dotingly back at him rather than at the camera. It was a perfect scene. And Maggie ached for what he'd lost, what both of them had lost.

She tried to memorize everything about the picture, the boy's hockey shirt and his old black Chuck Taylors. Did Max favored them because of this picture? Was he trying to emulate his long lost big brother—did he even remembered the photo? Or had he simply internalized a preference for Converse?

Brothers and shoes. It always came back to brothers and shoes with this case.

Why would the shoes from the bus station have been shipped to Bobby King's house? And what would someone with a connection to Bobby King stand to gain by fake-bombing the bus station?

Unless it was, as they had surmised, simply a distraction—one orchestrated by King himself?

What if King knew? Surely he knew he was being watched by the police—and they were watching the house because Guns and Gangs had decent intel that the weapons were being stored there. But when they raided the place—nothing.

What if the situation at the bus station had been a distraction —a way to pull all available units away from King's house long enough for him to move the merchandise, but not important or destructive enough that they would expect the police to actually investigate?

Hector had searched the security tapes over and over again with no sign of any of King's known associates. And besides—it was the shift manager, Vincent Reyes, who had suspected there was a bomb and pulled the fire alarm.

And Vincent wasn't pointing the finger at some mysterious figure, he was pointing it squarely at the brothers—at Oliver and Henri.

So why would Vincent Reyes lie? Was he scared? Did he take a bribe?

"What are you hiding, Vincent?" Maggie whispered.

She took out her phone and Googled VINCENT REYES, and she found doctor after doctor. Looked like Vincent had chosen the wrong career path. Then she Googled VINCENT REYES BOBBY KING. Still more doctors. Then simply REYES.

Reyes: A Spanish surname meaning King.

Of course.

That was why Henri could describe the shoes but not pick Bobby King out of a lineup. That was why the shoes had been shipped to King's house, but weren't there when they raided it.

Vincent Reyes was Bobby King's little brother.

CHAPTER 19

Oliver dozed off and on as they drove east across Ontario. It was a struggle for Max to keep his eyes open, and he longed to have Maggie on speaker phone, the comfort of her voice filling him in on the case or talking about her day. Had she gone to the bodega? Picked up her dry cleaning? He wanted to hear it all.

"I think I'm dreaming this CD now. What's so special about it anyway?" Oliver asked after a pothole jolted him from his light sleep.

"It's maybe the most perfect album ever recorded. He's a warrior poet and the master of the damn bridge."

Oliver snorted. "It's the only one you have, isn't it?"

"Only one I need," Max said, yawning.

"I can drive for a while if you're tired," Oliver offered, but yawns are contagious, and he only just got the words out before Max's weariness spread to him.

"Awesome, I'll pull over."

Max rolled his neck and shifted in his seat, trying to stretch his aching back. He jiggled his left leg and tapped absently on the steering wheel—anything to try and stay awake.

"You have terrible rhythm," Oliver said.

"What? No way, I'm a regular Neil Peart—"

"You keep tapping in between the beats. Sounds like you're trying to send Morse code or something."

"Oh yeah? You into Morse code?" Max asked, relieved to change the subject away from his own musical deficiencies.

"I was going to earn a merit badge."

"You know SOS? Dot-dot-dot-dash—"

"Everyone knows SOS. He even has a song where the beat sounds like SOS." Oliver pointed to the stereo. "If you hit them correctly."

"Really?

"It's on a different album. You know he has other albums right?"

"I did know that." Max rolled his eyes at the road instead of at the kid. He didn't actually know. "So what other badges did you earn? Robotics?"

"We did a little bit with circuits. Like, we had this kit where you would follow a lost in space story and learn it as you go. I like coding better."

"Coding, huh? Like programming apps?" Like programming an app to make a robot detonate an IED?

"Yeah, apps or games."

"What about rocketry? Was there a rocketry badge?"

"I don't think so. My neighbor used to build model rockets all the time, but I don't remember him earning a badge."

"You ever help?"

"I held the wings while the glue dried. It was boring. I'll stick to Lego. Snap and go instead of waiting while your hands get all sticky and gross."

"What kind of Lego? Those fancy remote-controlled ones?"

He could feel Oliver studying him, sizing him up once more. "We had my dad's old sets. Pirates and knights and prairie outposts and stuff."

"You know what I'm talking about though, right? Where there's gears and power to make them move? Ever use any like that?"

"Not Lego. Some other brand at the library once."

"You and Henri spent a lot of time at the library, huh?"

"I guess."

"You like to read?"

"Sure."

"Why that library, though?"

Oliver gave him a look, but said, "Henri liked the statues."

Kid had an answer for everything. "Did you ever—"

"You're doing it again," Oliver cut him off, rubbing his face and raking his hands through his hair.

Max almost apologized, but no, he was the adult and he was doing what he was supposed to do. Instead he said, "Hazard of the job, I guess."

"You must have a lot of friends," Oliver snarked.

It was going to be such a long night.

"You know, I am a cop. And someone planted an IED in a public building," Max replied, and he was pleased with himself that it didn't sound as sharp as it might have. "We think it was detonated by one of those robot kits from your library."

The kid stayed silent for a minute before meekly mumbling, "I thought you said you didn't care about that."

"If it was you, I maybe don't care so much. If it wasn't you, I've got some very grave concerns about who did it and why."

Now Oliver seemed as restless and fidgety as Max was. He wriggled around, adjusting the seatbelt and fiddling with the vent before opening a bag of M&Ms and setting them in the cup holder next to Max's phone. "Hey, you have a voicemail, did you know?" he asked, snatching up the phone before Max could get to it.

"Don't worry about it," Max said, reaching to take the phone back.

"From Magpie." Oliver held it out of Max's reach. "What kind of a name is Magpie? Want me to play it?"

"No, I don't. Give it here," Max said, still reaching blindly for the phone.

The next thing he knew, Maggie's voice filled the Impala, sounding exhausted and stressed.

"I said no." Max swerved onto the shoulder, slamming the breaks a little too hard so the car slid in the snow, almost off into a ditch. As he reached over to take the phone from Oliver, who sat frozen, biting his lip, the sound of ringing filled the car. The kid must have hit the call back button. "You didn't?"

"Oops," Oliver breathed, finally releasing his grip on the phone.

"Max?" Maggie's voice came over the speaker, strained and a little panicked.

Max gave the kid a death stare before killing the engine to save gas. He snatched the phone and plunged out into the cold.

"Max, god, are you okay? What's wrong?"

"Sorry. I didn't mean to wake you—I didn't mean to call back at all. Right now, I mean. It was an accident." So much for pretending he didn't have a signal.

"No, no. It's fine. I wasn't asleep. I was—I—may have caught a break in the case, actually." Now that she knew he was all right, the tension left her voice and she sounded excited.

"At two thirty in the morning?"

"Like I said in my message, the raid was a complete bust, so. Girl's gotta do what a girl's gotta do. Making up for lost time and all." An edge crept into her voice there at the end.

"I'm sorry I couldn't be there to help you."

"Couldn't," she scoffed. "It's fine. Like I said, I think I figured it out."

Without him, was the part she was saying without saying. She'd done it all without him.

"I knew you would," he told her.

"No, you didn't. That's just something people say after the fact. You didn't know, because it wasn't inevitable, and if I have solved it, then it's by accident. It's all completely random, like atoms floating around in space."

She was angry—at him—which wasn't quite fair after the day he'd had. "Don't be mad. I can't be in two places at once."

"I'm not mad," she insisted.

"You sure?"

Max stared up into the sky at the hundred million stars, so many you almost couldn't focus on a single one. Maggie would love it out here. He should tell her. He should bring her out here, to the middle of nowhere, just the two of them. Someday. If she'd give him the chance.

"Why would I be mad? You left me here to do all the work. And I've done it. So. Everything's fine."

"Did you want to come?"

"I wanted to be asked," she said, and her voice broke a little. She was pulling away, slipping further and further out of reach. So much for how this was all supposed to go. "What did you mean, you didn't mean to call me? How long have you had service?"

He didn't want to lie to her, but he also couldn't tell her the truth, not right now, not like this. "It's spotty," he said after not answering for too long.

"Don't lie to me." Her voice was cold.

"Why are you so mad?"

"Are you serious? Everything has been going wrong—"

"Not about the case. It's been longer than that."

She sighed. "You shouldn't talk and drive. Get home safe."

Lead with I statements, he could hear the department therapist advising him.

"You blame me for holding you back, don't you?" *So much for I statements.*

She didn't answer, but she didn't argue, either.

"I told you on day one, I didn't want to climb the ranks or wear a white shirt or be a detective. My job was to train you and yours was to move on. You're the one who didn't hold up your end of the bargain, Kyle. You were never supposed to stay. I may not be a good enough partner or a good enough TO, but it's not my fault you're afraid to take a goddamn test."

"I need to get some sleep."

"Don't hang up on me. How do I make this right?"

Tell her you love her, the hole in his heart screamed, but his brain told him now was not the time.

"Magpie?"

"I don't know if you can."

And he felt like the wind was knocked out of him, but maybe it was just a gust of cold air.

"Copy that," Max said before the line went dead, and he wanted to scream, so he did. He roared as loud as he could, fists clenched, and threw his phone into the snow.

Which of course was a ridiculous thing to do in the middle of the night on a dark highway.

Oliver peered at him through the fogging windshield still biting his bottom lip.

Max climbed back in the car and turned the key—at least he hadn't thrown those—but the engine backfired.

Startled, Oliver ducked for cover.

Max turned the key again, but there was another backfire and the engine remained dead.

He banged his hands against the steering wheel, feeling the kid's eyes on him the whole time. Maybe he could call CAA, but they'd probably freeze before a tow ever found them, and—oh yeah—his phone was out in the slush somewhere.

He got out again and slammed the door. It took a full five minutes to even find the lever to release the hood.

The passenger door opened, and Max barked, "Stay in the car. It's freezing out here."

"Do the parts have braille so you can fix them in the dark?" Oliver snapped back. Then he shined the weak beam of a flashlight on the engine.

"Glove compartment?" Max asked.

The kid nodded.

"Lucky us."

Even with light, of course, Max still had no clue what to do. He checked the oil. It was dark, but not dry. He peered at the battery, which had some corrosion but looked okay, he supposed. The fan belt looked intact too, as far as he could tell, and the spark plugs looked… plugged?

"I think—" Oliver began cautiously.

"Here, give me that. You should get back inside while there's still heat left." Max took the flashlight. Perhaps the smartest thing would be to find his phone.

"Let me help," Oliver said, reaching to take the light back.

"I don't even have a clue where to start, okay kid? Not a clue. We've got no tools, no phone. Our best hope is somebody comes by before we freeze to death."

Without another word of argument, Oliver stalked back to the passenger side, but Max didn't hear the door open.

"What are you doing?" he called, hoping the kid wasn't going to run again.

"Looking for your stupid phone."

"Just get in the car." Max walked over to the shoulder to search for it himself with the flashlight.

Oliver did get back in the car, but a moment later he got out again.

"You're letting the heat out every time you open that door," Max growled, sounding like his father, and hating himself more than he already did, which almost didn't seem possible, but there it was.

The kid didn't answer, but a moment later there was a loud banging that nearly gave Max a heart attack.

"What the hell was that?" he called.

"You're phone's over here. You threw it straight down," Oliver said. Then he slammed his door and the engine roared to life.

Max turned to see the kid smiling smugly and waving at him from inside the car. He spotted his phone, close to the front right tire, slammed the hood, and got back inside, sitting on his hands to warm them. "What'd you do?" he asked.

"Smacked the gas tank." Oliver held up a stick before tossing it in the back seat. "Your fuel pump might be toast. Guess they don't teach you about cars at police school."

"Only how to drive them really fast," Max said. "And kid? Thanks."

ANGRY AND HURT AND MISERABLE DIDN'T BEGIN TO DESCRIBE HOW Maggie felt as she showered, using Max's stupid red clover soap and his stupid shampoo so she smelled like stupid him all over. She dressed in the sweater Frankie had brought her to wear for the holiday party after shift. If only it weren't the same sweater she wore last year. As she pulled it down over her torso, she could feel Max's hands pushing it up, and she shivered. It was her favorite sweater, but she hadn't worn it, not once, since that night. And now, in her exhaustion, tears tried to sting her eyes, but she tamped them down. It was time to move on from last Christmas.

Maggie didn't know how Max was still functioning on so little sleep when one late night had turned her into a sniveling mess. Should she blame his being an ass on sleep deprivation and forgive him? Tears welled up again, but the adrenaline of closing in on her suspect would carry her through the day. Then she could crash. Alone.

Except she'd been over and over her notes, and still she only had a tenuous connection between her suspects. Reyes said he lived with his brother. He took the Dundas streetcar to work, which could be caught at any crossroad, including Regent Park, where King lived, but the address on his ID didn't match. He admitted to shopping online, and was fairly tech savvy which could lend itself to building and detonating the IED. She needed a warrant to search his work locker, his credit card history, and his phone.

"Morning," she rasped when Henri stumbled groggily into the kitchen where she was already drinking her second cup of coffee. "How would you like to help decorate the police station for our holiday party?"

"It's already decorated," he said. "And I'm supposed to go to choir practice with Selina."

"It's half decorated," Maggie assured him, because the admins always added a lot more on the day of the party. "And I'm sure *Selina* will understand you want to be there when Oliver gets back."

He stopped rubbing his eyes and seemed torn between two minds. "But she needs me."

"I bet after being gone so long, Ver needs to see you too."

"And he'll be here today? You swear?" he asked, bouncing up and down on his toes a little.

"Cross my heart and hope to... eat gluten-free gingerbread," she said, catching herself from using the morbid expression around this child who had lost so much.

Henri launched himself at her then, squeezing her tight around the middle and squealing. "Ver's coming home! Ver's! Coming! Home!"

THEY MADE IT TO THE STATION IN RECORD TIME, AND A FRAZZLED admin eagerly accepted Henri's help wrapping the desks in holiday paper to make them look like presents, stringing twinkle lights, sorting the gifts for the white elephant, and setting up an all-faiths holiday tree right in the middle of the squad room.

With Henri thus occupied, Maggie submitted her warrant affidavit before Hector had even taken off his coat.

"You look… chipper," the rookie lied.

"I'd be a lot more chipper if I could find the audio file from the 911 call," she said, clicking around in different time-stamped files on the shared computer drive, but unable to discern the rookie's system, if he had one. She and Max never had this problem. Maybe it was because he trained her, but sometimes it felt like they shared a brain.

"Here, let me." Hector sat down and Maggie scooted over.

"911, what's your emergency?"

"There's a bomb. At Bay Street Station."

"Did you see the bomb?"

"You have to come quick!"

"Stay calm okay? What's your name?"

"I have to go!"

Then the line went dead.

"I mean, it sounds like a kid, but does it sound like Oliver? Has St. James heard it?" Maggie asked. Forensics believed whomever called in the Bay Street bomb was the same person who called in all the others—the hoaxes all across the city, and that was the part she couldn't work out. Unless Vincent Reyes had struck some kind of deal or coerced Oliver and Henri, she couldn't figure out why they would have helped him.

"I don't think it was a kid," Hector said.

"You don't?"

"No, watch." He held up a shiny new smart phone.

"Look at you. Where'd that come from? Santa Claus?"

"Don't make a big deal. Listen."

"You better slap a waterproof case on that thing quick."

"Yeah, yeah. Listen." He tapped on the screen and spoke into it. "There's a bomb. At Bay Street Station," he said. "You have to come quick!"

Then he tapped some more and played it back for her. It sounded almost identical to the audio on the 911 call, except with a little less static, likely the result of the pay phone.

"Show me," Maggie said, and Hector pulled up the app on his cell, which looked similar to the model Reyes had used to show off his bus schedule app.

"You're a genius," Maggie said, ruffling his hair before trying to find the app on her own phone. "What's it called again?"

"This one's only available for Androids," Hector said.

"Can you get an app to remote control those fancy not-Legos?"

"Of course."

"So we just need to prove a connection between Vincent Reyes and Bobby King."

"What?" he asked. "Oh. Because Reyes means King?"

"Who even are you?" Maggie asked, and Hector grinned, pleased with himself. "Okay, so we've got means."

"Is that enough? The existence of two apps he might have downloaded? Shouldn't we, like, get his credit card receipts to see if he bought the fireworks or RoboZ?"

"I didn't say we could prove it yet. We definitely have opportunity."

"But wasn't he really busy with customers all day? And what if he has an alibi for when the other hoaxes were called in?"

"Hector, you're harshing my vibe here. The point is, we have a direction. And if the motive was to pull us away from the King residence while they moved the merchandise, then we should start by examining Vincent's phone and finding those shoes."

"You think he's dumb enough to hang on to them after we raided King's place?"

"King saw the warrant, but would he have shared it with baby bro? He probably figured it was an excuse to get inside. We weren't able to charge him with anything, and even if he did tell Reyes, people don't buy custom designed shoes and then turn around and throw them away."

"So let's go pick him up," Hector said, jumping up from the computer.

"Warrant's not back yet."

"It's rush hour. We'll have it by the time we get there."

The rookie had a point.

Except when Maggie parked in the lot across from the station, there was no email from the judge. She swiped to refresh, only to find a message from LinkedIn suggesting she apply for a variety of security guard positions across the city, and if this hunch didn't play out, she might have to consider it.

She dialed Dixon on speaker.

"Y'ello."

"Sarge, we're at Bay Street, waiting on a warrant. Any chance you could light a fire under Judge Allen so we can wrap this thing up before the party?"

Dixon sighed.

"I don't like that sigh, Sarge."

"I was at the courthouse this morning. Ran into Allen in the men's room."

"I hear that's where the deals get made," Maggie said, and Hector snorted.

"Not this time."

"Sir?"

"He was pretty clear. You don't have enough for a warrant."

"We have credible—"

"It's not enough, Kyle. The bench got burned yesterday by your credible testimony. Your witness is dead to them. They're not biting on this one."

Maggie slapped the steering wheel with her palm. "How are we supposed to get this guy without a warrant? Sarge, if we take down Reyes, we've got a very good chance of nailing King."

"Then find a way to make it stick. Without a warrant."

Maggie wanted to punch her phone to end the call, but Dixon hung up first, saving her the trouble. How had this case gone so wrong?

"I'm sorry," Hector said in a tiny voice. "If I'd done a better job with—"

"No." Maggie shook her head emphatically, and when the rookie didn't look at her she put her hand on his shoulder. "This isn't on you. Let's go talk to Vincent Reyes."

SHE ENTERED THE BUS STATION FROM THE SIDE WITH THE LOCKERS to catch Vincent by surprise. Hector was posted up out front in case the shift lead tried to rabbit. From this vantage point it was clear Vincent couldn't see much of anything happening by the lockers, not from the ticket counter on a busy day.

"Mr. Reyes?" she said, approaching the counter.

He looked surprised, but recovered quickly. "I'm working," he said.

"Should only be a minute."

So Vincent called for a coworker to take over his till. Then he met Maggie at the end of the counter, keeping it between them like a protective barrier.

"Interest you in a holiday special? Half-price fares out west," he said, almost cordially.

"Tempting. No, I was just in the neighborhood, well, the rookie had to pee," she said, rolling her eyes. "And I was hoping you could show me your backup battery thing again? I didn't catch the brand, but I thought they'd make great stocking stuffers."

"You mean this?" Vincent asked, taking the little Yoda tube from his pocket once more and holding it out to her.

"Yes!" she said. "How much juice does it give you?"

"Two, three full charges."

"Nice. And does it work with any type of phone? You use it with a…?"

"I have a Droid," he said, stepping around the counter and holding up his phone proudly.

"Perfect. I think this is the same one my rookie has."

"You can use it with any phone," he told her, showing her the USB input.

"Even better," Maggie said, handing back the charger with a smile, but she was looking at his feet. He wore Converse—not the infamous houndstooth, but another unusual design: green camo on the outside and brown camo on the inside, with dark brown stitching and laces, and sort of mud brown rubber. "Hey nice shoes," she said.

"Oh yeah? You like them?" he asked, shifting his weight nervously and glancing down at his feet like he'd forgotten they were there.

"You design those yourself?"

"Y-es?" he faltered.

"Very nice. You've really got an eye for detail. The thing is, Mr. Reyes, we'd like you to come to the station and tell us more about your interest in fashion footwear."

He looked at her for a moment with no trace of surprise in his gray-green eyes, merely resignation. Then he bolted for the door.

Hector stepped out in front of him, and despite being a full head shorter than the suspect, the rookie incapacitated him with a pop to the windpipe and an armlock that brought Reyes to his knees.

"Thank you, Mr. Reyes. I didn't have enough to arrest you before, but now I think we have no choice," Maggie said, cuffing him and helping him back to his feet.

Toronto,
Christmas Eve

CHAPTER 20

The kid hung on to the flashlight from the glove compartment. Maybe he was afraid they'd need it again—Max was certainly a little worried about stopping to get gas or breakfast. But in a way, it seemed like he needed something to hang on to. So when they reached the other side of Sudbury, and Oliver woke and started to return the light to where he found it, Max said, "Keep it, if you want."

Oliver looked down at the small, heavy Maglite in his hands and then looked back at Max frowning as if to say I don't need handouts from you.

"This unit's being decommissioned soon. No one will miss it."

"Thanks," Oliver said solemnly, laying it in his lap. "For everything."

"You're welcome," Max replied, realizing it was the first time the kid had said so.

"So what happens now?"

"Now we head to my place and shower before we meet up with your brother at the station."

Oliver tilted his head to the side and pursed his lips.

Max sighed. "We call Children's Aid, I guess. I'm sure Leah

will make the same arrangements for you that she did for Henri, whether with me or with Kyle, at least through Christmas."

Oliver turned his whole body away from Max and hugged his knees to his chest while he looked out the window. "Or you could not. You could let us go."

"You know I can't do that."

"We were doing okay. We'll stay away from Bay Street, I swear."

Part of Max wanted to agree. The system would do its best, but Oliver was right, they had done okay so far on their own. But the world didn't work that way, and anyway, the kids deserved so much more than just doing okay.

"Oliver—"

"Save it. Please. I know what you're going to say."

"Aren't you tired of having to take care of everything all the time? Wouldn't it be nice to let someone else take care of you for a while?"

"You can't count on anyone to take care of you but you," he said, and there was no argument left for Max to make.

Traffic picked up as they neared the outskirts of the city. And, as though Max's body knew its journey was almost at an end, aching exhaustion began to overtake him. His shower was going to feel amazing, and so would fresh clothes. "You're fine with stopping first, right?"

Oliver nodded.

"You sure? Because I could clean up at the station if you'd rather go straight there."

The kid shook his head.

"You hungry? There's probably something to eat around the place, but if not, the bodega on the corner might have Spaghettios."

"I lied to you before," Oliver blurted out.

Max stopped breathing. Was the kid about to confess to planting the IED? What had Maggie said—there's no such thing as coincidence? But when she told him she'd solved it, she hadn't mentioned the boys.

"About?" Max asked, forcing a calm tone out through his clenched jaw.

"When you asked if you should arrest me for anything. I lied."

Max gripped the steering wheel more tightly, but kept his gaze on the car in front of him. If the kid came clean about actually bombing the bus station with his brother inside, what would he do? What could he do? "Oh yeah?"

"I stole. Food mostly. Medicine sometimes. And I know it's wrong. And I guess I'm sorry if it hurt the people I stole from. But I take care of him. And I'll do it again if I have to."

"Oh." Max breathed, nodding his head as the panic in his chest began to ease. "Thanks for telling me."

"Still proud of me?"

"Yeah. For coming clean about that, you bet."

"Am I under arrest?"

"Well, I'm no priest, and this is no confessional, but how about we keep it between us, yeah?"

Oliver nodded.

"And, kid? Whatever happens, if you're ever that desperate again—where you feel like you have to steal to survive—find me. Or call me," he added, fishing a business card out of his wallet and tossing it to the kid. "It's okay to ask for help. Got it?"

"Got it," Oliver whispered, leaning his head against the window.

THE SECOND MAX UNLOCKED HIS APARTMENT, SELINA POKED HER head out of her own door.

"Oh good, it's you," she said. "I was afraid that Dixon character was back with more pho. This place has been like Union Station with all the people coming and going, up at all hours of the night. This must be the chorister."

"He used to be. Oliver, Selina. Selina, Oliver."

"You look like hell, Maxxy. Actually, you know what you look like? A Sim when their life meter is all the way down and they're about to sway back and forth before collapsing and pissing themselves."

Oliver laughed.

"Thank you?" Max had no idea what she was talking about, but it sounded accurate.

"Am I wrong?" she asked the kid.

"No, that's what he looks like."

Max chuckled and shook his head. "Thanks for keeping an eye on the place," he told her, ushering Oliver inside.

"Girlfriend?"

"Neighbor. I'll let you grab the first shower if you promise to save me some hot water," Max said, looking through the bag of clothes on his kitchen table. "I think these are for you."

He led Oliver down the hall to the bathroom, pivoting to the linen closet and pulling out a fresh towel for the kid. But when he handed it over, he did a double-take, looking back inside the closet. There were blankets and quilts shelved neatly beside the towels—blankets and quilts Max hadn't placed there, hadn't even laid eyes on for years.

The sound of the shower turning on shook him from his trance, and he turned toward the bathroom and beside it, the spare room, the one he had begged Maggie not to enter.

The door was open.

It was dizzying, standing in the hallway where the door was always closed, peering into another world, another dimension, but one he only faintly recognized now. Max lumbered forward, steadying himself against the doorframe. It seemed somehow bigger on the inside.

Everything was gone—all of it. Every scrap of his mother— gone—except for her quilt, spread neatly across the bed, and her wedding vase, filled with sea glass from their trip to PEI.

Max collapsed onto the side of the bed facing the sea glass. Her smell once pervaded the room so strongly you could swear she was right behind you. Now it only faintly lingered in the bedding and in the walls.

Rage bubbled up inside him until it burst into a crushing despair. And Max began to weep. Because he had known it needed to be done eventually, but it should have been him. And he wasn't ready yet. He was selfish, and he wasn't ready to let her leave him. And now that Maggie had seen his dark secret in its moldering, festering depression, she would leave him too.

He was still sitting there in the semidarkness, lit only by the light from the hallway, when Oliver peeked in looking tired but refreshed.

"I didn't use it all," he said timidly. "The hot water."

"Thanks, kid."

Oliver kept standing in the doorway like he didn't quite know what to do. Their roles from yesterday were now reversed, as Max grieved his mother all over again.

"You, uh, you know how to make coffee?" Max asked over his shoulder.

Oliver nodded.

"Perfect. Full pot. Extra strong," he said, rising for his own shower.

Afterwards Max stood before his bedroom closet wearing his only clean pair of jeans and staring at the shirts, too tired to make a decision.

"I like that one," Oliver said, pointing to a dark gray turtleneck sweater and handing Max a mug of steaming coffee.

"You're a saint." He set the coffee on his dresser and pulled the sweater over his head.

"Can I have some?" the kid asked, peering into the coffee.

Max drained half the cup, scalding his throat in the process. It wasn't very strong, but did parents allow their eleven-year-olds to drink coffee? Then again, did he have a parental right to say *no* to a kid he was expected to hand over to Children's Aid in an hour?

"Knock yourself out." He gestured toward the kitchen.

Once Oliver finished adding milk and sugar, Max was unconcerned. The concoction couldn't really even be called coffee anymore, and might contain less caffeine than some brands of pop.

"Do you think Henri will be mad at me?" Oliver asked.

All his life Max had longed to have a brother like Oliver. He'd tried to make Noah fill the role—Noah, who no one could see but Max, Noah who would sometimes say the mean truths Max didn't want to hear—sort of like Maggie. He'd been desperate to see her—up until their fight—desperate to hold her, and tuck her hair behind her ear, and tell her everything.

And now? Did she purge his spare room to get back at him for leaving? If it were anyone else, anyone in the world, he'd be done. But it was Maggie.

But what if she was done with him?

"Do you think he'll be, like, super mad?"

"Maybe," Max said. "But there's no one in the world he'd rather be mad at, and he's going to be really glad you're back."

FRANKIE WAS IN BOOKING WHEN MAGGIE AND HECTOR RETURNED to Fifty-One Division with Vincent Reyes in cuffs. She raised her eyebrows, but said nothing as the booking officer processed Reyes and took him to a holding cell. She followed Maggie and Hector to the staff lounge, where she watched longingly as they poured coffee.

"So good cop, bad cop?" Hector asked, studying the two bananas left in the fruit bowl and offering them to senior officers. When they both shook their heads, he took the nicer one and left the over-ripe one to languish until Maggie took pity on it and threw it away.

"No. You're going over to the library to sweet talk your way through every board member until they agree to release their security footage," Maggie said.

"You know the library board doesn't hang out at the library all day, right?"

"Then get them to call an emergency meeting. I don't want you to come back until they agree."

"And if they don't?"

"Then we're screwed," she whispered.

"So you got your guy?" Frankie asked a little too casually after Hector left the room.

"Looks that way," Maggie said, pouring her friend a cup of chamomile tea to make up for the coffee she couldn't drink.

"You found the evidence you needed?"

"Not exactly. But we will."

"Mags…"

"We totally would have, but they're withholding a warrant."

"Maybe they have a good reason," Frankie said cautiously. "Don't… blow your case on a hunch, okay?" She accepted the tea but set it down on the table and crossed her arms.

"I'm not going to blow it. I'm going to get a confession." *Fake it 'til you make it, right?* Maggie turned her back on her friend, emptying the coffee pot and starting a new brew.

"Love the confidence, but you're playing a dangerous game."

"Talk to Tony?" Maggie asked.

She meant to prove a point, but then Frankie said, "I talked to Tony."

"And?"

"Door number two." He wanted her to ride the desk forever.

"Did you tell him where to shove it?"

"No. Because he wants to be there."

"Yeah, but—"

"For now it's enough," Frankie said.

"This is really what you want?"

"For now. I'll have to start living vicariously through you though. So don't commit career suicide."

"I'm already in the midst of it. I've got to see it through."

"Have you heard from Max? How's that flu of his?"

"Should be back in commission any time." Maggie's stomach flip-flopped as she said it. It wasn't because she needed his approval. But she was excited about this bust, and she couldn't wait to tell him every detail. Even after their fight, she wanted him to watch her final interrogation from the observation room—their observation room—and she wanted to hear him say how proud he was of her. She wanted him to convince her she could do it on her own. How pathetically anti-feminist was that?

"Well. Go get him."

Maggie blinked. "I don't know where he is. I'm sure he'll come straight here, but I don't—I mean, I don't know if he'll be in the mood to talk."

"I meant Reyes."

"Right. Me too. Not sure he'll be in the mood to confess."

Frankie smirked. "Uh huh. I'm going to go throw up."

Maggie took a deep breath to steel her nerves, but the ragged sound made her more aware of her own sweaty anxiety. Frankie was right. She would have to tread carefully—oh so very carefully—if she was going to get the confession she needed on so little evidence.

So she took her time. She selected an unrefrigerated bottle of water, because the interview room would be stuffy and warm, and she didn't want Reyes too comfortable.

"You look a little sweaty, Vincent," she greeted him. "Need some water?"

Maggie placed the bottle just close enough to his cuffed hands that he could reach it if he really strained.

He stared back at her with small, badger eyes. "You're wasting your time, lady."

"My family are all out west for the holidays. I have nothing but time."

He shrugged as if to say, Suit yourself, playing it cool—whatever—he didn't care.

"What about you? Christmas Eve plans?" she asked.

"Why am I here?"

"We looked at your phone. We know you have the same voice modulating app that our hoax caller used from locations across the city. Every single time. That's a funny coincidence, isn't it?"

"The world is full of funny coincidences. The first and last soldiers killed in World War I are buried right next to each other, did you know that?"

"No, I didn't."

"A kid named Laura something released a red balloon, and it was found by another kid named Laura, same last name, same age. That's a funny coincidence."

"It's a heck of a coincidence," Maggie agreed. "Like a solar eclipse. Let's talk about your coincidences. There was another really interesting app on your phone—a RoboZ app. What would you need that for, Vincent?"

He didn't have a great poker face. He tried to maintain a chiseled disinterest, but his eyebrows twitched up for a second.

"You know the one I mean?" Maggie pressed.

"I don't know," he said, and it came out dry and raspy, but he refused to reach for the water. "I download a shit ton of apps to see what they do."

"This particular app is the same brand as the not-Lego robot used in the attack."

She chose the word *attack* deliberately, to rattle him, to make him feel like he was in deep enough trouble that he might consider ratting out his brother.

"Literally thousands of people have downloaded those apps."

"True. For the voice modulator, that's true. But the other one—the robot one? It's fewer than a hundred. I checked. They're really expensive toys. Do you often play with toys, Vincent?"

He didn't answer.

"Then there's the firework shop," Maggie lied, because she had nothing to lose. "They remembered you. You stuck out, buying fireworks for Diwali."

He blanched a little and finally reached for the water, wrestling to get the cap off with his cuffed hands, spilling it when he squeezed the flimsy plastic too hard. "Buying fireworks isn't illegal."

"No. But they keep meticulous records. They'll testify that you bought the exact model of forty second cake used in the attack."

Of course she was lying through her teeth, but she was in too deep to stop now. There were fireworks stores across the city, and they did booming business for the big holidays. No way they would remember Vincent, no way they would still have security footage to place him there.

"Isn't that hearsay or something?"

Maggie smiled. "Stick to train schedules, Vincent. Why did you visit the Lillian H. Smith Library?"

He swallowed and his knee began to bounce. She was so close. She had him.

"Why does anyone go?" He took a sip of water. "I needed a book."

"From the children's department?" she asked. "Do you often read children's books?" When he didn't answer she said, "We have you on camera."

"Someone told me I should check out *Origami Yoda*."

"But you left without borrowing a book, didn't you?" she guessed.

"The copies were all sticky."

"Did you buy your own copy?"

"No. I decided I didn't want to waste my time reading a book written for sticky little kids."

"You don't like children, do you, Vincent? You find them too noisy, too rowdy, too… sticky?"

"Is that a crime? I volunteer to work on Family Day so everyone else can be off with their brats."

"Do you also find them to be too observant? Too… what's the word… liable to notice your illegal activities?"

"I don't know what you mean."

"Is that the real reason you don't like those kids loitering around the terminal every day?"

"I don't like it 'cause they're a nuisance."

Maggie pulled out a chair and straddled it backwards like Max would do. "It's pretty cool you volunteer to work Family Day. I mean, why not, right? Who needs a day off in February? Maybe if my brother didn't live so far away, we'd all go to a movie or something. You said you have a brother, right? It's beautiful, don't you think—the bond between siblings? Take those boys for instance. They'd do anything for each other. I know I used to lie for my brother when he broke curfew. What would you do for your brother, Vincent?"

He didn't answer her question, but his knee stopped bouncing.

"I really do like those shoes," she said, shifting gears again to keep him off balance. "They're quite different."

"What can I say? I'm a unique individual."

"That you are, Vincent. You designed another pair of shoes, didn't you? With houndstooth and soccer ball skulls? Funny thing—it was a few years ago, but they were delivered to an address we've had our eyes on in Regent Park."

His leg started bouncing again, much faster this time.

"You live in Regent Park, don't you, Vincent? With your brother? It's not the address you gave us, the one on your license.

That's a UPS store around the corner. But you can't catch the Dundas streetcar from there."

He refused to look at her anymore, just stared at the water bottle in his hands. Maggie leaned forward, and spoke softly so he would have to strain to hear. "Was he angry at you? When we came looking for the shoes? Or did you do him such a huge favor he couldn't be mad, not at you? Was it your idea to create a diversion at the bus station and lure the cops away from his house? Or did he put you up to it? Brothers will do anything for each other, right? Did he force you against your will? Threaten you in some way?"

"I don't have a brother," Vincent whispered.

"Don't let Bobby King hear you say that. Formerly Roberto Reyes before he anglicized it and embarked on his life of crime. Clever, actually."

"I want my lawyer."

"You sure? It's Christmas Eve. Probably take a while to get a court appointee down here. And whoever they send will not be thrilled to be dragged out in the snow this afternoon, today of all days."

"I want my lawyer," he said again.

"Where'd he move the guns, Vincent? You tell me, we could make a deal."

"I want my lawyer," he said a third time, looking her straight in the eye. She had pushed too far. She wouldn't get anything more from him, not today.

CHAPTER 21

They drove to the police station in silence, and Max wondered if the kid felt as raw and exposed and anxious as he himself did. When he parked the old undercover unit in the back of the lot, a weight settled on his chest like an angry gorilla. By the time they walked through the doors, he could scarcely breathe. You would think he was being locked away on the wrong side of the bars.

"You're back!" the rookie called, trotting in behind them. "How—uh—how do you feel?"

"Like Wolverine when his body stopped regenerating," Max said, and it came out as more of a growl.

Oliver grinned.

"Where's the little guy?" Max asked, turning the corner to the squad room and scanning the crowded place for a sign of Henri.

The staff had done their best to convert the office area into something of a winter wonderland. Desks were pushed back, and fake snow and hand-cut snowflakes abounded, leaving just enough space to carry out any business-as-usual that might arise during the festivities.

The atmosphere overwhelmed Max with nostalgia for last year's holiday party: a single, almost perfect moment before it was swept away with the crumbs and wrappers and leftover dregs of spiked punch.

And then he saw her, stepping out of Interview Two, arms crossed in frustration, shaking her head and scowling at no one. She was beautiful, like the first rays of dawn peeking through the trees. She wore a black sweater—the same one from last year—and he realized he'd unintentionally donned the same sweater too, and he was so tired and it felt like some kind of *Christmas Carol Groundhog Day* do-over, and this time he'd get it right and erase everything he'd said and done wrong the last few days.

As though she felt him watching her, Maggie's eyes flicked over to Max, and her scowl transformed into the most radiant smile before giving way to a half smirk and disappointed eyes.

Like that, the spell was broken, and Max heaved a sigh. He hadn't breathed since first spotting her across the crowded room, a room which seemed to stand still, watching them. Did everyone already know his secret? And was her disappointment because he wasn't who she thought he was—because of his room, his life, his frailty?

She should never have opened that door. Like Pandora's box, Maggie had unleashed every memory, every pent-up emotion Max had battened down for years; they were roiling and churning within him now.

"Hey," she said from across the room, not exactly the running-into-his-arms welcome he'd imagined yesterday.

"Hey," he replied.

"You're back. Any luck?" she asked, and for a moment Max wondered how she could overlook Oliver standing right there. But then he realized she was talking past him, to the rookie at his shoulder.

The young officer stepped forward hesitantly, bridging the

distance between Max and Maggie, and glancing nervously from one to the other. "I convinced the library director to call an emergency board meeting. They're going to try and get enough members together for a video conference and put it to a vote."

"That's great," Maggie said.

"She wasn't optimistic. She reminded me about thirty-seven times that it's Christmas Eve."

"So I've heard," Maggie said. "Vincent's lawyering up."

"So that's it then?" the rookie asked.

"Maybe not," Maggie said, turning her gaze back to Max, lingering on his sweater for a moment too long.

Did she remember more about last Christmas than he thought she did?

Then she looked down at Oliver and said, "You must be Ver. I've got some questions for you."

"Can't it wait?" Max asked, a little more sharply than he meant to. "He hasn't seen his brother for three days."

"Then another hour won't hurt. Protocol says we separate the witnesses prior to interview."

Seriously? "Screw protocol," Max said.

"I guess that's on brand. You never were a big fan of protocol."

It was a low blow, considering Max had played it by the book where she was concerned for over ten years. "They're not suspects, they're kids. And I already interviewed him."

Hector's head turned back and forth from one to the other like he was watching a tennis match, and Max wished he hadn't started it, wished they didn't have an audience, wished a lot of things. He hadn't realized how angry he was at her, until it started leaking out in jabs and barbs.

"Has he looked at mugshots? Did you submit a report?" Maggie asked. "Do you have a statement in writing?"

"Yeah, I typed the report on my cell while I was driving across the province. He wrote his statement on the back of a Spaghet-tios label."

"Then I need to interview him. Properly. Before he sees Henri, before Reyes' attorney shows up. My case is hanging by a thread."

"Your case? Funny, I thought it was our case."

"Oh, our case? The one you demanded and then left me with?"

"I drove four thousand kilometers for the same case, partner. We each had our part, or haven't you ever played on a team?"

"I was on the chess team."

"Not sure that counts." Max shook his head. "Look, the kid doesn't know anything, okay? He's not the Magic 8 Ball that's going to help you solve your case."

"Ver!" a squeaky voice screamed, and Max turned to see Henri running across the room.

Oliver dropped to one knee, and the two boys clung to each other like they were drowning.

Everything—every ache in Max's neck and back, every second of lost sleep, even Maggie's utter invasion of his privacy—all of it was worth that moment.

"Where were you?" Henri asked, head still buried in his brother's embrace. "They said you went home."

"I did."

"Without me?" Henri asked, with the hurt tone of the one left behind. He pulled back to glare at his brother and punch him lightly in the shoulder.

Maggie looked like she wanted to do the same thing to Max, but the difference was he told her he was going.

"I didn't know what else to do," Oliver said. "So I went home to get Mama."

"You did?" Henri asked, looking at Max and beyond him to the station door. "Where is she?"

"She's with Papa."

"Oh," Henri said, nodding. "I thought so."

"You did?"

"What else would stop her from coming to us?"

Oliver glanced back at Max as if to say, Please don't tell him the whole truth.

Max nodded, a silent pact passing between them, and the kid turned his attention back to his little brother.

"Henri," Maggie said gently. "Why don't you go play with Hector and let me talk with Ver for a minute?"

The little boy nodded but didn't say anything.

"Can't you just give them five minutes?" Max asked.

"I really can't."

"Everything has to be on your terms, huh? Rest of the team be damned."

"You know, for someone who suddenly wants to be part of a team, you sure have kept me at arm's length the last—I don't know, five? Ten years? Partner."

That stung considering she'd been the one giving him the snow queen act recently. "Is that why you felt the need to go through my stuff? To get to know me better?"

"What?" He'd caught her off guard. Then her face reddened. "I—"

"My house, Kyle. My spare room. My everything. You had no right."

"Don't yell at her!" Henri said, pulling back from Oliver and scowling at Max.

Oliver shook his head, shushing his brother.

"St. James..." she began, but she didn't seem to know what to say.

"I get it, okay? You have to organize and label every aspect of your life. Put everything into tidy boxes or it doesn't make any sense. So which box do I fit in, huh?"

"Calm down," she whispered, glancing around at all of their coworkers who were frozen, pretending not to be watching them.

"I am calm. But Kyle, I told you—explicitly—you could take

my couch and put Henri in my room. What part of that involved my spare room? What part of that involved invading my privacy? Did you also throw away my signed Munro or my Cohen albums?"

"Don't get all high and mighty, Mr. 'There's spiders in my spare room.' I was trying to help."

"Help who? I didn't ask for help. You saw what looked like a problem and you had to make it make sense, like you always do. You just couldn't stop yourself."

Maggie grabbed his arm and dragged him into the staff lounge, away from prying eyes.

"A problem?" she whispered. "I looked in that room and saw more than a problem. I saw a cry for help, St. James. It wasn't normal."

"Everything I had left was in that room."

"And I sorted it for you. I bagged it, and yes, I labeled it, okay, you've got me there. And—if you'd care to calm down and ask—I schlepped the important stuff to your goddamn bedroom, and the things I thought you wouldn't want to keep are all in the closet until you give your blessing to donate them to charity. I may not have played hockey, but I'm pretty sure you can't have a team without trust. So if you can't trust me to not throw away something precious to you, then I don't even know why we're partners. And by the way, you're welcome."

Relief washed over Max, cooling the fires of his anger. Not just the blankets and quilt and sea glass, but everything was still there. She hadn't thrown anything away. "I—I was going to get around to it."

"I thought I was doing you a favor," she said. "But if you're this upset then when we're done here, I will happily dump every last scrap of it right back into a pile in the middle of your floor and you can close the door and hide from it for another five years. Or you can get crushed by it for all I care. Merry Christmas."

Max couldn't look at her anymore. It was all too much, and he was suddenly hyper-aware of their audience. From the doorway, Henri glared daggers at him and Oliver stared at the floor, and the poor rookie had followed them too, wide-eyed, like he was suffocating without the oxygen they had sucked from the room. He continued to glance from Maggie to Max like a child afraid to pick sides in his parents' divorce.

Was that what was happening? Were he and Maggie splitting up for good?

Castillo stood in the doorway too, holding a gingerbread house on a tray, shaking her head at the pair of them.

Max needed an exit, so he spoke to Oliver without actually looking at his face. "Will you answer a few more questions for Officer Kyle?"

The kid nodded, biting his lip and looking up at Max with a face full of second-hand embarrassment. He was a good kid. Max patted his shoulder and shoved between Castillo and the rookie to get away.

MAGGIE WATCHED MAX GO, AND SHE FELT LIKE EVERY DOOR IN THE universe was simultaneously slamming shut, never to be reopened. He was right, of course. He was always right when it came to her. But while her motivations for cleaning his spare room might not have been entirely selfless, her intentions were good, and it hurt that he hadn't thought so. How could he think otherwise? And why did he have to wear the same damned turtleneck from last year? She'd seen his closet. The man owned more than one nice shirt.

"Yeah, run away," she called after him. "It's sort of your MO, isn't it?" She'd burned the partnership to the ground anyway. Might as well throw another match on the flames.

Unfair as they were, her words stopped him and he turned back to face her. "Do you really want to do this here? Now?"

She shrugged. Who cared what anyone thought? There was already gossip that she and Max were together. Why not give them something real to gossip about for the next ten years?

"I had to go. You told me to go."

"No. I told you not to come back. You'd already left by then," Maggie snapped. She was changing the context of the words she'd whispered over the phone while lying in his bed. But it had the intended effect. His face, already rife with hurt and anger, now looked as though he'd been slapped, and he blinked at her.

"I don't know what you want from me," he said.

Anyone else might have yelled it, but not Max. Never Max. His tone was soft and sad.

"I don't know why you're the one who's mad. But I did the right thing here. If I hadn't been there, he would have died. Do you get that?" he whispered.

"No. No, I don't, because I've hardly heard from you. I don't know what happened—for hours at a time I didn't even know if you were wrecked somewhere on the side of the highway."

"I checked in."

"Not often enough."

And there it was, she realized. The admission she didn't want to make, even to herself. She was mad because he made her worry.

She studied his face, his narrowed eyes and the muscle twitching in his jaw, and there was so much emotion there that she couldn't unpack. She had to look away—at the floor, at his shoes. Not Chucks for maybe the first time since she'd known him, but regulation police boots. What had happened out there in the wilderness?

"You want to talk about me holding you at arm's length? What have you done except push me away until you needed something? I can't make nothing but small talk with you about the case and the weather, and then be the guy you call when there's a squirrel in your wall at night."

Maggie turned her back on him, her ears burning, and found herself staring at the empty fruit bowl.

"If there's a problem with your case, then solve it. Isn't that what you do best? But I am not one of your puzzles to solve," Max said.

And by the time she turned back around, he was gone.

Henri slipped his hand in hers, and Maggie looked down to see that he was also holding Oliver's. His mouth was set in a grim line, his eyes full of anxious worry.

"Hector," Maggie said to the rookie who was trying to pretend he wasn't hovering at her elbow. "Will you take Oliver to the soft interview? I'll be there in a sec."

"You bet," the rookie said, eagerly motioning for Oliver to follow him.

Henri squeezed Maggie's hand. "Don't be sad."

"I'm not sad," she lied, plastering a smile on her face. But his skeptical look made her smile begin to waver. "Not very sad anyway."

"Grownup stuff," he said.

"Grownup stuff," she agreed. "Why don't you go see if they need help setting up the karaoke?"

"Okay." He glanced back over his shoulder at her before finally leaving the lounge.

What would happen to him now? To both of them? She would have to call Leah soon and let her know Oliver was back safe and sound. But maybe it could wait until after Christmas.

"So St. James is back from the dead—and looking as fine as ever," Frankie said, setting down one of the gingerbread contest entries and trying to act like the entire fight hadn't played out before her eyes.

"Yeah, yeah. The prodigal son returns. Let's all throw a party."

"Okay, this party's not for him," Frankie said, "no matter how much you worship him."

Maggie snorted. "Right."

"What exactly happened?"

What had happened?

"I messed up," Maggie admitted. "Now he's pissed."

"Does he have a right to be?"

She shook her head but said, "Probably."

"Did you apologize?"

Maggie thought back over the whole embarrassing conversation. In fact she hadn't once said she was sorry. She had tried to turn it all back on him.

"You two are amazing." Frankie shook her own head. "It's like somehow you've been so in sync on the job for such a long time that you haven't had to actually communicate, so you're terrible at it."

"Says you," Maggie scoffed, but as usual, Frankie was right.

"Hey, I talked to my baby daddy. Now come look at this amazing gingerbread house Ma and I made. It'll melt your frozen heart."

The house was adorable, with a steep pitched roof that made it look like a church. They'd decorated it with fanciful Fluff icing-cicles and tiny sprinkles shaped like stars and snowflakes.

She couldn't believe Frankie had made it. "You hate baking."

"Sure, but, it's what moms do, right?" Frankie said, not looking at her. "Maybe I haven't tried it enough. This turned out okay."

"Who even are you?"

"I'm having a baby, Mags. I baked something for the contest. I'm not turning into a Stepford wife."

"I know."

"I get that you're mad about your case, and—whatever happened last Christmas—but you're kind of being a jerk. It's not Max's fault you're unhappy. He worked the same case you did, on way less sleep. And he brought you another witness. Maybe you should take a breath and go interview your witness."

Maggie swallowed the lump in her throat. She couldn't handle both Max and Frankie being pissed at her. They were the two best people in the world. If they were both fed up, maybe she was the problem. Not gun runners or runaways or even Christmas, just her. But how was she supposed to fix it when she had a case to solve?

CHAPTER 22

Max made himself useful by hiding alone in the Parade Room, sorting and cataloging the gifts his colleagues and their families had brought as donations to Covenant House for homeless youth. As he handled the roller skates and board games and plush toys and gift cards, he couldn't help picturing Oliver and Henri opening similar gifts around a Christmas tree that wasn't his, surrounded by well-meaning strangers.

You can't save them all, his father would tell his mom each time she brought home another abandoned kitten, injured rabbit, or fledgling sparrow.

Maybe not, she would answer every time. *But I can try to save this one.*

Raucous laughter invaded Max's hiding place from what sounded like the rookie trying to coax someone to start off the karaoke. A few people whistled, loud and shrill, and a round of cheering went up from the crowd as the opening notes of "All I Want for Christmas" began to play.

Max had to poke his head out when the singing began, only to see Castillo belting out the words in a rendition that would have impressed Mariah herself. Out of habit he looked around for Maggie, to see if her face was as shocked and impressed as their coworkers' were. Instead he spotted Oliver, already out of interview, sitting cross-legged in the back corner of the squad room atop a desk which had been pushed up against the wall. Dix leaned next to him, watching the festivities.

It made Max nervous, the two of them in cahoots, so he headed over.

"I agree," Dix was saying to the kid. "Parties suck."

"It's Christmas Eve," Oliver told him.

"I know that. Do you?"

"Tomorrow's Christmas."

"Solid math."

"Then what?"

"Then Boxing Day," Dix joked. He glanced down at Oliver and grew serious. "Then… whatever. Until it happens, anything can happen."

Oliver looked like he might cry, and it made the tightness in Max's own throat constrict so he stepped out where they could see him. "Hey," he said. "Where's that kid brother of yours? He hasn't convinced you to do karaoke yet?"

"I don't sing anymore," Oliver reminded him, pushing himself off the desk and walking away.

"It's a Christmas miracle! I thought I heard the dulcet tones of Max St. James returned to the living," Dix said. "Good to see you back, MJ. And you found the elusive older brother."

"I did."

"You happened to look up from your deathbed and there he was?"

"More like a fever-induced odyssey."

"Good, good," Dix said. "You and me should probably talk." He patted the space Oliver had vacated, so Max leaned beside him on the desk, another bystander to the revelry around them. "Did you have that strep throat that's going around?"

"I don't know. Maybe," Max said, hating himself for lying right to his oldest friend's face.

"Or maybe it was just the flu. You know what they say the best cure for flu is?" Dix asked.

Max knew it was a trick question, but what else could he do besides take the bait? "Tamiflu within forty-eight hours?"

"That or putting four thousand kilometers on a car that's scheduled to be decommissioned."

So he was caught. Should have known Dix would have seen right through him. In some ways, it was almost a relief. "Should I expect to be decommissioned?" he asked.

"You're lucky it turned out how it did."

Max nodded. "I know."

"It could have gone very badly."

"It almost did." Max still felt sick every time he pictured Oliver in the river.

"If you crossed provincial lines, or the border, I'm not sure I want to hear about it."

"I didn't."

Dix laid a heavy hand on Max's shoulder. "It's a good thing what you did, bringing him back. It was the right thing."

"I know."

"It also defied a direct order. I ought to suspend you."

"Let me save you the trouble." Max pushed off of the table and turned to look at Dix. But he couldn't meet his eyes, so he stared at his shoulder stripes instead. "I quit. Two weeks' notice or whatever you need, but I'm done."

"Good," Dix said, and Max was so surprised that he did look his old friend in the eye then. "Good, because I wanted to do you the favor our old CO should have done and let you go."

"I'm not that bad of a cop," Max protested, feeling unexpectedly stung by his friend's words.

"That's the thing, MJ, you're a great cop. But being good at something doesn't mean you should have to keep doing it if you don't love it."

Max slumped back against the desk again. In some ways he felt a million times lighter, but his stomach was twisted in knots.

"What about Kyle?" Dix asked.

"I don't want to talk about her."

"Maybe I want to."

"Not today, brother. Please?"

The sick churning in his gut was only getting stronger. Quitting without warning—when she was already furious with him? She might never speak to him again and without the chance of seeing her on the job, what else did he have?

"You've been partners a long time."

"Ten years," Max said, scanning the crowd again, and finally spotting Maggie exiting the interview room. God she looked amazing, even when she was frazzled and angry, and her hair, which she'd tried to wear down until she got fed up with it and stuffed it into a bun, wouldn't stay put.

"How long have you been in love with her?" Dix pressed.

Max sighed. "About ten years."

"But?"

Maggie looked around the party, locking eyes with Max for a second, before moving on, finding the rookie in the crowd, and motioning for him to join her.

"But we were partners. I kept thinking she'd take the D's exam and then maybe we could see if there was a *there* there. She kept not taking it."

"Why do you think that is?"

"I don't know," Max said. The thing about Maggie was, she always kept him guessing. Even when he thought he knew what she was thinking, she surprised him.

"MJ, I love you. But not talking about a thing, I'm told by my brilliant wife, is the surest way to destroy it. Don't ruin it before it really starts."

"Where is Leah? I had a question for her." Max craned his neck to scan the whole room, but there was no sign of his friend's wife.

"She left."

"Already?"

Dix shifted uncomfortably and scuffed his foot against the floor. "Didn't like her Christmas present, I guess."

"Why'd you give it to her here?" Max asked. Dix would never learn how to be romantic. He hoped it wasn't the date night kit he'd suggested that turned her off.

"Because I had to beg her to even show…. She wants to split up, MJ. I've been sleeping here for a week."

"What?"

"Happy New Year," Dix said, an unenthusiastic imitation of a party host.

Max didn't know what to say. Leah kicking Dix out was about as alien as, well, actual aliens. "You guys'll get through it." He bumped his friend's shoulder. "You're the most rock-solid couple I know."

"Not sure what that says about you."

Dix without Leah? Max had introduced them himself when he was a rookie. They were a matched set, each the other's right-hand. "I'm sorry, brother. Maybe she just needs some time."

"Speaking of needing time, what's this I hear about Kyle going through your mom's stuff?"

God. Did everyone know? "News travels fast."

"It does when you're yelling it down the halls. I thought you did that awhile back?"

"I did. I started to. I got it all off my dad's plate and…" The heat was rising behind his eyes again. What was wrong with him? Was it the holidays or lack of sleep?

"Five years, MJ. That's a long time."

"It was too much."

"I know."

"I couldn't—even throw out the junk. I couldn't look at the pictures, let alone hang them." He looked up at the ceiling to stop any tears from coming and cleared his throat. "Every time I tried, I shut down. Or disappeared down a bottle. Or got a tattoo. Or wound up next door at Selina's." He rubbed the back of his head. "So I quit trying. Like as long as I had her stuff, she wasn't really gone."

"You should have called me. I'd have done it."

"I thought it should be me. Thought it would bring some kind of closure. Eventually." And now the chance had been ripped away from him, and at the end of the day, maybe that's what closure was, and maybe he didn't want any part of it.

"Well, it's done now." Dix looked at him, his face too full of a sympathy Max didn't deserve. "Maybe find closure in that."

Maggie was surprised by how quickly the public defender arrived, and she sent Hector to get the woman settled. The case must have come through right when she was returning from lunch or maybe she rushed to Fifty-One Division eager to have things over and done quickly so she could knock off early for Christmas Eve.

But when Hector emerged from Interview Two he raised his eyebrows at Maggie and said, "I think you're going to need a bigger boat."

Maggie's confusion must have been clear in her cocked head and squint because he added, "If that chick drew the short straw for a round of pro bono at Legal Aid, then Reyes might be the luckiest son of a biscuit-eater to ever grace a holding cell."

"She's not an underpaid, over-worked, under-slept do-gooder on her last ounce of Christmas cheer?"

Hector shook his head.

"Did Vincent make the call himself?"

"Dunno."

"Find out," Maggie said, taking a breath and heading into the shark tank.

Even with the rookie's warning, she wasn't prepared for the trim and exquisitely coiffed figure wearing a three-piece woolen suit and five-inch Louboutin heels with toes so pointed you'd almost need to have one or two digits removed in order to wear them.

The lawyer fixed Maggie with an icy stare, and Maggie felt instantly frumpy in her best sweater, jeans, and sensible shoes.

"I'm Officer Kyle," she said, screwing up her courage and extending her hand.

"An officer?" The lawyer shook Maggie's hand and then eyed her own before wiping it with a handkerchief. "Your detective was too busy to meet with me? Must be quite the party," she added with a sniff.

"I'm running point on this case," Maggie said, clenching her hand into a fist at her side.

"I see." The lawyer examined her acrylic nails as though Maggie's hand was so rough that shaking it might have scratched the paint.

Vincent watched the entire exchange with a smug smirk Maggie wanted to smack right off his face. He knew as well as Maggie did that she'd already lost.

"Carol Lewiston. You'll be releasing my client immediately."

"I don't think so."

"You have nothing to hold him on."

"I have quite a bit actually. Suspicion of conspiracy, willful destruction of property, interfering with an investigation, and child endangerment to start."

"Where's your evidence?"

"We have plenty of evidence," Maggie bluffed, "but we tend to save it for court."

"A phone app? A pair of shoes?"

"Custom shoes, entirely unique as corroborated by the manufacturer and placed at the scene by a witness. And they were delivered to the residence of a known criminal, which is reason enough to detain your client."

"Really? That's the best you've got? My client has no knowledge of any such shoes. There's obviously been some kind of mix-up."

"I'm sure the post office will have a record."

"Forgive me, Ms. Kyle, maybe you're new at this, but I'm not. And I can assure you that you have absolutely nothing. No prosecutor would touch this case. But we both know that, don't we?"

"Your client—" Maggie began.

"My client is a misunderstood boy who has been repeatedly hounded by your department because you were too inept to see what was right in front of you—children perpetrated this crime. And I will make sure the judge sees it that way too. Now, if I have to request a writ of habeas corpus for Mr. Reyes, then I promise you the very next thing I will do is file a harassment suit against your department—and you personally," she threatened.

Maggie wasn't unfamiliar with the tactics of this Narnia-esque ice witch. But familiarity didn't make Carol Lewiston any less terrifying, and if she was going to regain control of the case then she needed to get out of the room, catch her breath, and think of a plan B. "Excuse me one moment," she said, moving to the door.

"That's what I thought."

Outside, she was careful not to let the door slam shut, but she sagged against it, blinking back the tears of frustration threatening to fall. She closed her eyes and focused her breath, and when she opened them again she spotted Hector and both boys huddled around a computer.

"Whatcha doing?" Henri asked, when she joined them. He shrugged off Oliver's arm and tugged on Maggie's sweater hem.

"Talking to a suspect," Maggie told him.

"Was it the King?"

"Who?" Hector finally turned away from the screen and shot Maggie a look as Oliver tried to shush his brother.

"It looked like the King," the little boy said. "You know, the King of the Bus Station?"

"Did you name him that?" Maggie asked.

"Everyone calls him that."

"He's the one with the shoes, Henri? The one who chased you?"

The boy nodded. "You don't think he saw us, do you?" he asked, shrinking back into Oliver's side.

"No. He's been in there all day," she assured Henri, but he and his brother exchanged worried looks. "Why do you think they call him the King?" Maggie pressed.

"They're making fun," Oliver said quickly. "Because he struts around like he owns the place."

"I wonder if that's the only reason," Maggie mused. "Hector, any word on the attorney?"

The rookie handed over a mostly blank document detailing everything he knew about the phone call: the number, owner unknown, and the duration of the call, a whopping two minutes and eighteen seconds. "Unregistered," Hector said. "Seems like our boy called a burner."

"So she's not from Legal Aid."

"Explains a lot."

"What are you on the trail of?" she asked, leaning over his shoulder to see what he was researching so intently.

"This," he said, leaning back proudly and turning his monitor to give her a better look.

He'd compiled a list of Carol Lewiston's past cases, mostly corporate law.

"What is this? What am I looking at?"

"She's a shark, but she doesn't do criminal defense," Hector explained. "Never has, except for one minor possession of weed a few years before it was legal."

"So where'd she come from?"

Across the room, Carol Lewiston stepped out of Interview Two and looked around, scathing and impatient to leave. She barked orders at a passing admin who scuttled off to Dixon's office.

"Exactly," Hector said, highlighting case after case where Lewiston represented companies like Bobby's Best Auto Salvage, Junk Junk Junk Removal and Demolition, and King Kong Kash. She had litigated contract negotiations and civil suits all over the city.

The names rang a bell. "Are those—"

"Bobby King's companies," Hector exploded, then clapped his hand over his mouth like an over-eager little boy.

"She's on retainer," Maggie said, pretending not to watch Dixon speak with the lawyer before making a beeline right for her and the rookie.

"Who else you going to call when baby bro gets pinched on Christmas Eve?"

"This should be enough for a warrant—"

"What's the hold up?" Dixon asked, hands in the air. "Your boy's lawyer's kicking up an awful fuss. I thought you were releasing him?"

"Waiting on the paperwork," Maggie fibbed, "but listen—"

"This paperwork?" the sergeant asked, picking up the release documents from Hector's desk.

"Yep, that's the paperwork," Maggie sighed. "But Sarge, listen, Carol Lewiston is Bobby King's lawyer."

Dixon followed Maggie's gaze back across the room, where the lawyer glared at the clock, arms crossed adversarially. "I'm losing patience, Officers," she shouted over the "Mistletoe and Wine" karaoke someone was struggling through.

"I don't care if she's the Virgin Mary about to give birth on my floor, you've got three minutes to cut Reyes loose."

"He's guilty," Maggie whispered, as Dixon started back toward Lewiston. "I'm more certain of it than I've ever been of anything else in my life."

"That's not how this works, Kyle," Dixon said. "Can you prove it?"

"Not in court."

"Then you have to cut him loose."

"Everything okay?" Max asked, walking over to witness Maggie's second utter failure of the week because why not?

"Fine, thanks," she snapped.

"Are you the detective?" Lewiston asked Max, stomping up to them in her clicking high heels.

"Again, I apologize for the delay, Ms. Lewiston," Dixon said smoothly. "There was a mix-up with your client's paperwork. We'll have you out of here in a jiffy."

"I did it," Oliver announced, from behind Maggie. "I put the bomb inside the locker."

CHAPTER 23

For Max, everything happened in slow motion, like being underwater. Everyone turned to face Oliver. Maggie went completely pale, rolling her eyes heavenward. Dix's face screwed up in confusion, and the brash woman whose suit screamed over-priced lawyer raised her eyebrows in delighted surprise.

"We both did it. Together," Oliver added. "Henri and me. We made it out of fireworks and RoboZ toys."

"Knock it off," Max said in his sternest voice. To the adults he added, "Kid's exhausted. Doesn't know what he's saying."

Maggie forced a laugh. "Kids."

"My client and I will be on our way," the lawyer said, eyeing Oliver in a way that made Max uncomfortable.

The kid shrunk behind him a little. "I do too know what I'm saying." His voice was small and less sure than before.

"Stop talking. This isn't a game," Max whispered sharply. Then he shrugged and offered the lawyer his most charming smile, repeating Maggie's helpless, "Kids."

"What is it they say, Detective? Out of the mouths of babes?" she said, with all the artificial syrupy sweetness of a bowl of aspartame. Then she held out her hand, demanding the paperwork Dix was holding.

"Deal with this," Maggie pleaded to Max through clenched teeth before stalking into Interview Two behind the lawyer and acting sergeant.

Max gripped Oliver's shoulder tightly, and the kid glanced up at him, licking his lips, but allowed Max to march him into the soft interview room.

"All right, let's hear it, tough guy," Max said, pushing the kid firmly down into a chair.

The rookie came in with Henri, and Max pointed to the chair next to Oliver. Henri read the room and scrambled into his seat without a word, eyes the size of saucers glued on his big brother.

"Come on, kid. You sure had plenty to say back there."

"I told you. We put the bomb inside the locker together," he said, and Henri's head snapped from Oliver to Max and back again like a wide-eyed yoyo, but he still didn't say a word.

Max glanced at the rookie, whose own face was the picture of confusion.

"Why?" Max asked.

Oliver shrugged. "To see what would happen."

Max caught himself leaning forward, hands on the table, an intimidation stance, so he pulled out a chair and slid into it.

"How'd you make it, Henri?" he asked.

The little boy's eyes grew even wider, and he glanced at his brother.

"Don't look at him, look at me. How'd you make the IED?"

"Science," Henri whimpered.

"You already know," Oliver said. "A robot kit from the library and fireworks."

"What size cake?"

"Biggest one we could find."

"How much did it cost?"

"A lot more than we had."

"How'd you ignite it?" Max fired his questions quickly, trying to trip the kid up.

"A timer on the robot."

"But what ignited it?"

"Matches?"

"How'd you get the kit?"

"Stole it."

"When?"

"Can't remember. We steal a lot."

"Oliver," Max said, shaking his head and pinching the bridge of his nose.

"Officer?" the kid asked, staring past him.

Whatever rapport they had built up seemed to have vanished, as though Max had only imagined it. "Is he telling the truth?" he demanded of Henri, but the little boy just stared back at him, his eyes darting periodically to his brother, his mouth opening and closing, unable to speak.

"Why confess now?" Max asked.

"You and me agreed to tell the truth," Oliver mumbled, but he wouldn't look Max in the eye.

"I don't think you are telling the truth."

Oliver rested his chin on his fist. "You can think what you want."

"Why would you put both a bomb and your little brother in the same set of lockers?"

"So he could trigger it if anything went wrong."

"Weren't you worried about maybe blowing him up?"

Silence. Then, "It was only fireworks."

Max stood up and rubbed the back of his head feeling betrayed for the second time that afternoon.

"Do we need to sign something or what?" Oliver asked, his voice shaking a little.

Max sighed. "I'll get a notepad." He jerked his head at the rookie to follow him outside.

"What the hell was that?" Maggie demanded from across the room. Dix did his best to shush her, but they were once again drawing curious looks from the fringes of the party.

Max and the rookie joined them at the door to reception, where Maggie watched her suspect collect his keys and wallet. His lawyer flashed them all a bright, sparkling grin.

"He's lying," Max said.

"You sure about that?" Dix asked.

Was he? Not really, but he had a little faith left. "I can tell when he's lying, and when he's telling the truth, and right now he's lying about telling the truth."

"You've only known him for two days," the rookie said skeptically.

"And you've only been a cop for two minutes," Max snapped.

"Easy," Dix said.

"The question is why?" They all fell silent at Maggie's statement. "My theory about Reyes makes sense. All the pieces fit. This doesn't." And then the rookie drew a deep, reluctant sigh. Her head jerked up. "What? Hector?"

"I was researching the lawyer. I was only half paying attention."

"What did you do?" Max demanded.

"The kid kept asking what would happen if they had done it."

"And you said?"

"I said they'd probably go to juvie."

Max closed his eyes. "Together."

"I don't understand," Dix said.

"I think Oliver believes foster care would split them up."

"Sounds an awful lot like what you believe," Maggie said, her tone accusatory.

"There's a reason people think it. He probably figures they'd be somewhat together in juvie."

"Those are two messed up little dudes," the rookie said.

"No." Max turned back to the soft interview room. "Just desperate."

"What are you going to do?" Maggie asked, following closely behind him.

"Reason with them."

But when he opened the door—the room was empty. The boys, and their backpacks, were gone.

MAGGIE WATCHED MAX SCAN THE EMPTY ROOM LIKE HE WASN'T quite comprehending the emptiness—like when your brain misfires and tricks you into seeing something else. He even checked behind the door.

Then he stepped back into the squad room and spun in a circle, searching the crowd of fellow officers.

But they weren't there. They'd done a runner, again, and they weren't even wearing winter coats over their hoodies.

"Check the washrooms," Maggie told him, springing into crisis mode. "Hector, check the parking lot and the alley."

"I'll put out an APB," Dixon said.

Hector dashed off, but Max still stood there, shaking his head, raking a hand across his mouth and over his stubbly chin as his eyes darted back and forth like he was studying a map inside his head.

"St. James?" Maggie asked. "The washrooms?"

He looked at her as though she was speaking Cantonese.

"You really think they just slipped off for a pee? They're not here, Kyle."

"Fine, I'll do it myself."

And she did, because she had to do something.

But Max was right. They weren't there—not in the ladies' or the men's, not in the staff lounge, or the janitor's closet—they weren't anywhere.

She returned to the squad room in time to see Max pulling on his leather jacket.

"You're leaving?" she asked. "You think you're going to magically bump into them in a city of two point eight million people?"

"It's better than nothing," he said. His voice was soft and his face was calm, but in his eyes and under his tone was a mournfulness that almost surprised Maggie.

"Stay here. Help me follow the evidence," she said. "We'll find them together."

"Kyle, there is no evidence," Max said over his shoulder as he strode past Hector, who was on his way back inside. For a moment Maggie wasn't sure if he was referring to the kids or her case.

"No sign of them," the rookie reported, watching the senior officer leave.

Frankie approached with a stack of mostly empty cookie platters. "What's up?"

"The kids took off," Hector told her before snagging the last melting snowman cookie on her tray.

When Frankie and Maggie both turned glares on him he said, his mouth still full of cookie, "What? I'm feeding my feelings."

"Are you okay?" Frankie asked Maggie.

"Trying to think where they could have gone."

Frankie set the trays down on the desk beside her. "What can I do?"

For a moment Maggie wanted to tell her friend to go back to the party, she'd do it on her own, but she couldn't. Not this time. "CCTV footage," Maggie said. "Maybe we can figure out which way they went."

Frankie nodded and sat down at the closest computer.

"Anything?" Dixon called as he hurried back across the squad room.

Maggie and Hector shook their heads.

"I've issued the APB and sent their photo to the news stations, so pretty soon people will be checking every outhouse, hen house, dog house, gingerbread house—"

Maggie squinted at him.

"Sorry. I've been told my humor in times of stress is less than charming."

"Do you think we could get our warrant now? Reyes' lawyer saw Oliver, she has to know they're the witnesses even if he did confess. That could put them in danger."

"I'll try," Dixon said, sitting on Frankie's desk and picking up her phone.

"Amber Alert?" Hector suggested.

Maggie weighed the option. "There's no actual evidence of imminent danger."

"But you just said—"

"There's a difference between getting a search warrant and a province-wide Amber Alert," she explained.

Hector nodded and smacked his palm against his head like it might help him think. "Does imminent danger of freezing to death count? The temperature's dropping fast. It'll plummet as the sun goes down."

"Where would you go? If you were them?" Maggie asked no one in particular.

"Home," Frankie suggested.

It was as good a guess as any.

"If only we had, I don't know, a massive CB radio or something," Maggie said. "To alert the long haul drivers."

"We do." Hector grinned and held up his cell.

"What?" Maggie and Frankie asked together.

"There's an app for that," Hector said, walking off a little way and fiddling with the device.

Dixon slammed down Frankie's desk phone and shook his head. "No dice on the warrant."

"Did you tell them—"

"Kyle, I explained the situation."

"Yeah, but did you downplay it or—"

"No dice, Kyle."

Maggie groaned. She would have to be more careful in how she spent her goodwill with judges on her next case. It was truly at a premium.

"So the rumors are true. It really is all party, party, party at the ole Five-One," Boyd teased, walking up in an ugly green sweater bedazzled with garland and flashing lights.

"What are you doing here?" Hector asked his TO.

"I heard there was an ugly sweater contest, but it looks like I may have been punked."

"You want some coffee?" Frankie asked.

"Always," Boyd said. "You know me well."

"Perfect. I'll take a ginger tea, and these three need coffee too. Thank you so much," she sang sweetly. "Oh and those cookie trays need to go to the staff lounge since you're heading that way."

"Aye, Captain," Boyd said, collecting the platters.

Hector grinned. "You're so bossy," he whispered to Frankie.

"It's one of my finest qualities."

"Any luck?" Maggie asked.

"Truckers haven't seen them, but they'll keep a lookout and let us know if they do."

"Maybe they haven't left the city yet, that's a good sign," Dixon said. "Nice work, rook."

"And I got a call from the library director. She's sending over the security cam footage now." Hector collapsed into his desk chair and woke up his computer.

Maggie ruffled his hair and when he ducked away so she couldn't muss it further, she pulled up her own chair between him and Frankie so she could see both screens.

Boyd returned with the requested beverages, and Maggie accepted her coffee gratefully, but her stomach was too nervy to drink it. He hovered for a minute, watching them and then asked, "Anything else?"

"Pull up a chair and grab a CCTV camera," Frankie suggested.

"No, wait," Maggie said. "Can you call the transit authority and make sure they saw our APB? I want every driver alerted, those kids don't get on a bus, a train, a ferry..."

"Your bus station kids? They're both gone?" Boyd asked.

Maggie nodded.

"Oh shit. I'm on it," he said, sitting down at a desk opposite the rookie.

Maggie's heart surged with affection for her friends all joining the search. Especially after Max bailed on her—again— and after all that talk about being on the same team.

"I've got something," Hector and Frankie both said.

"Richmond and Jarvis," Frankie added.

Maggie leaned over to study her friend's frozen monitor.

"Could be them, right?"

The footage was dark and grainy. "I couldn't swear to it," Maggie said. "But it sure looks like them."

"So, what, they're heading back to the bus station?" Dixon asked, leaning over Frankie's other shoulder.

"Ma'am, you're going to want to take a look at this," Hector said.

"Call St. James. Maybe he can get there faster." Maggie leaned over to look at Hector's monitor. There, frozen in time, was the image of Vincent Reyes stealing the not-Lego kit right off the desk of the children's librarian.

CHAPTER 24

It was tricky, navigating the overflowing parking lot at Grace Church. For half a second, Max wondered what could be going on. But of course, it was Christmas Eve. For everyone else in the city time wasn't standing still and speeding up and slowing down all at once. He gave up on the lot and parked illegally in the alley.

The carol service was already in progress when he entered, and he hovered at the back, thankful for his height but a bit overwhelmed by where to start. Kids are small and chameleon-like in a crowd, and his hopes of finding them were fading fast. Still, he climbed the stairs to get a better view.

Spill-over seating had been set up with folding chairs in the loft, and Max skimmed the dimly lit faces, knowing without a doubt the boys weren't there. The church, filled to bursting with the faithful, was a small-scale diorama of how impossible it would be to locate two small children in the whole of Toronto.

He squeezed past the solemn church goers in their creaking folding chairs, ignoring their irritated looks, and picked up an old brown blanket, forgotten in a corner. Had it been theirs? It held a faint whiff of stale cigarettes mingled with adolescent sweat.

Staring out over the congregation from above, Max thought he spotted them several times, only to have the kids in question shift their weight or turn their heads, and he realized he was wrong. He'd entered dangerous territory, seeing them everywhere he looked, because he wanted to.

Where was his moose guide now?

Scanning the loft one last time, he caught a woman's eye— Leah Dixon gave him a wan smile. He returned her greeting with a low wave, intending to head back downstairs, but she patted the empty chair next to her.

He felt like something of an interloper, but Max squeezed in beside her and kissed her cheek. "Merry Christmas, Leah," he said.

She squeezed his hand. "I missed you at the party."

"Some party."

Leah snorted. From her coat pocket she withdrew a Christmas present, a long, thin box still wrapped in festive gold paper. She stared at it for a moment before whispering, "Is he cheating on me, MJ? I need to know."

"What? No!" Max said, completely shocked by the suggestion. Dix was an idiot, always capable of saying the wrong thing at the wrong time, but he wasn't a cheater.

"This is jewelry. He hasn't given me jewelry in years. Last year he gave me an Instant Pot. And I love it, but—"

"Come on. You think he thought of this on his own? He just wanted to give you something that wasn't an Instant Pot."

She handed it to him, her eyes begging him to open it for her.

As quietly as he could, he lifted the tape and peeled away the paper to reveal a maroon felt jewelry box. He tried to hand it back to her, but she wouldn't take it. So he snapped it open. Inside was a sterling silver chain, a bracelet with two dangling charms and a third, by itself, not yet attached.

Leah put one hand to her mouth and accepted the box with her other hand.

"Aquamarine," she whispered, pointing to the first charm. It was a ball of silver starfish surrounded by pale blue bubbles.

"Does it mean something?"

"It's Julia's birthstone. And peridot," she said, running a finger along the other charm: a tree of life with bright green leaves. "That's Emmy's and my mom's."

Well done, Dix.

She picked up the loose charm, a compass with a small amber-orange stone in the center. "Topaz," she said.

"What month is topaz?"

"November."

So it was Dix's birthstone, and also the month they got married.

"He didn't attach it," she said.

"Maybe he's leaving it up to you. Look, Leah, I don't know what happened. But he loves you. More than I've ever seen anyone love another person. Ever. I only hope somebody loves me like that one day. Even an idiot like Dix."

A tear rushed down Leah's cheek and she wiped it away with an embarrassed grin. "He is an idiot," she agreed, squeezing Max's hand again.

"Yeah, but he's our idiot."

She laughed. "Thank you, MJ. I heard you found Henri Thibault's brother?"

"I did."

"Good work."

"Oh yeah, real good. They've run away again." Max crumpled up the wrapping paper in his palm until it was a tiny ball. "They're gone, and this time I don't know where to look."

Leah put her hand on his arm in a sort of motherly way. "You thought they might be here?"

He nodded. "Where would they go? I know there are places—hangouts."

"I don't know."

"Leah, if it was Emmy? Or Julia? What would you do?"

"Ping their phones, call their friends, check my mom's house."

"Say you did that. All of those things. And you still came up empty. Then what?" he asked, reminding himself of Oliver's constant question. *Now what? What happens now?*

She sighed. "MJ, you cannot go in there as a cop. You have to turn that part of you off."

"Done."

"I'm serious. You also can't go in there as a bleeding heart who has to save everyone."

"Just these two," he promised.

She studied him skeptically for a moment, but then she seemed to accept him at his word. "There's an old linseed oil factory on Wabash."

"Near the train tracks?" Max asked. He'd seen the old building plenty of times. As kids they would throw rocks to try and break the windows. They would dare each other to spend the night inside, too, although he didn't know anyone who actually had.

"Lots of runaways hole up there. I shudder to think how my girls might find out about it, but if I looked everywhere else, that's where I'd go next."

"You're an angel."

"I could come with you," she whispered, gathering her coat and purse.

"Actually, could you stay here in case they do turn up?"

She nodded and squeezed his hand one last time. "You found him once," she whispered. "You can do it again."

❄

The library security footage was all they needed to finally secure a warrant. Fifteen minutes later, Maggie and Hector pulled up outside the coach terminal, and Boyd parked his own cruiser right behind them.

Maggie hadn't bothered to change, but Boyd had removed his ugly sweater to match their uniformed rookie. The ticket clerk slumped on the counter with her cheek resting on her fist, but the moment she saw them, she scrambled to sit up straight and attentive.

"Evening," Maggie said. "I'm Officer Kyle, these are Officers Hector and Boyd. You are—?"

"Sarah?" the girl said, glancing nervously around the nearly empty station.

Maggie looked around too. There was no sign of the kids, and her heart sank. "You haven't seen either of these two boys, have you, Sarah?" she asked anyway, passing the photo to the girl.

"No, not today. Are they in trouble?"

"Not with us. Miss, we have a warrant to search the employee file and locker of one of your coworkers, Vincent Reyes."

"The King of the Station?" Sarah asked, rolling her eyes. "God I hate that guy."

"Is he here?" Boyd asked.

"No. I was supposed to take the bus home to Kingston, but when I walked in my manager said I had to cover his shift."

"Sorry about that," Maggie said. "We arrested him this morning."

"Shocking." The girl lit up with interest. "What'd the creep do? Did he finally snap and kill somebody?"

"Would you be able to point us to his locker?" Maggie asked, holding up the warrant. "And pull his employee file?"

"Sure." Sarah slid off her stool. "I don't have access to the files, but I might be able to get into the payroll system."

"Nothing illegal." Boyd pointed at her and she frowned but led them all to the locker room.

Vincent's locker was secured with a red padlock.

Sarah leaned against the doorway, watching the officers decide what to do next.

"Thanks for your help," Maggie said by way of dismissing the curious twenty-something. "You'll try to get hold of a manager who can access those files for us?"

The girl sighed. "Totally," she said, slouching off back to the ticket counter.

"Now what?" Hector asked, giving the red padlock a half-hearted tug. "Pick it?" he added a little too enthusiastically.

"Maybe next time," Boyd said, holding up a pair of bolt cutters.

"Well aren't you… prepared." Hector's face was full of admiration.

"Always," Boyd bragged.

"Yeah you are," Hector agreed.

Maggie glanced from one to the other, sensing a little something more than collegial banter between them. "So get on with it?" she said.

Boyd winked—Maggie was undecided whether it was directed at her or the rookie—and then he turned dead serious and with a steady hand, cut right through the padlock.

All three of them stared at the closed locker for a moment longer.

"Would you like to do the honors?" Boyd asked Maggie, sweeping an arm in invitation.

Maggie took a breath, and as she lifted up on the latch, she briefly wondered if it could be booby-trapped.

She jerked it open before she could chicken out.

Inside they found basically everything. Hector whistled.

"Shoes?" Boyd asked, eyeing the houndstooth running shoes with interest.

"*The* shoes," Hector agreed.

"Bingo." Maggie pulled on a pair of latex gloves and held up a plastic bag with a Lillian H. Smith Library sticker and barcode on it, which contained a few leftover RoboZ pieces.

"Sorry?" Sarah peeked in from the hallway. "My manager gave me her password." She offered Maggie a printout of Reyes' employee file.

"That's a different address," Hector said, looking over Maggie's shoulder, "than the one on his license. That's—"

"Bobby King's address," Maggie finished for him.

"Also," Sarah interjected, "those kids you were looking for were on the news."

Maggie's mouth went dry. "What for?" she asked, swallowing her panic.

"Caught trying to sneak across the Rainbow Bridge into the States," Sarah said.

"Niagara Falls?" Hector asked.

"Guess so."

Maggie tried to calculate the time in her head. If they had hitchhiked they could have made it in an hour and a half. Faster if the driver was in a hurry.

"What time did we cut Reyes loose?" she asked Hector.

"Around two o'clock."

"That could have given them enough time. Barely. Boyd, you got this?" Maggie asked.

"Yep. Go."

Maggie set down the baggie and handed Boyd her gloves. "Someone needs to head over to King's place, see if our boy Vincent is there."

"I'll let Castillo know," Boyd said, taking out his cell phone.

"Hector, call St. James. I'll try to reach border control."

"On it. What are you going to do then?"

"I guess start driving to Niagara. You coming or staying?"

Hector looked to Boyd for guidance, and the senior officer jerked his head toward Maggie.

"I always wanted to see the Falls in winter," Hector said.

CHAPTER 25

$\mathcal{I}$t was nearly dark when Max parked on the street alongside the factory. The chipped, hundred-year-old bricks were covered in even more graffiti than the last time he'd seen the place. It bordered a park, but a tall chain link fence circled the perimeter.

A couple of kids stopped playing basketball to watch Max as he placed his hands on top of the fence and heaved his weight up until he could get a foot on top and jump over.

God that took too much effort. Maybe it was lack of sleep, but he was really starting to feel old, and also he may have pulled a groin muscle. But he was in, and he hadn't broken his neck. Today that amounted to a win.

He circled the yard, imagining the countless numbers of kids who must have sought shelter there, not to mention those who came to tag the walls, to ride their now abandoned skateboards, to cause general mayhem and who knows what else.

Empty beer cans and broken hockey sticks littered the area, and in the growing darkness, Max tripped over a heavy wool blanket reeking of urine.

Finally he spotted an ungraffitied piece of plywood propped

against the property, and when he shifted it, he found a small window he could squeeze through.

The hair stood up on Max's neck as he imagined whomever was inside, watching him, waiting to see what he would do next. But the boys could be in there, and if they were, he had to find them. It occurred to him that he should tell someone where he was about to go—just in case—and he pulled out his phone. Both Maggie and the rookie had called, but neither left a message.

He dashed off a text to Selina and lowered himself through the old window before he could change his mind. Inside, he was met with a fierce stench, like sewage and mildew and dinosaur sputum. The ground felt simultaneously sticky and slick. Thank goodness for his boots.

Stupidly, he hadn't replaced the old cruiser's flashlight, which he had so cavalierly given to Oliver. He was glad the kid had it, but was now forced to fiddle with the one on his cell phone. Light out and taser closer to hand, Max stepped through the apparently empty room, keeping to the perimeter, straining his eyes and ears for any sign of life, until he tripped over what appeared to be another blanket, except for two bright eyes staring up at him. "Sorry!" he whispered and knelt down toward the child who skittered away into the darkness.

A tidal wave of nausea threatened to engulf him at the idea of Oliver and Henri living in such a place, or any child, any human being, really, here among the rats and grime. And as much as he wanted to find the boys, part of him hoped he wouldn't find them here.

Max almost fell through a hole in the floor but his light found it in the nick of time. A sketchy-looking ladder led down the hole to the basement. The rumble of faint voices and scent of wood smoke drifted up from below.

Phone in his mouth, he descended the ladder into the bowels of the old building.

Aside from pillars to support the floor above and the odd

mattress and lawn chairs, the place was mostly empty. A fire crackled inside a rusty oil drum. The drafty broken windows couldn't possibly provide quite adequate ventilation.

"Somethin' you want?" a voice asked, and a tall boy with brown dreadlocks stepped out of the shadows.

Max dropped the phone to his hand. "Looking for someone."

"You a cop?" the teen asked, scanning him up and down, guessing where his weapons were.

He considered playing dumb, but the teenager looked like he could smell a cop before they entered the room. What he probably wasn't used to was anyone being straight with him.

"Not today. Not in any official capacity. I'm trying to find a couple of kids," he added, holding up his phone to show the old picture of the boys. "Oliver and Henri. Seen them?"

The teen studied Max's phone for a long time before shaking his head. "Nah. They ain't here."

Max sighed, and it felt like his whole body deflated. In a minute there would be nothing left but a sack of skin, like a giant lawn ornament the day after Christmas.

"Ever seen them around anywhere?" he asked. "They're brothers. About eight and eleven? Been on the streets a couple years. Little one has to be careful what he eats."

"Nah man. I ain't seen them two kids. They in some kind of trouble?"

"No. Listen…" Max took a business card from his pocket and offered it to the teen along with fifty cents for a pay phone. "If they do turn up, will you please give them this and ask them to call me?"

"You want them to call you?" the kid asked, surprised, Max supposed, that he wasn't being asked to narc on them instead.

"I'd really appreciate it."

He studied Max's card for a minute before pocketing it. "You wanna flash that picture around? See if any the other guys seen your boys?"

Max nodded gratefully.

"Can I hold your gun?"

"Sorry," Max chuckled, and the kid shrugged and turned in the direction of the flickering firelight.

"I'm Bash, by the way," he said.

He led Max to the center of the seemingly empty room, where the campfire could light him up for all the shadows to see. Then Bash whistled and said in a commanding voice, "This here's my pal James. He wants to show you a picture." He stuck his hand out, and Max surrendered the phone.

One by one the kids began to re-emerge around the fringes of firelight, and for a moment it was like a scene from *Peter Pan*. "Oliver and Henry," Bash said, showing first one kid and then another—dozens of them, the youngest even younger than Henri. "Seen 'em?" Bash asked each one.

One after another they shook their heads 'no' and melted back into the shadows.

"Sorry man," Bash finally said. "Spacey thought she maybe seen them once, but she couldn't remember when. Or where."

"I seen 'em," a girl about thirteen said, looking over Bash's shoulder at the phone as he was handing it back to Max. She wore her hair cut short and offered a crooked-toothed grin. "Little guy calls him 'Ver.'"

Relief flooded through Max. "You saw them tonight?"

The girl sagged, like maybe she'd been hoping for a reward. "Hell. You never said tonight." Then she spit on the ground for emphasis.

"Where you seen 'em at, Chlo?" Bash asked.

"Over near the dollar store. Offered the big one a poke, but he wasn't buying."

"Which dollar store?" Max asked. "When?"

"I thought you wasn't doing that no more, Chlo," Bash scolded.

The girl shrugged at them both. "It was a couple months ago

anyway," she said over her shoulder before disappearing like the rest.

"Sorry, Copper," Bash said.

"Thanks for trying." Max pocketed his phone and handed the teen sixty-two dollars—all the cash he had on him.

"What's that for?"

"Christmas dinner?" Max suggested.

"You ain't gotta."

"I know," Max replied, pressing the bills firmly into his hand and wishing he could do more. "Bash, if you couldn't come here, where else would you go?"

"Dunno. Church?"

"I tried there."

"Every church?"

"You know I don't have that kind of time. Is there another place like this, maybe? I won't tell them you sent me. Please, Bash."

"What are you going to do when you find them?" The teen kicked his worn-out running shoe at a crack in the floor.

"Take them home and give them dinner. Tuck them into a warm bed. File papers to become their guardian."

Bash stared at Max hard, and Max didn't blink.

"There's a shelter on Gerrard. Near the college. They might look the other way when kids come in ain't got folks."

"You mean they don't report you to Children's Aid?"

"Not so long as you mind your business and don't overstay your welcome."

"Thank you, Bash," Max said. "I mean it. Take care of yourself."

Bash walked with him back to the ladder and up to the floor above, trusting Max a little, but not quite enough to turn him loose inside the sanctuary.

"Hey, if you ever get jammed up—remember you have my card, and you call me okay? I'll do what I can."

"Good luck, man. Sure wish someone was looking for me the way you're looking for them two kids."

"Maybe someone is. Merry Christmas, Bash."

The boy shook his hand. And Leah had been right. Max wanted to save them all.

❄

"Come on," Hector moaned at the bumper to bumper traffic on the Queen E.

Maggie pulled up the traffic app on her phone. The highway was a solid red line all the way to Burlington, and the terrible, tinny jazz pouring through her phone speaker was already threatening a migraine. "Do these apps have history? Did they have enough of a head start to beat rush hour and still make the five o'clock news?"

"I think so? They must've right?"

Finally there was a click on the phone line. "Canada Border Services, Niagara Falls," said the same nasally voice who had placed her on hold seventeen minutes ago.

Maggie took the call off speaker and said, "This is still Maggie Kyle from the Toronto PD."

"Oh right. Sorry, Toronto. Nothing I can do for you. Have a nice night."

"Are you serious right now? You can't even look at a picture and tell me if it's the same kids?" Maggie asked.

"No point. No kids here."

"It was on the news."

"But they were Canadians, right? We don't exactly worry about folks leaving, do we now?"

"Even little kids?"

"Listen, Toronto, you get caught on the way in. So if they were caught, it's the Americans that have them, and I would not want to be them."

Maggie couldn't tell if he meant the kids or the American border agents. "Can you put the Americans on the phone then?"

"You're funny. But you know it's separate buildings, right?"

"Do you have their number?"

"Why would I?"

"Doesn't this kind of thing happen all the time?"

"Why would it?"

She hung up on him and roared in frustration, tempted to throw her phone through the windshield. "Border cops are the worst," she growled, and punched UNITED STATES CUSTOMS NIAGARA FALLS into Google.

"Worse than this traffic?"

"The worst!" she said again while she listened to another recording about approximate wait times for crossing the border.

Finally, the recording offered her a touchtone menu, but no matter which option she pressed, she couldn't seem to find anyone to answer her call.

"Speak to an operator!" she tried shouting at the phone, even though it was not voice operated.

"Go figure," Hector teased. "No one working the phones on Christmas Eve."

"Yeah, okay, I get it, Christmas Eve," Maggie said. "But isn't this friggin' Homeland Security? Are they allowed to take a night off?"

Hector shrugged. "I mean, they're Homeland Security, but we're, you know, Canada."

"Did you get through to St. James?"

"No, and his voicemail's full."

Maggie flushed, remembering all the messages she'd left that he apparently hadn't deleted, and flipped on the lights and sirens, but there was nowhere for the other cars to go. She tried Max's number but, like Hector, got no answer and no voicemail.

"What is wrong with you people?" Hector asked the drivers who were not pulling over to let him pass. "Shouldn't you all be home by now?" Then he swerved onto the left shoulder to use it as a passing lane.

"What about you, rook?" Maggie asked.

"What about me?"

"Shouldn't you be home? With your family? Why are you out here with me—after shift—on Christmas Eve?"

"To make it right."

"Hector," Maggie said firmly, "it is not your fault they ran. They were probably always going to run from the moment we reunited them."

"I sure didn't help matters."

"Did you have plans you had to cancel?"

"Not really," Hector said. "My mom's Greek Orthodox, so we're still almost two weeks out from Christmas yet."

"Really?" Maggie asked, suddenly realizing how little she knew about the younger officer.

"Yeah, I mean basically we celebrate the twelfth day of Christmas instead of the first, and until then, we starve ourselves."

"So no baklava tomorrow?"

"Why is that always the first thing people think of?" he joked.

"Because it's delicious. And also, it wasn't, I promise. I definitely thought of lamb, Windex, and wedding cookies first. Big fat Greek wedding cookies."

"Respect."

"Which part?"

Hector honked his horn at a car that was drifting onto the shoulder. "The part where you sound like you've eaten your weight in wedding cookies."

The rookie's phone dinged.

"Was that a text?" Maggie squirmed in her seat, looking around the front console for Hector's phone. "Was it St. James?"

"I don't know," Hector said softly. "I'm driving."

"Where's your phone? I'll check?"

"Probably wasn't him. He's not a big texter. What's the deal with you and him, anyway?"

"What deal?" Maggie asked, turning away to look at the ocean of traffic to her right.

"You guys are like your precinct's dream team—everyone says. Now you're not even talking."

The phone dinged again.

"Come on, hand it over. It could be a lead."

Hector sighed, but he fished his phone out of his pants pocket and glanced at it instead of passing it to her. "It's from Boyd," he said.

"Want me to respond?"

"No."

"Maybe he has a lead?"

"He doesn't. Look, I'm sure St. James is busy running around trying to find them, same as us. Living the dream. Cops gonna cop."

"Why did you become a cop?" she asked. "I mean other than the sexy uniform and sweet hours?"

He glanced at her. "You going to try to talk me out of it? Since I'm obviously doing such amazing work?"

"You're doing fine. Just making conversation."

Hector took a breath. "Death notifications," he said.

"What? Seriously?"

"When I was ten, the police came to tell my auntie that her twenty-two-year-old son had been killed in a car wreck. At the time, they believed he was under the influence of something, but actually, he had a seizure. Their delivery could have been… kinder. And I swore to myself if it were me, I'd do better."

"Wow." It was maybe the most substantive answer Maggie had ever heard.

"Few years later I was at a friend's house when an officer had to notify the family that his dad had an aneurysm at work and didn't make it to the ER. I watched the officer really carefully, and she was so compassionate. Gentle but strong, you know? It didn't change the tragedy, but it helped them keep their dignity. And I thought, what a terrible job, but what a noble service."

"You're really something, Hector," Maggie said. "Have you had to do one yet?"

"No. Not yet."

"Normally I'd say I hope you never do."

"Yeah I know. So what about you? Why'd you want to become the youngest woman to make detective?" he asked.

"I like puzzles," Maggie said, turning on the radio so Hector wouldn't dig any deeper.

CHAPTER 26

Speeding down College toward University, Max had to keep reminding himself he couldn't storm the shelter as though it were the Bastille. It was such an obvious place that he was kicking himself for not checking there first. Probably the closest shelter to the coach terminal, the boys must have known about it. They'd have walked right past it every day. But they kept on walking, choosing instead to sleep in a church.

He passed the Lillian H. Smith Library—would Oliver and Henri have had time to sneak inside before closing? Hiding away in some reading nook to spend the night under the watchful eye of the great stone griffins? And if he didn't find them at the shelter, were there any favors left in the universe that he could call in, to get inside that library after hours on Christmas Eve?

His phone rang, and Max nearly dropped it in his eagerness to see if it was his partner.

It wasn't.

"Selina?" he answered. "Are you at my place? Are the kids there?"

"No, I'm at the gingerbread house—"

"I don't have time for this right now. Please go home, and only call me back if you see the boys," he begged before hanging up on her protests and shoving the phone back in his pocket.

While he was with Bash the rookie had texted **OTW 2 NF**, which Max assumed meant they thought the kids had gotten a bus traveling to Ottawa and then on to Newfoundland. Even though he couldn't fathom a reason for them to go there, it took every ounce of self control not to drive straight to the capital. If they weren't at the shelter, he'd break speed limits driving east.

Hey St. Jude Mission was a nondescript brick building that from the outside might as easily have been an office space or dispensary.

Max's phone began to vibrate again just as he arrived, but it still wasn't Maggie.

"Selina, unless you're calling to tell me Oliver and Henri are sitting at my kitchen table, then I'm sorry, but I've got to go."

"I told you, I'm at the gingerbread house," she whispered. "Did you see my text?"

"No. Why are you still there?"

"Something's not right."

"I cannot fixate on this with you. It'll be gone in a couple of days."

"A couple of days will be too late. Something's going on right now."

"Selina, I'm hanging up," Max said, digging his fingernails into his palm to keep from screaming.

"I saw a light flickering," she whispered.

"What were you doing, watching it with binoculars? It was probably someone having a smoke."

"It definitely wasn't. Too rhythmic. So I ran down here, and there was music."

"Music at a gingerbread house on Christmas Eve? That's unheard of."

"It wasn't Christmas music, Maxxy. Look at my text," she whispered a little louder.

So Max opened his messages. She had sent him a video that took forever to load, but when it finally stopped buffering, it showed a first person view as Selina crept up to the strange little house, where a light seemed to flash off and on through a crack between the wall and the floor.

"Blink-blink-blink-blink… blink… blink," video-Selina whispered as she crept closer still. "That's Morse code isn't it?"

Oliver was right. Apparently everyone did know SOS.

Finally the video got close enough to the house for Max to hear music—it was Jason Isbell, a song from one of his other albums, and the beat kind of matched the flashlight SOS.

"I'm on my way," Max said, "Don't do anything."

He tucked his head down to keep the wind out of his dry, exhausted eyes as he hustled back to the car and nearly walked right into a man carrying a large box.

"Sorry, sorry, sorry," he said, and they did an awkward sort of dance to steady the box before Max continued on without ever really looking up.

"Max?" the man called after him.

He stopped to look back—and found himself looking into the wrinkled face of his father. He seemed somehow smaller than Max remembered.

"You okay, son?" his father asked.

Seeing him there, so unexpectedly and so ravaged by the last several years, evoked a visceral memory of being nestled together on Max's twin bed reading *The Incredible Journey*. Max was overwhelmed with the urge to hug his father and ask for help.

"What are you doing here?" he asked instead, completely unmoored. "Are you staying at the shelter?"

"What? No. We had a few late donations for the food drive, so here I am. Do you… want to go get some dinner?" his father asked with the hesitance and eagerness of a kid at a middle school dance.

"I can't, I'm sorry. I've got to go," Max said, walking slowly backwards.

"It's just," his father said, shifting the heavy box to get a better grip, and Max's instinct was to help share the weight of it, but there wasn't time. "I know we never really talked the way you and your mom did, or even your grandad, but I—I do—I mean, I always…"

"I know," Max said, shrugging. "You told me you loved me when you thought I was asleep. They told me when they knew I was awake."

His father's frown deepened, and Max felt like shit. He hadn't meant it that way. Why did everything always come out wrong?

"I'm sorry, Dad, truly, but I'm on a case, and I really gotta go."

Then he left his father standing there, holding the heavy box of canned goods, and hurried back to his vehicle so he could race to the ridiculous gingerbread house with lights but no siren.

We never really talked, his father had said, and it was true. They were never on the same page with words. They always had to fight to find ways to connect, like the time he brought Max his first *Wolverine* comic. Max was probably ten or twelve, grounded for two weeks and suspended for fighting with some kids who called him chief, and a smoke signal savage and feather-headed bow-bender, and more that he wouldn't repeat in front of his mother. Even though he was grounded, his father had snuck into his room and handed over the comic about the tough-as-nails antihero.

After that, Max would hold back a little when the bullies came at him, pretending he *was* Wolverine and if he let himself go the claws would come out and he'd kill them all by accident.

"Look at the sky," his father had advised him, sitting on the edge of his bed awkwardly patting Max's shoulder. "If you think you're going to cry, look up and count to twenty—fifty—a hundred if you have to. But don't let them see you cry."

At the time, Max had believed his tears would bring shame on the house of St. James. But the only alternative to tears was anger, and he had swallowed that, too, until he became the emotionally constipated specimen who had yelled at Maggie tonight instead of telling her he loved her.

It had always been a perplexing moment for Max, such tender understanding followed by the callous warning, as though his father's own mortification should Max be caught weeping on the playground would be the end of everything.

"TWELVE DAYS OF CHRISTMAS" CAME ON THE RADIO SO MAGGIE scanned to another station, which was playing a pop rendition of "I Ain't Gettin' Nothin' for Christmas" that was, impossibly, more horrible than the original. She scanned again, only to find Bing Crosby plaintively crooning "I'll Be Home for Christmas." Too depressing. The next station played Gayla Peevey's campy "I Want a Hippopotamus for Christmas," but it reminded her too much of Henri and their impromptu snowball fight, and her throat started to constrict. She scanned to Elvis's "Blue Christmas," but honestly, sometimes that one was also too depressing, and if you're not in the mood for the King, then you don't deserve music, so she turned the radio off completely.

"Whatever happens with this case, you're pretty badass, you know," Hector said, regarding her a little longer than she was comfortable with considering he was driving.

"Whatever."

"You are! Teach me your ways."

"You don't want to be like me." Maggie motioned for him to turn around and watch the road.

He complied, but said, "I could do worse."

"Look at you. So full of potential." Maggie fiddled with her cell phone, willing it to ring. It didn't ring.

Hector's dinged though, and again he checked it and dropped it back in his pocket. "Still not him."

They were silent for a minute until Hector finally asked the question Maggie knew he wanted to ask. "So how come you aren't a detective?"

She checked that the volume was up and set her phone down in the cup holder, then folded her hands to stop fidgeting.

"Test anxiety doesn't disappear with your last college final. Besides, riding with St. James—it was fun. He's a bit of a mystery, even if he doesn't want to be solved."

Hector laughed. "What are the rules about that, anyway?"

"What, how many times you can sign up for the exam and then not show up to take it?"

"No, I mean, dating someone at your precinct? There's got to be rules, right?"

"Yeah there are rules. I think you have to fill out a form. You can't ride together or report to each other."

"But what about you and St. James?"

"Oh my god, we're not... we never... that really is what everyone thinks?" Maggie asked, horrified.

"Well yeah."

She groaned and buried her face in her hands.

"So that's a no? 'Cause I would get it if you had a thing for him, he's totally awesome."

"Why the sudden interest in rules?" Maggie demanded.

That shut him up. Or at least made him think carefully about his next words.

"Our division isn't getting any new rookies next year," he said.

"So?"

"So unless I've bungled this case so badly they decide to get rid of me, I'll get cut loose. No new rookies for the TOs means Boyd will need a new partner, you know, long-term."

It took Maggie a minute to connect the dots. And then it hit her—the questions, the texts, the wink back at the bus station.

The rookie had a thing for his TO, just like she had, and maybe it wasn't completely unrequited. "Oh," she said. "Oh!"

Hector checked his mirror and changed lanes to pass a slow-poke, but Maggie could tell he was really avoiding her eye.

Finally her phone began to ring in the cupholder, rattling some spare change.

"St. James?" Hector asked.

Maggie took a breath and answered, "Tell me you have them."

"I need backup. What's your 20? How soon can you get to that gingerbread house near my apartment?"

"What, the monstrosity *Selina* keeps going on about?"

"Yes. How soon?" He sounded out of breath.

She punched it into the GPS. "Thirty-five, maybe forty minutes. Traffic's terrible."

"I could make it back in twenty," Hector said, pulling an immediate U-turn to drive the wrong way down the shoulder until they could cut through the barrier that divided the highway.

"Did you guys really go to Ottawa? The kids are here. I need backup."

His tone was strained and unnerving. "Ottawa? If you need someone now, then call it in. We're on our way."

Max hung up, and Maggie tossed the phone down and rubbed her face. Ottawa? "You want my advice, Hector? If you think there may be a *there* there, then get as far away as possible."

He glanced at her with a frown that said she was crazy.

"I'm serious. Transfer divisions, come to Fifty-One if you have to, but don't ride with him."

"Why not?"

"I told you. You don't want to end up like me."

CHAPTER 27

$\mathcal{T}$hirty or forty minutes? What was he supposed to do for that long? He could call Dix or Boyd for backup, but he didn't want Dix or Boyd, he wanted Maggie. At least he could scope out the situation, make sure it wasn't another crazy Selina scheme and his own imagination running wild.

He parked a block away so as not to arouse suspicion. Then he crept along the side of the gingerbread house, listening. There was shuffling inside, as music from the alternative station drifted through the walls, along with the rumble of deep voices engaged in an animated discussion.

Suddenly aware of a presence next to him, Max reached for his gun.

"There's at least two of them in there," Selina breathed in his ear. "Men."

Max dragged his neighbor a few meters across the empty parking lot and into a dumpster-lined alley.

"I could have shot you," he said.

She yanked out of his grip. "You could have broken my arm."

"Never ever sneak up on a policeman like that."

"My bow arm," she added, incensed. "Never ever grab a cellist like that."

"What are you still doing here? I told you to go home."

"Reconnaissance," she whispered, as maddening as ever.

"That is a very dangerous and stupid thing for you to do. Go home."

"Are you calling me stupid? Where's your backup?"

"They'll be here. Home, Selina."

"I can't believe you. Where's your girlfriend?"

"My partner is on her way."

"You two have a fight or something?"

"Selina…" She was always too perceptive for his own good.

"Fine. But you tell her this is my collar. I've been warning you about this brick heap for days."

"Not even close. You've been watching too much *Law and Order*," Max whispered, pointing down the alley in the direction he wanted her to go, and watching until she was completely out of sight.

Even if she was right, if two men were inside with the boys, it wasn't necessarily nefarious. He needed to get closer, to listen at the back door that stood ajar.

Maggie and the rookie were still at least ten minutes out by Max's watch, so he texted Boyd to standby just in case. If the kids were actually in danger then he was losing precious time, and if they weren't, then backup was unnecessary and he was kneeling in the cold for no reason.

But if the window looking out on the parking lot and alley was a real one, he needed to be very careful about how he approached without leaving more tracks in the fresh snow.

He was calculating the best path when the back door opened and a figure stepped out, backlit, but slightly illuminated by the bright candy decorations of the house. The guy wasn't very big. Max could easily take him, especially if he wasn't well armed and Max caught him by surprise.

The shadowy figure took a few quick puffs of a cigarette before flicking it to the ground, and when he turned to go back inside, Max glimpsed his face. It was the weaselly kid from the bus station, the one Maggie liked for the IED: Vincent Reyes.

HECTOR MADE GOOD TIME. THEY HIT TORONTO IN FIFTEEN, AND Maggie didn't kill the siren until they were a few blocks away.

"So how do we get to Santa's Village?" he asked. "Wait isn't that his car?"

It was the same rundown Chevy he'd taken to Pickle Lake parallel parked in front of a less rundown apartment complex. "Pull in behind him."

"It's kind of a small spot. Maybe I should—"

"Park, Hector."

So he tried to, but he pulled up not quite far enough and then turned the wheel not quite sharp enough and had to pull back out and try again. When he pulled out for a third attempt, Maggie grabbed the wheel.

"Stop," she said.

He gave a sheepish look and she tried to soften her tone as she unbuckled her seatbelt.

"It's easier without an audience. I'm going on ahead. Just park. Doesn't have to be here."

"Don't tell Boyd," he pleaded.

"He should let you drive more. One block that way when you're done. Can't miss it."

She grabbed her vest from the trunk and continued on foot, not looking back to see how Hector was coming with the parallel parking.

The place was lit up with all kinds of Christmas lights and flood lights and projector lights that made the candy decorations sparkle. It was an eyesore, a little off-putting for its garishness, but it was the urgency in Max's plea for backup which most unnerved Maggie.

When she reached a shadowy section of sidewalk, someone stepped out from behind a large bush, blocking her path, and Maggie had her gun out before she recognized the shadowy figure as Selina.

"Sure hope you brought the cavalry," the woman said.

"What are you doing here?" Maggie whispered, shoving her gun back in its holster.

"Wait, are you seriously it? Trust a man to foul it up."

"I swear, Selina, if this is some ruse to get us to investigate your spooky haunted house, I will arrest you myself."

"The gingerbread house is the center of everything. You guys should have listened to me days ago."

"Get out of here." Maggie brushed past her rather than waste more time arguing.

"Like I told Maxxy—this is my collar," the woman whispered after her.

The house was situated on a corner, and Maggie darted across the shadowy side of the street to get a better look: one door—closed—and two windows—frosted—on the front; one more window—frosted—on the side facing the cross-street; a small, empty lot bordered the other side large enough for one or two cars or maybe one larger truck to park. No sign of Max.

The whole thing was probably about four meters squared. If Max was inside, anyone else in there must surely already know it.

Drawing her weapon once more, and staying low to the ground, Maggie skulked further down the street so she could cross again in the shadows. She would hug the alley created by a dry cleaners and a dumpster, and hopefully come out the other side with an unobstructed view of the back, without being seen herself.

Her pulse beat loudly inside her ears, as though she'd been

running, but she strained to hear through the quiet night, to step silently and aware. There was another shadowy figure ahead of her in the darkness, kneeling behind the dumpster. It could be an indigent, a criminal, a drunk. But from the profile—the hatless hair spiked up a little in the front, the chiseled jaw and sloping shoulders, the little movements as he adjusted his weight on his knees—she knew it was Max.

Almost as though he felt her watching him, he turned. Their eyes met, and her stomach flip-flopped when she registered his own clear relief at seeing her. His posture relaxed a little and his mouth crooked up on the left side. Regardless of their cruel words slung carelessly in anger, they were still partners. He was glad she was there, and she wanted nothing more than to go to him. Then he snapped back to business, returned his gaze to the house, and motioned for her to stay low. Maggie knelt down beside him and immediately regretted it as the cold, wet snow seeped through her jeans.

They watched the house in silence for a few minutes, but nothing was happening. At one point she thought she might have seen a shadow flicker across the window, but surely it was only her eyes playing tricks on her patience.

"St. James," she whispered.

He raised a finger—she thought to shush her—but then he pointed at the house, where Hector had just slipped around from the front. Silently and efficiently, Max leapt from his hiding place, put a hand over Hector's mouth, and pulled him behind the dumpster.

"You could have texted me!" Hector whispered.

"Where's the fun in that?" Max asked.

"This place is creepy," Hector said. "Are they in there? The kids?"

"They are."

"You saw them?" Maggie asked.

"No. Selina sent me a video of an SOS from Oliver."

"Are you kidding me right now?" Maggie shook her head. *"Selina?"*

Max gazed at her in the faint glow of the obnoxiously cheerful gingerbread house. "It's them," he said, closing his mouth and then opening and closing it again like he wanted to say more.

She stood up. "So let's go get them."

Max yanked her back down out of sight. "They're not alone. Did you hear the part about the SOS? There's at least two guys in there, but I've only put eyes on one. "

"And?" Maggie's wrist still tingled from where he grabbed her, even though he was wearing soft, warm gloves. She shook her head to clear it, trying not to focus on the dread building up inside her.

"Can we go back to the part where the kooky lady sent you a video?" Hector asked.

"She's not kooky."

"She's pretty damn eccentric," Maggie replied.

"Trust me, it's them. Can you do that, please? For once, just trust me."

"I always trust you."

Max snorted. "Always—?"

"Could we maybe not do this right now?" Hector asked. "I trust you, okay? Who's inside?"

"Reyes."

He gave the dread inside Maggie a name, and her stomach sank like she was on a roller coaster. If Max was right then Reyes had, what? Followed the boys when they left the police station, lured them or snatched them and brought them here?

"If it is Reyes," she began.

"It is," Max assured her.

"Then it's gotta be King too, right?"

"Bobby King?"

"They're brothers," Hector explained.

"Okay," Max conceded. "But why this place? What's the connection?"

"He has connections all over the city," Hector reminded Maggie. "Why not this place?"

"He's right." Maggie tried to picture the list Hector had made earlier in the day before everything went sideways. "Some kind of auto salvage…"

"King Kong Kash," Hector said.

"Junk Junk Junk."

"Bro likes alliteration." Hector shook his head.

"Junk Junk Junk," Maggie repeated. "That's it. It's a demo and removal service. Ten to one it's scheduled to haul this place off the day after Boxing Day. What better place to hide the guns?"

"That's a lot of conjecture," Max said.

"Everything's here. I know it." Maggie whipped out her phone and texted Boyd to bring ETF. "The guns, the ammo. It's all here, it has to be. That's why we didn't find it at his house." She looked up to see Max staring at her in admiration, and it made her feel flustered. She didn't need to be flustered right now, so she moved away from him.

"But here?" Hector asked. "This place is a shoebox."

"And the public has access all day long," Max whispered.

Both valid concerns, but Maggie was certain she was right. She slipped out from behind the dumpster and crouch-walked to the back of the gingerbread house.

There was a door marked "Do Not Enter," presumably for Santa and his elves to go in and out on smoke breaks without ruining the illusion. It was cracked open to accommodate an extension cord which ran to a humming generator that supplied the outside frosting with its icicle twinkle. "Last Christmas" was playing and Maggie couldn't help rolling her eyes at the universe.

"You shouldn't have brought them here, Vinny. They're just a couple of dumb kids. Now we're going to have to get rid of them." She had only spoken briefly with King, but it sounded like him.

"They're brats. I want to get rid of them."

"You don't know what you're talking about. It's messy, Vinny."

"I'll take care of it."

"It's messy, you understand? I don't like messy."

Maggie reached out to coax the door open a tiny bit wider, but Max grabbed her wrist, startling her.

He shook his head once.

She pinched her fingers together to show him she only meant to open it a smidge.

He shook his head again and held up a closed fist that turned quickly into what some would consider an *okay* signal, but the gesture was actually their own shorthand to wait—the ASL gestures for the letters E-T-F.

She tapped her watch in frustration. They were running out of time. Then she made a circle in the air with her index finger. Unless they looked around, they would have no way to get their bearings on the inside.

Max frowned and rolled his eyes, but inclined his head in acquiescence as the men's argument escalated.

"I said I'll take care of it," Vincent yelled.

"Like you took care of the diversion at the bus station?"

"It got the cops off your back, didn't it?"

"Maybe next time a diversion that doesn't put them on yours."

Using her pen, Maggie coaxed the door open about a centimeter more. Then she slid down onto her belly and peeked through the crack. Her entire view was blocked by a mountain of wrapped packages. She rolled over and sat back against the building.

Max raised his eyebrows in question, and she shook her head, so he slid down beside her to take a peek himself. When he looked back at her, it was like he read her mind. The gift wrap.

That's how they hid the weapons and ammunition in plain sight. It was kind of ingenious.

"What's the plan?" Hector whispered. "There's three of us and only two of them."

As though they were one person, Maggie and Max snapped a finger to their lips, and then they all slipped back to the dumpsters.

"What?" Hector asked. "We can take those guys."

"There's only two that we know of," Maggie explained.

"And there are two hostages," Max reminded them. "Little kids."

"So we wait for backup?" Hector asked.

Maggie and Max looked at each other. He was the rule-breaker, the one who never waited for backup, and for once she agreed. But she could see in his eyes that he was torn. Something about the last few days had tempered him, made him more care-ful. What an inconvenient time for him to trade in his impulsive Chucks for cautious leather boots.

"What if we got that kooky lady out of the bushes and had her create a diversion? She could knock on the door or something?"

"Did you rent your uniform from a costume shop?" Max asked.

"They gave it to me for free, for thinking outside the box," Hector sassed.

"It wasn't the worst idea," Maggie said.

"We wait for ETF."

It aggravated Maggie that he was making an executive deci-sion for all of them. "They're talking about getting rid of the boys. I don't think we have that kind of time, do you? Hector brings the car, tells her she can't loiter or something, and they have a fight—a nice loud one. Hear me out," she said, raising a finger to shush Max before he could object again. "They're across the street, totally safe. We can give her a vest, they'll have the car for cover. Just loud enough and long enough for you and me to slip in behind that pile of Christmas presents.

"I don't like it," Max said.

"I think it's brilliant," Hector marveled at her.

"Backup will be here any minute," Max argued.

"Perfect. Then they'll have our backs, but I'm not waiting. Are you with me or not?" Even as she asked it, Maggie knew he'd say yes. He would always say yes.

CHAPTER 28

When Max had first turned to see Maggie sneaking up to his hiding place behind the dumpster, for a moment the whole world felt right again. If the kids hadn't been in danger, if it were just them and the bad guys, he'd have held on tight, drinking her in. But they had a job to do. Everything else would have to wait.

Now he remained outside the shed door while Maggie and her adopted rookie went to find Selina. The world was spinning off its axis worse than ever, and nothing about any of this was right. This brash, impatient desperado wasn't Maggie Kyle. His partner had never charged in half-cocked trying to save the world, not once in ten years. That was his shtick. And this time even he could see there was too much at stake.

He shot off an anxious text to Dix and another to Boyd. Where the hell was ETF?

Inside the gingerbread house, Reyes and King's argument grew louder, and Henri began to cry.

"You better shut him up," Reyes growled, kicking something— the wall, by the way it reverberated back to Max—immediately the crying was stifled as Oliver softly shushed his baby brother.

"Your girlfriend's in," Maggie whispered, popping back up right behind Max and breathing into his ear. "You ready?"

"Ready to call it off," Max whispered back. "She's a civilian—untrained—unpredictable. We need to wait for ETF."

Maggie's lips were set in a flat, determined line, but her eyes were wavering. His conviction was shaking hers.

Then a shriek in the street startled everyone into silence, even the arguing brothers, and Max and Maggie scrambled around the corner of the building in case one of the perps burst outside for a better look.

"Ma'am, I need you to calm down," the rookie yelled.

"Calm down? Don't you tell me to calm down and don't you come any closer, either! You hear me, pig? Swine! Hog! Boar! Boor! Don't touch me," she screamed.

Selina always had been dramatic.

"Ma'am, I'm going to need you to go back inside your house," the rookie shouted at her. "Put the tree branch down."

Max scuttled back to the door and peered through the gap. The diversion appeared to be working, both Reyes and King stood at the window squinting out at the street.

He held up three fingers at Maggie, and she nodded one curt nod, then scrunched down, poised to leap inside. But Max gestured for her to take the lead. It was her case after all.

She grinned at him and held up her own three fingers, then two, then one.

Max threw the door open wide, tensing his shoulders in anticipation of an almighty creak, but nothing came and Maggie ducked inside and out of sight behind the gift box mountain. As she brushed past him, Max noticed her figure in the soft black sweater and he realized with a wave of dizzy nausea that she'd taken off her vest.

He tried to catch her wrist and then her eye, to wave her back out and call off the op while Selina and the rookie were still going at it, but she actively ignored him, the choice made, and he knew it was too late. Like so many things, the only way out now was through.

"Somebody help me!" Selina hollered. "Tell him to keep his filthy pig hooves off me!"

"Keep your voice down, ma'am. This is a residential area."

"I don't care if it's a damn cathedral in the dark before the dawn, I have every right to stand out here in this yard if I want to!"

Reyes and King were still glued to the window, and so Max slipped in and slowly eased the door shut before taking up a post opposite Maggie. From this vantage point he could see Oliver and Henri in the corner, Oliver's left arm around his little brother's shoulders, the other hand clamped tight over Henri's mouth. They stared at him in disbelief and he put a finger to his lips.

He wanted to take off his vest and force Maggie into it, but they hadn't yet invented silent velcro, so he'd have to settle for a wish and a prayer. He looked at her, and she looked at him, and then she held up three fingers once more and wiped her face on the shoulder of her sweater.

Two fingers. He crouched low for leverage.

One finger.

Sirens blared in the distance, breaking the men from their trance, almost as though it alerted them to the intruders behind them.

Max and Maggie both jumped out. "Police! Hands in the air," they shouted in unison.

From two sides of the tiny room, they trained their guns on the criminal brothers, Maggie at Reyes and Max at King. Reyes pointed back—first at Max, then at Maggie, then back at Max again—frantic and frazzled, baby's first crime.

Max needed to make his way in front of the boys, but he was on the wrong side. Maggie was closer if she could navigate around the gift boxes that had her pinned in but at least protected.

"Merry Christmas," she said. "Drop your weapons."

Calmly, smugly, Bobby King turned his own gun away from Max, pointing it instead right at Oliver's curly brown head.

Oliver's eyes widened and then shut tight, and he squeezed Henri closer.

"No," Max blurted out, then grimaced. King knew he had the upper hand.

"Perhaps you should drop your weapons, officers."

"Can't do that," Maggie said.

"What a shame," King replied, releasing the safety on his weapon.

"Game's over, King. Don't add killing innocent kids to the rap. Let them go, nice and slow," Max said, as the distant sirens grew closer with the pace of a backward snail.

"Now, now, officer," King said. "My brother may be naive, but see, I'm trying to teach him. Lesson one: a hostage is worth its weight in heroin. Double, when it's a kid."

"What do you want?" Max asked, trying to keep him talking while Maggie inched around the other side of the gift pile.

"Stop," King said, motioning her back to her corner with his pistol.

"You want safe passage?" Max asked. "You want a plane? We could probably get you a plane."

"You?" he scoffed. "You're nothing but a lemming with a badge. You couldn't get me a bicycle."

"So what's the plan?" Maggie asked. "You going to hide out here until it melts in the summer sun?"

"It's not real gingerbread," Reyes snarked.

"Yes, I know, thank you," Maggie replied. "But you can't stay here forever. It's going to be hauled away in what, two days?"

"What's going to happen is this: you're going to surrender your weapons to me," King said. "And then you're going to call off your friends out there and tell them it was all a false alarm.

We'll go about our business, and if you play nice, no harm, no foul."

"And when we're done, we'll burn this shit-hole to the ground. And not with fireworks this time," Reyes added.

"I have a better idea," the rookie said, bursting through the door holding the C7 Rifle from the back of his squad. "Freeze mother truckers, you're outnumbered now."

His explosive entrance startled Reyes, and then everything happened very fast.

Reyes fired at the rookie.

The rookie jumped behind the packages with Maggie.

Boxes began to avalanche toward King and the kids.

King fired at the rookie.

Bullets seemed to ricochet everywhere at once. The building must have a metal frame. Maybe under all the papier-mâché the walls were actually corrugated aluminum too.

Maggie dove toward the kids, using the falling packages for cover.

King yanked a second pistol from his boot.

Max itched to shoot him, but the kids and Maggie were too close.

King fired another shot at the rookie with his right hand and at Maggie with his left.

Max lunged at King, reaching for his taser.

There was a sick thud.

Maggie slammed to the ground and skidded into the wall.

Max fired his taser at King, full force and close range. The big guy fell to his knees, dropping both guns before landing on his face. Max kicked the guns to the rookie, all the while keeping his own pointed at King. The rookie whacked a distracted Reyes in the back of the head with the butt of his rifle.

"Kyle? You okay?" Max asked, afraid to take his eyes off King, even for a second. Afraid of what he would find.

"Yep," she gasped.

"You hit?" he asked, sneaking a look at her, but he already knew.

"Yep," she gasped again.

Her face was white and there was blood spatter smeared on the gingerbread wall behind her.

THE IMPACT STUNNED MAGGIE, KNOCKING HER BACKWARDS INTO the wall, and she was a little surprised it held, surprised she didn't just crash right through it into the snow. It wasn't the first time she'd been shot in the vest, but like every time, the force and the pain were shocking. Gasping for breath, she tried to assess the damage, but the only thing she was certain of was that her left shoulder and upper torso were on fire. The bruise was going to be massive.

She slumped against the wall, watching Max and Hector wrangle Reyes and King until her vision grew dark and splotchy, and everything sounded like it was under water. If she didn't catch her breath she might faint.

She tried to stretch her arm to shake out the numbness, but the movement caused a searing pain and a wave of hot nausea to shoot through her.

How ridiculously humiliating if she fainted in front of the kids, the perps, the rookie, and worst of all, Max.

God she was hot.

Had she worn a tank top under her sweater? Could she take it off?

Or at least the vest? It wasn't the sweater, it was the vest making her swelter. So many layers.

She reached for the velcro, but she couldn't find it. It had been right there a minute ago—when she pulled off her vest to give it to Selina. There wasn't a spare one in the car.

But that meant she wasn't hit in the vest. She was just—hit.

Maggie vomited down her front and surrendered to the black that surrounded her.

WHEN SHE CAME TO, SHE WAS FLAT ON HER BACK AND MAX WAS hovering above her. Kissing her? Was this some kind of fever dream? Had a dream ever hurt this badly? His lips would feel cool against her clammy skin.

"What are you doing?" she tried to ask, but the words wouldn't come and she didn't even care. Maybe she was going to die, but not without letting him know how she felt.

So she kissed him back.

But his lips felt wrong and then he pulled away and jumped back, peering into her face with concern. He hadn't been kissing her at all. He was checking to see if she needed CPR.

God how embarrassing. And with throw up breath, too.

"You're back," he whispered like he was witnessing a miracle. He studied her whole face with a concerned frown and brushed the matted hair from her forehead. "I think the bullet went through and through."

"Is that good?" Henri whispered, squeezing her right hand, and Max nodded and gently touched her hair again before using his hand to put pressure on her shoulder in an effort to staunch the bleeding.

"Where is she? Is she okay?" Dixon called before his rosy-cheeked face swam into view, Frankie and Boyd on either side of him. "You're going to be fine, Kyle, you hear me?"

She tried to answer, "Yes, sir," but her throat was still too dry for actual words.

"Of course you are, you're going to be fine, because you are fierce and you are mighty. And why the hell would you let her come in here without a vest?" he demanded of Max.

"Obviously I didn't realize—"

"She doesn't need a man telling her what to do," Frankie interjected. "She's a grown-ass woman, and she makes her own decisions, stupid or otherwise."

A siren wailed in the distance and Maggie felt like throwing up again.

"Reyes and King?" she gasped.

"Back of my squad," Frankie said. "You think these guys would let them get away? Your partners let you lie there and bleed until they got those two secured."

"We brought down Bobby effing King," Hector said, kneeling down on her other side, next to Henri.

"Good work, rook," Maggie whispered, because whispering was easier.

Suddenly everyone was being ushered away from her to make room for the paramedics, but she didn't want them to go. Max only stood, reluctantly, when a medic knelt beside him to take over the pressure on her wound.

"Come on," someone said, and there was a tug on her good arm.

"No," Henri cried, as they tried to take him away. "No, no! I have to hold her hand so she won't be scared."

Maggie rolled her head over to look at his red, teary face. "It's okay," she lied. "I'm not scared."

"I am," he whimpered, and another tear rolled down his cheek.

"Come on, kiddo," Max said, picking Henri up, and Maggie wished he could pick her up like that and make everything okay.

"What's your name?" a gentle paramedic asked, taking her pulse and examining her wound.

"Maggie," she whispered.

"I think I've seen you around, Maggie. I'm Aster. If it's all right with you, we're going to get you over to St. Mike's, okay?"

"Thank you."

"On the count of three, we're going to slide this board under you," Aster the paramedic said, but everything was happening so quickly that Maggie was shifted onto the spinal board before she was ready.

"I think my back is fine," she gasped as her shoulder blades immediately dug into the unforgiving plastic and began to ache, almost badly enough to make her forget she was shot.

"Probably so," Aster replied before counting off a lift to place her onto their gurney and wheel her out to the ambulance.

They paused outside and it was so cold all around her, yet she was still burning up, like sitting outside in a hot tub on a freezing day. Voices and commotion and flashing lights overwhelmed her and made it hard to breathe. If her mom were here she would be yelling to get Maggie a blanket and for everyone to shut up.

Finally she was lifted up and into the ambulance, and Max climbed in beside her.

"10-24," he said softly, the police code for job done. He stared at her like he wanted to say more, and Maggie wanted to say a hundred different things at once, half of them beginning with "I'm sorry," but she was still having trouble forming words.

"You riding with us?" Aster asked.

"Yes," Max said, but then immediately frowned and shook his head. "Sorry, no." To Maggie he added, "The boys. You're tougher than one lousy bullet, you hear me?"

"10-4," Maggie acknowledged, hoping her disappointment wouldn't be too obvious.

Max smiled. "I'll be right behind you, Magpie. Promise."

He opened and closed his mouth like he wanted to tell her not to die en route, and she whispered back, "Promise."

Then he was gone, and Aster slammed the doors behind him. "Well he's handsome as hell," she said, taking Maggie's arm to check her pulse and blood pressure again.

He's my partner, Maggie would have said proudly, if she had the strength.

Tears pricked her eyes when the paramedic put an IV in her arm, and she felt so stupid because it was only a needle, and she'd been shot for heaven's sake. But she was *shot*, and every part of her ached, the spinal board most of all, so bad she didn't want to inhale and crying was about all she could do.

I'll cry if I want to, popped into her head, and she thought she was chuckling but it came out as a sob.

Again she imagined Max holding her, smoothing her sweaty hair off her forehead—how safe she would feel—and it made her angry to want him there. Because Frankie was right—she didn't need a man to tell her what to do, and she didn't want to need one to make her feel safe. But she did want Max around. Just to be there because everything was better when he was, and god, why had she spent so much time pushing him away?

Aster squeezed her hand.

"Sorry," Maggie whispered, wanting to wipe her face but unable to because of the IV tubes. "So stupid," she added.

"You'd be surprised how many tears have been shed inside my ambulance. But everything's going to be okay."

"Everything?"

"No doubt. I have a policy against losing patients on Christmas."

CHAPTER 29

There was no question that Max would leave the scene to follow the ambulance. ETF had arrived only minutes before Guns and Gangs, and together they took over processing the gingerbread house, leaving Dix to oversee Boyd and the rookie, joking that he had to make sure Fifty-One Division got credit for the bust.

Oliver wouldn't look at Max as he climbed silently into the back of the undercover and helped a sniffling Henri with his seatbelt. There were so many things Max wanted to say to the kid, but he didn't yet trust himself to say anything right, so he held his own peace.

"Is he allowed to drive this fast?" Henri asked as they sped down Queen Street in the wake of the ambulance.

"He's the frickin' police," Oliver whispered back.

Henri was quiet for a minute, nothing but sirens and sniffling to ring in Max's ears. "What if she dies?" he finally whispered.

"Shut up," Oliver told him, and Max glanced in the rearview to see the kid's face set like stone, staring out the window, but he was still holding his brother's hand.

"But what if she does, and it's all our fault?"

"Then she does. But it'll be my fault, not yours."

It sort of killed Max, but he still didn't know what to say. He felt the weight of the same guilt Oliver did, heavy on his own shoulders.

He pulled up to the ER right behind the ambulance and jumped out, eager for a glimpse of his partner.

"You can't park here," a security guard said.

Max flashed his badge and kept going.

"You still can't park here," the guard called after him.

"It's okay. He's the frickin' police," Henri yelled over his shoulder as he and Oliver trotted along behind Max.

The hospital staff were waiting, and Maggie's gurney never stopped moving as it was surrounded by doctors and nurses.

"Female, thirty-three, GSW right scapula," a paramedic reported to the receiving nurse. "BP is eighty over sixty and falling, heart rate one-twenty."

An orderly stepped in front of Max, blocking his path as they wheeled Maggie through the double doors leading to surgery. "They'll let you know, as soon as there's something to tell."

Henri dodged around the orderly, running toward the closing doors, but Max snatched him up and held him tight, glad to have a job to do. "Sorry, bud," he said. "We have to wait out here."

They turned back to the dismal waiting area as Castillo and Selina hurried in.

"Have they taken her back? How'd she look? Did she say anything?" Castillo asked, and Max shook his head because the thought of her pale, sweaty face and closed eyes threatened to choke him.

Castillo flopped down into a chair, and Max set Henri down to join her.

"What a mess, eh?" she whispered, leaning her head against Max's shoulder, her fingers worrying the hem of her blouse.

"I'm sorry we dragged you away from your family," Max said.

"It's fine. The smell of pork belly and flan…" she grimaced. "I was desperate for a break."

Oliver curled up in the corner by himself, and Henri wiggled into the seat with him, leaving an empty chair for Selina next to Max.

"I almost forgot." Castillo took a small gift-wrapped package from her purse. "I snagged your white elephant gift from the party."

Max stared at it, wrapped with perfectly crips edges in Maggie's Astro Santa paper. "I didn't bring anything," he said.

"It's okay. Mags didn't take anything."

He accepted the present from Castillo, and tore away the paper. It was a wooden picture frame, which held an old four by six photograph that Max recognized instantly, though he couldn't remember ever having seen it. It was him—baby him and Noah wearing the same old hockey shirt—actual Noah, in living breathing technicolor, not a figment from his brain.

Max looked up, bewildered, half-expecting to see the ghost boy standing in the hospital waiting room tilting his neck to view the photo, but there was only Oliver and Henri and his friends surrounding him.

Curious, Henri slid off his chair and came over to see the photo. Then, at Selina's beckoning, he hesitantly climbed onto her lap and allowed her to wrap her arms around him and rest her chin on his head, studying Max.

It felt like the entire world was staring at him, waiting to see what he was going to do. He leaned forward, resting his arms on his knees, the frame dangling between them. Maggie's blood had soaked his watch band when he was applying pressure to the wound. He took it off, his grandfather's watch, ensconced in the ruined leather cuff, and a wave of grief knocked into him. What he wouldn't give to have his grandfather, steady and comforting, with him right now.

He rubbed fruitlessly at the blood, but there was so much of it, and it had seeped deep into the cow hide. Maggie was a part of the band now.

A small finger reached out, gently traced the outline of Max's moose tattoo, and he looked at Henri, offering him a weak smile.

"How's our girl?" Dix asked, bursting into the waiting room like a tornado, Leah at his side.

Max stood to meet them. "They're working on her," he rasped.

"Oh, MJ," Leah said, offering him a hug that nearly broke him.

"She'll be okay," Dix said. "It's Christmas."

Max snorted.

"I've found two foster families who can each take a boy tonight," Leah whispered so the kids wouldn't hear. "So far, no one can accommodate them both, but I'll keep trying."

Max looked up sharply. "I thought I'd get the same emergency deal you had with Kyle."

Leah's face softened. "Are you sure? With everything that's happened—you need to be here."

She was right, but Max was also sure, one thousand percent sure.

"Hi," Selina said, stepping up and wedging herself between Max and Leah. "Selina. Not eavesdropping, but I actually need to get to choir practice. I could take them with me, and then put them to bed at your place and hang out until you get home."

"Who are you?" Leah asked, tilting her head to the side.

"My neighbor. Is that allowed?"

"We'll have to run a background check," Leah said. "You have choir practice on Christmas Eve?"

"It's a long story," Selina sighed with a great deal of insinuated drama. "But Henri's been practicing with us this week."

"You're a lifesaver," Max said, hugging Selina and sort of not wanting to let go. "But I don't think you'll have the same luck with that one." He nodded to Oliver, who still refused to make eye contact. If there was a gulf between them at the station before, now there was an entire ocean.

"Oh I don't know," Selina said, bumping Max's shoulder with her own. "I always was best with the tough guys."

"True."

Selina turned to tell the boys the new plan, and Max couldn't shake the feeling that he had to say something to bridge the chasm between himself and Oliver, or the silence might grow too insurmountable, like it had with his own father.

But everything he could think of to say rang in his ears in the Inspector's voice. Regardless of his own hurt and anger, asking questions he already knew the answer to, like, *Why did you run off again?*—or telling Oliver things the kid already knew, like, *I'm really disappointed you lied to me*—might make Max feel temporarily better, but it would only widen the rift.

"Please," Henri begged his brother. "It's the only thing I want for Christmas. Mama said singing is like a wish and a prayer, remember? Un voeu et une prière."

"You'll have to wish it for both of us this time, okay?" Oliver said, turning toward the door.

"Oliver," Max said, stepping over and laying a hand on the kid's shoulder.

He pulled away from the touch, and Max let him go.

"That was quick thinking tonight, the SOS with the flashlight. I'm really proud of you."

Oliver didn't respond, but Henri tugged on Max's pant leg and in a tiny voice he asked, "Aren't you mad at us? For lying and running away?"

Max knelt down beside Henri and brushed his hair out of his eyes so he could look at him man to man. "The most important thing is that, no matter what, you never do it again."

Henri nodded solemnly, and when Max held up his fist, the little boy bumped it, and then he took Oliver's hand to walk out with Selina.

❄

When she awoke after surgery, the first thing Maggie requested was a drink of water. The second was to see her best friend.

Max looked awful—tired and rumpled, with dark circles under his soulful eyes and deep worry lines etched into his brow. He had never looked more handsome to Maggie.

"Merry Christmas," he said with a nervous laugh as he collapsed into a chair and took hold of her right hand like he might never let it go. Her stomach did a little dance that made her glad of the antiemetics in her IV.

The way he looked at her—up and down and all over like it had been decades since he'd seen her—she suddenly wished she'd asked for a mirror and comb before he came in. But nothing in his face seemed to find her lacking.

"I'm sorry," he whispered. "I'm so sorry."

"You told me to wait for backup."

"I know, but I'm still sorry. I'll never stop being sorry."

He was staring at her so intently. The beep of Maggie's heart rate monitor, the loudest sound in the room, began to speed up. She glanced at the gossipy screen, willing it to shut up before it gave her away.

"St. James, it's okay."

"No, Kyle, it's not, because I love—" he froze, and his eyes flicked to hers, shooting electric heat across the surface of her skin. "Your sweater," he finished. "I love your sweater. Like, more than anything. It's maybe my favorite sweater ever. And the thought of bullets… tearing holes in your…" He swallowed.

His hands were trembling, and Maggie tried to squeeze them still.

"Tearing holes in your sweater… it kills me. Because I should have made double sure that such a perfect sweater was protected by a vest. And even if they can patch up the holes, even if—I don't know if I'll ever be able to forgive myself, because every time I see—your sweater—I'm going to see those bullet holes and know it was my fault."

BEEP. BEEP. BEEP. Maggie almost ripped the pulse oximeter off her finger, but even her hazy brain knew it would only send an army of nurses to interrupt them.

"It's just a sweater," she whispered, trying to memorize his face without looking directly at him.

"The warmest, smartest, most beautiful sweater I—"

"Bad news," she interrupted him, taking her hand back to dry the sweaty palm on her hospital gown. "They had to cut it off me. Sweater's toast. I really hope you're not actually talking about my sweater."

Max smiled shyly and leaned on the bed railing, dropping his head. "Don't be mad, but I called your mom."

"Oh god," Maggie groaned. She didn't want to talk about her mom right now. "Where's my phone? I'm sure she's left a hundred 'I told you so' messages."

"Not unless her plane has WiFi. She took the redeye. Dix has gone to pick her up from the airport."

A new sort of flutter stirred in Maggie's chest.

"My mom doesn't fly. Whose poor mother did you call by mistake?"

"She'll be here in an hour," Max said, brushing some hair out of her face and tucking it behind her ear. Hot tears pricked Maggie's eyes. She hadn't realized until that moment quite how desperately she wanted her mama.

Max held up the photo Maggie had found—the one she framed for his Christmas gift. He held it up, and then held it to his heart, and the ache for her mother burst back into tender butterflies again.

"I'm sorry I went through your stuff, I shouldn't have—"

"It's fine—"

"No, I—I really wasn't trying to invade your privacy. I just wanted to be there for you like you've always been there for me. To put things back how they used to be between us."

"Don't worry about that right now," Max said, setting the picture frame on the side table where he could still look at it.

"Are you kidding? This is the best time to talk about it—I'm on so many drugs right now! I got shot last night. I was friggin' shot! I could have died—I was pretty sure I was going to."

He tried to shush her, but Maggie had more to say.

"In the ambulance, all I kept thinking about was you, and you and me. And how we used to be partners—really partners, and I—"

"I don't want to be partners anymore," he blurted out.

And it was a good thing she was on so many meds because the pain of those words should have knocked her out.

"Oh," she said, trying to reorient herself from the conversation she thought they were going to have to the one that was actually happening. "So, are we breaking up? Like, professionally? 'Cause your timing kind of sucks. I'm in the hospital."

"I don't want to be a cop anymore."

Maggie was dumbfounded. And pain killers are weird, so she actually thought to herself, I am dumbfounded, oh my gosh, dumbfounded literally means finding yourself dumb and unable to speak, I never thought about that, I'm dumbfounded again.

"Dix reminded me of something tonight. Ten years ago, I tendered my resignation."

"What?"

"Walked into the staff sergeant's office first thing in the morning and gave him my two weeks' notice. I didn't want to train a rookie, and I told him he better assign mine to somebody else because I wouldn't be there come month's end."

The pain in Maggie's shoulder was starting to move up her neck into her head, and she pressed the button to send another drip of morphine or oxy or whatever they were giving her. "What are you talking about? You never quit."

"Sarge begged me to reconsider. Said if word got out that I quit on my rookie's first day, it would make things awfully awkward for them. I guess he knew me better than I knew myself, because after that, I couldn't do it. Even when you were a total pain in the ass, riding with you kept me going."

Maggie's head felt like a balloon, like it had detached from her body and was watching all of this play out from above, a bystander to the whole thing, instead of a participant. "And now?" she asked him.

"It's not enough now."

"Oh," she said, deflating like the balloon and trying to hold back another wave of tears. It wasn't her, it was the medicine.

"I want more," he whispered, taking her hand again.

"More?"

"I love you, Magpie. I've loved you from the moment you walked into the parade room with your too big, extra-starched uniform and your feisty green eyes, hiding behind that overconfident laugh. Your hair was pinned up so tight, I would have bet if you let it down your spine might collapse, but all I could think about was how long it would be if you did let it down. How far would it go, and was it curly or straight or in between? I didn't want to be a cop anymore, but I had a reason to get up in the morning, and I figured I could be a cop forever if it meant partnering with you every day."

Maggie felt like there were actual gears in her head, turning in slow motion, forcing their way through thick mud, trying to catch up. "But now you want to...?"

He swallowed and scratched his head. "Sacrifice being together all day so we can—you know." He was blushing now, and he swallowed again. "Be together all night," he added sheepishly, coughing a little to clear his throat after he said it.

"St. James!"

"Hey, you kissed me, lady."

Maggie grinned stupidly. "You mean you like me?"

"How much oxy did they give you?" he asked, bewildered.

"You *like* like me?"

"I mean, this isn't sixth grade, but yeah. Can I kiss you?" he asked hesitantly.

"I didn't get shot in the mouth."

So he sat down gently on the bed and leaned over to kiss her—first on the forehead, tentatively. Then when she didn't shatter, he kissed her on the lips, and she felt as though she could finally breathe again.

Toronto,
Christmas Day

CHAPTER 30

Oliver still wouldn't speak to, or even look at, Max when he returned from the hospital to find them munching on Selina's gluten-free, choir-approved breakfast of bacon and apples. But the kid had apparently agreed to sing with her boys' choir that morning, and he looked visibly relieved when Max told them Maggie was being discharged. He didn't run around like a maniac the way Henri did, but he smiled and nodded.

The choir was scheduled to perform a Christmas Day show at a retirement community called Kensington Terrace—his dad's retirement community, as it happened—and the boys seemed to fit right in with the other kids. Selina always did have a knack for helping disparate individuals find common ground.

Max milled around trying to make awkward conversation with the choir moms and dads until he was rescued by the arrival of the Dixon clan.

"MJ, you clean up pretty good," Leah said, reaching out to brush lint off his sweater. Three charms dangled from the bracelet on her wrist.

"Merry Christmas." Max kissed her cheek. Over her shoulder

he saw Oliver approach in a breathless, wide-eyed state. "What's up?" Max asked.

The kid held up a black necktie. "Henri got the last clip-on, and I have no idea what to do with this," he said, still not looking Max in the eye.

"I can help with that," Max said, leading him into the men's room. "Jump up here."

He helped Oliver to kneel on the counter facing the mirror and then stood behind him, adjusting both ends of the tie. "The trick is to start with this part the length you want to end up with. Then cross over like this. And pull it through. And around, and through. See?" he said, talking through the steps as he tied the knot for Oliver. He was kind of reveling in the moment, to be honest, and hardly noticed the door opening, as he snugged the knot and straightened the tie. "It's not too tight is it? You can still sing?"

"That's a mighty fine Windsor knot, son," a voice said as Oliver jumped down, and Max turned to see his father.

"I learned from the best," Max said.

"Thanks," Oliver told him shyly, and paused at the door.

"Something else?" Max asked.

"This kid, Finn, practiced an encore, but he's afraid no one will call for it except his mom. So, could you? After 'Joy to the World'?"

"You got it," Max said, and Oliver nodded again and left.

"Max—" his father began once the door closed.

"I'm sorry about last night. I was working, and things were a bit… intense."

"I heard," his father said, and when Max tilted his head in question, the Inspector shrugged. "I keep up. I still have some friends on the force. I'm really glad your partner's going to be okay."

The door burst open, and Henri came running into the washroom wearing his clip-on tie. "Will you fix my tie too?"

"Sure," Max chuckled, putting him up on the counter, facing him toward the mirror. Then he pretended to go through the motions of tying a Windsor once more.

"Thanks!" Henri said when he was done, and then scampered back to the door. "We're on in five!"

Max's father studied him with a bemused expression. "I'm trying to do the math here," the Inspector said.

"Don't hurt yourself. It's all pretty new."

"Good for you," his father said, and he seemed like he meant it.

"I should…" Max gestured toward the exit.

"Yeah, I should…" his father pointed at the urinal. "I hope we can talk after."

When he rejoined the Dixons and their daughters, Max found them standing with Hector and Boyd, waving over Maggie and her mother.

Maggie looked exhausted and stiff, her movements slow and measured, but her color was back, and she was whole, and she had never looked more incredible. Max couldn't tear his eyes off her.

"Ma found an open Thai salon," she explained of her blow out and sparkly crimson nails. "I feel almost human again."

"You look—"

"Are you the young man who let her go into that place without a bulletproof vest?" Mrs. Kyle demanded.

"I am so sorry," he said.

"Ma! He didn't let me do anything. It was my choice, my consequence."

"I hope you put a bullet in his brain pan," Mrs. Kyle whispered to Max as they took seats near the back.

"Ma, you watched *Serenity*," Maggie cooed, and her mom patted her face gently.

The lights dimmed, and then Selina and a pianist began to play as the choristers emerged from the back. They walked up the aisle singing "Angels We Have Heard on High," and took their places on the makeshift stage. Their flawless treble voices made Max nostalgic for the old days, for the Christmases when he was small, when his grandfather was still alive and teenage angst had not yet set in—when his mom would dance around the kitchen humming along to Brenda Lee while she baked sugar pie and dressed the turkey.

"I always loved to hear you sing," his father whispered from the row behind, patting Max's shoulder awkwardly, thrusting his emotions into a tailspin.

Between songs, Selina stepped out to address the gathered families. "I know you were all expecting my boys' choir today. About half of them got sick, little Petri dishes, some with strep, some with stomach flu. At the eleventh hour, a few of the girls from my other choir graciously agreed to give up their Christmas mornings, along with two more boys—my neighbor's kids, Oliver and Henri. So when Oliver asked to sing the next one, how could we say no?"

The next one turned out to be "What Child Is This?" Tears immediately sprang to Max's eyes. He could almost feel his mother sitting beside him as Oliver sang—Oliver, who didn't sing anymore. His voice was perfect and pure, and when the final note ended, the kid sought Max out in the crowd and raised his eyebrows as if to ask, Are we okay?

Thank you, Max mouthed, and Oliver grinned and nodded his head.

After Finn's Gaelic encore, someone dimmed the lights even lower, and the kids lit candles to sing "Silent Night." Max was overcome once more with memories of Christmases past, singing the same hymn, first in the choir, then just in church with his mother's hand in the crook of his arm.

When the lights came back up, he hurried over to congratulate the boys with his whole posse in tow.

"Did you hear me sing 'Merry Little Christmas'?" Henri asked, jumping into his arms.

"I heard! You were so great," Max said, and Henri jumped back down to run off with his new friends.

Then Max turned to Oliver, but he realized a moment too late the kid was facing the corner wiping away unrelenting tears.

"Sorry," Oliver said. "Sorry, I'm sorry."

Max's first instinct was to pass on his father's advice for keeping the tears at bay, suddenly understanding that it was his own embarrassment his father had been trying to prevent, but he swallowed the words and said what he'd always needed to hear instead.

"For what?" he asked, cupping the kid's neck so he could look him watery eye to watery eye. "If you can't cry at Christmas, when can you, eh?" And Oliver buried his face in Max's side and wept, while Max held him tight.

He looked around sheepishly at the group he had led over, all trying to act like they hadn't witnessed the adolescent's tears.

"She'd be proud of you. I know I am," his father said.

"I'm considering a career change," Max announced, because why not rip the bandage off before he got used to his father's pride? "Social work," he added, and Leah beamed at him.

"Will it make you happy?" the Inspector asked.

"I think so."

"Good. Life's too short to live someone else's dreams, son," he said, offering Max a manilla envelope.

"What's this?"

"Your mom always seemed to know what you needed. Not like me. But I ran across it the other day, and I thought... maybe she was trying to tell me."

Max peeked inside the envelope and saw what looked like his own adoption papers. "Dad..." he breathed.

"You never asked me, so I thought... but... she always meant for you to have them."

He stared at his father for a long moment, until he remembered they had an audience. "You remember Maggie Kyle?" he asked, finally letting go of Oliver, and putting one arm around Maggie while he introduced the rest. "This is her mom. And Dix? His wife Leah, and you know Hector and Boyd. Everybody—my dad."

"You know my name?" Hector asked, in awe.

"You didn't think I thought it was 'Rookie' did you?" Max replied, and everyone laughed.

LEAH DIXON WAS THE PICTURE OF GRACIOUSNESS, MAKING ROOM AT her holiday table for Maggie, her mom, Max's father, the boys, and even Selina. Maggie still couldn't believe her mom had boarded a plane and flown from Vancouver to Toronto—three glasses of Chardonnay or not. Among her mother's many fears, flying was the worst, but Maggie was so glad to have her there with her.

At the Dixons' no one would let Maggie lift a finger. She sat in her staff sergeant's comfortable recliner while the festivities swirled around her, and every time her mother caught her eye, she would hold Maggie's face in her hands and just look at her.

"It's okay, Ma," Maggie kept saying. "I'm okay."

"My strong, beautiful girl, of course you are," her mother would reply.

It was cozy and lovely, curled up by the fire, replaying the choir's performance in her head. When they had sung a special arrangement of Pachelbel's "Cannon," Maggie's imagination ran a little wild and she saw herself walking down the aisle to same melody. But now her pain killers were beginning to wear off, and doubt was creeping into her sludgy brain, lapping at the edges of her anxiety, until finally she realized why. Max may have confessed his love for her—at least her drug-addled mind sure thought he had—but what about last Christmas?

"What's wrong?" her mom asked, catching her frowning.

Maggie shook her head.

But mothers always seem to know, don't they? "He went that way," she said, nodding down the hall.

MAGGIE FOUND HIM LEANING IN THE DOORWAY OF THE DIXONS' laundry room. "If you were playing hide and seek, I think the other kids may have forgotten," Max said to whomever was on the inside. "Talk to me, kid. Who're you hiding from?"

"You, I guess," Oliver replied.

"10-4," Max said, and Maggie could hear the hurt he was trying so hard to keep out of his voice. "Should I go, or...?"

"I didn't want you to realize I'm a huge sissy crybaby and change your mind about things."

"No, never," Max said, entering the room fully, and Maggie crept further down the hall. "The crying thing—scientists say it's healthy," he told Oliver.

The eleven-year-old was sitting against the dryer, in between two laundry baskets. He picked up a towel from the pile on his right and started to fold it, placing it in the basket on his other side. Max slid the basket over and sat down next to him, leaning against the washer.

"It's a physical way to process your feelings instead of bottling them up and getting an ulcer like me," Max went on, and boy if that wasn't the truth. "Look, the holidays are hard for lots of people. They're excruciating after you lose someone. One minute you're fine, you get swept up in the holiday cheer, and then in an instant you're crushed under the guilt of daring to feel okay because how could you? And then you sort of ache with the absence of them. I'd like to say it gets easier—maybe eventually it does."

Maggie felt a little guilty, spying on such an intimate moment, but she couldn't pull herself away. She was caught between wanting to give them their privacy and wanting to wrap them both up in her arms and protect them from every bad thing.

"You want to know what I miss the most?" Oliver asked.

"If you want to tell me."

"Just… being held. And I know it's super dumb because I hold Henri all the time, and he holds on back, but it's not quite the same, being the one doing the holding. And I didn't even know that was it, but then earlier…" He started to cry again, and the tears came faster than he could swipe them away. "You held on to me, and I didn't… want you to…"

"I'm sorry, Oliver, I should've—boundaries—I—"

"I didn't… want you to stop," Oliver blurted through his tears. "Like, ever." He wiped his nose on his sleeve.

"Oh," Max said with a little smile. "Okay, deal."

"But it's not though, is it?" Oliver asked. "I mean, this—you and us—it's just for now, right? That's what foster parents are—temporary, until the next thing or we turn eighteen or whatever—and that's okay, I mean, you didn't ask for—it's not your job to—and we don't expect—" the poor kid stammered.

"Oliver—"

"I mean we're really grateful—"

"Oliver, listen. You and your brother have been on your own a long time—"

"I know," Oliver whispered.

"A long time, so long it didn't seem fair for me to make any kind of permanent decision without your input. It wouldn't be right. What do you think, I make a habit of driving halfway to Nunavut to wrangle runaways? 'Cause I don't."

Oliver snorted a sad sort of laugh, and Max put his arm around the kid hesitantly, but he didn't pull away. He sort of melted into Max's side.

Maggie leaned her head and good shoulder against the door-frame, watching them.

"You and me, there's something between us now, okay? No matter what, we're family. Nothing's going to change that. But you guys deserve—I don't know what's going to happen between Maggie and me, but you guys deserve a mom and a dad, with normal jobs and normal lives, with siblings, and a dog if you want it. No matter how I feel, I want that for you. So yeah, I made a reversible decision just for now, just until things calm down and we could talk about it. In case, you know, you want to reverse it."

It was a kind of perfect picture. Maggie had never thought about Max having kids, but watching him with Oliver, she knew it was exactly what was meant to happen.

"Oh," Oliver said, wiping his face again. "That's a really good point. Why would we want to stay with some weirdo who saved our lives—twice—when we could have a dog?" he laughed, and Max laughed too, holding him close and resting his cheek on Oliver's head.

Maggie stepped inside then so Max could see her.

"I think dinner's done," he told Oliver. "Wash up when you're ready, yeah?"

The kid nodded and Max pushed himself to his feet and met Maggie in the hall, his face crinkled with concern. "You okay?"

"Pain meds are wearing off."

"Want me to take you home?" he asked, patting his pockets for his keys.

"After dinner. My mom's going to get a hotel for a few days. I think I'm going to stay with her."

Max's face fell, but what had he thought she would do? Move in?

"Okay," he said. "Or—you could not. I don't know if you've heard, but I have a pretty great spare room now. No spiders or anything. You guys could each take a bed and I could build a blanket fort with the boys in the living room."

Maggie chuckled at the image, and Max took her hand.

"What's really wrong?" he asked.

It was now or never, Maggie told herself. No more dancing around half truths and assumptions. "Everything you said before —were you just swept up in the moment? Because you thought I was going to die?"

"No, it was all the things I realized while I was driving back and forth across the province."

Maggie looked down at the floor. She wanted to believe him. Max touched his forehead to hers, interlacing his fingers with her good hand. "Tell me?" he said.

"I can't make the pieces fit," she whispered.

"Which ones."

"You said you loved me. And I sort of believe you because you always take the brown banana. And I used to think it was because you liked them, but nobody likes them. You do it so I don't feel like I have to."

"Guilty," he whispered.

"But then there's last year. At the holiday party."

Max pulled back to look at her. "I didn't think you remembered."

Her cheeks burned. "I wasn't that drunk."

"You never mentioned it."

"I was humiliated," Maggie said. She felt weak, faint. She needed to sit down before her knees buckled. He could tell, and he guided her back to the living room and knelt beside her chair. "I was… heartbroken," she confessed. "I had imagined that moment for eight, nine years, and then—well my fantasy never ended with rejection."

"Rejection? No, no, no, no," Max said, leaning back on his heels. "Is that what you thought?"

"That's what it felt like."

"No."

"You stopped."

"You were drunk—or I thought you were. And we were in a dirty interview room at the precinct party. I didn't want to take advantage of you in a filthy room at a work party. I wanted it… to be nice."

Warmth flooded Maggie's belly. "So you're saying… you wanted it?"

"Yeah, Magpie. I've replayed it a thousand times, and kicked myself a thousand more for not taking you home and pouring coffee down your throat until I knew you were sober, and then at the very least kissing you senseless."

"Oh," she said.

So much time. They had wasted so much time being awkward and having hurt feelings, all because Maggie had pretended to be drunk and Max had behaved like a gentleman.

He kissed the inside of her wrist.

"So a social worker, huh?" she whispered.

He smiled sheepishly and raked a hand through his hair so it stood up at all angles like he'd just rolled out of bed. "Better late than never."

He kissed her cheek.

"I guess that means it's time I took the detective's exam," Maggie said, and this time, she had a feeling she would actually do the thing, no regrets.

"Better late than never," he whispered again, as she sank into the chair and his lips found hers, testing her strength and tasting her eagerness, his tongue darting in her mouth like she was the last drink of water left on earth.

Banff,
7 months later

EPILOGUE

$\mathcal{M}$ax gazed out at the tall evergreens and imposing mountains, like sentinels watching over everyone in the world that he loved. The cabin had been an excellent choice.

"Nervous?" Oliver whispered at his elbow.

Max looked down at least a few centimeters less than he used to, and put his arm around the boy. He shook his head, turning back to the mountains.

"It's okay if you are," Oliver reminded him.

The twelve-year-old walked out to lean on the veranda, and Max wondered if the trees reminded him of his old home.

"What about you?"

Maggie had confided her worries to him that she and Oliver were cordial but hadn't really bonded deeply yet. She felt like Oliver was his and Henri was hers, and feared there might be hurt feelings over Henri needing his brother a little less as he came to rely on her a little more. It was why they'd decided to ask Henri to stand up with Max today, and Oliver to stand with Maggie.

The boy turned, tilting his head. "It's like Dix said. Restoring the natural order of things."

Max chuckled. "When did he say that?"

"When you two couldn't keep your hands off each other at New Year's," Dix answered, and Max turned around to see his oldest friend standing in the bedroom wearing a trim cobalt jacket and matching Chuck Taylors.

Max whistled. "You look good, brother," he said.

Dix held up a eucalyptus boutonniere matching his own. "Wife sent me to fix you up."

Max lifted his chin to give his former sergeant access to his lapel, looking past him to where Henri stood on a chair facing the mirror while Max's dad helped him with the real bowtie—not a clip-on—Henri had insisted he wear for the big day.

They chatted comfortably together—about what, Max couldn't hear—as his father straightened the little boy's tie.

"That'll do." Dix took a step back to look over Max's full ensemble, white shirt, charcoal blazer, black Chucks, and he nodded approvingly. "Social media ready if I say so myself."

"What do you know about social media?" Max teased.

"Oh ho, the comedian. I have just as many kids as you do, remember?"

"We're not allowed on social media," Oliver said, and Max grinned.

"I'm glad you're here," he told Dix.

"We saved each other's marriages. I think we're even. Now don't get all soppy or my makeup'll run." Dix squeezed Max's elbow.

There was a tentative knock at the door, and everyone turned.

"Hide," Dix said, shooing Max away. "It might be the bride."

Max rolled his eyes, but before he could step back out onto the balcony, Andrew Boyd poked his head in, Hector right behind.

"Max, buddy, a uh… rather intimidating Mrs. Castillo ordered me to inform you that she will not be asking Maggie to agree to obey you today."

"She said it's non-negotiable," Hector added, and Max burst out laughing.

"She also said we're starting in five minutes, with or without you," Boyd added, laughing himself as he stepped further into the room to shake Max's hand.

Hector did the same. "Sure you don't want to come back to Fifty-One Division?"

Max shook his head and Dix said, "I wouldn't let him if he tried."

"I thought we agreed not to talk shop, Jabberwocky," Boyd said, throwing his arm around the rookie's shoulder as they left the room.

In the far corner, Oliver and Henri whispered in rapid French—low and fast enough that all Max knew for sure was they weren't discussing lunch.

"You ready?" his father asked him.

Was he? Most definitely. His dad passed him the small vase holding three white roses.

"You heard the lady. They're starting with or without you."

"Thanks, Dad," Max said, then he took the roses and joined the boys—his boys—who stopped whispering immediately.

He handed each their own rose, keeping one for himself. "Like we practiced," he reminded them, and they nodded solemnly.

Then he led the way out onto the wraparound porch which connected to the open doors of the cabin's main living room, where their friends and family were gathered and waiting.

"Ready?" Hector asked, and Maggie nodded tightly, although she felt like she hadn't taken a full breath since waking up before the sun. It was ridiculous to be nervous. Only twenty of her nearest and dearest were there to watch her walk down the world's shortest aisle, and one was a napping infant. "You look beautiful," Hector said, adding, "Detective," as a shy afterthought.

"It's not official yet."

He shrugged. "You finished the rotation. You'll be cracking cold cases in no time."

"I think they're about to start," Frankie said, handing Maggie her bouquet of blue hydrangeas. Mrs. Castillo had graciously agreed to preside over the ceremony and she ran a tight ship.

"Gonna throw that?" Hector asked.

"I might. Why, you want to catch it?"

He shrugged. "She'll have her hands full with the baby, so who else is going to?"

"Baby or no baby, Corbin Hector, I will shove you down that mountain if you get in my way, don't think for a second I won't," Frankie said.

He laughed a high, uncomfortable laugh and ducked out of the bedroom where Maggie had been getting ready.

She watched him go, peeking out into the main room that opened onto a balcony and breathtaking view of the Cascade Mountains, framed by an arch of ivy, eucalyptus, and more hydrangeas. The intoxicating earthy fragrance drifted back to her on a soft afternoon breeze.

Her mom nudged her back from the doorway before anyone could catch a glimpse and whispered, "My precious girl," squeezing one of Maggie's shoulders in each hand.

"You're not disappointed about the dress?" she asked, running her hands down the simple, ecru A-line sundress, sprinkled with flowers and complemented by a pair of off-white Chuck Taylors.

"My darling. You've never done anything traditional in your life. Why would I be disappointed?"

Then Selina's violin started up the familiar prelude of Pachelbel's "Cannon," and over Frankie's shoulder Maggie glimpsed Max and Dix stepping inside from the balcony.

She sucked in her breath at the sight of him in his dapper suit and Converse, his hair spiked up messily the way she liked it best.

He laid a white rose on an empty chair next to his father, and Maggie's heart broke a little that she would never meet his mom.

Then he stepped back into place in front of Frankie's mother, and the boys came inside, Oliver rocking a dark vest, and Henri in his little hipster bowtie. They, too, held white roses, which they placed gently on two empty chairs next to Maggie's father, before Henri joined Max and Dixon, and Oliver stood on his own, awaiting Frankie and Maggie's arrival.

"Look at them in their little suits," Maggie whispered.

"Yeah, the fellas clean up pretty good," Frankie teased.

Oliver lifted his chin and took a breath, and suddenly four more children jumped onto their chairs—Maggie's niece and nephew, Cora and Tommy, and both of the Dixon girls. Ignoring their parents' desperate attempts to make them sit down, they faced forward, focused and intent.

A nod from Oliver, who was watching Selina, and they all began to sing, with Henri gleefully managing the treble descant Oliver had carried last Christmas, the older brother now harmonizing in a counter tenor.

Tears sprung to Maggie's eyes as the sweet voices filled the cabin. She glanced at Max, but his jaw had fallen open in surprise and he stared at the boys. Oliver's eyes flicked up at him and a cheeky grin spread across his face.

When she'd heard that arrangement last December, Maggie had pictured herself walking down the aisle. It was honestly the only thing that made her agonize over the decision to hold the wedding in Alberta so her mom wouldn't have to fly again—to almost settle for a church she didn't belong to or even a rented hall, where Selina's whole choir could attend and perform.

"Don't cry. You'll smudge your makeup," her mom whispered, kissing her hair and smoothing the fluttery sleeves of her dress.

"Well they should have thought of that then." Her voice wobbled, but it made Maggie laugh to say it.

"You are so loved," her mom said before heading down the aisle to her seat, as though those parting words wouldn't be the very thing to push Maggie over the edge into tears.

When she reached the wedding party, her mother lovingly cupped Henri's face in her hands, and then Oliver's, and the boys beamed back at their adopted grandma. They were family already.

"See you down there, Nene," Frankie said, kissing her cheek before taking her turn down the aisle to stand beside Oliver.

Oliver. So maybe he didn't resent Maggie's closeness with his little brother after all, didn't see her as a usurper like she feared. Somehow, she knew, he had managed all this—the wannabe conductor—across three households and a four hour time difference. This must have been what kept the children so busy downstairs yesterday, where their parents joked they were plotting world domination.

Selina nodded to Maggie and winked, her cue to start walking, and she floated down the makeshift aisle to Max and her boys—her boys.

But before she took Max's hand she raised her eyebrows at Oliver in question. It was all him, right?

He returned a small smile and inclined his head in confirmation, a little pensive, in case she didn't appreciate the surprise.

"Thank you," she whispered, and this time he returned a huge grin with his nod.

Maggie squeezed his arm and handed her bouquet to Frankie, as Mrs. Castillo—newly ordained in the province of Alberta— smiled benevolently at them, ready to begin.

Then she reached out without even looking, and Max's hand was there, ready to catch hers. Partners to the End.

ACKNOWLEDGMENTS

Writing a book can be a massively lonely and solitary experiment. And yet, it would be impossible without an incredibly supportive, and at times collaborative, team behind you.

First and foremost, I owe everything to my best friend and husband, DJ, who holds my hand on the roller coaster and has the courtesy to only freak out when I'm calm. Thanks for giving me the moon and stars, and for taking care of the pup when I need to escape to the mountains.

As I write these words, I'm beyond lucky to be sitting in my happy place, surrounded by many of my herd. An early, pivotal draft was actually completed at the first Writerly retreat in this very cabin on this glorious mountain, so it's only appropriate for me to thank my crew for their boundless love, endless support, many beta reads and pep talks: Christian Berkey, Angi Black, Jen Davenport, Jennifer Iacopelli, Tabitha Martin, Megan Paasch, and importantly, Megan Orsini, my first critique partner, my ticket into this group of talented introverts, and the person who read the first three chapters of the first draft of this story and said, "I think you finally found your genre," even though I didn't know you were right for another five years.

Mark Benson, our fearless founder: you taught me to dare mighty things.

Krista Walsh, who patiently read more drafts than anyone could ever be expected to, talked me off more than one ledge, and who, with Sarah Blair, encouraged my dream and generously answered a thousand questions along the way.

DeAnne Hays, who answered countless late night "does this

make sense?" and "how does this sound?" texts—I owe you some Oscar's.

Emma Tennier-Stuart, Hannah Long, and Jessie Parker, whose keen eyes for detail and nurturing support have been invaluable.

Brenda Dyck and Melissa Boyce, who adopted me as a Canadian sister. And my biological sister, Susan Semadeni, a wonderful writer in her own right, who picks me up when I'm down and reminds me how to fly.

And of course my parents, who taught me to love all kinds of stories, to believe that I could tell them, and to never give up.

Ann Doyan and Kaitlin Littlechild—my book is so much richer thanks to your kindness and generosity. Erika Donovan, who read and gave me notes on the very first version, the screenplay, way back in the day. You fanned the flame of my hope and dream.

My fantastic cover designer, Bran Cedio at Crowglass Design, and my audiobook narrator, Karen Gundersen whose passion and brilliance picked me up and dragged me over the finish line.

To so many friends and family who have cheered me on from the sidelines—your enthusiasm and encouragement mean the world to me.

The musical inspiration behind Selina's choir was the magnificent Robert Prizeman, whose transcendent harmonies have grounded me in moments of stress and inspired me more times than I can count. May he rest in peace, and may his legacy live on in the voices of future choristers.

And to you, dear readers, thank you for taking a chance on this little labor of love. Happy holidays.

ABOUT THE AUTHOR

Rose Prendeville is an honourary Canadian and librarian living in Middle Tennessee with her husband, the world's cutest dog, and a garden full of bees, where snow is a rare treat and cicadas are the soundtrack of summer. The award winning author is passionate about books with happy endings and their ability to brighten a sometimes dismal world.

If you enjoyed this book, please consider leaving a review at your favorite marketplace.

If you'd like to read the story of Max and Maggie's undercover op at the country-western bar, scan the QR code and sign up for Rose's newsletter or visit: 
 roseprendeville.com

BOOKS BY ROSE PRENDEVILLE

Last Blue Christmas

The Unknown Birds

Brides of Chattan

Mistress Mackintosh and the Shaw Wretch

Lady Len and the Mysterious Mac

Maggie and the Pirate's Son

Tennessee Hebrides

Grace on the Rocks

A Faire Affair

www.ingramcontent.com/pod-product-compliance
Lightning Source LLC
Chambersburg PA
CBHW061041190726
48286CB00006B/1562